the
Echoes
of
Us

the
Echoes
of
Us

EMMA STEELE

MLP

First published in Germany in 2023 as *Die Sekunde zwishcen mir und dir* by
Verlagsgruppe Droemer Knaur

First published in Great Britain in 2024 by
Mountain Leopard Press
An imprint of HEADLINE PUBLISHING GROUP

1

Cataloguing in Publication Data is available from the British Library

ISBN 978 1 8027 9533 2 (Hardback)
ISBN 978 1 8027 9534 9 (Trade paperback)

Typeset by IDSUK (Data Connection) Ltd

Printed and bound in Great Britain by Clays Ltd, St Ives plc

HEADLINE PUBLISHING GROUP
An Hachette UK Company
Carmelite House
50 Victoria Embankment
London EC4Y 0DZ

www.headline.co.uk
www.hachette.co.uk

To Ben, Flora and Daisy

ONE

2019

JENN

If he could only see inside her mind right now, he would know how much this means to her. Just being in the car with him. Gazing out the steamed-up window into the darkness, she watches as houses and streetlights flicker by like a blurry reel of film. After a moment, she reaches up to wipe at the glass, leaving a smudge at the centre. The ghost of her reflection smiles back.

And then it catches her again; that awful, sickening, plummeting feeling in the dark of her belly.

Turning quickly in the passenger seat, she looks over to Robbie's large hands on the steering wheel, up to his rough stubble and mess of dark hair. She's always thought he was too tall for the space; a clown in a toy car, with his knees almost jutting into the dashboard. She places her hand on one now, tries to just focus on him and the love she's feeling. She's so glad she came back.

'What are you smiling about?' he says softly, covering her hand with his own. And then he does it, squeezes twice, like all those times before. *I love you.*

She tilts her head back against the seat. 'Nothing, I'm just happy.' She smiles.

Memories from the past whirl around in her mind: the first time they met five years ago, falling in love, moving in together. A thousand amazing moments fill up her chest like bubbles. Other memories flit briefly through her head too, but she pushes them away. They don't matter anymore.

Last night was perfect, their first night together after eight months apart. That moment when he opened his door, the almost disbelief in his eyes, the familiar scent of him. They paused for only a few lingering seconds before his hands were on her skin and his mouth was pressed against hers and they were backing into the bedroom, frantically, urgently, shedding each other's clothes like no time had passed. *Oh god.* It was like how they were when they first met five years ago: twenty-five and drunk on love.

Then afterwards, as they'd lain together in the dark, he'd produced a small gift – a packet of jellybeans. She'd laughed into his chest. *Oh, the beans!* They'd meant the world to her, even though she had no clue where they would go from there.

The clenching sensation in her stomach starts again, needling at her, pushing at her. *Tell the truth.*

'How was your shift anyway?' he asks, and she smiles automatically.

She's fine, it's OK. It will all be OK.

'Good, great really,' she nods decisively. 'I'm enjoying being back at it.'

She'd missed medicine; the feeling of being needed by people, of using her brain in the way it had been trained. It had been strange walking away from it all for a time. It had been strange walking away from everything for a time.

They slow down to a junction and she looks out of the window to where Edinburgh Castle sits up on its lofty crag in the distance. She's always loved the way it can be viewed from all angles of the city: a lighthouse on the rocks. The engine reverberates beneath them as the wind buffets against the steel cocoon.

'Was it absolute bloody chaos?' He smiles.

She laughs, hearing all the familiar words between them resurface. 'Yes, yes, it was absolute bloody chaos. You know what it's like.'

'Well, they're lucky to have you back,' he says. 'Like me.'

She loves the way he just says what he means straight off. He's like that about everything – good and bad. She's always struggled to articulate anything difficult, anything that's bothering her. The last thing she wants is to burden people with her problems. *To be pitied.*

There's a beeping sound from her backpack and she reaches down into a side compartment, retrieves the scratched phone pocketed there. Pulling it out, she draws the screen to her and in a split second she feels the life drop out of her.

No, no, no, not now. *Not yet.*

Her heart is thumping against her chest.

Oh god. She wishes the traffic lights would just turn green again so they could move. Her body feels frantic, and there's a fizzing in her veins. A surge. They're at the front of a queue of cars, caught between two moments in time.

'It's green,' she says, looking up at the bright circle above. Her voice is suddenly panicked, even to her own ears, and she realises her thumb nail is pressed into the opposite palm.

'You alright?' Robbie asks as he presses down on the accelerator and they lurch forwards, over the junction and down the arterial highway towards the city. Soon they'll be back home, and she can get out of the car. Her body stills for a moment at the thought, a scintilla of peace. She tries to imagine them going for a walk in the Pentlands this weekend, where they've spent so many happy moments together, the rugged hills sucking them in for whole days at a time. She thinks of the gorse and the heather; the Scottish sky spinning its roulette wheel over them each time.

Her heart stops beating for a split second and she closes her eyes, wishes she could erase this moment in time. It feels like someone else is manipulating her mouth, speaking these words; an alien imposter sent here to destroy her life.

'I've got to tell you something.'

The air seems to drain from the vehicle and, for a moment, she wonders if he heard what she said.

'What's up?' he asks, but she can hear the uncertainty in his voice – the change mirroring her own.

'Maybe we should wait until we're home.'

'Wait for what? I don't understand.'

She can't bring herself to answer, and tension seems to radiate from the other side of the car.

'What's going on?' he presses, his voice troubled now and it takes all her strength just to hold it together. Her cheeks are hot, and when she opens her eyes, looks at her legging-clad legs, they are shaking.

Up ahead, she can see another junction coming and wills the lights to stay green. Please just keep the car going. Please don't let it turn red. She allows herself to look over at Robbie and his eyes are stressed, hands welded onto the wheel. As they approach the lights, it starts to turn amber, but it's too late for them to safely brake. *Amber gambler*, Robbie would have probably said on another day, as they soar across. She feels him glance at her. Movement on the road ahead. Something skids across from the other side; headlights rush towards them.

TWO

1999

JENNY

Sunlight catches the glittery silver of her new wellies and they wink back up at her. Two fishies by the sea. She smiles, feeling a cool breeze dance across her face. Below her boots, there are snake-like ripples of sand. She's always thought the beach floor looks funny with the tide out. Like it's forgotten to put clothes on.

Looking back up, it's so bright Jenny has to squint out at the waves, which scuttle out into the distance. Seagulls float through cotton clouds, and salty freshness floods her nose. She shades her eyes, feeling the weight of layers on her shoulders; a scratchy fleece underneath her berry-red jacket, both of which are far too big. Her dad always buys things baggy – *to grow into*, he says. As the afternoon sun touches Jenny's raised arm, she feels a sudden heat. Then, just as quickly, it's gone, and spring winds flip black strands across her eyes, cutting the world into shoelaces of colour.

Across the water lies Cramond Island, a lonely bump of brown and green, as though one day it waded out too far and got stuck. People can actually get to the island now that the tide is out – her dad says it's one of seventeen that can be walked to from the Scottish mainland. He knows lots of stuff like that. She wonders what it might be like at night, if any ghosts roam the shores dressed all in white. Maybe one day she'll get to find out.

'Jenny, over here!' a voice cries and she turns. Her mum is standing near jagged rocks, hair flying around her head as she beckons with a pale hand and excited eyes. She's wearing her long green coat and too-big wellies today. They make her look funny, like she's a child dressing up in adult's clothing. Picking up her yellow bucket from the sand, Jenny runs over, a few scallops and pen shells rattling around on the buttercup plastic. She hears the wet slap of sludgy ground as she goes, the wind hurtling in her ears. Her mum dips down again, looks at something.

'What is it?' Jenny asks, stumbling to a halt as she sees the pool of glassy water, like a hundred others they have gazed into together. 'What did you find?' She wonders if it's a shore urchin, or perhaps a blenny – a pipefish maybe? Her mum is excited, so it must be good. They've been coming down to this beach since she can remember, the whole ten years of her life. She knows every creature that could possibly live in a rockpool: the sweeping curve of the whelks, the shiny loops of the ragworms – the regulars that are the anemones and winkles. Then Jenny sees it shifting, weaving under the freezing water.

'A brittle star,' she breathes, leaning forward onto her knees. Long octopus-like arms creep out of the water, and the strange creature starts to pull itself over rocks. It looks so familiar, but she's only ever seen them on the pages of her animal books.

'It's a good spot, isn't it?' her mum says.

'Dad said we couldn't get them on the east coast?'

From her crouched position, her mum looks out towards the water where the brittle star must be headed, eagerly twisting its body back to the sea. She smiles, her cheeks a bubble-gum pink, eyes crinkling up at the sides.

'Perhaps he just fancied an adventure.'

After a lingering moment, her mum shifts on her haunches, and lifts an empty cowrie from nearby sand. She dusts it off lightly, before dropping it into an ocean-blue bucket with a clatter.

Jenny looks about herself and sees her dad a little further up the beach where the ground is firmer. He's kneeling heavily in the sand, navy jumper rolled up on his hairy arms. As he pats around today's construction, curls flap by his wind-burnt ears like a dog. Jenny runs the short distance between her parents, energy coursing through her legs, her arms, all the way to her fingertips. To the left, grassy hills rise up and away from the promenade – great for rolling down in summer. A dog walker passes by, but there is no one else on the beach, oddly. Today, it is just them.

In front of her dad lies a perfectly carved castle, with turrets, a drawbridge and a deep moat. It's huge, and just marvellous. In his job he builds actual houses and buildings and things – places she's seen the blueprints for in his messy study. But down here, he makes it up as he goes. All so Jenny can score it at the end.

'So, what will it be?' her dad says, and she smiles up at his bushy eyebrows and too-big ears – like hers.

After a little pacing around and pressing one finger to her lips, she comes to a dramatic halt. 'Nine point six,' she says, and folds her arms with a nod. Looking up, she knows he's delighted, by the way his smile pushes into his cheeks. But he would never say it. He never says all that much – not like her friends' dads, with their goofy jokes and silly voices. Not like her mum. She watches as he brushes his hands on the front of his cord trousers, hard grains on soft ridges. But it only seems to make him look sandier, and his palms are still covered. She wants to laugh, and thinks how much she loves him.

'Marian,' he calls into the wind, and Jenny turns. Her mum smiles across at them. He gives her a small, beckoning wave, and with that gesture, Jenny knows it's time for home. Hot Ribena will be served and she might get a chocolate bourbon if she's lucky – her mum will sneak her another later when her dad's not looking. Then, as he starts to prepare dinner, her mum will wash her shells in the kitchen sink, and tell her stories, as the evening light from the kitchen window turns her hair a sunset red.

With her dad on one side, and her mum on the other, they say goodbye to the castle, and walk back off the beach towards the sea of rocks. Jenny takes her time, leaping from stone to stone. There are crocodiles below, and she must avoid them or risk falling into their toothy mouths. Snap. She feels the sharpness through the rubber of her boots, but her ankles hold steady. One day she'll go somewhere like in the books, with jungles and fast-flowing rivers – up mountains so high they disappear into the clouds.

On reaching the promenade, Jenny looks back down onto the beach. She takes a final mental photo of the castle, sees the beach pulling the waves slowly back up itself. It will disappear soon. As she's about to turn, something catches her eye along the sand. She blinks and squints, but there's nothing actually there. A shiver goes down her spine, and she has the strangest feeling that she's been in this exact moment before.

Her mum calls it the *faraways*.

'Everything OK?'

She looks round at her dad, who raises a questioning eyebrow, before wrapping one arm around her shoulder. Her mum is already up ahead. She drifts up the grassy slope, blue bucket swinging in the breeze. A kite appears in the sky above, its green material waving at her playfully. As she runs ahead to see it better, the world seems to go hazy, and it's as though the kite blurs away to nothing.

THREE

2014

ROBBIE

Green material waving above me. I'm somewhere loud and packed. What the hell is happening? Vaulted ceiling above, green bunting strung wall-to-wall. Fiddle music blasting, drunken chatter swims in and out of my ears. My heart is hammering and there's a dull pain at the side of my head. It pulses.

People are swarming all around me, mainly men, all a bit pissed-looking, all with a drink in their hand. There's a bar along the back wall, a mirror behind it. I know this place. It's that Irish bar, in The Cowgate. I used to come here when I was younger.

But where's the beach? Where's Jenn? And why the fuck was she so young? Like a version I saw once in a battered photo album, from before her dad left. She looked about ten, eleven maybe? They called her Jenny.

Am I dreaming?

When I wake up, I'll roll over to Jenn and say, *I had the strangest dream, where I couldn't wake myself up. And you were there, but it wasn't you*. And she'll just smile and roll her eyes like I'm being daft as usual.

I look into the mass of people and a feeling rushes through me, like I've been in this exact moment before. But my thoughts are blurry, like a high-speed train whizzing by. I can't think straight.

A roar of laughter. A few guys walk towards me, drinks in hand.

My heart leaps.

I know them – from school. That's right. Doug, Rory and Gus. Absolute liabilities. Shit, I haven't seen this lot in years now. I used to go out drinking with them loads though after I got back from Chamonix.

Before I met Jenn.

The guys come to a stop beside me and my panic lifts slightly. Perhaps I'm not going completely mad. Did I hit my head or something? Did I come here to meet them? Some sort of reunion maybe. I start to think frantically about what happened earlier, how I got here.

Perhaps I've had way too many pints tonight and it's caused some sort of epic memory lapse.

Except I don't actually feel drunk at all right now.

I feel pretty fucking sober.

Gus pushes back his surfer-blond hair and takes a sip of his pint, entirely oblivious to me standing here. I'm about to say something, when I see someone coming out of the shadows over to the right. The familiar form of a woman appears, pale white and slim, with dark pixie hair. I breathe a sigh of relief, even though my head is alerting to me something. Veering quickly over to her, I wait for her to clock me, for those big green eyes to light up.

She walks straight past.

'Jenn—' I start, but am immediately silenced at the sight of another figure moving away from the bar, cutting across the room at the exact moment she passes.

Time seems to stop, as they crash into each other blindly, his pint spilling over her and the floor as she stumbles back with a 'shit'. My stomach drops, as a twisted recognition creeps through me. He's too tall, and dishevelled, his jawline thick with stubble and hair unkempt. He looks as though he doesn't wash, but a glint of an expensive watch on his wrist suggests something else. He starts saying he's sorry, and with some light-headed alarm, I realise what I'm looking at.

It's me.

And Jenn's hair is short, like before. She's carrying that blue coat she used to love – the beer stain never completely faded. I've experienced this whole scene before. This was where we first met. This was it, the day that changed everything.

I reach out to a high table beside me, but I can't seem to catch my breath.

What's happening to me?

Jenn starts to walk away from him finally, and I can't help chasing after her. 'Hello?'

But my voice sounds cut off, muted, like the volume is turned down. There's no carry, no follow through. I try again. I shout at her. But she can't hear me. It's like I'm somewhere and nowhere at all.

She stops briefly for some napkins at the bar, wipes vaguely at the stain on her coat. A thought occurs to me and I turn to the mirror along the wall.

I'm not there.

I have no reflection.

A pint glass on the bar. I reach my hand out to touch it, find that it's cold and firm. Disturbingly real.

I feel like I'm about to pass out. But who would care? I'm not even sure this is happening.

A hand on Jenn's shoulder in the mirror. She turns sharply, an almost hopeful look in her eyes.

It's him again.

Me.

'Hey,' she smiles, a question mark across her face.

'The thing is,' he starts, and he breathes in. 'I've got this rule that if I spill a drink on anyone in an Irish bar, I've got to buy them one to say sorry.'

Oh god, did I really say that?

She smiles up at him, but then her eyes seem to catch something over his shoulder. 'I think my friends might have already got a drink for me actually,' she says, almost apologetically.

He raises his hands to the side. 'God loves a trier.'

As my old self walks away again slowly, Jenn bites her lip, like she does when she's thinking something over.

'Hey,' she says after a moment, and he looks back a little too quickly.

Play it cool.

'Maybe I could just have one,' Jenn says, and raises her eyebrows. 'I mean, you do owe me an apology for the body slam.'

He grins, just as the band kicks off with another song.

'Fisherman's Blues'.

'I've got a better idea first,' he says, and before I know it, he's taken her hand, led her away. Weaving into the throng of people in front of the band, he spins her around quickly so they almost seem to disappear into the mass of people. They dance together like that for the rest of the song, spinning and laughing, both of them grinning like crazy.

And without understanding why, I move closer, unable to take my eyes off them.

Eventually the song stops, drums crash out their ending and they pause in front of me to catch their breath. He claps loudly in the air, shouts his appreciation at the band; wolf whistles. He's sweating, small beads forming at the top of his brow.

He's a fucking mess, but the way she's smiling up at him.

She looks so damn happy.

'I'm Robbie,' he says, in the lull before the next song.

'And I'm Jenn.'

A moment later and they're back dancing again, their hands still joined together, and I can almost feel the light touch of her fingers on mine; sense her smiling right beside me.

JENN

It's cold and dark outside on the cobbles as she waits. Old Town buildings loom up all around her: the castle up on the right, the Irish bar to her left. Pubs are in the process of shutting up, people roaming around everywhere, shouting to each other, stumbling. She looks towards the door, and as the last of the stragglers come out, her heart starts to beat quickly.

And then she sees him, walking out of the light of the Irish Bar towards her; and her heart does a little leap. He shrugs a winter coat on as he approaches, hair a riot from their dancing.

God, I fancy him.

'Didn't think you'd get rid of me that easily?' he says, smiling down at her in a way which makes her stomach flutter. 'Sorry, the coat queue was massive.'

I was so worried he'd disappeared on me.

'I was giving you thirty seconds,' she says, 'and then I was off to find a late-night kebab.'

'A kebab girl then?' They start to walk away over the cobbles together. 'You're a woman after my own heart.'

She laughs, but it's sort of weird – she's got the strangest sense of *déjà vu*, like they've had this exact conversation before, this exact night. Shaking the feeling off, she tries to focus on the here and now.

'So, where is it you live?' he says, over the smashing sound of bottles.

'Just five minutes up that way, Tollcross.' She points over to the left.

'Cool. You're on my way.'

Her stomach flutters again with anticipation.

'Are you making sure I get home safe or something archaic?'

'Absolutely,' he grins. 'It's the gentlemanly thing to do, surely?'

'Uh huh,' she smiles. 'Just so we're clear here, nothing's going to happen tonight.'

'I never said it would.'

He takes her hand in his, and she feels something like an electrical current right through her. They drift up towards her flat, chatting about everything and nothing. She tells him she's a doctor, he tells her he's a chef, and she finds herself bursting into laughter every two seconds as he chats about stupid stuff at his restaurant. She's not sure she's ever sparked with someone like this before, but the timing is just so crap.

How is she only just meeting him now?

Outside her blue front door finally, they stand under the hazy glow of a streetlight.

'Do you fancy a drink at mine?' she says, nerves flooding her suddenly. 'I mean, don't worry if you need to get home.'

Robbie smiles at her. 'I absolutely do not need to get back home.'

She nods. 'OK then.'

Leading him up the dingy stairwell, she feels the tension all around them; that atmosphere before something happens between two people. Opening the flat door, she lets him into the cramped hallway, and she wonders what kind of place he lives in. She got the sense earlier on in the Irish bar that he's from a bit of money, and has a 'normal' type of family. Self-consciousness jabs at her.

Her life is a little more complicated.

They're standing so close in the dark now, eyes on each other, and for a moment she thinks he might kiss her right there by the coat pegs.

She swallows. 'I'll just go get us a couple of drinks, OK?'

Ushering him into the living room, she goes to find something, anything, drinkable in the kitchen. She scans the fridge, spies two bottles of beer behind some mouldy-looking cheese at the back; Susie's boyfriend must have brought them over. 'Sorry, Paul,' she mutters to herself, before taking them through to the living room. As she approaches the door, she pauses briefly in the dark hall to see Robbie leaning awkwardly on the small sofa, one arm along the back, like he's trying really hard to seem nonchalant. Suppressing a smile, she walks in and he looks up sharply.

'Here you go,' she says as casually as she can, and passes him a bottle, before sitting down on the other side. They both take a sip of their beer at the same time.

'So, just you living here?' he says finally. He's drumming his fingers lightly on the back on the sofa, and she gets the impression he never really sits still.

Or is he nervous too?

'No.' She shakes her head. 'I live with another girl from the hospital right now, Susie.'

'Oh, cool, cool,' he says, leaning forwards slightly. 'She here then, tonight?'

'No, she's staying at her boyfriend's.'

'Great, great,' he says, a little too enthusiastically and she smiles. He reddens. The space between them seems to have closed in now somehow. Their knees are tilted towards each other, practically touching. He shifts his arm along an inch further, and she sucks in air, knowing instinctively what's about to happen.

Her skin prickles, and for a bizarre moment she has the feeling that someone else is here in the room with them too. But when she glances around, there is nothing.

As she turns back, he kisses her, their mouths pressing roughly, urgently, against each other. He tastes metallic, oddly familiar, and she's not sure she's ever felt so alive before. He wraps his arms around her and she forgets every thought in her head, losing herself in time.

ROBBIE

A purple bed. Two figures under the sheets, threaded through each other. It's Jenn and my other self again. Light shines in under an old blind and the air is heavy with the scent of sleep and last night's alcohol. Jenn laughs at something my other self has said, that wonderful peal of noise, and he smiles back, entranced.

I must be dreaming still about the first time we met – going back up to hers, our first kiss, our first night together. But it's just so strange how it all keeps going like this, how it all feels so very real.

I'm ready to wake up now. But I'm also not. I want to stay in this moment a little bit longer.

When everything in my life changed.

I wasn't even supposed to be at the Irish bar that night. I was supposed to be working at the restaurant. But at the last minute, Matt switched with me for the Friday – some gig he wanted to go to apparently. I checked in with some guys from school, headed to meet them for pints as early as I could. We bounced around from bar to bar, and as I listened to their tales of promotions into 'proper' jobs – lawyers, accountants, surveyors – I started to miss the Alps again. I wasn't sure where my place in Edinburgh was anymore.

Looking back, I was completely lost. No clue. No plan.

But when I met Jenn that night in the Irish bar, something anchored in the pit of my stomach.

She was different – weirdly tall, with short hair. Not my usual type at all. But the way her eyes crinkled up when she smiled at me, I just melted.

And I didn't want the evening to end. Not because I wanted to sleep with her – I did, at some point, of course – just not the first night. Because even then, I think I knew we were on the verge of something important.

We talked until the sun came up, too excited by each other's company to actually fall asleep. She didn't tell me too much about her past come to think of it – didn't seem to want to speak about it. But I had all the information I needed to know. She was awesome and that was all that mattered. At some point she told me her favourite sweets were jellybeans, and I told her I'd buy her some the next day.

Because I just knew I had to see her again.

The other Robbie starts kissing her again, and I remember that feeling so well now; that intensity in the pit of my stomach, that hold she had over me. Then without warning, I think about the day she left me four years later, without any explanation.

A lightness in my head again, that pulse growing heavier against my skull, thumping insistently. I try to keep my eyes on them, but the room seems to get brighter by the second, and the image of them together on the purple bed fades out like a photo left too long in the sun.

* * *

ROBBIE

I'm back in the driver's seat. The car. My hands are welded to the wheel. Outside, the front window is that bright, bright circle of light, now glaring at me. And sitting beside me is Jenn. But I can't seem to turn to her. I cannot move my limbs.

This is where it started.

Here, in the car, driving home.

I remember now. We were talking about her work; I was squeezing her hand.

I love you.

But the rest of our conversation is blurry for some reason, and nothing is moving now. I can see dust particles suspended in the air between us, sparkling in the light. My heart is racing but I can't seem to do anything.

Then it moves. The beam inches just the tiniest fraction towards us, and I know in that moment that it's something big on the other side of the glass. Maybe a truck, maybe a bus – I'm not sure. But it's coming for us.

And she's seen it too.

FOUR

2001

JENNY

The street is foggy as they head back from their walk – *the haar*, her dad calls it. She hears a noise in the white sky above, a seagull strayed too far from the sea. Her dad walks beside her, both of them in matching green wellies and navy waterproofs. It's weird how she's almost as tall as him at only twelve. She can't help walking to the same rhythm as him: *left, right, left, right*. He looks over at her and smiles.

Eventually their house comes into view, and she wonders what her mum's been up to today. Probably resting, maybe a spot of painting. She seems to get so tired from everything these days. But not her dad – he's got endless energy, even if he doesn't actually say very much. They spent the whole afternoon rambling along the beach and in the nearby woods.

Walking up the drive, she hears the crunch of their boots on the gravel as the blue gables of Larchfield come into view, ivy pouring down one side of the door. The downstairs windows are glowing with warm light and it looks so cosy in the cold. She loves the way their house is tucked out of sight by tall trees; in the summer the garden is bursting with her mum's flowers. She's always thought it was like a fairy house.

Opening the heavyset front door, her dad steps into the porch. He stops for a moment, sniffs the air.

Burning.

In a second, he's striding into the hall and Jenny swiftly kicks off her wellies at the door and follows.

Mum.

Through the smoky kitchen doorway, she sees her dad run across to open the window. Her mum is leaning against a cupboard, apron on, eyes swollen.

'I'm sorry,' her mum's saying through sobs.

'It's alright.' Her dad crouches down beside her, places one hand on her shoulder. 'What happened, darling?'

Her mum covers her face with her hands. 'I just,' she sniffs, 'I was just trying to help out because Margaret asked me, and then I burnt one batch, so I started all over again and I—'

'Shhh,' he soothes, holding her now. 'What were you helping with?'

Jenny watches it all from the doorway – this isn't the first time she's seen her mum fall to pieces. But her dad will sort it out.

He always does.

Her mum's hands drop finally. 'I was in town getting a few bits and pieces while you two were out and I ran into Margaret, you know Margaret from the school? Mrs Hamilton,' she says, glancing briefly at Jenny. 'She was asking if I could bring things in for the senior school bake sale tomorrow, so I said I would do some cakes, but I've still got to prepare for the art class I'm taking tomorrow and I've just got so much to do.'

'Look,' her dad says gently, helping her mum up off the floor. 'Why don't you just go and have a lie down and I'll bring you a tea?'

'No, no,' she says, shaking her head resolutely. The plastic apron has a highland cow on the front and it's all bunched up, so it looks as if the cow is in pain. The red strings have come undone at her sides. 'This is for me to do.'

'Darling,' he says, touching her arm. 'Don't worry about it. Jenny will help, won't you, Jenny?'

He looks over at her and she nods, smiles. She loves baking with him. 'Definitely.'

Her mum looks between them both, pauses. 'Well, OK then. I'm sorry about this, it's just I didn't feel I could say no.'

'Don't worry.' Her dad smiles. 'But it will be fun for us, don't worry. You go and sit down.'

Her mum finally smiles, her face lovely and bright now. She unhooks the apron from over her neck and lays it on the back of a kitchen chair. With a final pause, she walks out of the room.

'Now, let's think about what type of cake we should make for the bake sale,' her dad says, turning to Jenny with a piece of chocolate debris. He snaps off half for her, before eating his own.

Watching her dad across from her, she suddenly realises how they do the exact same thing; both chewing on one side of their mouths, except he does it on the left and she does it on the right, so it's more like a reflection. It's sort of funny because they look the same too, with their dark hair and green eyes.

Like mirror images, her mum says.

ROBBIE

Through the open window, I gaze in at the kitchen scene in front of me.

What the actual fuck is happening?

I feel like I can't get a moment to think, to process. One moment I was in the Irish bar watching myself, the next, in the car with Jenn. Now I'm trapped outside this house because I can't turn the fucking door handle. I can't get in.

Just breathe, Robbie.

OK, what do I know? We were driving back from the hospital and we were talking. I was holding her hand and then suddenly a truck was coming towards us – a big one. But I couldn't drive away; we were suspended in the car somehow. Our bodies are trapped there but I'm also bouncing around these places – the beach with child Jenn, then the Irish bar with older Jenn, followed by her flat and now what appears to be her childhood home. Which means what?

This isn't a dream.

The words come to me from nowhere.

My stomach drops out of me.

What if the truck's already hit us and I just can't remember?

What if I'm dead and this is the afterlife?

26

I look down at myself – same New Balance trainers, same jeans, same red hoody I was wearing in the car.

Fuck, maybe I'm like the guy in that film, *Ghost*, Jenn made me watch; just following her around but she can't see me.

I pinch my hand as hard as I can. It hurts. The skin goes white then pink. I rest my hands on the window ledge in front of me. It's, of course, solid.

Thank fuck.

Not dead.

I just need to wake up from whatever this is. I shut my eyes. Think as hard as I can about waking up. *Wake up, Robbie!*

Nothing.

I open my eyes.

Fuck, it's bloody Baltic out here. I rub my hands together, blow on them, before running back around to the front door. Trees, bushes, an old swing set all flash by; gravel crunches beneath my trainers.

Standing in front of solid oak, I reach out to the handle, hold it. I still can't turn it though – like my hand won't connect or something.

Bollocks.

I run back over to the kitchen window. She's still there. Does she know I'm here? Is the Jenn I know in there somewhere?

I imagine telling her about it after; she'll never believe me in a million years. And maybe I won't either. I can chalk it down to the excitement of the last twenty-four hours with her.

She came back.

I watch as Jenn wipes flour from the surfaces and her dad sweeps the floor – or at least I assume it's her dad. I've never actually met him, of course. I just saw him once, in that photo album Jenn has from before he left.

Photos. There's loads of them on the far wall, all different sizes. Ducking under the window, I try to get a better look. It's weird seeing Jenn in her childhood like this, and I can't help wondering if she told me about all this once, or showed me photos and now I'm just conjuring it all up in my mind, inserting myself in memories I was never part of. Seems vaguely unlikely given how little she told me about her childhood. But, at any rate, seeing her here now, in this warm, secure setting, like my family – I'm just surprised. I got the impression it had always been dysfunctional.

Most of the pictures are hazy, faint outlines of a child on a swing, or blurs of people on a beach. My spine tingles. One in particular is clear though. It's of her parents on what looks to be their wedding day. Just barely, I can make out the words *Marian and David* scrawled in a corner. It's got to be the early eighties from the looks of it, with her puffy dress and his penguin tux and that slightly bleary colour quality to it. But the thing that strikes me the most is how ecstatic they both look. They're walking towards the camera, and she's looking beyond the lens, with her mouth slightly open as though about to call to someone. She's stunning, with her flowing red hair and band of white flowers around her head. Glowing. But it's him, the way he's looking down at her, gazing at her as though he just can't quite believe his luck.

Where did it all go wrong?

The pulsing in my head starts again, a humming in the ears and I can't quite make out the features in the photo anymore. I see the blurry shapes of Jenn's dad stacking the dishwasher, Jenn getting out fresh mixing bowls, a set of scales. The scene in front of me starts to dull, smears like wet paint, until all that is left is that kitchen light – a bright circle shining in the gloom.

FIVE

2014

JENN

A bright light, shining in her eyes. She blinks down to see a warm kitchen below and immediately smiles. Mulled wine bubbles away on the hob and on the table in the alcove are bumper bags of crisps, a variety of liquor – vodka, gin, rum, a keg. Half a bottle of cheap wine is flanked by two ruddy glasses on the sideboard and, at the heart of it all, is Robbie, in his cinnamon-scented chaos, smiling at her.

'Looks good on you,' he says, and she follows his eyes down to her torso, the stars and the sparkle, the woolly flakes over an upside-down snowman.

'Uh huh,' she laughs.

She knows he's joking, obviously. His sweater is about four sizes too big and drowns her lanky frame. But the way he's looking at her. *Oh, that look.* She feels her cheeks heating up.

'I can't believe you have more than one Christmas jumper.' She smiles, diverting attention away. 'They're so naff.'

'Naff?' he says, in mock horror. 'Never say that around my family, they love this kind of shit.'

'Well,' she laughs, 'I can safely say mine did not.'

She stops when she realises what she's just said; sees his questioning expression. A familiar heavy feeling creeps up on her, the one that settles in her stomach when anyone mentions family, or Christmas, or anything that other people perceive as normal. But a moment later, she's pushed it away. She's not dealing with it now – not tonight.

'You do realise I'm not going to go all Bridget Jones on you,' she says quickly, indicating at his front. 'With your reindeer jumper. I'm not just going to fall in love with you, Robbie Stewart.'

There's a moment between them, a look that says everything. She can feel her stomach fluttering as she realises the word that now hangs between them. Then he smiles.

'So, what I'm hearing is, I'm a bit of a . . . what was he called? Mr Darcy? Is that it?'

He cocks his eyebrow at her and she can't help grinning, shaking her head. As he crosses over, her heart leaps, thinking about their afternoon in bed watching films, having sex and eating jellybeans – they'd just about made it out the door to get provisions for the party tonight. Only five weeks since they met each other, and she's experienced more fun, more excitement, than she possibly has in her whole life. Every time they see each other feels surprising: what they'll eat, ('Mexican or Mediterranean, Jenn? Hell, I'll just make you both'); what they'll do in the evenings if they're both off – there's always some great party or comedy night or obscure movie that Robbie's desperate to see; what sweet, yet hilarious message he'll send to her at work – *I like you more than Tabasco sauce on eggs, have a great day*, or *I like you more than* Top Gun *on a hungover Sunday, have a great day.*

And she loves who she becomes with him too: the happiest, most spontaneous version of herself. She can't imagine a time now when she didn't know Robbie; when she didn't feel this enormous pull to him.

As he places his hands on her waist, she smiles up at him.

'Exactly how many Christmas jumper parties do you attend each year out of interest?' she asks, looping her hands round the back of his neck.

'Oh, you know, I'm a man about town. Everyone wants a piece of me,' he grins.

'Is that so?'

She can smell the nutmeg and clementine peel on his fingers, the vanilla from the pod he'd deftly split down the middle just an hour ago. His lips are still stained a berry red from sampling the mulled wine – apparently a necessity at any good Christmas party.

She feels a flutter of apprehension about tonight, his friends should be here any minute; the first time she's met any of them. They've been in such a bubble before now.

Is it about to pop?

'I meant to ask,' he says, after a moment. 'What do you normally do for Christmas? You going to Cornwall?'

That curious look again; she tucks her hair behind one ear.

'To see my mum? No, I'm actually working.'

'At Christmas?' he asks, horrified, and she laughs.

'Some people do work at Christmas you know?' she says, with mock seriousness.

'But Christmas is for getting drunk in front of *Jurassic Park* and passing out!' he cries, pauses. 'You could always, I mean, you could come around to my parents after your shift, if you like?'

'Oh god, I'd love that,' she says, meaning it. 'But I'm not off until eight, maybe nine. It will be too late by the time I get there, seeing as I've never met your parents before . . . I could come over Boxing Day though?'

'I'll take it,' he says, and kisses her again.

The doorbell goes, cutting through the moment and Robbie pulls back dramatically. 'Here we go.'

Twenty minutes later and the kitchen seems to have ballooned with people, all laughing and chatting away. She's introduced in quick succession – guys from school, folk from the restaurant and its lively owner, Matt. They're all friendly, all loud, just like him. *So, you're Jenn,* they say, with knowing smiles and sideways glances. He's never been in anything with a girl longer than a few months, she knows.

She offers them drinks, though most pull out their own bottles, plonk them on the table, in the fridge – there's a drill evidently. Doorbell goes again, more people arrive. Robbie's chatting to everyone, buzzing, eyes alight.

He's in his element.

Eventually, a short, good-looking guy suddenly appears in the doorway. He's got dark hair; almost aquamarine blue eyes and he's wearing a slightly smarter green Christmas jumper. Robbie throws up his arms jubilantly before he marches across and they do a clap-on-the-back hug.

Marty.

She recognises him from photos she's seen online, and she feels nervous again – this is Robbie's best friend, the guy he grew up with. *Like Katy*, she thinks, and feels sad for a moment.

Walking back across to her, Robbie says, 'Jenn, I'd like you to meet my idiot pal, Marty.'

'Good to finally put a face to the name,' Marty smiles. 'I've heard lots about you.'

'Oh really,' she says, raising her eyebrows at Robbie, but she can't help feeling secretly pleased. She turns back to Marty. 'Do you fancy a drink? There's, well, every liquor you can possibly think of.' She sweeps her hand across the table.

'I'm sure there is,' Marty says with a laugh, 'but I'll just have one of my beers, thanks.' He indicates at the four-pack he's carrying.

'This one's a lightweight.' Robbie shakes his head.

She doesn't know if she's imagining it, but she's sure Marty grimaces briefly at the comment.

'I'm just going to grab a cold one for me,' Robbie says, placing an empty can on the sideboard. 'Jenn, you need anything?'

'All set, thanks.' She nods at her still-full wine glass before he bounds off to the fridge.

'So,' Marty smiles when he's gone, 'Robbie's still introducing me as Marty then.'

She looks at him, confused.

'It's really Chris,' he says, 'but my second name is McFly, so Robbie dubbed me Marty at school.'

'Like . . . the band?'

'No, like Marty McFly in *Back to the Future*?' He raises one eyebrow, but there's no disdain there. 'Because of my apparent height deficit.'

'Ah,' she says, as it falls into place: the eighties film with Michael J Fox. She watched it once when she was younger.

'So, should I call you Chris then?'

'Nah,' he grins, 'Marty's fine.' He nods around the room. 'Bit nerve wracking meeting everyone in one go tonight I'd imagine.'

She breathes out finally, nods. 'Totally. But everyone's so nice.'

'Just wait until later,' Marty says, pulling one of the cans out the pack. 'This lot will be hanging from the rafters and you'll be chasing them out of here.'

'I'll look forward to that,' she grins.

Robbie arrives back, beer in hand. He looks between her and Marty, both grinning away, and smiles. 'So, I was thinking, the three of us could go to this gig in town next Thursday if you're keen, Marty? It's that Scottish band we used to love, you know, the one where the guy goes apeshit at the end of every set.'

'I'd like that,' Marty says, then pauses. 'But I'm afraid I can't.'

'Don't tell me it's work again.'

'Well, sort of.'

Robbie rolls his eyes at Jenn. 'He can't help himself, honestly. Work, work, work.'

Marty rocks forward on his toes. 'Well, what if I said the work's in New York?'

Robbie's mouth opens. 'What the fuck?'

'Yup, I got a job there. At an asset management company.'

'Mate,' Robbie says, grinning now, 'that's amazing. You've always wanted to work there.'

'Congratulations.' Jenn smiles too.

'Thanks,' Marty says. 'So, what do you think, you guys going to come out and visit me or what?'

'Too fucking right we are,' Robbie says. Then his face falls. 'Shit, I'm really going to miss you, mate.'

A twinge in her chest. She loves how much he loves his friend.

'Ah, you'll be alright, I'm sure,' Marty says, but he's clearly touched too.

'Hang on,' Robbie says, his expression changing again, 'what happened to that Claire girl? I thought you guys were all loved up?'

Marty smiles. 'Claire's a great girl, but I think there's a bit more to love than just hanging out with someone.'

Robbie shakes his head, still in shock evidently. 'I just don't understand how I didn't hear about all this before?'

'Well, you've been somewhat occupied recently,' Marty says, a spark in his eye.

Robbie looks across at Jenn, then, pulls her closer to him. His expression is so openly adoring, so unselfconscious after what Marty just said, that her stomach fills with butterflies.

When they finally turn back to Marty, he's looking at them in a strange way, almost like he's trying to work something out.

Or work me out?

But a second later, new voices boom from across the now-packed kitchen and he and Marty are over to them, guffawing and laughing again. The moment passes.

Taking a sip of her wine, she smiles, thinking about how much she likes Robbie's loud and colourful world, full of parties and trips and fun.

It's so different from hers.

Sometimes she wonders why he's even with her.

What if this is just a fling?

The thought makes her dizzy suddenly and she veers quickly across to the kitchen sink, smiling at people she's been introduced to as she goes. Grabbing a glass from the drying rack, she pours herself a water and gulps it down. She's just never felt this way with a guy before, like her world's been tipped upside down, and now she can't see straight.

A noise behind her and familiar arms go around her waist again. Looking up at the reflection in the window, she sees Robbie standing behind her, his mouth lifting at the sides, and she melts back into his chest.

'Look,' he says quietly, and points forwards over her shoulder.

A wisp of snow catches on the kitchen window, then another. As she turns back to face him, he takes hold of her hand.

'Come on,' he says, pulling her from the busy kitchen and along the smoky corridor of his flat. Picking up keys from the hall table, he opens the door and they traipse out onto the cold tenement landing, down two flights of stone steps to the ground floor.

Inserting a rusty key into a shabby-looking door at the back, Robbie pushes it open and icy air immediately rushes at her body. But instead of finding the basic patch of green she was expecting, she's faced with perfect luminous snow with sugar-dusted foliage around the sides. It's so very dark, but the tenement windows around them are lit up like candles.

She exhales, her breath misting out to nothing in the sky.

How long has it been snowing? Her feet sink in, making muffled imprints as she goes, and from the middle of the garden she looks up, into the great void above. A million tiny feathers start falling again, like pillowcases have been split in the sky.

'It never snows in December anymore.'

'I know,' she hears him say, 'and I'm sure it did loads when I was a kid. Though sometimes I wonder if I just imagined that.'

Looking back down, she realises he's watching her, a soft look in his eye. The world is a hushed white around them, and she casts her mind back to her own childhood winters: blue plastic sledges, white rocky slopes – her dad in a grey hat. It seems so oddly vivid for a moment.

'You didn't imagine it,' she says eventually.

A solitary flake lands on her eyelash, and she blinks the cold weight of it away. A thousand more drift down around her, growing thicker by the second, and suddenly Robbie is right there in front of her.

'I wanted to talk to you earlier today about something actually,' he says.

'What is it?' She looks up at him quickly, heart hammering. Perhaps this is it after all. Perhaps he's changed his mind.

All too good to be true.

'Well,' he says, breathing in. 'I just wanted to check if we're a couple?'

He says the word *couple* like it's a funny thing, like it's a silly expression. But his eyes are all sincerity, nerves.

Then suddenly she's grinning, as his words sink in.

He feels the same.

'I think we might be,' she says, and kisses him deeply.

When they finally break apart, Robbie reaches down with his bare hands and scoops up a heap of snow. He packs it together, eyes flashing with mischief.

'You do realise you're missing your own party right now,' she says.

He shrugs. 'What of it?'

Taking a step towards her, she starts to back away from the newly formed snowball in his hands.

'Don't you dare,' she laughs, waggling a finger at him.

Running under the beam of his kitchen window she has the oddest feeling that they're being watched – out here, in the snow, together. She looks up sharply, but there's nothing there behind the misty glass. Just a feeling.

A sense that they're not alone.

Two weeks later

ROBBIE

Long grey lockers ahead of me. A green vinyl floor beneath my feet. A bench down the middle of the space. No windows, but there's blue tinsel strung up along the top of a pin board with flyers on it. I don't know this place. My heart is racing. I can't get my bearings. This is relentless, being flung around from place to place with absolutely no warning of when it will happen, or where I'll go next.

At least I was in my flat before; remembered the Christmas jumper party I'd hosted there five years ago.

Yet another bizarre playback of stuff I've already been through.

And that image of the two of us out in the snow, when I asked her to be my girlfriend – I'd totally forgotten about it. Fuck, I was so nervous she'd say no. After all, I knew how different we were, how out-of-my-bloody-league she was. But there was just something about her that sent my pulsing racing. She was so different from all the other girls I'd dated in the past with their sparkly skirts and dull conversation. Jenn was intelligent and kind and she made me want to do better. *Be better.*

She made me want to actually go home at the end of the night, rather than to endless after-parties. She made me want to take her out for brunch, so we could argue about what the ideal breakfast was (she thought bacon butty, I thought full English), then go and see my parents for a bloody tea. She made me want to think about the future because, for the first time in my life, someone really believed in that future.

Believed in me.

A clattering noise from somewhere. Shit, I really need to figure out where I am. Glancing around, I try to identify something else, anything else.

That smell.

The air is thick with antiseptic, soap and something else I can't put my finger on, something unappealing. That's it – hospitals. I never did like those places. I only went inside a couple of times when I was younger, for some drunken injury or other, usually caused by me mouthing off after the pubs. Jenn finally found the scar on my chin after I'd shaved off the stubble. I remember her running a finger along the curved length of it as we lay in bed. *It's like you're always smiling somewhere*, she'd said.

Footsteps behind me. I turn sharply to see her passing through a doorway in blue scrubs. My heart lifts at the sight. We're in Jenn's hospital then, in Edinburgh.

Moving across to a locker, she clicks the padlock dial around before opening the door with a metallic thunk. In one graceful movement, she removes her baggy top before dropping it in a nearby container. She has a tight grey t-shirt on underneath and she looks so slim now, her shoulder blades protruding out slightly from the thin material. She takes off the trousers, revealing black leggings underneath, and dumps them too. It's so reassuring somehow to see her here, in her normal working environment.

Somewhere inside myself, I finally clock that each place I go to is a real moment from her past. Not mine.

Is this time travel?

Don't be stupid, Robbie.

I can't help thinking about that truck, how close it was. How real it was. Then nothing, followed by all these places in her past.

What does that mean?

I feel sick.

I turn to see a slightly shorter girl, with pretty wide-set eyes and sandy hair in a ponytail. It's Hilary.

I was at her wedding just yesterday.

In the real world at any rate.

'Hey.' Jenn smiles at her, as she retrieves her bag, her blue coat. 'That you done?'

'Yeah, thank god,' Hilary says, sitting down on the bench and looking up at her. 'Shitty day, should have left an hour ago. At least we can go and enjoy Christmas Day now, right?' She starts to pull off her trainers. 'Time to get absolutely sloshed.'

Classic Hils. Before, at least.

'Totally, you deserve it.' Jenn takes the band off her head which keeps her hair back.

Putting on her jacket, she swings the backpack up on two shoulders and takes her helmet from the locker before shutting it again. Just as she's heading to leave, Hilary twists back to look at her

'Oh, Jenn, I meant to ask . . . '

Jenn looks back, fingers on the door handle.

'You heard back from the hospitals in Sydney yet?'

Jenn opens her mouth to speak, closes it again.

'Yeah, yeah I did actually. I got offers from both in the end.'

'Oh my god, that's fantastic! When are you going?'

Jenn pauses for a moment before replying. 'Well, I don't think I'm going to go anymore actually . . . '

'What?' Hilary says, aghast. 'But you were so excited about it? Australia was your dream?'

I don't understand, she never told me anything about this. Not once did she say she wanted to go and work abroad.

Jenn smiles as she holds open the door. 'Dreams change,' she says, and with a mischievous expression she walks through. 'Merry Christmas, Hilary.'

Hilary twists around on the bench. 'You've met someone, haven't you? I knew it! It's that guy from the Irish bar, isn't it? Come on, tell me!'

But Jenn simply grins, before walking out. Just in time, I slip through the door behind her.

Outside is pitch black and icy cold after the heat of the hospital. I shiver in my hoody. It's insane the amount I can feel. Everything just seems so bloody *real*. Exactly the way it would have been.

There's grit on the concrete and I remember the snow came and went this year, leaving icy brown mounds around the city by Christmas. Snow in Edinburgh never lasts long. It seems like a world away now. I follow her as she heads towards the bike rack, feeling like a stalker and protector all at once.

'Jenn,' I call out to her back, but she just shifts her backpack further up onto her shoulders, walks with purpose. I feel so lost. The white hospital buildings loom up from the darkness around us, like something from a futuristic society. Lights are on in every window and lamps illuminate the pathways connecting it all. I always thought it must be a bizarre place to work; this world that just keeps running day and night without stopping. Patients going in constantly, coming out sometimes: the endless cycle of birth and death and everything in between behind those walls. I've just never had the compassion for it. The idea of examining people, touching their skin and god knows what else, makes me feel a little ill. But Jenn, she's different from me. She lights up helping people. It's what makes her tick.

What made her leave it all behind?

At the bicycle rack now, she comes to a halt in front of a black one with yellow flashes and starts to fiddle with one of the locks until it releases and she pulls the bike free. A figure appears from nowhere behind her and she spins around, eyes alert to danger, before her mouth lifts at the sides, recognition in her eyes.

'What are you doing here?'

Turning, I see the other Robbie standing beside me, holding a plant pot. A ruby flower flares out the top of it.

'Well, I thought I'd come and keep you company,' he says, smiling in the dark. He's wearing a black beanie; heavy Gore-Tex jacket and his cheeks are red raw from the wind. What does he look like? Wearing his snowboarding gear around Edinburgh, carrying a plant.

'But it's so late?' she says. 'You should be drunk and watching *Jurassic Park* by now.'

She seems genuinely apologetic. She's always hated putting other people out.

He shifts position slightly, looks lost for words for once. 'Well, I've spent quite a lot of time with the family today already. Just thought a change might be nice.'

'A change,' she repeats.

'Yeah.'

She peers at the plant, arches an eyebrow.

'Oh, yeah,' he says, as though just remembering he's holding it. 'This is for you. My mum wanted you to have it.'

'Seriously?' she says, eyes lighting up, unnecessarily delighted. 'That's so kind. I love Poinsettia.'

'That's it!' he cries, tilting his head back to the sky briefly. 'I could not for the life of me remember the name on the cycle up.'

'I'm sorry, you cycled with a plant?'

'Well yeah, I'd had a few drinks with dinner. Thought best not to kill myself in a car getting here.'

I notice the silver bike behind him, propped up merrily.

'You're *such* a weirdo,' she says, eyes creasing.

'You're not totally normal yourself, you know, Jennifer Clark,' he says softly. 'Spending Christmas alone.'

'Christmas night,' she clarifies, holding a finger up. 'I have been working remember.'

He rolls his eyes. 'Yes, yes. You are a better person than me, I get it.' But there's no malice there. He's just smiling stupidly at her.

'Anyway,' he says, hunching his shoulders. 'It's bloody freezing out here. Let's get going.'

As she hauls her bike out towards his, she looks up at him, and there's this expression, like she can't quite believe he's here.

Watching them ride off, I wonder if I'll be able to go with them too, and I start to run across the tarmac, past the parked cars and up the grassy verges. But then they disappear ahead of me into the darkness, and I feel myself fading away again, disappearing too. Her words from the locker room, about Australia and turning down jobs, ring in my mind, and it dawns on me that Jenn gave up a continent for me.

She gave up another life.

As my head starts that thumping again, I look down to see a ruby red leaf below me on the ground, from the Poinsettia I gave her; the 'Christmas star' she called it later as she set it on the kitchen sill.

That was a Christmas to remember.

It hits me.

Oh god.

Oh no, no, no.

SIX

2002

ROBBIE

An explosion of red sparks in the sky. Fireworks.

Darkness again. Freezing cold air.

It's pitch black now, other than an enormous bonfire ahead of me. There's a roar from it, a crackle of burning and the rich stench of wood smoke fills my nose as the flames torch the night sky.

Pulsing in my head. I press my hands to my temple.

It comes crashing down on me like a wave.

Life is flashing before her eyes.

A noise escapes from me, and there's an ache in my chest, like someone's crushing it. Everything feels peculiar suddenly. This can't be happening.

Can it?

But a feeling in my gut is telling me it is.

The truck must have skidded on ice into our lane. She saw it coming towards her, and thought she was about to die. She's

47

reliving her life memories. Oh fuck, I've heard of this type of thing before – near-death experiences. All that out-of-body stuff.

That's exactly what this is.

But why am I watching it too?

Holy shit.

I try to breathe.

We need to stop this. If I can just wake her up, haul us out of her memories, then perhaps I can swing the car right into the other lane. I can't go left – there's a pavement, wall, then a row of houses behind it; we'd both be dead.

But we were suspended – how do I even know everything will go back to normal? How do I know I'll be able to move right away?

My mind is spinning, nausea rising.

I need to find her, now.

Stumbling forwards, I see kids and adults everywhere, running around, shouting, screaming. An explosion sounds behind me again, and I turn sharply, look up to see a blue firework smashed to bits across the night sky. I'm at some kind of bonfire night, a school one maybe. A few teenage-looking boys stalk past in their jackets and hats. Their faces are all blurry. *What the fuck?* A shiver goes down my spine. I look over at some adults holding plastic cups at the side. Same thing.

A shimmer of light – there, I see a figure a little further out to the side, standing in the darkness, with a sparkler. A girl. Walking quickly over I know it's her, I know it's Jenn, and my heart fills up inside.

I'm running now, breathing ragged. She's taller, older than she was in the kitchen. She's wearing a woolly hat with a large bobble. Her legs look lanky beneath her duffel coat. Thirteen, I'm going to say, like those boys. She looks so alone here, so isolated in a field by herself.

The sparkler is still going, but it's half-way down now, and still she doesn't take her eyes of it. It seems to be pulling her to it, hypnotising her, like she's glazed over. *What's she doing?*

'Jenn,' I say, knowing it's pointless. I've tried this already.

'Jenn!' I almost shout now.

She doesn't move, doesn't look up from the light.

I move closer, place my hand on her shoulder, to make her feel my touch, but she doesn't even flinch. She doesn't know I'm here, right beside her.

I feel terrified. I'm shaking. 'You have to listen to me, you have to hear me.'

Down and down the sparkler burns on the charcoaled stick, and she's got no gloves on. Where are her parents? Why is she out here alone?

Through all my own panic and fear, it dawns on me.

This must be after her dad left.

The sparkler is getting very low now, spitting angrily. I don't understand what she's doing. It could burn her.

'Drop it, Jenn,' I say, my voice steelier now, but she doesn't look up, doesn't hear a thing I'm saying. She just watches it, burning and burning.

49

'Come on. Drop it, Jenn,' I try again. I want to shake her, tell her to look up, listen to me.

As the sparkler hisses to the bottom and the sparks flash just above her fingers – she starts to cry, tears pouring down her face. Just before the sparks are about to hit her skin, I swing my hand towards it.

And everything goes black.

Six weeks later

JENNY

The fairy lights flash from the Christmas tree, but they're all out of sync. The top row is blinking slowly, and the bottom row strobes like crazy and it's hurting her eyes. Her mum threw them up yesterday on Christmas Eve, which seemed pretty late to do it.

Her dad always got the tree up at the start of December. They'd go to the garden centre together, just the two of them, and she'd pick the best one, the tallest of the bunch for their high-ceilinged living room. But she'd always make sure that there was something odd about it, a crooked branch, a discoloured trunk. She doesn't like them being too perfect. Then they'd put up the decorations together at home, with hot chocolate and Christmas crooners in the background. Only the oldies. *The most wonderful time of the year.*

She checks her watch again, a chunky purple one her dad got for her thirteenth birthday in October. Her throat catches,

It's still only one in the afternoon, so there's plenty of time. He'll be here. He has to come back for Christmas dinner.

For a moment, she thinks back to the day he left them, with no note, and no warning. It had been September, when the leaves had just started to turn orange. She'd tipped from her warm bed that morning onto her sheep's wool rug – the one her dad got her at a farm shop up north. She was excited because it was a Saturday and they were going on a day trip to Culzean Castle: her dad would already be down in the kitchen making sandwiches, and her mum would be in bed still, trying to get those final extra minutes before the day started. Tripping down the stairs, she listened out for the familiar hum of the kettle, the sounds of early morning activity.

But even as she turned at the foot of the stairs, she could see the kitchen was quiet, empty. She looked at the old clock in the hall, the hands pointed sleepily to eight o'clock. *He can't still be in bed, can he?*

She went back up the stairs then, two at a time, and an anxious question mark started forming at the back of her mind. She opened the door slowly – feeling a little awkward about running in now that she was no longer a child – and looked towards their bed, the place she'd snuck into every morning when she was younger; the sleepy pocket she liked to nestle into at dawn.

Her mum still had her eyes shut, head resting on her hands, which were pressed together like a child pretending to sleep.

But her dad wasn't there either.

'Mum,' she said softly. No movement. Her eyelids were puffy, like she'd been crying the night before.

'Mum,' she said, louder this time, and she saw the signs of stirring, her lips opening and shutting like a codfish. She was about to speak again, when she stopped. Because in the space where her dad should have been, the sheets were pulled up to the pillow, tucked neatly under. *Like he's made his side already*. And even though Jenny had known he could still be somewhere else in the house, could have popped out for some milk this morning, that cover pulled up high had made her whole body lurch.

A burning smell floods her nostrils suddenly and the memories evaporate. She gets up with a jolt, runs out of the living room, through the hall and into the kitchen. *I wish it could be Christmas every day* is blasting from the radio, and the room is filled with thick smoke. She wades through it, coughing.

'Mum?'

She sees her pulling the green roasting tin out of the oven and onto the side with a loud clank.

'No, no, no.'

She looks so lost in her festive red dress and bare feet; her gloved hands held high like she's about to do some sort of strange dance in the fog.

'I've ruined it,' she cries, lowering her arms.

Jenny walks back over to the hob, reaches up to turn the fan on as she's seen her dad do a thousand times. She looks around at the messy work surfaces, the pots and pans bubbling over.

The smell of burnt potatoes wafts from the tin on the side and her stomach sinks. Why did she leave her mum to handle it all? What was she thinking?

But she can sort something else for them. She's been doing most of the cooking recently anyway. Looking in the fridge, she scans the contents, imagining how proud he'll be of her taking control of everything. He'll say that he's sorry he's not been in touch but he's been far away designing some new amazing building. He'll say it was a secret project, one that he couldn't even tell his family about and that's why he left without warning. He'll say that there was no phone signal, no way to get letters to her either, but now he's back and he'll never leave them again. He'll say all of this just as soon as he gets here.

He has to come back.

She pulls out leftover chicken from a shelf finally and puts it on the sideboard. They could have it with some pasta, a little sauce? Yes, that will work. Lifting the apron from the back of the kitchen door, Jenny ties it around herself.

'You go sit down, Mum,' she says in her best Dad voice. 'I'll bring you a tea.'

For a second, her mum looks like she'll say no. Her mouth starts working at the sides, and a noise comes out, but then she clamps it shut. Nods. She looks so tired, with purple half-moons under her eyes, and Jenny feels worried. *Will Mum start taking the art classes again? Do they have any money?*

'You're a good girl, darling,' her mum says, walking towards Jenny and kissing her cheek. 'I'm sorry I spoilt it. Silly me. I'm just . . . struggling with everything. I might need to go and lie down for a moment. I'll come back and help clear all this up though.'

'That's OK,' Jenny says brightly, 'I'll do it, don't worry.'

With another nod, her mum walks out of the room, disappears. Turning back to the kitchen, Jenny sees the room is a state. She sighs. *So much to clear up.* But she has to make this better – has to make this better for her mum. She goes to the window to open it and start airing the place out. But just as she's about to lift it up, she sees a circle of mist appear right in front of her eyes, like someone's standing on the other side, breathing on the freezing glass.

Her heart beats faster for a moment. The *faraways* again. She quickly wrenches the window open.

SEVEN

2015

ROBBIE

Pulsing. I press my hands to my temples. Light floods in from windows high up, shining in on strange split columns below. I squint around. There are multiple levels of stained-glass windows and a grand organ. The place is huge and cavernous, stretching out to four points like a cross, and there are people everywhere, wandering, drifting almost.

Their faces are all blurry again, but I can still see they're wearing shorts or dresses – clothes for hot weather – with sunglasses perched on heads. Some have cameras in hand, some are sitting down in pews up ahead, heads bent in prayer. This is a cathedral.

And for a brief moment, in the calming expanse of this place, I feel calm too.

Then I remember, and it's like waking up in the morning and being hit by the shit thing.

Like how it was after Jenn left me eight months ago.

But so much of it isn't making sense to me still. Like why am I seeing her memories too? And why does it keeping jumping around in time? One second I'm in her childhood, the next, it's us.

And how the hell could I suddenly knock that firework out of her hand? I couldn't do anything before; I couldn't even open a bloody door at her house.

But none of that matters right now. The main thing is finding her, warning her about what's happening to us; telling her that none of this is real, and what's actually fucking real is that truck. Because I know she's in there somewhere, I know she's starting to sense that I'm here. I saw it on her face in the kitchen, when she looked out at me.

Or through me.

I just need to figure out where she is. But where is this place? There's a trace of something in the air, something like the incense Fi used to burn in her room when her hair was pink and she listened to Metallica.

Sagrada Familia, the cathedral in Barcelona.

That's it! I remember visiting as a teenager once, with the whole family. But if this is Jenn's memory, then how am I here?

Suddenly I know when this is, this day in her world. Jenn came here alone. On our first holiday abroad together.

Right, think, Robbie. Where is she? This place is huge, a maze practically. Weaving my way through tourists, I look out across the sea of heads: black, brown, blonde and grey ones all scattered like marbles. Voices in all different accents, mingling together. I can't see her anywhere. Oh god, this is literally like trying to find a needle in a haystack.

Stay calm, Robbie. What would Jenn do?

Wait. Surely if this is where I started, she's going to come this way at some point? That's what's happened everywhere else after all. Craning my head up to the magnificent ceiling, I know instinctively this is the best plan. This is all I've got.

The sound of Spanish voices nearby. It starts coming back to me; this holiday. We'd been going out for about nine months at the time. We bobbed around the south of France for a week, before finishing in Barcelona for a few days – it was all either of us could manage with work at that point. We took trains or drove rental cars between places, taking in the scorched land-scapes as we went. We strolled along the promenade in Nice, drank too much cheap wine in the cobbled backstreets of Montpellier, walked hand and hand down Las Ramblas like the tourists we were.

She definitely regretted letting me book the accommodation in Barcelona. Gràcia, I think the area was called. What a disaster. But by the end of the three days, we kind of liked the place: the way the bed sagged in the middle and we rolled into each other every clammy night; the way we played heated games of cards with a bottle of wine before heading out in the evenings; how the shower was either scalding hot or freezing cold in the mornings. I remember her coming out of the bathroom that final day of the trip, pink towel wrapped tightly around her, skin blotchy, eyes tired from the night before. The Spanish sun shone through the lace curtains and covered her shoulder in patterns of light. People called to each other on the street below, cars trundled by, and we had one final day left before we flew back in the morning.

'You planning to get up any time soon?' she teased, taking a long green dress out of the wardrobe. Dropping her towel, it landed in a puddle at her feet and she slipped the dress down over her sun-kissed body.

I pulled my hands down over my face in bed. I felt rough and I needed water urgently. The room felt like the surface of the sun. Far too many sangrias the night before. Far too many beers in that bar-cum-club we went to after.

'God, I feel like hell,' I said, closing my eyes.

'Aw, poor boy,' she replied, turning around. 'Well, we can always get some food before Sagrada Familia, that should sort you out. Always does.'

My heart sunk. I'd forgotten about going to see the cathedral that day.

I found the Gaudí stuff a bit weird, and I'd seen it all before. But I'd been up for going along – before that hangover kicked in. The last thing I wanted to do was traipse around a crowded tourist attraction.

'Why don't we just go sit on the beach today?' I suggested. 'We're both struggling. We could get some lunch, some beers. What do you think?'

She went to pick up her brush from the bed, hair still straggling wet at her neck. She raised her eyebrows slightly.

'Well, I feel OK actually. I stopped drinking when we got to the club remember?'

I didn't remember her stopping. But I did recall shots for me. Lots of shots.

'And this is our last day here,' she continued. 'We had the whole afternoon on the beach yesterday?'

'And wasn't it a treat?'

'Yes,' she smiled, starting to drag the brush through her wet hair. 'But I really want to go see this place. We can go to the beach after?'

'Do you really want to walk around a cathedral today? Seriously?'

For the rest of the holiday, we'd pretty much been on the same page: eating, sightseeing, eating again, drinking, having lazy holiday sex. More holiday sex. We'd barely had to think about it. But now, something felt off.

'Yes,' she said, 'I do. We won't get another chance.'

'Sure we will. We'll come back another time?'

'Robbie,' she said, holding the brush out in front of her now. I could immediately sense she was tense. She never actually said my name out loud. Or if she did, it was the whole *Robbie Stewart* affectionately. 'I just really want to go see this final place, OK? I've been looking forward to it.'

'Why?' I asked, pinching the bridge of my nose with my fingers now. 'It's not that interesting, it's . . . odd looking.'

'Because . . . ' She stopped for a moment, as though about to say more. 'Because I just do, alright?'

My eyes blinked open and I looked across at her. I was getting annoyed now. I didn't like feeling like I had to do something just because someone made me. I sat up in bed, the white sheets scrambled around me. 'Look, why don't you just go by yourself then if you really want to? I'll head down to the beach. We can just meet up after.'

She looked confused.

'Are you serious?' she said. 'On our last day?'

'Yeah. I just don't want to go, OK?'

'But it would mean a lot to me. This particular cathedral means a lot to me.'

'But it's my holiday too,' I said, tired, pissed off. 'And I have to be back at the restaurant tomorrow night. You've got another day off. Look, I just want to relax today. It's not a big deal is it?'

I could hear the coolness in my tone, the provocative under-layer. But it was just another church, just another weird stone building. What was her problem?

'Fine,' she said after a moment, her face stony. 'Do whatever you like then.' She went to pick up her satchel and slung it over her shoulder. Picking up her sunglasses from the side table, she walked over to the door. She paused for a moment only, hand resting on the wood, before opening it and heading into the corridor. As the door had shut, I'd sensed her figure going down the corridor, upset and alone, and despite how peeved I'd felt, I'd already known I was in the wrong.

I just didn't understand why.

Faces around me suddenly come into focus – mouths, eyes, noses, just as a girl walks by me, so close I could almost touch her. She has a flowing green dress on and a long-sleeved top, which shows off her lean physique. She looks so cool, so fresh – beautiful.

It's her.

I follow quickly behind, up towards the front of the cathedral. 'Jenn!' I call, but she just keeps walking. 'Jenn,' I say again. Nothing.

Coming to a halt, I see that we're now standing beneath the incredible dome, which flares down in yellows and golds like an enormous sunflower. She cranes her pale neck up, face basked in a pool of light, and although she looks in awe – like every other tourist in this place – I can also see the tension in her face, the sadness in her eyes.

'Jenn, you *have* to hear me,' I say, placing my hand on her arm. She flinches, looks at it with an alarmed expression on her face.

She can feel me.

Yes, Jenn, yes! I'm here!

For a moment, I think I've done it. She's looking straight at me, forehead creased, lips slightly parted. Then she shakes her head, wipes a hand down her tired-looking face. With a final glance above, she turns and walks through the crowds, towards the open doors at the back of the cathedral. *Shit.* I start to follow her again, weaving through the throngs of people, but it's like she's moving too fast. There are too many people between us, around us. I can't get to her.

For fuck's sake.

'Jenn,' I cry into the cavernous space above. But she just keeps on going. She has no idea what's happening.

'Come back!'

JENN

When she gets back to the hotel it is late afternoon. The pavement underfoot has started to cool, the sun is sinking wearily into its sandy bed. She likes the way there's such a clear delineation between night and day in southern Europe, the way the sun rises and sets at the same time. It's steady and predictable and there's something about a solid black sky she likes – the stars shine that little bit brighter. In Scotland the light and dark are always changing, pushing and pushing against each other. No day is ever truly the same.

As she passes through the rather forlorn-looking entrance to the hotel, flip-flops slapping on the white-and-blue tiles, she wonders where Robbie is at this moment. Likely on the beach, she supposes.

Well, she'll be damned if she sits around waiting for him to get back now. She's going to have a shower, get changed and head out by herself. She's not wasting this last evening crying over him.

It's just, she feels so anxious in her chest, like she can't settle. She tried to enjoy today by herself, of course she did. But she was just too distracted. This is their first holiday abroad together as a couple, and that means something to her. *Doesn't it mean something to him too?*

As she reaches the top of the stairs, she crosses the tiny corridor to their shabby wooden door, lets herself in. Immediately she sees him, out on the balcony, behind a film of lace curtains which wave back into the room. She stops for a moment while he doesn't know she's there, looks at him. He's holding onto the bar ahead of him tightly and the back of his neck seems strained.

She walks across the room, and pushes back the lace. Only the sound of her shoes scuffing on the terracotta balcony makes him turn.

'I'm sorry,' he says, and she knows in his soft brown eyes that he means it, that he's been waiting here for a while. But she also knows that he still doesn't get why, and that she should tell him the truth – tell him why she wanted to go so much. *But should the reason matter? Why can't he sense it's something I needed?*

'I didn't stay long on the beach in the end,' he says.

'Too hot?' She manages a small smile.

He nods slowly, before reaching out for her hand and holding it closely in his own.

'I'm so sorry,' he says again, 'I love you so much.' Then he squeezes twice, a signal to her body of that love, which spreads through her hand, up her arm, across every part of her. She can't stand this tension between them. It feels all wrong, and it's just a blip anyway, isn't it? All couples argue from time to time. And she's just so relieved he's here.

'I love you too,' she says, before folding herself back into him.

Three weeks later

ROBBIE

Light again, warm. But a garden this time. Tall trees at the back, manicured, extensive lawn; the rockery I used to play in as a child. It's home. The sky above is pink, and there's a lingering smoky scent of barbeque.

A clink of cutlery. I turn.

It's us. My parents, me and Jenn, my sisters and wee Struan. No Max though.

'That was delicious, my love,' Mum is saying to Dad across the table. 'You outdid yourself.'

Her light brown hair rests neatly on her shoulders and the mint shirt she's wearing, open slightly at the neck, reveals a V of pink from an afternoon outside. Everyone makes enthusiastic noises in response, empty bottles of Dom Perignon glistening in the dimming light between them.

This was that dinner we had, not long after Jenn and I got back from Spain – August I think it was.

But why is Jenn coming back to it?

I'm starting to realise that the memories we come back to are significant in some way: the first time we met, the first Christmas without her dad, our first fight in Barcelona. A lot of firsts.

And that moment before she walked away in the cathedral, when I put my hand on her arm, she definitely flinched. She might not have heard me calling to her after, but she definitely

64

felt my touch. I don't know how exactly, but it feels like my impact on these memories is growing.

What else can I do then? Could I pick up that Champagne bottle? Shit, I could really use a drink. A bit of numbness would go a long way right now. I go to pick it up, try to wrench it off the table, but it doesn't budge. It's like it's stuck, or I have no strength. I try the glass beside Mum next, Fi's, Jenn's, but it's all the same.

Nothing.

'Shit,' I say, backing away from the table. But no one looks up. No one can hear me.

I don't get it.

'You know, Dad,' I hear my other self say, and look up sharply. 'I've found this great new technique for cooking meat on the grill. I could show it to you sometime if you want?'

'Ah yes,' Fi smiles from across the table. 'I forgot we had our very own Jamie Oliver here.'

Fuck's sake. Always the same, even in a memory. No one in the family ever takes me seriously.

Dad sips his wine, looks across the table at the old me. His face is rosy from the sun, but his eyes look bored under his fop of salt-and-pepper hair. 'That sounds fun, we'll do that some time.'

Predictably, he turns his attention to Fi. 'So, Max is at a conference in New York this week, is that right?'

'Yup.' Fi knocks back a large glug of wine. 'Seven whole days and nights. Must be quite the conference.'

'Excellent opportunity for him, and how's your work going at the moment, Kirsty?' Dad asks, immediately pivoting his attention to golden child number two. 'Any sign of that associate job yet?'

'Not officially,' she smiles, her eyes perking up at the sides like Mum's. 'But they've basically said it will be the end of this year.'

'Clever girl,' Dad nods. 'Mackenzie Brown are lucky to have you, I still remember doing my traineeship there. Great lads. Great firm.'

God, it's all just as bad as I remember. What the hell is his problem? It's like he still just sees me as the baby of the family, but I'm actually an adult, if he hadn't noticed. And I've been working as a chef for years now. It's not some fucking hobby.

Under the table, Jenn reaches for Robbie's leg, squeezes it.

'Fuck, why can't work just leave me alone for a minute?' Fi says, looking down at her phone. It flashes angrily back up at her.

'Your son can hear that,' Mum calls out, indicating with her chin at Struan. But he just smiles a toothy smile.

'He's heard far worse.'

'That doesn't make it any better, you're a psychologist for goodness sake,' Mum says, getting up from the table.

Fi shakes her head, takes another drink of wine.

'We actually watched a psychology programme the other day, didn't we, my love?' Mum says to Dad across the table. Classic backtracking.

Dad laughs. 'If you can call it that.'

Mum turns to Fi hopefully. 'Did you see it?'

Fi raises her eyebrows wearily. 'What was it called?'

'I can't think of the name, but it was all about unexplained human experiences. Phenomena and things like that.'

Robbie makes a noise beside her. 'What, like paranormal shit?'

'Language,' Jill says, exasperated.

'That's not psychology, Mum,' Robbie says, 'that's just hooey.'

I swallow.

I had no idea.

'Actually, it's called anomalous psychology,' Fi cuts in, pulling Struan onto her lap. She wipes his greasy face with a wet wipe. He squirms in her arms, desperately trying to get off.

'What's that?' Jenn asks, leaning forwards.

I forgot how Jenn and Fi always talk about psychology together. *I just find it interesting why people do what they do,* Jenn said while she read a book Fi had lent her once. She spent all those years studying the human body, and still, she can't get enough knowledge.

That's one of the things I love most about her.

'So, anomalous psychology is the study of the unexplained, essentially,' Fi says, her usually serious blue eyes glittering. 'Human experiences that might be called paranormal. It's an attempt to explain them using psychological and physical factors.'

'So, in essence, disproving them then,' Robbie smiles.

Fi shrugs. 'Not necessarily.'

'Do you mean things like ESP?' Jenn asks.

'Yeah, and out-of-body experiences, near-death experiences, that sort of thing. Though actually those experiences are fairly common, and aren't really associated with anything paranormal. In fact, an article in the world's leading medical journal even implied that our sense of self is not simply what our physical body does, but might exist independently of it.'

The hairs on the backs of my arms stand up on end.

What did she say?

'Alright, Freud,' Robbie teases. He picks up the stack of plates from the table and stands up.

'I'm just answering Jenn's question,' Fi retorts, and I can tell instinctively that the conversation is over.

Fuck. There was something about what Fi was saying – it could explain how I've ended up in this situation.

I need to know more.

'I'll take those inside,' Jenn says to Robbie and stands too, ushering him to sit.

'Hey,' Fi says as she goes, and Jenn turns. 'I've got a book on all that stuff somewhere I'm sure, just if you want to read more without Robbie interrupting?'

'Yeah,' Jenn nods. 'Yeah, that would be great, thanks.'

JENN

While the family continues to talk, Jenn slips away across the flagstone patio, towards the open kitchen door. The sunny South face of the enormous 1920s house smiles down on her as she goes.

In the open-plan kitchen, Jenn sets the china plates down by the sink and they land with a gentle clatter. They look old, perhaps very old, with the little string of pink roses around the white edge. Outside the mock-Tudor window, the family is laughing again on the cooling patio.

She feels so at home here, so in love with this group of people who have welcomed her into their fold like she's one of them.

She can't count the number of times they've been over to Robbie's parents' house now; popping over for coffee and biscuits, drinks and dinner, or just swinging by to say a quick hello if neither Jenn nor Robbie are working. Jill and Campbell always welcome them with open arms, particularly Jill, who's all chatter and maternal warmth. Robbie is her baby, the youngest child of three and the only boy. And he clearly adores Jill too, always hugging her and getting her cups of tea; checking if anything needs sorting around the house.

But she doesn't understand why they treat Robbie like they do sometimes – all that downplaying of his job. She doesn't get it. He could totally set up his own restaurant and make a success of it, she knows he could. *Why are they funny about it?*

As Jenn starts to run hot water into the enormous Belfast sink, footsteps on the stones outside make her turn to the door and she smiles to see Jill coming in with another pile of plates.

'Oh honey, you don't need to be doing that,' she says, seeing Jenn at the sink. 'Don't be silly.'

'It's fine,' Jenn says, rinsing a plate and putting it on the draining rack. 'Gets it done faster.'

'Shoo,' Jill sings playfully, waving her away from the sink. 'Go and help yourself to some more fizz in the fridge.'

'OK,' Jenn concedes with a laugh. 'Do you want one?'

'I really shouldn't, but I may just have a drop more,' she smiles. 'Oh, and just grab us some fresh glasses, the ones outside will be warm by now.'

Pulling open the enormous fridge, Jenn reaches for the open bottle, hears the scrape of glass against plastic as she draws it out. She goes to the ancient-looking dresser and takes down two flutes before pouring them both a drink. She probably doesn't need any more either but the day has been so lovely and the air is still warm and she wants to float along in this fuzziness for a little while longer.

Placing a glass down next to Jill at the sink, she looks back out into the garden and takes a sip.

Jill turns to her as she's rinsing a side plate, a watchful look in her eye.

'You're a good girl, you know, Jenn.'

The comment takes her by surprise, and she remembers another kitchen, another mum. *You're a good girl.*

She doesn't know what to say, and so looks down at the sandy flagstones, the cracks beneath her feet.

But Jill doesn't seem to notice any pause. 'And you get on so well with the family . . . I hope it works out with you two.'

Jenn starts. She could never break up with Robbie, it just wouldn't happen. It would be like losing a limb. She thinks about the last ten months (has it only been ten months?), about

70

every dinner he's cooked for her, every time he's made her laugh, every passionate kiss they've shared in the darkness of night and the dewy light of dawn. She thinks about all the places she now associates with him too – the tiny Lebanese restaurant around the corner they've claimed as theirs after a particularly hilarious night involving tabbouleh and her handbag, the spot on the canal where they bickered about receipts, the museum where they had hurried, euphoric sex in the loo, the cinema in town they went to two months ago, where she'd asked him in the dark why he was being so quiet and he'd just said it out loud – what she'd been feeling in her gut too – that he loved her.

'I'm not going anywhere,' Jenn says.

'Good,' Jill smiles, a trace of worry in her sparkly eyes. 'Because I like you two as a couple. He's better.'

Jenn takes another sip, heart rate elevated slightly. 'What do you mean?'

'Oh,' Jill says, turning back to the basin and recomposing her face into a smile. 'I didn't mean anything. Perhaps I've had enough fizz already.'

Jenn replays the lunch earlier in her mind, the way Robbie had been talking about ridiculous blunders at the restaurant; asking for recommendations for their upcoming long weekend in Skye; checking if Fi wanted them to look after Struan for a night before they go. He'd been warm and caring and funny. Like he always was.

Wasn't he?

Jenn waits patiently for Jill to speak again, but instead she looks out the window to where Robbie is now swinging his nephew around by the arms on the manicured green lawn. Struan is shouting with glee as Fi sits nearby, glass in hand. And a lovely smile spreads across Jill's face as the light settles on her laughter lines.

Drying her hands on a tea towel, she says without looking at Jenn, 'Now let's head back outside again.'

Jenn opens her mouth to speak, but senses the moment between them has passed. There's no picking at that thread of conversation today. Before she leaves, Jenn looks out the window to see Robbie swinging Struan around yet again. Struan's giggling like crazy, as his uncle's strong arms propel him around and around like he's about to release him up into the now-amber sky. She starts to feel dizzy as she looks at their spinning figures. She touches her fingers to her forehead and shuts her eyes for a moment.

EIGHT

2003

ROBBIE

Thumping in my head. Paint smell. Instant coffee. Pictures of sunsets on a wall and spikey plants placed on random tables and cupboards. Spotty teenagers dotted around some sort of chaotic art studio. I'm not in a school now, am I? Oh god, I fucking hated school. It was effectively a posh prison, filled with a lot of over-privileged kids and teachers who hated me. *Always pulling pranks and never listens,* one particularly damning report said.

This must be Jenn's school at least. I see her now, by the window, sitting across from some guy. Unlike the rest of the class, all with their heads down sketching, Jenn's looking up and out through the large industrial panes at the puffy white sky beyond. *What's she doing?* She looks glazed, that way you get when your eyes kind of blur and you're not even sure what you're staring at anymore.

I've got to get her attention in this memory.

I've got to jolt her awake.

But how? I tried to pick up stuff at that lunch and nothing happened.

Maybe I should try smaller? There! On a table. A blue and white rubber. *Could I?* Taking a deep breath, I place my thumb and forefinger around it.

Come on, focus.

But even though I can feel the soft texture, hold it where it sits, I can't actually pick it up. It's not connecting.

Looking back over at Jenn, I can almost feel a clock ticking through me like a metronome. There's no time for this. I have to wake her and show her what's actually happening to us. I have to try to drive us across to the other lane if I possibly can.

Putting my fingers around the rubber again, I think about Jenn this time, focus my mind on her.

I lift it.

Oh my god, it worked! If anyone could see me right now, holding a rubber up like some sort of golden nugget, they'd think I'd gone mad. But no one can, and there's no time for celebrations.

I throw it at her and she flinches; touches the back of her head. *Yes!* I wait for something to happen, for the car to appear again. Anything. I close my eyes.

Nothing.

Opening my eyes, I see Jenn turn to someone sitting behind her, whisper something. The name *Katy* is written in dark font at the bottom of her picture – black hair tied neatly in one braid over her shoulder, golden-brown skin, pretty dark eyes, something twigs at the back of my mind. The rubber is on the floor between them. No, no, no, she thinks Katy did it!

Suddenly she mouths something to Jenn, which looks like *What are you doing?* and spreads her hands. But she's smiling. After a moment Jenn nods, and they both turn back again. They're doing portraits of whoever is opposite them. Jenn's is pretty good actually, even at that age; I always forget her mum's an artist. But there's something familiar about the face on her page, something needling at me. That boy opposite – the almost white-blond hair, pale blue eyes and serious expression. *Is that . . . ?*

'OK everyone,' a voice says from the front of the studio. A small woman with curly blonde hair glances at her watch. 'That's time. Pencils down.'

A heave of a sigh fills the room, as kids slap their pencils down and sit back on their stools, stretch out. A few of them at the back have blurry faces again. What the hell is it all about?

Then it dawns on me – this is her memory. Of course she can't recall everyone fully. It's only if they were close by that their features are clear, like she's sketching them out mentally.

I look over at Jenn. She isn't stopping, and she looks so anxious suddenly, pressing her pencil down into the paper so the lead starts to split.

'Jenny, stop,' the teacher calls from the front of the room, and Jenn looks up, her cheeks red. Across from her, the boy tries to smile at her. But she's looking down, eyes focused on her drawing. And I'm sure of who he is now. Duncan, the guy she dated before me. He's much younger, sure, but it's the same guy. Good-looking enough I suppose, in a pale type of way.

I didn't realise she'd known him since school?

As the teacher comes by to check over their work, she pauses at Jenn, a serious expression on her face.

'Come speak to me after class, Jenny,' she says quietly, before turning to the rest of the room. 'Just leave your drawings on the desks, please, and I'll collect them after.'

As she walks away, Jenn exchanges a look with Katy who mouths *What's going on?* Jenn just shakes her head at her, eyes anxious.

The bell screams through the school suddenly and everyone stands up, slinging their backpacks over their shoulders and filtering out of the studio. Katy gives her a small wave as she walks out behind the other blurry faces in their white shirts and striped ties.

Quickly, Jenn makes her way over to the teacher's desk and I follow behind, feeling like I'm about to get a telling off too.

'Why don't you take a seat, Jenny?' the teacher says, indicating at a plastic blue chair. She lowers herself down onto her own and I catch a trace of that instant coffee again, a minty smell too.

Jenn does as she says, hugs her backpack to her.

'Look, I'm really sorry about going over the time,' Jenn starts, 'but I just got distracted and I—'

The teacher puts up her hand to stop her.

'No, no, that wasn't why I wanted to speak to you, Jenny. Not at all. Don't worry yourself with a silly portrait. I just wanted to check if you were OK?'

Jenn looks nervous, caught out.

'I heard about your dad,' the teacher says, slowly. 'That must have been . . . hard. For you and your mum, I mean.'

So that's what this is about. I never really stopped to think how Jenn must have handled him leaving. But then, I guess I always just assumed he was a bit of a shit and it was for the best. Now, after seeing all these memories, these moments, I'm not so certain.

'How is she?'

Jenn blinks. 'Mum?' she says. 'Oh, she's fine.'

'Fine?'

'Yes, we're OK.'

The teacher's brow furrows slightly. I understand her pain. Jenn can be like a wall sometimes with private stuff – I never really got why.

'She teaches art over at the community centre, doesn't she? Your mum?'

Jenn nods. 'Yes, sometimes.'

A pause.

'You do know you can speak to me, don't you? You're a very clever girl, Jenny, but it's OK to be sad for a while too, to stop. Do you understand? In a situation like this, when you're thirteen, that would be totally normal.'

'What do you mean exactly,' Jenny asks, 'a situation like this?'

'Well,' the teacher says, clears her throat. 'When a parent has left the home—'

'It's not like that,' Jenn says quickly. 'He's coming back.'

The teacher doesn't initially say anything, just sighs, nods eventually. What else could she say? *No, he's never coming back?*

'Anyway,' she eventually continues, 'the Gaudí project you're working on right now, I'm happy if you just want to put it aside for a bit?'

'You don't like it?' Jenny asks, a concerned expression on her face now.

'No, not at all! I think it's brilliant, all those technical sketches of Sagrada Familia, the colours you've used. Did your dad teach you that?'

She swallows.

Hang on a second. Gaudí. Sagrada Familia. Her dad.

'Yes,' Jenn says.

Oh my god.

I'm such an idiot.

That's why she wanted to go to that bloody cathedral. I cover my face with my hands, even though no one can see me right now. He's an architect. She had an art project. They must have been working on it together before he left. Of course, she wanted me to come with her that day in Barcelona, and I just threw it back in her face. *It's not a big deal?* I'd said.

I wish I could understand what she's thinking in these places. It's like I'm watching a movie of her life, but have absolutely no idea what's going on in her head.

Standing up suddenly beside me, Jenn hooks her bag up onto one shoulder and smiles a tight smile at the teacher.

'I'd better get off to maths now, if that's alright.'

The teacher looks surprised, but stands up slowly too, nods. 'Right, OK then. But just remember, Jenny, I'm here any time you need to talk.'

'Thanks,' she says, and smiles brightly.

As she almost sprints away, I jog behind her, trying to push Gaudí from my mind. This isn't the time to be worrying about this stuff, what I did or didn't do. I'll talk to her about it when we're both out of this situation and safe. I'll say I'm sorry. I'll say anything she likes.

I've just got to wake her up.

JENNY

Out in the industrially lit corridor, Katy is waiting for her still with a bag of crisps. But as soon as she appears, Katy stops eating, wipes the greasy yellow flakes onto her blue jumper. She's so happy she has Katy still, her best friend since they were little, and the only thing which makes her feel OK these days – that and her course work. Every time she does well in a class, she feels better; she feels normal for a moment.

'What was all that about?' Katy asks, wide eyed.

Jenny pauses. She can't stand this twisted sensation in her stomach whenever her dad gets raised, like she's going to be sick. She doesn't want to talk about it, with anyone.

'Just stuff about my project. I'll fill you in on the way to maths.'

Katy nods and they start walking down the corridor in silence. At least it's maths next. She likes the way there's a definite answer to everything, that you have to work through each step to get there. It makes sense to her, and she likes it when things make sense.

Nothing made sense when her dad walked out.

He didn't even give her a goodbye, or leave any kind of note or even say that he loved her. Not that he ever actually said that, but she always felt it. *Didn't she?* All she knows for certain is that it's been exactly four months since he last said goodnight to her and turned off her bedroom light.

Sleep well, Jenny.

'Quit thinking about that project,' Katy says and laughs. Jenny blinks at her.

'Hey,' she quips back, 'quit throwing rubbers at my head in class, will you?'

Standing in front of the white brick wall, Katy gives her a funny look.

'I didn't.'

NINE

2015

ROBBIE

Pain in my head. Thumping, getting dimmer now. I crack my eyes open. I know these walls, these painted-white bricks, the rubbish bins below. I know where I am. It's the restaurant – or outside it at least. I see this bloody wall at the back of the building several times a week. The same alleyway, the same peeling red door, the same kitchen.

Thank fuck.

And now I know I can get to Jenn. I know I can impact on these memories, even if it's only in small ways: I just have to focus on her and then it happens. I think that's why I could knock the firework out of her hand but not pick up the champagne bottle. That's why I could throw the rubber.

And she knew it wasn't Katy.

She knew.

I saw that look of confusion on her face just before the memory cut off.

But Katy reacted when Jenn mentioned it. I still don't understand how this whole thing works. When I threw that rubber, everything seemed to adjust around it, including her friend. Which means Jenn's subconscious must be working really hard to keep up; to the point where even people's reactions are changing from what they actually were.

Even hers.

She's not coming out of this easily.

Katy.

That's why I know the name, the face. Jenn pulled out a picture of her once after I asked her who her best friend was at school. She started telling me how awesome Katy was, how I would have loved her too, but then suddenly she got all cagey and put the photo away; said they hadn't spoken in years. She was like that with a lot of stuff about her past, looking back. I knew her dad had left and it had been a bit unexpected. I knew she had a strained, slightly distant, relationship with her mum, but like with the Katy thing, she just didn't want to go there – those topics seemed to make her uncomfortable. So I let it go, moved the conversation on to something lighter.

Why dwell on the past anyway?

Footsteps behind me. I spin around to see a younger Robbie and Jenn walking down the alley. From the coffee cup in her hand, and the paper bag from my favourite bakery in his, I can assume it's some point in the morning. The sun is up in the sky, but there's a slight edge to the air, a few golden leaves on the alley's tarmac. Autumn.

'Here we are,' he says, sticking the key in the lock. Opening the door, he gestures inside with a flourish. 'Where the magic happens.'

She laughs and follows him. I tail behind quickly – I'm not getting locked outside again. I don't know how long I have in this memory, and I have to try and get to her again. The door shuts with a clunk, and we're standing in the shadowy kitchen. He flips the lights on and suddenly the room is flooded with brightness. It bounces off the white walls and stainless-steel counters. There's a calendar by the oven. I squint at it – Saturday, 26th September. We'd been together for almost a year at this point.

'Wow,' she says, looking around smiling. 'So, this is a proper kitchen then.'

'Eh, I wouldn't exactly call it proper,' Robbie says, switching on the oven. 'It's not the biggest but it does the job, I suppose. I'm still not entirely sure why you wanted to see where I sweat away everyday though. You've already been in the restaurant with Hils?'

She shrugs, places her near-empty coffee cup down on a surface. Maybe I should knock it over, spill what's left. But what's that going to do? *Shit, think, Robbie.*

'Because this is where you spend all your time when you're not with me,' Jenn says. 'It's a big part of your life?'

He scratches his head and leans one hand against the island. 'Well, if you put it that way. I guess I do know a weird amount about medicine for a non-medical guy now.'

'You love it really,' she continues, before lifting herself up to sit on the counter behind. Her long legs swinging happily.

After the first holiday, that first fight in Barcelona, it had been surprisingly easy to just forget, to go back to having fun together. It was a blip, and we were back to Jenn and Robbie in no time: the couple who had such a great time together, the couple who were so in love.

'Oh hey,' she says, pointing at the floor, 'what's that?'

'Huh?' Robbie looks down at a card on the floor and laughs. 'Another one.'

'Another one?'

'Marty,' he says, walking over before bending to pick it up.

'One of his postcards?'

'Yup.'

He turns the card around to Jenn. It's a chicken wearing sunglasses against the backdrop of the American flag.

Jenn laughs. I remember that one. That was when Marty was still working in the States and was also still my most prolific bachelor friend. We were always sending stupid postcards to each other's work – just our way of staying in touch.

'What's with the chicken anyway?' she asks, nodding at the postcard.

'Because of his name, remember. Marty McFly, *Back to the Future*?'

She looks lost.

'*Nobody calls me chicken*,' he says in an overkill American accent.

'OK ... ' she says and laughs, 'it's vaguely coming back to me.'

'Well, that's our evening sorted,' he grins.

'It must have been so fun when you guys were travelling together,' she says from her perch. 'Seeing the world, doing what you liked.' There's the hint of a sigh there.

'So much fun,' Robbie smiles, his eyes alight.

'I can't believe you guys climbed into the Trevi Fountain.'

'When in Rome.'

'Literally,' she says with a gentle eye roll.

I remember that moment in Italy, how young and carefree Marty and I had been. How life had seemed like my own personal theme park, just brimming with opportunities. Jenn and I talked about our travels early on and I remember being so surprised when she said she hadn't really been anywhere interesting yet – she'd always been so busy with exams and jobs apparently. I said I couldn't understand why she hadn't just jetted off after school or during university summers holidays, taken a student loan even, but she did her usual ducking of the conversation; pestered me about where I'd been instead.

I stopped pressing her after that; never did get to the bottom of it, come to think of it.

'Another coffee?' Robbie points at her empty cup.

'Oh, yes please,' she says, and he walks over to the massive machine at the side, switches it on at the back. The lights flash red at me.

Time is running out.

Without saying a word, he goes across to the fridge next, pulls out a couple of Tupperware boxes. Setting them out on the counter next to the paper bag, he starts making one of my old favourites for her – haggis and cheese croissant. She would always be so exhausted after a long shift week, and I'd present her with these platefuls of food because she'd forget to eat otherwise.

'You weren't ever tempted by the whole uni thing after?' she asks, as he sets the tray in the oven.

'No way,' he says, smiling at her briefly. Turning back to the coffee machine, he untwists the heavy coffee handle.

He lifts a bulbous pack of beans up from the shelf below, starts scooping some into the grinder. 'I wasn't stupid or anything. My grades were alright, but I'd seen Fi and Kirsty go off to university, and it all just sounded so . . . normal. I didn't like the idea of knowing exactly how my life would be. First uni, then a job, then marriage, boom, boom, boom, you know?'

'So, how did you end up at the top of a mountain?'

Robbie's finger hovers over the 'on' button.

My stomach twists.

A white beach, people dancing. Me and Marty in neon vests. Him grinning at me on a Thai beach.

'Well,' Robbie says, finally pushing it, and the memories, away too. 'We were in Thailand and this school friend of ours said he was working in a kitchen in Chamonix by night, snowboarding by day, and it just seemed like a really great opportunity for me.'

I swallow. Moving on.

'Sounds it,' Jenn says, wistfully. 'So, then you were there for the next five years?'

'That's right,' he says, walking over to the fridge and pulling some milk off a well-stocked shelf. He turns back to her, frowns slightly. 'I've told you all this before, haven't I?'

'Bits maybe,' she smiles. 'I like hearing about it though. What happened next?'

'Well . . . then Marty went off to university in Bristol and I stayed in Cham. Tend to find that once you go to the Alps, you either leave after one winter or not at all. Suddenly a season was a year, then a year was two years, and so on.'

He pours the milk into her coffee and presents her with the oozing croissant.

The smell is incredible.

She smiles thoughtfully and takes a bite. 'God, this is amazing. Haggis and cheese should not be this amazing.'

'Right?' He grins. 'And that's the other reason I came back actually.'

'Why?'

He looks excited now, and for a moment, I really miss that point – when it was still easy to dream big, and aim high with my career – just have fun with it all.

'I want to open up my own restaurant at some point,' he says. 'It's been great working for Matt and everything, but I want my own place in the Old Town, Scottish fare but with a European twist. That's the plan.'

'I think I like that plan,' Jenn says, placing the cup down beside her. Her eyes are shining and I can see that she was really lit up by the notion, this ambition of his for more. I can almost feel the sparks in the room, the atmosphere filled with the possibility of tomorrow and everything after.

I start to feel strange again and my breathing quickens because I know the next place is coming soon. The light is starting to fade, and I could be going anywhere, her childhood, our relationship – the car?

I have to do something, anything.

As the room starts to disappear, I smack my hand into her cup with everything I've got.

'Wake up, Jenn!' I cry.

Porcelain crashes to the floor, and she immediately gasps. The last thing I see is her terrified expression, her eyes darting frantically around the room, and then I hear her voice.

'Who said that?'

Three weeks later

JENN

One year ago. It was one year ago to the day when she met Robbie – on Hilary's birthday in The Cowgate. And now here she is, unpacking her clothes into his drawers, placing her textbooks and notepads on the top of the chest. Their lives are intertwining like the inosculation of two trees and her heart swells at the sight. She is home.

He is her home.

They didn't really need to think about whose flat they would move into. Susie had started talking vaguely about moving in with Paul when their lease came up and Robbie owned his place in Marchmont already. And he didn't suggest she moved in as much as begged her to. 'OK,' she'd said eventually, before he'd picked her off the ground with a whoop of happiness.

Some overly upbeat pop song starts up on his radio clock now and she can't help doing a little happy dance to herself.

'Jenn?' She stops, turns. He's smiling widely at her through the door, cheeks pink from the exertion of carrying her stuff up the wide tenement steps.

For a moment, she feels embarrassed, but a second later he's dancing towards her, daft Robbie moves that make her laugh to her belly.

God, he makes her laugh. He even still sends those silly *I like you more than spicy tuna rolls, have a great day*, messages to her work every time she goes in. Perhaps he should have upgraded the message to *I love you* by now, but Robbie's never one to be serious. Of course, he said it that first time at the cinema, and in Barcelona after that fight they had, but she's not totally convinced he's said it since.

She's being silly though. She knows how much he loves her: in the squeeze of her hand, in the way he looks at her, cares for her (he even asked her to move in for god's sake!)

He makes her mad as hell too, of course: the way he's always losing his wallet and keys and she has to find them, the way he dumps his sweaty cycling kit anywhere he pleases, the way he never actually cleans up after making one of his extravagant meals.

But the way he kisses her – it's like nothing else.

When he's beside her finally, he takes her in his arms and spins her around. Her face hurts from smiling so hard.

Coming to a halt finally, he says, 'Is it time for fizz yet?'

'Why not?' She's heady with the moment. 'Let's celebrate!'

'Atta girl,' he grins and disappears down the corridor, past the boxes of shoes, past the bin bags of homeware she brought. Not that she needed to bother with the kitchen so much. His is well prepped with peelers, dicers, poachers and blow torches. Every inch of his cupboards is stuffed with spices and herbs and condiments. She'll probably never cook again, she thinks, and smiles.

Like with her dad.

The thought catches her, and she has a flash of her dad in that warm kitchen, peeling potatoes at the sink, chopping onions on a scratched board. He never actually said he loved her either, come to think of it.

What if Robbie leaves too?

Her stomach contracts painfully, and for a moment she can't breathe – just that notion that she could become so very bound up in someone again, only for them to disappear on her. And it was different with Duncan somehow – she never once worried about what might go wrong, or if he would leave her.

A popping noise from the kitchen makes her startle, and she hears the clink of glasses, imagines him pouring in the Champagne they got from Jill and Campbell to say congratulations. Pushing thoughts of the past away, she hears Robbie's heavy steps in the hall and turns as he walks back in grinning.

'Here you go,' he says and passes her the fine-stemmed glass. 'Here's to us. Thank you for moving in with me.'

It seems such a funny thing to say, *thank you*. There was no bone in her body that didn't want to move in with him, it felt more like the pull of gravity than anything else. And despite everything that happened with her dad, despite feeling all alone in the world at times, she just knows that *this* is it; she knows what she has with Robbie is on another level.

And she won't let the past ruin it.

Taking a large gulp of the drink, she sinks half, and places it down before stepping towards him. Before he can even speak, she presses her mouth hard against his. His body reacts in response, moulding his own mouth against hers, like they have done so many times before, like they do without thinking. He tastes metallic and warm and it drives her on, her hands pulling, clutching at him. She feels the growing hardness against her, knows that she created this response in him in a matter of seconds. It's like breathing to her, this need for him, this desire.

After a moment she realises he's still holding onto his glass.

'Put it down,' she commands.

'Absolutely,' he replies, and claps it roughly onto the chest of drawers, before they fall back onto the bed, onto her jeans, her tops, onto his pyjama bottoms, her favourite blue coat. Back onto her notepad, which says in a familiar spidery scrawl, 'I'm here.'

ROBBIE

I'm in the kitchen now. The empty bottle of champagne sits on the worktop, something's cooking on the stove. Onions and something else: hot dogs, that's it. The light outside has faded.

But did Jenn see the note? Did she read it?

Everything just cut out again. And I'd finally managed to use a fucking pen. I wrote actual words.

But she wasn't looking. She was too wrapped up in him.

Me.

I had to try something else – the speaking out loud certainly didn't achieve anything at the restaurant, because she can't fucking see me. It was exhilarating I guess, to know that she could actually hear me – that I still had a voice – but what the hell did I think would happen?

Of course she was terrified.

I can't help wondering what else I could actually do though, how far I could push it. If I threw a pan into the window, would it break? If I lit a flame in this building, could I burn it down? But as tempted as I am to try something bigger – something more extreme – that terror on Jenn's face stops me. They're her memories after all, and I can't go messing with them, making them all twisted and confusing like that. What if it changes them permanently? What would that do to her if we get out of this?

Shit, I don't know anything about what happens when we get out of this. Can I just drive the car away immediately? Or will I still be frozen in the seat, that truck rushing towards us, and all of this will have been for nothing?

92

I run through everything in my head now, all the things I know I can at least do in the memories when I think of Jenn – touch her, move things around her (small things), speak to her out loud. I have some control here at any rate, I just don't understand what the point of any of it is though. I don't understand why I can do any of this stuff if it all just scares her.

What is the point?

I head out of the kitchen to see if I can find the note, when I hear laughter from the living room. I know that riotous laugh.

Fi. Her, Max and Hilary came over that night, to celebrate Jenn moving in. I did a hot dog night for everyone. I remember now. Through the open door, I catch a glimpse of them all in the warm light, sitting around with glasses in hand, and I can't help thinking about how happy I was that day, how just the idea of her moving in made me so bloody excited. I just loved her so much – the way she was always up for trying new cuisines, the way she was just as into music as me, the way our humour would often be surprisingly in tune and we'd end in stomach-hurting fits of laughter about nothing at all.

So it didn't matter that she woke annoyingly early on Saturdays, or left her hair on the side of the bath after showering, or made her tea wrong – 'you don't squish the bag against the cup,' I remember telling her so many times.

All I wanted was to be with her.

I have to get that note. If Jenn sees my handwriting, maybe it will remind her of what's happening. Maybe that's the level of jolt she needs?

I head towards the bedroom again; stop.

Is that why we keep getting thrown from one memory to another? Because I keep scaring her? Like when you're having a bad dream and you try to change it; switch to something else. I think of the sparkler, touching her arm in the cathedral, shouting at her in the restaurant – the memory moved swiftly to another one each time.

Fuck.

But how the hell else am I supposed to wake her?

Walking into the living room instead, their voices get louder.

Jenn, Hilary and Fi are chatting away on the sofa, the lamp light making Jenn's smiling face glow, but Hilary looks awful now that I look closer. Her eyes are red and her face is blotchy.

My other self sits on an arm chair pulled up beside Jenn, one hand resting on her knee. He laughs at something she's just said.

Max is sitting on the chair across the room, an almost-empty tumbler in one hand, his phone attached to his other.

He looks up suddenly, wiggles his glass at Robbie. 'Could do with a top up, mate.'

Fucking knob. I've never understood what Fi sees in him.

But my other self seems too happy to be bothered by him on this particular occasion – the day Jenn moved in.

'Sure,' Robbie says, with only the slightest frown and stretches up to his full height. He goes to take Max's glass, turns back. 'Anything for you girls?'

'Yes please,' Fi and Hilary say in unison.

Jenn smiles up at Robbie. 'I'm alright, thanks.'

After he's left the room, the girls turn back to each other.

'So,' Fi says, turning to Hilary, 'I was hearing you just broke up with someone, what happened?'

Hilary shakes her head. 'I just don't know. One minute things were going really well, and the next . . . ' she throws one hand up, sighs.

Ah, yes, another break up. I remember. But this was nothing new, it was just classic Hilary. She was always dating arseholes before – and she'd always predictably wind up here with Jenn, glass of Sauvignon in hand. I'd rustle up some tapas for them, easy dishes they could eat while speaking, and then just leave them to it. Cooking was the one thing I was good at, so it gave me a kick too, knowing how much people enjoyed my food.

Plus, there was something about Hilary that I just got. We were both a bit of a mess before someone came along and changed that.

'Bastard,' Fi says, shaking her head.

'It will be OK,' Jenn says gently, 'honestly Hilary, you'll know when you find the right guy.'

'Will I?' Hilary doesn't look convinced.

I wish I could speak to her, tell her it's all going to come good and to stop stressing out.

'How's work going?' Jenn asks Fi eventually, clearly trying to keep the mood levels up.

Hilary's break ups had that sort of sobering effect over a room.

'Oh fine, crazy.' Fi quaffs her drink. 'The waiting lists are just mental.'

Jenn nods. 'Tell me about it.'

Fi's eyes light up. 'Oh, I meant to say I finally remembered to bring that book with me this time.' She reaches down into her handbag – the bright red one Mum gave her for Christmas – and pulls one out. 'That's if you still want to read it?'

'What book . . . ?' Jenn asks, before her face breaks into recognition. 'The psychology one? Oh, yes!'

The book.

'I just had no idea people studied those types of experiences in that level of depth,' Jenn says, taking the shiny blue tome from her.

'Well, they're pretty common actually,' Fi replies, 'particularly in trauma . . . Actually, I had an odd case recently,' she continues.

'Here we go,' mutters Max.

'What was it?' Jenn says over him.

'Shared-death experiences,' Fi says. 'Ever heard of them?'

I stop. Look up.

Jenn is shaking her head. My pulse quickens.

'Neither had I,' Fi says, 'until this patient started talking about seeing his brother, who lived at the opposite side of the country, standing at the end of his bed one night. Next day, guess what happens?'

'He gets a restraining order?' Max jokes, without looking up from his phone.

Fi doesn't even acknowledge the quip. 'He finds out his brother had actually died in really traumatic circumstances. A machinery accident.'

'I feel like I've heard of that kind of thing before,' Jenn says slowly, like she's trying to recall information from the back of her mind.

'Probably. In Victorian times they used to be called deathbed visions, you know, seeing loved ones walking towards a bright light and all that. But then when I looked it up, I saw this doctor in America had actually coined the term *shared-death experiences*.'

'Sounds like nonsense to me,' Max grunts.

Shut up, Max.

'I thought that too, initially,' Fi says sharply. 'But there's a whole raft of documented experiences on the phenomenon. All healthy bystanders sharing in someone's last moments, usually a loved one, and they all come out of it with greater knowledge of some sort. There are reports of actually seeing the person's life flashing before their eyes, like a three hundred and sixty-degree experience – the dying person relives it, while the other person watches. There's a whole chapter in the book on it if you want to read more about it.'

Oh my god.

This is it.

This is what's happening to us.

It must be.

Shared-death experience. I repeat the words quietly to myself. Everything she's saying matches what's happening to us: Jenn reliving all these moments, me seeing it all, the fact that it's a well-documented phenomenon.

I need to know more.

Footsteps in the hall; the other Robbie walks into the room. *Shit.*

'Here we go,' he says, Max's refilled glass in one hand and a fresh bottle of prosecco in the other. He tops up Fi and Hilary's glasses, before taking Max's glass across to him. Max is just putting down his phone as he takes the drink.

'That's that all booked then,' he says and takes a sip.

Fi looks across at him. 'What's what all booked?'

'*Las Vegas, baby,* for ten days over New Year. Can you imagine the carnage?'

'What this?' my other self says, looking between them.

But Fi doesn't even seem to hear the other Robbie. She looks shocked.

'What do you mean you've booked it?' she asks, eyes wide.

Max raises his eyebrows. 'I mean, I've booked the flights, and Greg has booked the hotel. Booked it.'

I remember this.

Things were definitely tense between them that night, looking back. But I'm not sure I fully took it in with the excitement of Jenn moving in that day. Sure enough, the other Robbie walks back out of the room a second later, without actually hearing Max's answer. In my defence, I'd asked Fi a question, and she hadn't responded

'You can't actually be telling me you've booked to go away over the holidays,' Fi says once he's gone, 'the holidays we both agreed to take off with Struan.'

Max casts his eyes up. 'I told you about this, for Greg's stag? He was best man at our wedding if you don't recall.'

Fi looks livid, and I guess I can see why.

Ten days for a stag is a little extreme.

'And I told you, that's a stupid time of year for a stag, if you don't recall,' Fi bites back. 'I said why don't we take Struan to Lapland or something? Spend time as a family for bloody once!'

Hilary starts to get up from the sofa now, mutters something about needing the toilet. Jenn follows swiftly after, the book in hand, but not before she glances back at Fi, a worried expression on her face.

Although I half want to keep listening to this, I know I need to concentrate on reading this book while I can. Heading out the room, I'm relieved to see Jenn sitting on our bed in the room next door, the book now open on her lap.

I can still hear Max and Fi going though – Max is shouting that she can't keep suffocating him, and Fi is saying that he doesn't care about his child. Discomfort washes over me.

Did I ever ask about her marriage after that?

Pushing the thought aside, I walk around behind Jenn to read what she's reading, but so much of the opening pages are blurry, like Jenn's forgotten a lot of the detail.

Shit.

The spatting next door crescendos when Jenn turns the page and I see it.

The heading reads, *Attributes of a shared-death experience,* with a few bullet points still legible below.

- *Observers speak of time being suspended during the SDE, then restarting once the SDE is complete.*
- *The observer is generally aware that the SDE is happening, but not necessarily the person dying.*
- *SDEs often involve some sort of 'goodbye' at the end, where both parties are aware of what's happening.*
- *The dying person is sometimes accompanied by the observer towards death, but the observer is stopped from going any further.*

I look down the rest of the page, but that's it. There's the stuff about the three hundred and sixty degree-review review Fi mentioned too of course, but other than that, the page is all blurred smudges. I scan through the rest of the document – nothing. There's nothing else to see.

Shit.

The place has gone silent again now, and a second later I hear heavy footsteps in the hallway, the door slamming shortly after. Jenn immediately gets up and heads back in, with me following closely behind. Somewhere in the distance, I can hear Hilary and Robbie laughing away now, oblivious to what is happening here. Fi is sitting on the sofa when Jenn walks back into the living room, head in her hands, but she looks up sharply as Jenn clears her throat. From the splotches of red on her pale, pretty face it's quite clear she's been crying, and I have this overwhelming urge to hug Fi; make her feel better in this moment.

But I know inside myself that that's not really her in there: just a memory Jenn's kept; just a sad, frustrated apparition of my sister.

'You OK?' Jenn asks softly.

Fi wipes under her eyes, sniffs before reaching for her drink on the table. 'Yes, all fine, thanks. Max has just gone out for a cigarette.'

Now that I think about it, he never actually came back that night. Something about the babysitter being sick and him needing to look after Struan. I was too busy preparing the hot dogs to think much of it though.

'Do you want to talk about it?' Jenn says to her now.

Fi smiles, a genuine smile, and I'm glad that Jenn was checking up on her at least.

'Thanks,' she says. 'Maybe another time.'

Jenn nods, sits down next to Fi.

'Well, I have a question about that book then,' she says, and I know Jenn well enough to see that she's largely trying to distract Fi in this moment. Fi looks up at her with a sad expression, but she seems grateful too.

'Sure, fire away.'

'In one of these shared-death experiences,' Jenn says, 'does the person always die at the end? The one having the life review, I mean.'

I feel sick as the scent of hot dogs drifts towards me. I can't breathe.

Please don't say yes.

Fi turns to her, a heavy expression on her face. 'Usually.'

As my head starts to pound again, I exhale.

I'll take usually. Usually doesn't mean yes. Usually doesn't mean always. There's still a chance.

And now I know from that book that I can definitely drive the car away when the shared-death experience stops – when time restarts.

I just have to figure out a way to wake her.

And quickly.

TEN

2003

JENNY

Food vans, disco-lit rides and people surround her. She can smell burgers, chips and warm grass. Looking through the funfair she sees Katy and Laura standing away off together, chatting. They already bought candy floss from a stall earlier, but she doesn't really like the stuff – too fluffy and it leaves a funny aftertaste. Plus, the apple was cheaper.

'That'll be fifty pence, sweetheart.'

Fishing coins from her pocket, Jenny counts them out on her palm. Sunlight bounces off the silver before she hands them up to the guy in the van.

'Thanks,' she says, taking the sticky red apple from him and walking slowly away across the green grass towards her friends. The sun makes the top of her head hot as she takes a bite, the sugary outer layer giving way to juicy flesh.

Pumping music grows louder as she approaches her friends, and she starts to make out the neon lightning bolts and stars on the cars as they slow to a gradual halt. Katy is fiddling with her phone again – probably her mum. She's always right on Katy's back, asking what she's been up to that day, if she's remembered this thing or that. Jenny feels sad, as she realises her mum doesn't even know where she is right now. Not in a mean way or anything but, well, she didn't ask. Jenny left her on the sofa earlier watching some cookery show, even though she knows her mum hates cooking.

It seems a little silly that Katy's mum is checking up on her to be honest. They are thirteen, after all, and some of the kids at school have even started drinking, going to the pub. As she reaches the girls, Laura turns, a wisp of candy floss pinched between forefinger and thumb. Her sparkly nails dig into the delicate sugar, kohl eyes widen.

'We're totally thinking the waltzers next. Are you up for it?'

Laura says it with an almost-American accent, which is annoying because her family went on holiday to California a couple of weeks ago and now that she's back words like *sidewalk* and *garbage* have found their way into her vocabulary.

She was supposed to go to Florida with her parents this year – her mum had finally agreed to a plane trip. Her stomach sinks at the thought and, for the thousandth time, she wonders where he is, why he never came back.

Sleep well, Jenny.

The world feels silent for a moment.

'Jenny, did you hear what I said?' Laura says, her string-thin browo pointed down.

She pushes images from her mind, says, 'Yeah. I'm up for it.' Taking another chunk out of the sickly-sweet apple, the taste brings her back to the present and she sees that people have started to trickle down from the ride.

Every year around festival time they bring this fair to the Meadows and she loves it; the scrambler, dodgems, the coconut shy, she can't get enough. But the waltzers are her favourite. That feeling she gets when the car is pushed around, and the world just spins and spins until her stomach leaps up into her throat. Last year she came here with her dad – just the two of them – and she went on every ride going. He watched from the side, smiling, hands in pockets. An overwhelming sense of sadness rushes over her, and suddenly she's not so sure she wants to go on the ride after all.

Chucking the remains of their food purchases in a nearby bin, the girls step up onto the metal platform with a clunk. A guy in a black t-shirt immediately swoops over to take their money. Her chest contracts. There isn't much left in her clip purse. As Jenny offers out a pound, she looks up at his pale, spotty face and he gives her a sly smile. She looks away, feeling immediately uncomfortable. He's a bit older, seventeen or so.

Sliding onto the slippery, still-warm seat, she watches the guy slam the metal bar down across the front of them before giving the car a rough shove. The car does a lazy spin and the girls laugh. But that uncertain feeling creeps up on Jenny again. She brushes it off.

'He was totally eying me up,' Laura says, when it starts to slow again.

'No, he wasn't,' Katy replies, shaking her head. 'He was looking at Jenny.'

She feels herself growing hot. 'He just smiled.'

'That means he fancies you,' Laura shoots back, eyes hardening. Her lips are all shiny with lip gloss and her blonde hair is a flat yellow.

'Guys smile if they like you,' she continues. 'You should totally go speak to him after.'

Laura's daring her, she knows that. But the idea of going up to that guy makes her want to die.

'No way,' Jenny says, and wishes the ride would just start so she can end the conversation. Sometimes she wonders why her and Katy started hanging around with Laura – they don't have much in common with her after all. But one day she just appeared, and at least everything was a little more exciting with three.

The music suddenly gets louder, and she can feel the ground giving way from underneath them. They rise up, then dip down as it circles around the booth at the centre.

'Here we go,' Laura says and does a drum roll on the bar. Jenny grips it tight, the metal pinching at her skin. The guy is over on the other side, flipping each car around, and she realises it will be their turn soon. Looking out into the loop of world around them, she wishes she was back on solid ground. Gleeful cries blast in from another ride as they pass, and quickly fade again. Loud, low, loud then low. Painted carousel horses bob by, red and white stripes, green grass, faces. Her heart quickens.

There's a thump on the metal behind them, and suddenly the guy is looming above their heads, hands clamped on the back of the car.

'Ready?' he says, but he doesn't wait for an answer, just grins and pushes hard. And then they are spinning, around and around they go and her stomach is flying this way and that and her heart is thumping – but it isn't the fun feeling from last year, or the year before that. She doesn't like this. Beside her Katy and Laura are whooping with excitement, hair flying up behind them. Jenny closes her eyes and tries to stop the out-of-control feeling, but it only makes it worse.

'Stop,' she says, to no one in particular. Neither friend looks over at her. Neither of them hears her over the racket.

'Stop!' she cries, louder this time. Her chest feels like it's going to explode.

Katy finally looks over as the car slows just a little, brows creased. She's confused. *Are you OK?*

A second later and Jenny feels the weight of hands press down on the car again, and it spirals into oblivion once more. The world disappears into streaks of colour. She can't stand this. Why didn't the guy hear her? She starts crying now, heaving in gulps of air. *What's happening to her? Why is no one helping?*

'Jenny, are you OK?' Laura is saying now, and she feels the touch of her hand.

'Stop the ride!' Katy is shouting. She's waving her hands like mad in the air, and Jenny knows this is embarrassing, but she just has to get off. The guy is over on the other side and he doesn't seem to notice.

'Stop the ride!' Katy is shouting at him again, and stabbing her finger at Jenny. 'She's having a panic attack and she needs to get off. Right now.'

He finally looks over, gives them an unconcerned look, before disappearing behind another car. Up and down they go – around and around like a spinning top.

Laura's overly made-up blue eyes loom large beside her like in a nightmare. 'It's going to be OK,' she says dramatically, lights strobing red and blue against her skin.

Jenny tips her head back and closes her eyes. *Make it stop, make it all stop.*

Then, she feels a sensation, as though the booth is digging its heels in hard. Like someone has caught hold of it and forced it to stop spinning. Her breathing evens out slightly, but she keeps her eyes tightly shut. The ride is still going, but the car is no longer spiralling. Blood rushes to her head, and everything feels very odd.

ROBBIE

When I look down at my hands, they're still clamped to the back of the car. What the hell just happened? The ride has finally come to a standstill, and I watch as the girls get up, step out. Katy rushes around to Jenn's side to help her out. Laura looks more confused, annoyed even, as she steps off the platform, like she's not quite sure what all the fuss was about. But I saw it in Jenn's eyes, that anxiety, that sheer terror.

Like her world was falling apart.

One minute I was standing on the grass wondering how the hell I could try to contact her this time, and then I was running towards the platform, walking around the ride, veering between the cars. I just had to get to her; had to help her.

My heart is pounding still. I stopped it. I stopped the waltzer car.

The girls are retreating across the field now, but I know she felt it this time. I know she sensed me.

Just turn around.

And then she does it, looks back towards the waltzer car, towards me.

'I'm here!' I cry, waving like mad at her. She can see me, hear me too, I know it; her eyes are darting about everywhere. She looks terrified but I'm so relieved. I've done it. She's going to wake now. We'll be back in the car and time will start again like Fi's book said and I'll swing right; press the accelerator down hard.

She looks away again, back towards her friends.

No, no, no!

An animal noise escapes from me and I tip my forehead down onto the back of the car. *Nothing is working.* That pulsing begins again, lights flash around me and I know I'm being pulled to someplace else.

'Wake up, Jenn,' I shout at her receding form across the grass.

'Wake up, Jenn, goddamnit.'

ELEVEN

2016

JENN

She can hear the swishing, almost like whispers, as their legs move through the tall grass. Evening sun glints through the trees ahead and she wraps her arms about herself, burrowing down further into one of Robbie's old, grey hoodies. After a moment, he stops, lifts Struan down from his broad shoulders.

'Go for it, little guy,' he says, and a second later Struan's off, the chestnut top of his head darting away through the greenery.

'Is he—' she starts.

'It's fine,' Robbie reassures her. 'It's totally enclosed here, don't worry.'

She nods, relieved. They often take Struan out for a walk when they're all back at his parents', but usually just around the local streets or perhaps the park. It gives Fi a break, but Jenn also secretly loves it. It's like they're borrowing a little bit of family life for a moment, a little piece of solidity she's never really had before. She's always wanted to be part of a big family: siblings, cousins, nieces, nephews, all congregated together for dinners and birthdays. Both of her parents were only children.

'How come we've not been to this field before?' she says, looking about herself. It's not a field really, more like a paddock. It was along the road from his parents' house, up a little track between some of the other grand houses in the area.

'Have we not?' he says, looking confused. His forehead creases at the centre as he thinks about it. His hair ruffles in the spring breeze.

'We used to come here loads as kids, even though we weren't meant to. Kirsty always used to worry we were going to get into trouble,' he smiles, shaking his head. 'We even had a rope swing there,' he says and points at a large tree nearby. 'But someone cut it down eventually. It was deemed *unsafe*. Bloody kill joys. Fi went nuts.'

Walking under the thick branch protruding out, Jenn stares up at the weathered creases of bark, the twists and ripples of time. She thinks about everything it's seen over its existence, every nest of fragile life, every child's weight it's held up – there must be a lot of stories in its veins.

'Look!' she cries, after a moment. 'It's still there.'

'What?' He stands beside her.

'The rope swing,' she grins, pointing up at a faded loop of dirty white around the bark.

'Well so it is,' he says softly.

There's something about finding this small piece of Robbie from the past that delights her. As though she has been given another fragment of him, something nobody else has. And, for a moment, she can see that small boy in this field again – a little older than Struan perhaps – running around, tying rope swings onto trees he shouldn't, refusing to march to someone else's drum. She can still see that spark in his eye sometimes, that defiant look he gets.

He turns to her. 'Do you know what Mum reminded me of today?' His breathing quickens.

'What's that?'

'We've been together for exactly eighteen months now.'

He swallows, takes a breath in.

'So, is this your way of telling me you've had enough?' she teases. 'I mean, it's a bit harsh taking me out to a field to do it . . .'

Without another word, he pulls her into him, kisses her beneath the old branch, under the layers and layers of green leaves which reach high above them.

After a moment, he draws back, smiles down at her, and she's not sure she's ever felt so alive and yet so peaceful at the exact same time. Because, for the first time, she can truly see it: the glimmer of a real future with him.

And she knows he's seen it too.

As they walk away from the tree, towards where Struan is now brandishing a stick, as though warding off invisible pirates, she has the distinct feeling that the Robbie from another time is still here in this place too. Standing under that branch behind them, watching them go. The wind picks up through the trees like a howl – a call to them from beyond.

*   *   *

ROBBIE

In the car again. Hands on the wheel. Foot on the accelerator.

Yes, I'm back!

I just need to drive away.

Try pushing my foot down – still frozen.

Try moving my hands – still stuck.

Shit.

Why can't I move?

Time is suspended.

Fi's book. From the corner of my eye, I see that Jenn's still watching that truck come towards us. It's even closer this time, I know it.

I just need to see her face. I need her to see *my* face so she can see what's happening, wake up, and we can drive away from here. I need to talk to her. I imagine yelling, screaming, wrenching my hands off the wheel and turning to her, telling her that she needs to stop thinking we're going to die, because we only just got back together.

She only just came back.

But nothing changes. Those dust particles keep floating and my heart keeps pounding and I can't think straight.

113

My head is filling with an image, a favourite moment, of me and Jenn lying on the grass in the Meadows, side by side, staring up at the puffy spring sky as the birds climbed and then dove above us. I smelt freshly cut grass, the scent of possibility in the air. Then I turned my head to her, took in the makeup-less face and short hair, wondering how I could still love her that much after years together. Other pictures start flooding my mind now: of me and Jenn getting caught in a freak hail storm in the Pentlands and laughing so hard it hurt, of us getting lost in the car up North where there was no signal so we had to listen to the best of The Beach Boys on repeat, of countless dinners with our friends and nights out just the two of us and waking up to her face every morning and everything and everything.

Why did you leave?

As I look into that beam of light coming towards us, another light appears in my mind. It feels like I just saw it moments ago, but it's a world away too.

It's green.

Jenn, in the car beside me. She was looking up at the traffic lights, she was saying those words. She sounded panicked I remember; something was worrying her. There was a beeping noise from her bag, a shifting of limbs. An intake of breath.

I've got something to tell you.

TWELVE

2005

ROBBIE

I open my eyes, heart pounding. It's dark.

Am I still in the car?

Dim light rises, spreads out. A sofa. A person on it.

Marian.

Fuck.

Still in the memories.

She's sitting alone, her face occasionally illuminated by a TV ahead of her. She's wearing a dressing gown and resting her head against a faded cushion. An empty bag of crisps lies on the living-room table, an untouched mug of tea. Canned laughter occasionally fires out into the room, but she's not smiling. She looks tired. This doesn't look like their house though. A street-light outside the bay window flickers slightly – I think we're in a flat. They must have moved.

I've got something to tell you.

Oh god.

The car. Jenn's memories.

No, no, no, I have to get back to the car again. She was trying to tell me something before this all happened, I remember now. My heart is racing. Can't breathe.

OK, calm down, Robbie.

I inhale, exhale.

Just think.

She was about to speak, then the truck came towards us, then we went back into her memories. Now it won't stop.

My thoughts merge together, collide.

Hang on.

What if Jenn's *still* trying to tell me something? Something important. Not deliberately, but what if her subconscious is doing all this? Pulling me into her world, showing me everything, making me watch until I find out what she wanted to tell me.

Because she thinks she's going to die.

She has a secret.

Maybe that's why I can't move in the car. Maybe that's why I keep coming back to these memories. Fi said that people come out of shared-death experiences with greater knowledge. So, maybe this is it?

I have to find out her secret in order to wake her.

It might be a long shot, but it's the only one I've got, and if I'm right, I can stop the crash from happening.

I can stop it.

But the truck is almost on us. We can't have much time.

Shit.

A noise. Jenn walks in. She looks so different. And not just because she's older, sixteen if that, but because she looks so very un-Jenn. Her face is thick with makeup, hair poker straight and she's wearing some sort of strappy black dress. I can count on one hand the number of times Jenn has worn anything but jeans, unless it's something properly formal, like my parents' ruby wedding anniversary or Marty's engagement party.

Someone else appears behind her, blonde and heavily made up too. It's that girl, Laura, from the waltzers. Her eyes are bleary and she sways forward slightly. Overly sweet perfume fills the air, undercut by sour alcohol. I knew girls like her at school, the ones who looked older than they actually were, who went to the pubs early and dated older guys. Why is Jenn still hanging around with her? Where's Katy?

Jenn sucks her breath in. 'Mum,' she says. Marian turns. 'That's us away out now, OK?'

My heart softens, that familiar worry in her voice. She might look different on the surface, an alternative version, but she's still in there. The real Jenn.

Marian leans forward and looks up at the two girls. For a moment she seems confused, as though she's not entirely sure what to do. Finally, she says, 'Where are you girls off to then?'

'A party,' Jenn replies quickly, 'but if you're not feeling well, I can stay?'

I swear there's a pleading look in her eyes, as though she wants her mum to say something; to stop her. Her dad would have.

Laura hiccups, before covering her mouth.

Come on, Marian, say something. Surely she'll stop them going wherever it is they think they're going.

But she just nods. 'OK then.'

'Oh,' Jenn says, 'there's dinner on the hob if you want any, veggie stir fry, and I've put the hot water on for a bath.'

Marian smiles a limp smile. 'Thanks, darling.'

'Well, later, Mrs Clark,' Laura says and prods Jenn to leave the room, whispering something in her ear as they go.

Marian tips her head back against the sofa, resumes watching the TV with that lifeless expression. And I've never been so annoyed at her before. For not being there for Jenn when she needed it most. For not understanding her own daughter. Without warning, the room starts to fade like I'm blacking out, and I think about all the things Jenn's never told me.

All the things I'm only seeing now.

JENNY

The lighting is dim at the party, the music muffled under the buzz of chatter and a haze of smoke has settled across her eyeline like the haar that used to come into their old garden. Around the living room people sit on sofas, chairs, the floor. Bottles of cider, beer and spirits are littered across the glass coffee table. From where she's perched awkwardly on the arm of a sofa, Jenny can see Laura doing shots with a group of girls from the year above in the corner.

Pretty much everyone from sixth year is here, with only the odd fifth-year student dotted about, and Jenny feels uncomfortable because she doesn't really know any of them, doesn't know who to talk to. It was Laura who got invited, through some guy she's been dating. Katy was going to come, but then her mum said she didn't want her at a party with alcohol. She looks at the barely touched drink in her hand, bright blue and sickly tasting. The colour reminds her of a trip to Deep Sea World with her dad when she was younger, that dreamy view from under the shark tunnel with the lights glinting through. She'd like to be there instead right now.

'Hey,' she hears a voice say, and turns to see a familiar face, tufts of white blond hair above. Duncan. She has a fleeting image of him in biology, tilted over a Bunsen burner, goggled eyes concentrated on the task assigned.

'Hi,' she says and a curious sense of relief immediately floods through her. He looks different outside of school, more relaxed in his blue t-shirt and jeans. He's got a beer in his hand. It's almost full still.

'You enjoying the party?' he asks.

'Um, sort of,' she says.

A knowing look passes between them.

'Yeah, I don't really know anyone here either,' he says. 'I don't usually go to these parties.'

'How come you're at this one then?'

'Oh, I play football with Eric.'

She nods, thinking of the guy who opened the door earlier with his slick of black hair and creepy smile. *Hot*, Laura had whispered to her once they'd gone in, before she'd dumped her in a corner.

'So,' Duncan says, looking slightly unsure of himself now. 'I think we're both taking all three sciences for Highers, right?'

She smiles. She hadn't actually noticed he was too. 'Yeah, I'm trying to get into medicine, if I can.'

'Me too.' He grins.

There's a cheer from beside them on the sofa, two guys wrestling each other and one of them knocks into the side of her. She almost falls off but Duncan steadies her with his hand. She can't help laughing, which makes him laugh too.

'Hey, do you want to go outside for a bit?' Duncan says. 'I think some people are out on the patio.'

'Sure.' She nods. Looking across at Laura's back again, she doesn't suppose she'll care where she is. And some air would be good, some other chat. All that's waiting for her at home is a dark flat.

Slipping off the sofa arm, she grabs her jacket and the two of them veer past people into the crowded hallway. Duncan opens the door for her and a rush of cool autumnal air hits her face as she steps out onto the porch. She hears the bass beat still thumping behind them as she walks down the steps, rhythmic and fading.

The next day

ROBBIE
Music. A radio is playing quietly. I'm in a bedroom, and it's nuts. The walls are covered floor to ceiling in prints of paintings – they

look kind of familiar, famous probably – and there are clothes all over the floor, all over the massive bed. I thought I was messy, but this is in a different league.

No one else is here, but the photos of Jenn and Katy around the vanity mirror tell me all I need to know.

Is this soon after the party?

Jenn and Duncan. It felt weird watching them walk off together. Like they have this shared history I have no part in.

Did she think about him when we were together?

I suppose these are the moments I've really got to pay attention to: the places I never was, the conversations I never heard. These must be where I'll find her secret.

But Jenn's the one who's good at games, mysteries. Not me. She's always loved end-of-night Pictionary, or Who Am I? I can see her now at my parents', a yellow post-it stuck to her forehead, Dolly Parton scrawled over it in my childish handwriting. And she would always put so much effort into it, so much enthusiasm. *Am I human? Am I an actor?* She would keep going until she got it right. She would never give up.

It's my turn not to give up.

The bedroom door opens and I freeze.

'Oh my god, you have *got* to tell me everything,' a voice says, and Katy catapults in. She's wearing some sort of red fluffy jumper with sequins across the front. Jenn's behind her, shrugging off her grey cardigan. It's warm in here.

Katy drops down on the bed and looks up at Jenn expectantly. But Jenn just smiles, takes a seat on a massive pink blow-up chair.

'There's really not much to tell, I didn't stay long.'

'But *something* must have happened,' Katy presses, 'there must be some gossip, surely?' She frowns.

'Honestly, nothing happened, you didn't miss a thing,' Jenn says reassuringly. 'I just hung out with Duncan for a bit and then we left.'

'Duncan?'

Jenn blushes, like she's said too much.

'You didn't say anything about Duncan. Duncan Anderson you mean? Isn't he like, super smart? Like *you* smart? Did something happen with him?'

Jenn lets out a surprised laugh. 'No. We just walked home together, that's all.'

'That's all?' Katy leans back on her hands. 'Well, he's a bit quiet really, I'm not surprised.'

'He's not that quiet,' Jenn says, almost defensively. 'He's nice. We had a nice chat.'

Katy gives her a look.

Duncan. This must be when she got to know him. I looked him up online once. I was curious to see who it was she'd been with for the five years of university. I remember Duncan's profile picture: nice smile, nice hair. Nice guy. I forgot about him two seconds later. They'd broken up, she was with me now and that was all I needed to know.

'Anyway,' Katy says, 'I still can't believe Mum wouldn't let me go. We're sixteen. We're basically adults now. Your mum's so cool like that.'

I wouldn't really describe Marian's blatant depression to be cool. But Jenn doesn't say anything, just smiles.

'Hey,' Jenn says, getting off the chair and moving to the bedside, 'is that from the family shoot you guys did?' She points to a white frame, between hairbrushes and alarm clocks and a lava lamp. It's of Katy's family I presume, in black and white. Katy and an older boy are standing between their parents, all with thick black hair and golden-brown skin, other than her dad standing to one end, his white skin the same colour as the background. They're all grinning at the camera like it's an advertisement for some Stepford estate. Cringe. My parents made us do that too, prancing around barefoot on a beach somewhere.

'Oh god, isn't it awful?' Katy says and I look up at her. 'Isn't it just the most embarrassing thing? Mum loves them though. She got so many printed off, I'll show you the living room later. It's hideous.'

Jenn picks it up, looks at it for a moment. 'It's not so bad,' she says softly.

That longing in her eyes. This is clearly what she wanted; what she used to have.

Does this have anything to do with her secret?

'Hey, you want to stay for lunch?' Katy asks and Jenn looks up. 'Mum's doing chicken cafreal. Or do you have to get back?'

'I'd love to stay, thanks,' she smiles. 'Mum's painting today, I don't think she'll mind.'

But what I suspect she means is, *I don't think she'll notice.*

What feels like seconds later, and I'm standing in a communal garden, like the one outside mine and Jenn's place. It's chilly, but her mum is sitting at the end of the green in front of a canvas painting. Her back is to us, draped in a cream shawl, and she looks so lonely suddenly; so isolated out here by herself. Jenn wanders past me in her grey cardigan, carrying a chipped mug of something steaming in her hand. The sun behind me is low in the crisp blue sky, shadows starting to stretch up the brick walls around the sides.

I have to fight the urge to call out to Jenn again. But I know now that it just ends up freaking her out. I need to listen instead. Watch. I follow behind her, the shapes on the canvas become more distinct the closer I get: bare trees, an old bench at the back. I'm no art connoisseur but I think it's good.

She's standing behind her mum's shoulder now, and the dimming sun catches it briefly, illuminating the greens and browns, the almost dream-like flecks of gold.

'It's lovely,' Jenn says.

Her mum startles, looks up at her. She's pale still, drawn.

'Jenny, you scared me.'

'Sorry,' Jenn says and passes her the mug. Marian takes a couple of small sips, her bony fingers pink with the cold under streaks of paint. 'Thank you. How was Katy's?'

'Good, I had lunch there.'

'That's nice.'

Jenn pauses, like she wants to say something else.

'Why do you never try to find him?' she says eventually.

'Sorry?'

'Dad. Why did he leave? Why aren't we a family anymore?'

It's such a direct question, but then I think of the photo in Katy's bedroom – those four smiling faces.

'Jenny,' she says quietly, not looking her in the eye, 'we can't keep going over this. Stop pushing it.'

But Jenn's eyes remain steady.

This clearly isn't the first time she's raised it.

'I've been looking for him, you know.'

'What do you mean?' Marian says, turning to her. Her forehead is creased.

'The internet, architect firms, projects, councils. I've looked everywhere, but I can't find him. It's like he's vanished, but people don't vanish, Mum. They just don't. You have to have heard something from him. He has to have told you something?'

'Jenny, I—'

'Tell me something, Mum, because I just miss him so much.' Jenn starts to cry suddenly, tears streaming down her face. 'I can't keep wondering.'

Marian covers her face with her hands, like it's all too difficult for her.

'Please Mum,' Jenn continues, 'please just tell me what happened—'

Marian's hands drop.

'He hit me.'

The words hang like invisible daggers in the air. My heart is hammering against my chest. Jenn's must be too, because I can hear her breathing. For what seems like ages, the two of them just stay like that in the garden, frozen in time. Marian's cheeks are stained red.

'What do you mean . . . hit you?' Jenn asks eventually.

Marian shakes her head, like a child refusing to speak. 'Forget I said anything.'

'Mum,' Jenn says, standing above her now. Her eyes are wide and searching, but Marian refuses to look at her. 'Mum, please.'

· Marian is gripping her paintbrush, staring down at it like the answer to this situation is in its chipped shaft. But Jenn doesn't move, doesn't let up. This is too important, clearly.

'It was in the September,' Marian starts finally, so quietly I can barely hear her. 'Your dad had been working a lot, if you recall, some big project, and I'd been trying to keep out of his way. I'd been trying to keep out of his way quite a lot by that point . . . he was different, you see. I was doing the dishes late one night, my hands were all slippery and I dropped a pan on the floor – that giant one we had for soup? It made such a noise, and your dad, your dad suddenly appeared out of his study. And his face. Jenny, I'd never seen him look so angry. He said I was making a racket and why couldn't I just stop being so useless for once? And then he came towards me and he hit me, hard.'

'No,' Jenn says, shaking her head.

'Yes,' her mum presses, voice trembling. She looks at the painting as though picturing herself back in that kitchen, behind the canvas. 'That was the night he left us. But I tried to stop him,' she says, wiping at her eyes now. 'He started packing his bags and I told him that I loved him, and that I forgave him. I just couldn't bear the idea of him leaving . . . fool that I was.'

Jenn just stares at her, like she's unable to take it in.

'He agreed to stay initially,' her mum continues, 'and we went to bed as normal. But he must have got up once I'd fallen asleep.'

'No,' Jenn says, more firmly this time, 'no, I don't believe it. Dad was never like that. You've got this wrong.'

'I haven't,' Marian says, her own eyes filling up with tears once more.

Jenn starts shivering, and I'm not sure if it's the chill in the air or because of what she's been told. I want them both to keep talking, in case this is something to do with it. *Her secret.* It could be, couldn't it? Because this is properly traumatic stuff.

But why would Jenn have kept this from me? He wouldn't be the first abusive husband. And anyway, I agree with Jenn that it doesn't make any sense. Everything I've seen, everything I've witnessed in her childhood, suggests he was a good guy.

'I don't believe you,' Jenn says eventually. 'Dad was the kindest, most gentle person I know.'

'Jenny, I'm telling the truth. You might not have noticed it, but he would have sudden bursts of anger sometimes. That was the only time he hit me, but his temper had been getting worse for a while. I actually wondered if he'd been drinking – his father was an alcoholic, did you know?'

Jenn shakes her head. 'I don't want to talk about this anymore.'

Marian looks like she might be about to say something else, but then she nods, the paintbrush lying wearily on her knee now. All the colour seems to be sapped from around us, and I just can't visualise these new images of her dad that her mum has produced. It's as though she's given Jenn an outline of a picture, one of those paint-by-numbers things, but there are no details – no numbers to follow.

As Jenn walks back across the garden, my mind starts to buzz: if her dad didn't do this, does that mean her mum's lying?

But why would she do that?

Her words about psychology buzz in my mind again, why she was so into it – *I just find it interesting why people do what they do.*

Just before she disappears back into the dark tenement, Jenn glances back across the lawn, at her mum settling in front of the canvas again, and there's this utterly bewildered expression on her face, like her whole world has been crushed. She goes inside finally, the scuff of her feet echoing on the stone.

As my head starts to thump again, her mum reaches for a plastic bottle on the grass, before pouring turpentine across the top of her painting. It bleeds purple, green and brown, drowning out the gold flecks; dissolving all the light.

THIRTEEN

2017

JENN

She's just finishing painting her nails gold at the living room table when the flat buzzer goes. She looks up.

'I'll get that.' Robbie grins, and bounds out of the room to get it. Screwing the top back on the polish and placing it on the table, she smiles too.

Marty's back.

She can't help thinking of all the photos Robbie's showed her online of his and Marty's travels together: Robbie and Marty at Sydney Harbour, Robbie and Marty at the top of Machu Pichu, Robbie and Marty at a Full Moon party with luminous bands around their heads and orange vests on. They were the kind of boys that could get away with it – Robbie with his height and rugged dark looks, Marty with his cheeky smile and bright blue eyes. They looked exactly like what they were: kids having the time of their lives, not a care in the world. And for a moment, she couldn't help it. She felt jealous. Jealous that they got to just take their parents' money and fly off into the abyss the year after school. Jealous that it didn't occur to them to take a paid job because they had to.

Life for her at eighteen had been somewhat different.

But as she hears the door opening, she can't help smiling. It will be great to see Marty again; great for Robbie to have him back in Edinburgh.

She looks around the living room, at the tea lights burning in jars and the fire lit in the grate – the first this autumn. Bowls of crisps are set out on side tables and the mantelpiece too, little touches that she thought would be nice before the dinner party. It still feels funny holding dinner parties for some reason. At twenty-eight, it's like they're on a bizarre cusp: not quite adults, no longer kids. Somewhere in between.

She hears the sound of back slapping and laughing in the hall, then heavy footsteps into the room.

'Jenn!' Marty says, walking forwards and leaning in for a kiss on the cheek. He's wearing an expensive-looking shirt, and his hair is neatly cut, jawline smooth when it brushes against her own. He looks older, but in a good way.

'Long time no see,' he says.

'I know,' she smiles. 'Actual years.'

'Since Robbie's Christmas party, I think it was. Just before I left for New York.'

'Oh, god,' Jenn says, 'I had far too much mulled wine that night.'

'I think everyone did,' Robbie adds, coming back in with a bottle of beer and giving it to Marty.

'All those broken promises about trips over.' Marty shakes his head in faux disappointment.

'Oh, come on,' Robbie says, 'I saw you in Dubai last year.'

'*Early* last year. And that was the worst attempt at a boys' holiday I've ever seen.' Marty turns to Jenn. 'He would not get off his phone to you. Always texting in restaurants and walking out of bars. The boys eventually hid it under a sun lounger one day—'

'Hey, hey, enough,' Robbie says and laughs.

Jenn can't help but smile. She remembers those ten days they had apart just over a year into their relationship, the sheer ecstatic torture of it, how they'd sent each other texts day and night, and each time she got one her heart leapt out of her chest. They'd had time apart before, of course, both of them had busy lives after all, but ten days in different countries still felt like forever somehow.

It made her realise something big was happening between them. Something she'd never experienced before; might never experience again.

'Where are you going to work here?' Jenn asks.

Marty turns to her. 'Oh, just a small hedge fund in town.'

'*Oh, just a small hedge fund in town,*' Robbie mimics with a smile. 'Marty's doing pretty well for himself these days.'

He's being sincere she knows, but there's a bitterness there too.

'What made you come back?' Jenn asks. She feels strangely comfortable with Marty even though they've only met once, as though she's friends with him by osmosis. All the stupid postcards around the flat, the drunken phone calls after the pub when Marty's night is just kicking off across the water.

Marty shrugs. 'I'd just had enough of it, I guess, the life over there. I loved it, don't get me wrong, but I've always been a bit of a home bird.'

Jenn nods, wonders what it must be like to live abroad. That was her plan once too, after all.

'So,' Marty continues, looking between them, 'is that three years you guys have been together now?'

'That's right,' Robbie says, and loops his arm around Jenn's middle. She almost can't believe it herself. Has it really been three years already? *She still loves him so much.*

'What happened with that girl you were seeing in New York?' Robbie asks. 'Tiffany? I thought it sounded serious.'

'Her name was Tory,' Marty says slowly, 'and no, it just didn't take off in the end.'

'Ah that's a shame, mate. Another one bites the dust.'

Marty smiles. 'Plenty more fish and all that. Anyway, I might meet someone at your wedding?'

Robbie almost spits out his drink. His arm drops from around Jenn. 'Wedding?'

A look of confusion crosses Marty's face. 'Sorry, I was only joking, guys. I just assumed . . . ' he tails off. 'Don't tell me you've lost your sense of humour since I've been away, Robbo?' he says quickly, and laughs.

'Jesus,' Robbie says, starting to laugh too, but it's stilted. Uncertain.

Jenn feels odd suddenly. Was it such an appalling idea, getting married to her? She's not sure she wants to get married if she's being honest with herself – too many people staring at her, too complex with her family. But commitment, yes, she assumed they were on that path.

Aren't they?

Before she can process anything further the doorbell goes again.

'I'll get that,' she says, knowing who it will be. She's not going to dwell on it this evening – she's probably overthinking it anyway. They're only twenty-eight after all. Barely any of their friends have significant others. *Stop being so needy.*

Walking into the hall, she recomposes her face as the boys laugh away about something in the background. She pulls open the flat door to find Hilary standing on the other side, a vision of glossy hair and preternaturally tanned skin. In one hand is a bouquet of pink and purple flowers, in the other, a glittering wine bag.

'Hey,' Jenn smiles widely and reaches in to hug her.

'Is he here yet?' Hilary whispers, walking inside. She shrugs off her cream coat, the scent of rich perfume fluttering out of it. Jenn takes it from her, hangs it on a hook. She's wearing a tight pink dress, strappy heels, and suddenly Jenn feels under-dressed in her standard jeans and black top. They hadn't planned to set Hilary up with Marty exactly, but it seemed fun to even up the numbers, given Kirsty and her new man were coming. And Jenn knew he would probably be her type – Marty would probably be any girl's type.

'Hils,' Robbie says as they enter the living room and immediately walks towards her. He gives her a big hug before stepping back and smiling. 'Did you get away from work OK today? Amazing the three of us all managed to get a Saturday night off.'

'Oh, are you a chef too?' Marty asks quickly, eyes brightening at the sight of her.

Hilary beams at him, cheeks flushed.

'No, no, I'm a doctor. Like Jenn.'

'Excellent,' Marty says, his eyes focused on her. 'What kind?'

'Same as Jenn again, A&E.'

'Wow, that's impressive. Oh, and I'm Chris,' he says and laughs. 'Got ahead of myself there.'

'What happened to Marty?' Robbie cuts in. He's smiling but he looks confused.

'God, haven't introduced myself as Marty for a while now,' he says, smiling at Hilary still. 'Time to grow up.'

Jenn feels if she were to put her hand between Marty and Hilary, it would be caught in a crossfire of invisible sparks – the ones at the start of something, when everything feels great and it's all about the fun. No expectations, no confusion.

'Right,' Robbie says, oblivious, and claps his hands. 'Booze. What can I get you, Hils?'

'Oh,' she says, 'anything is fine. Here, this is for you guys.' She passes Robbie the bag.

'Ah, you're a gal after my own heart,' he grins, glancing in at the bottle before turning to Jenn. 'Prosecco for you ladies?'

'Yeah, sounds good,' she says, trying to read him, this man she knows like the back of her hand. Or thought she did. *What's he thinking?*

'Back in a moment, folks,' Robbie says and walks out of the room, like everything is totally fine, like he doesn't have a care in the world. As Jenn watches him go, she hears the door buzzer. *Kirsty.* She's about to get it, when the candle at the centre of the living room table flickers rapidly, as though a gust of wind has caught it. The hair on the backs of her arms stand up, and she shivers.

Two weeks later

ROBBIE

A long, dark room. People drinking at wooden tables. Floor to ceiling windows, cobbled alleyway outside. Neon lighting flares up behind the bar. I'm in the West End – I know this place well. I look around for Jenn. They're in the corner: him with a pint in hand, her with a white wine. He's in a green sweater and she's still got her blue coat on. Likely autumn, so not long after the dinner party. Though I didn't quite get *why* I was seeing that dinner party. What did Marty coming home have to do with anything?

I cross over to them, past a couple of empty tables. Must be mid-week. We used to like going out for dinner and drinks on random nights if neither of us had a shift and we weren't working the next morning. After all, we didn't always get weekends off at the same time. We'd go to a restaurant first: Korean, Greek, Turkish, wherever we happened to land upon. Then we'd head out for a few drinks, maybe more, before heading back up the road, talking and laughing about our days.

Quietly, I edge my way onto the wooden bench beside Jenn. I don't want to scare her, stop the flow of conversation. *Listen carefully, Robbie.* There might be something here.

'I saw Hilary at work today,' she's saying, and takes a sip of her wine.

'Oh yeah?' Robbie doesn't sound particularly interested. 'How's she getting on?'

'Good.' She raises her eyebrows.

'What's that look about?'

'Oh, I just heard there's already been a second date with Marty. Think it's going pretty well.'

'Really?'

'He didn't mention it?'

Robbie shakes his head, takes another drink.

'That's great though,' he says, 'they'd be a great couple.'

'Yeah,' Jenn says and starts to fiddle with the stem of her wine glass. She looks like she wants to say something else, but he's on his phone now, scrolling, laughing. *He's always on that bloody phone.*

She clears her throat nervously and he glances up.

'Do you remember that wedding comment Marty made?'

'What wedding comment?' he says, looking blank initially, then his face changes. 'Oh, yeah, the not-so-funny joke?'

She half laughs, twirls the stem in her fingers.

'You weren't annoyed about that, were you?' he asks. 'I mean, you're not actually wanting to get married right now or anything?'

He looks troubled, the colour seeping out of him. *Could he be any more obvious?*

'No,' she says, 'but I suppose I just wondered . . . '

'What?'

'Well, if . . . if we're on the same page here?'

He smiles at that, takes her hand. ''Course we are. We're having a good time, everything is good, right?'

Jenn nods but she doesn't look totally convinced. Of course she isn't, he's given her nothing of any substance here. Even I can see that. *Why isn't he saying anything more?* My stomach is churning. This was the first time we ever discussed the topic of marriage and I gave her absolutely no reassurance. Is this really what I said?

Taking a final sip of her wine, Jenn sets her empty glass back down.

'Another one?' Robbie says quickly, making to stand up.

'No, I can't tonight I'm afraid,' she smiles woefully. 'I've got the MRCEM Intermediate, remember? And we've been out so much the past month.'

'Seriously?' Robbie says, looking more put out than is warranted.

'Well, yeah, I have to pass it to specialise.'

'Didn't you say you get more chances to pass?'

'Four, yes,' she says slowly. 'But the next one isn't until spring and I have to pay each time. Plus, it looks really bad if I fail.' She shakes her head nervously, like the idea terrifies her.

'OK . . . OK,' Robbie says, holding up his hands. 'I was just thinking we hadn't been out, just the two of us, in a while, but that's fine. I'll go and settle the tab then.'

'Hang on—' she starts and he turns to look at her. She sighs, smiles. 'Maybe just the one more.'

He fist punches the air.

'But last one, OK?' she adds.

'Atta girl,' he grins, 'I promise you'll be in bed by ten and up cramming by eight.'

'Deal,' she says, looking at him with so much love, so much trust.

I feel awful, knowing what's coming.

'I'm sure you'll ace it,' he says, feet already pointed in the direction of the bar. 'You always do.'

Five weeks later

JENN

Putting the key into the lock, she lets herself into the dimly lit hallway. Light from the kitchen is leaking into the corridor and she hears the dull grate of plates, the clank of cutlery being pulled out of a drawer. On the side table next to some green tinsel, lies her coffee cup from this morning, deserted in a spin of expectant energy. She'd been so excited about today, so confident that she'd done enough to pass that exam. Now she just feels so shit. Even the mug seems to taunt her with its picture of a Spanish señorita on the front, clicking her heels and fanning herself. They picked it up on a weekend to Madrid a few months ago. *Your sassy mug*, Robbie dubbed it.

As she shuts the door behind her, the noises stop in the kitchen and he appears under the archway.

'I didn't hear you come in there. Congratulations!' he says, grinning as he walks towards her, 'I've got the Champagne chilling, the Chinese food just arrived—'

'I failed,' she says quietly, simply. Dropping her bag on the floor, she picks up the mug from the side and walks past him. She can feel his eyes on her back, pressing, searching, but she can't talk about it anymore.

Opening up the dishwasher, she places the mug inside, the señorita now head down in the dark. *Could he not just have put it in earlier? He's been here all day.*

'But,' he starts, 'are you sure?'

'Of course I'm sure,' she snaps, knowing how unlike herself she sounds. But she's panicking. *This has never happened before.*

'But you're always working so hard,' he says, at a loss, 'I don't get it?'

She takes a breath in, all her thoughts on the cycle home whirring around together now. 'No, I'm not always working so hard, I just go to work as normal,' she says steadily. 'I never actually study. I'm always out with you, or our friends, or your family, or trips away. I just need to focus if I'm going to do this. Things have to change. You might be able to duck out of shifts in your job, but I can't keep doing all this spur-of-the-moment stuff.'

His expression drops, all that jubilant warmth seeping out of him.

'I think you're overreacting a bit here, Jenn,' he says eventually, 'it's just one exam. You can just take it again?'

'That's not the point. Do you know how bad it looks to repeat exams? How it could affect my job prospects?'

'Jesus, Jenn. Calm down. It's not the end of the world.'

She covers her eyes with her hands. He's not getting this. *He doesn't understand how important this is to me; what it was like for me.*

'Look, I'm sorry,' she says, feeling like she might burst into tears of frustration at any moment. 'It's just been a really hard day. I'm going to go to bed.' She walks quickly out the room, so he can't see her cry.

'What about the Chinese?' he says, and she stops briefly, but doesn't turn. She knows it's ultimately her fault for not just going home when she needed to study – that's on her – but why did he have to actively lead her astray? Why couldn't he have been the responsible one for once? Why couldn't he have just supported her when she needed him to?

He's still not supporting her now.

'Fuck the Chinese, Robbie,' she says and walks out, the tears starting to fall now.

In the bedroom, she heels off her trainers, pulls off her leggings. The bed is unmade, the duvet crumpled into the centre where Robbie left it earlier, but she doesn't care, just pulls it up and over herself, hoping that she'll somehow fall asleep and forget this day ever happened. Tomorrow she'll get up and study, make sure that this never, ever happens again. Looking at her watch, she sees the faded peach flowers, the long hand ticking over it.

'*Please* wake up, Jenn. We're running out of time.'

Jolting up, she looks sharply around the room. *What was that voice?* Her heart is beating so fast. But there's no one in the room, obviously. Lying back again, she tries to soothe herself, the way she's done since she was thirteen. *It's going to be OK, Jenn, it's going to be OK.* But she feels so shit. So shit for failing, so shit for snapping.

So shit that Robbie's not here beside her now.

Through the fog of her thoughts, she hears the cork of the champagne in the kitchen, the sound of one solitary glass being poured. Hot frustration rises up in her, and she shuts her eyes; lets herself fall down, down, down into nothing.

FOURTEEN

2006

ROBBIE

Light blurs, focuses. The pulsing in my head subsides. I'm in the hallway of another flat. It's the same kind though – old tenement style. Wooden skirting runs around the surrounds and there's a stripy rug on the floor, chipped boards. A big, colourful canvas is hung on the wall beside the door, a vase of fresh flowers on the side table alongside a photo of Jenn and her mum.

Their flat again. Except this time, it looks better. Cheerier somehow. Sunlight is flooding from the living room, which is neat and tidy now. No sad mother on the sofa or bad TV shows. Things must have improved a bit.

Thank fuck we're out of the last place, our place. I couldn't stand watching us like that, watching Jenn like that, upset and lying in the dark while I drank our Champagne alone. How did I not know she was crying? I should have comforted her, instead of drinking.

And I shouldn't have spoken out loud there either – scaring her didn't exactly help anything.

Again.

A metallic sound at the door. A swooshing noise. Letters start to drop down onto the floorboards. Pounding feet, fast and drawing closer. I turn just as she flies towards me – a gangly teenage Jenn in yellow shorts and a white t-shirt – and I have to step quickly to the side. I have no idea if she could feel I'm here, but I don't really want to find out right now. Then she's down on the floor, searching, shifting the letters, until she grabs a large brown one, clutches it, shreds it open. Her breathing is laboured, hands shaking as she pulls a sheet of paper out from it. She reads it, then she's screaming and laughing, and screaming again.

I start smiling too, can't help myself. This moment is infectious and I don't even know what's going on. Her mum appears, eyes wide, drying her hands on a tea towel.

'Is it—' she starts.

'I did it!' Jenn cries, jumping up and clutching the paper. Tears stream down her face.

Marian hugs Jenn to her, daughter towering over mother, and the immense pride is clear. Pulling back finally, they both look down at the sheet of paper together, before grinning at each other.

'I wish I could let him know,' Jenn says after a moment, and Marian's face immediately changes. She starts wringing her hands on the stained tea towel again, even though they're obviously dry.

'Well, I wouldn't think too much about that today,' she says, in a forced cheery voice. 'Better just to celebrate. We could even go out for dinner after school as a treat? At that restaurant you always stop outside. You know, the trendy one with the flowers around the door? We could take Katy?'

'Mum,' Jenn says, almost firmly. 'We can't afford that place. You know that.'

'Oh,' Marian says, then nods. She looks confused. 'OK, you're probably right.'

It's so weird seeing a child having to have this conversation with a parent – Jenn was always the sensible adult, because she had to be. Is this why she didn't want to rack up student loans for travelling? Because she always tried to keep her and her mum out of debt?

I never once thought about money when I was growing up. I never really even think about it now. Mum and Dad bought the flat years ago, so, other than bills, what I earn is mine to do with as I please.

Things were clearly not as easy for Jenn.

She looks back at her mum.

'You must know where he is,' she tries again. 'This would mean so much to him. I know it would.'

Marian shakes her head. 'I don't know where he is. I don't know where he went. I told you what happened . . . '

'But Mum, he wouldn't just do that. I know he wouldn't—'

'What are you saying?' Marian asks sharply. It's the first time I've seen her raise her voice. 'I'm not lying.'

Jenn opens her mouth to speak again, but the flat buzzer goes. Both of them jump, as do I and we all turn to look at the door. Then it goes again, like someone is shouting at them.

'Who could that be?' Marian asks, unmoving. And suddenly it's like she's back to that childish state, lost and confused in the darkened hallway – a rabbit caught in the headlights.

Jenn picks up the intercom, as a high-pitched screeching leaks out into the hall. 'Come on up,' she smiles, pressing the button to release the door. She looks back at her mum. 'It's Katy.'

With something like relief on her face, Marian lets out a sigh, drops the tea towel. There's a slamming of the main door downstairs, followed by feet up the steps. *Shit, don't stop speaking.* Is this the reason her relationship with her mum is so bad now? Because Jenn didn't believe her?

I only met Marian a couple of times over the years. Once when she came up here and we had a fairly stilted dinner at the flat. Once when we went to London to see friends and her mum happened to be there too. And both times Jenn became this anxious version of herself. Like the experience triggered something in her. But, yet again, when I asked her about it, she clammed up. So I moved the conversation along to something more fun for her.

Or something more fun for me?

A knot forms in my stomach.

What if her mum has something to do with her secret and I missed it?

The sound of feet on the stairs gets louder and Jenn unlocks the door, opens it up just as a flurry of dark hair, green hoodie and pink pyjama bottoms appears on the landing.

'I got an A in art, and four Cs!' Katy screeches, clutching her own torn envelope in one hand. 'Did you get what you need?' She looks as though she hasn't taken a brush through her hair in weeks. *Is that cereal in her hair?*

I like Katy though, she seems interesting. Why is Jenn not friends with her anymore?

'I did,' Jenn nods. Katy rushes to hug her and they stumble back into the flat. They start jumping up and down, their faces glowing with happiness, as the morning light floods in on them. Jenn looks so carefree now, so excited and almost child-like again.

Marian stands to the side slightly, a bit bemused.

'Congratulations, Katy,' she says eventually, as the girls finally slow down to a halt. 'Which art school do you think you might go to?'

'Oh, I have no idea,' she breathes. 'Isn't it wonderful?'

Marian smiles, nods.

The house phone rings on the hall table, and Jenn reaches for it quickly, still grinning away to herself.

'Hey,' she says. 'Yeah, yeah I did. You?' A pause. 'Congratulations, that's amazing. Yeah, I'll catch you in a bit.'

Jenn replaces the handset and looks up.

'Who was that?' Katy asks, still bouncing. She can't seem to stand still.

'Oh, just Duncan, asking how I got on.'

Katy rolls her eyes and smiles. *'Just Duncan,'* she mimics. 'He's so in love with you. Who else would call you first thing in the morning other than moi?'

'What's this?' Marian says, looking between the girls, like she's trying to be involved.

Jenn blushes, shakes her head. 'He's just a friend. And anyway, I haven't heard from him all summer.'

'Uh huh,' Katy says and starts dancing to non-existent music again. She twirls Jenn around in the middle of the hall, the light getting brighter and brighter in my eyes.

'We'll see.'

Two weeks later

JENNY

Rain spatters against the library window and Jenny looks up and through the glass at the grey wobble of sky beyond. Summer is officially over then.

Turning back to her textbook in front of her, she reads through the homework from biology this morning. She knows she likely won't need any grades in her final year of school, not given her Higher results, but still – you never know.

'Hi Jenny,' a voice says quietly and the familiar form of Duncan appears on the other side of the desk. His hair is slick with rain, cheeks pink from the cold, probably from playing football. He smiles at her before dumping the backpack on the floor and pulling out his own textbooks. Ever since they spoke at the party last year, they've had a routine of coming to the library to study at lunch. They push each other on, checking in on each other's progress. It's probably why they both did so well.

'What section are you on?' he whispers across at her as he sits down, opens his textbook. His hair is blond even with wet in it, his eyes a clear blue. There's a smattering of freckles across his nose and she knows already he will grow into his still paling looks, like she can see an older version of him already somehow, stubbled and weather beaten. Good looking. *An old head on young shoulders*, as her dad used to say.

'I'm on skeletal muscles,' she replies, tapping her pencil on the page.

She's fascinated by the human body, ever since she broke her arm a few years ago falling off a bike. Despite the pain, she'd felt so calmed by the doctor's steady presence at the hospital, the way she had been examined, x-rayed; how the cast had been secured on her arm.

That's why she wants to be a doctor, so she can learn to make people better too. Help them when they need it most.

'Hey, did you see Katy around?' she asks. 'I thought she was coming here.'

'Katy?' Duncan says, looking up. 'I think I saw her going into the art department earlier.'

'Ah right.'

'That will be weird for you guys, huh?'

'What will?'

'Oh,' Duncan says, 'I'm just assuming she'll be off some-where random when we all leave here. She's always struck me as an ... adventurous type.' The way he says it is so careful, like he's trying not to say anything wrong. It's sweet.

She smiles. 'Yes, you're probably right.'

She knows Katy still has no idea what she's doing yet. It isn't really in her nature to make decisions ahead of time, but then, Katy doesn't really have to.

Not like she does.

They'd stopped hanging around with Laura by the end of fifth year, though whose choice that was remained largely unclear. All Jenny knew was that she had to get good grades, and in order to do that she couldn't go out to parties every weekend. There always seemed to be this tense knot in her stomach, driving her forwards, driving her to take care of things. Her mum was still a community arts worker – part time, so she could still do her painting – and it wasn't enough. Certainly not enough to have anything left over for them. *Why did Dad leave us with nothing?* So, she did a paper round in the mornings, on top of care home shifts at the weekend. And she found she liked it – that feeling of being in control of her own money finally. In control of her own life. She could earn it for herself now, protect herself.

'You thought any more about which universities you'll put down?' Duncan asks suddenly, his pen resting on a page of neat, precise notes.

I need to get into Edinburgh. I can't leave Mum.

'I think Edinburgh still,' she says casually.

He smiles, cheeks slightly pinker. 'Yeah, that's my top choice too.'

'Well, I'm sure you'll get in. You're top of the class.'

'Joint top,' he corrects and she grins at him.

'Well,' he says, 'maybe we'll end up in medical school together too.'

She gets this glimmer of something in her chest, this feeling, like he's said something she already knows. Like she's remembering a dream she had last night and it's all just coming back to her again.

Her faraways again.

Smiling across at him, she says, 'Maybe we will.'

ROBBIE

The two of them have their heads back in the textbooks and I can see why they got on. You would never find me in a library at school, spending extra time studying. I imagine for a moment if me and Jenn had been at school together when we were younger. What would we have thought of each other? Would we have even spoken?

Maybe timing really is everything.

But why do I keep seeing this guy? What's this got to do with her secret?

And how close is the truck now?

I'm suddenly aware of just how glib I'm being about this whole thing. A fucking truck is about to smash into us and I'm just loitering around a library. Is there some sort of way I could alert someone? Cross the void somehow?

My phone. Why the hell didn't I think of that before? I pat down my pocket for it. Shit. It's not there. Must be in the car somewhere.

I look around behind me, at the shelves of books, the scattered desks. My heart leaps. A computer.

Would it work?

Walking across, I can see it's an older model, clunky in comparison to today's slim-lined models. But it's still a computer. This is stupid though – there's no way a computer will work in her memories. Get real.

But then, maybe there's more to these places than I know?

I sit in front of it, look back at Jenn. She's speaking in hushed whispers with Duncan, eyes locked on his, and I feel a pang of envy for what's to come between them. A part of her life that I had no place in. But what happened with them? And just how much about her life has she not told me about?

With an uncomfortable feeling in my chest, I turn back to the computer. I double click the mouse on the desk and the screen springs to life. Bloody hell, this is old school. I remember being on computers when I was a teenager, downloading music illegally and chatting online with my friends. Fi used to go mental at me because she couldn't use the house phone.

Quickly, in case I'm running out of time, I click on the internet icon, wait as it chugs over, loads. So slow. OK, what should I try? Anything, I suppose.

In the search bar I type the words *emergency services*. The screen goes blank for a moment and I wait. Nothing.

Nice try.

What was I planning to say to them anyway? *Hey police people, I'm currently having a shared-death experience with my girlfriend. Send help?*

Idiot.

I just wish I could contact someone.

I wish I didn't feel so alone.

As I watch that timer symbol spinning round and round, the pulsing starts in my head again. Spots of light in my eyes. The books around me in the library start to fade out.

'Come on.'

The timer keeps whirring and whirring.

Goes blank.

FIFTEEN

2018

ROBBIE

'Robbie.'

Voices, laughter. That comforting smell of hops. My heart rate rises as shapes begin to sharpen again, refocus. The thumping in my head lessens.

'Robbie,' the voice says again, only louder this time.

I blink to see Jenn standing next to me at a bar, the lower shelf of which is lined with decorative old books. She's in leggings, trainers and that purple oversized sweater with the hole in the shoulder, like she's just come from work. She's holding two pints.

Can she . . . ?

No. She's not looking at me, she's looking past my shoulder. My stomach sinks.

Like it would be that easy.

Turning, I see my younger self across the room at a table with Matt. They're chatting away, laughing loudly about something, oblivious to Jenn. Looking back at her, I notice two further bottles of beer and a few bags of crisps on the bar beside us.

Fuck's sake. Why's Robbie not helping her?

After a moment I hear Jenn sigh, and she walks by me. Following behind, I try to work out what memory this is.

Where we are is easy enough, at least. Oak surrounds, well-trodden carpet, dusty books everywhere, Steve behind the bar. This is our usual post-work haunt – Burn's Bar.

On the wall, the chalk board says *June bar menu.*

So about six months on from that sad night after her exam results then. Spring time.

But I still can't place this specific night.

'Oh shit,' Robbie says, seeing her coming over. He stands up quickly at least.

Well done, mate.

'Sorry, I meant to come and help, sit there,' he ushers to a stool. 'I'll get the rest.'

'Thanks,' Jenn says and edges down. I sit down on the booth seat opposite, leaning in so I can hear above the din.

'Cheers for this,' Matt says and holds his pint up to her, before taking a sip. His round cheeks are flushed pink under the lights, bald head looking particularly shiny.

'No problem.'

'That you off duty now then?'

Jenn shakes her head. 'No, sadly not. I'm on for the next four days, just thought I'd drop in for one on the way home, since you were all here.'

'That your excuse then, eh?' Matt grins and takes another sip. 'Not just checking up on him?'

What?

Jenn looks confused for a moment, and I am too. My neck feels hot. What would she have to check up on? And why the fuck would Matt say that? He's probably just drunk already I guess – trying to be funny. That's what he was all about. Good food, good booze. Good fun.

Jenn doesn't reply to his question, but a curious sparkle appears in her eye. She shifts in her seat. 'I've actually got some great news I wanted to share with Robbie,' she says, glancing across at the bar.

I turn briefly. He's chatting away to Stevie – about the football no doubt.

'I couldn't wait until he got home,' she says and I look back at her.

Oh?

Matt smiles woozily. 'Fantastic. At least someone's got great news around here.'

Jenn pauses. 'How was the restaurant tonight?'

The clock on the wall tells me it's only ten, a sure sign of a poor evening, and I remember this stage now: the lagging custom, that feeling of being sluggish and underworked in the kitchen – I listened to a lot of podcasts.

'Fucking dead is how it was,' Matt says, cutting through my thoughts.

'Well, it's only Tuesday I suppose?' Jenn tries.

'Nah, nah it's not that.'

'It's not what?' Robbie says, reappearing finally with the two bottles and crisps. He puts one bottle in front of Jenn and the other at the side of the table.

The extra bottle, Jenn coming after work – this night finally comes back to me.

Things did get a bit tense actually. But nothing bad? Nothing that wasn't forgotten about the next day?

'I was just saying that the restaurant is taking a fucking nose dive,' Matt says.

Robbie doesn't respond, just sits down and takes a drink. He looks kind of rough now he's across from me. There are bags under his eyes and his face is a bit bloated, his green t-shirt all creased. I'd been going out a bit more at this point, I guess. But then Jenn was always working or studying for some thing or another. I wasn't just going to sit around by myself in the flat.

'It's just the nature of the game,' Robbie says to Matt eventually. 'Sometimes a restaurant is the shit and sometimes it's—'

'A pile of shit?' Matt finishes and laughs morosely.

Jenn bites her lip.

'Just gotta keep with it,' Robbie says to Matt. 'You'll see.'

A figure appears alongside us and I look up to see familiar feline eyes, bow-shaped lips. Liv. She starts peeling off her leather jacket, revealing a strappy black top, olive skin – not a lot of her figure is left to the imagination. My stomach clenches with guilt.

But I'm being daft. It's not like anything actually happened at this point – not before Jenn left at any rate. We were just pals.

Men can have female friends, can't they?

'Sorry, sorry I'm late, guys,' Liv says, pulling out her earphones.

'Don't tell me you're still playing that horrendous music you had us listening to in the kitchen earlier.' Robbie raises one eyebrow at her.

Liv pulls a face at him, before grinning. 'Are you still going on about it, seriously?'

'Yes, it was that bad.'

'You're just too old to get it.'

Robbie smacks his hand to his chest. 'Ouch!'

'What music was this?' Jenn says, after a moment.

'Oh sorry,' Liv replies, placing her jacket down on the stool and sitting next to her. 'You must be Jenn?'

I can see Jenn taking Liv in, like most people do. *She'll cause trouble when she's older, that one,* Mum used to say. She used to come over to the house with her family a lot when we were younger. Our dads would kick back with beers in front of the rugby while our mums drank wine in the kitchen. They'd put on a film in the snug for Liv or something – she was a few years younger after all – but she'd spend most of the time following me around the house, trying to wind me up. I never really paid her much attention though.

Not back then.

'This is Liv,' Robbie says. 'Remember I said we had someone filling in for some shifts after Craig left?'

Jenn's face finally breaks into a smile of understanding. 'Ah yes, you're a family friend, right?'

'Sadly yes,' Liv says with a faux sigh and Robbie lets out a bark of a laugh.

'She's just helping out while she sets up her business,' he says, more to Liv than Jenn.

I feel a bit odd suddenly.

Why is this weird?

'So, what's the business then?' Jenn asks it in a friendly way, like with everyone she meets, but she definitely looks a little tense.

'Craft gin,' Liv answers and takes a sip of her drink. 'I'm going in with a couple of guys I know from school.'

'Wow, that's really cool,' Jenn says.

'And then you can supply my restaurant when I open it,' Robbie adds, still looking at Liv. 'Just don't tell Matt,' he whispers behind one hand, and Liv grins back at him.

My chest contracts. *Is he . . . flirting?*

'So, have you been thinking about that again?' Jenn asks Robbie quickly, 'opening your own place?'

Robbie's face immediately stiffens, and I remember this moment so clearly now – how irritated I was by her question out of the blue like that; it wasn't the time to get into the details. It felt like she was needling me, showing me up. But sitting here now, it's no fucking wonder she asked the question. I raised it.

'Of course I've thought about it,' he says flatly. 'What, did you think I'd just given up?'

Jenn visibly flinches, and it's painful to watch. He's being so cold.

'No, I never said that,' she says.

'I'll do it when the time is right, OK? Setting up a restaurant takes a lot of work and planning.' He glances at Liv, like he thinks Jenn wouldn't get it or something.

I could kill the old me right now.

Liv looks between them awkwardly. 'I think I'm going to nip to the ladies.'

Once Liv's out of ear shot, Jenn turns to Robbie, her eyes searching his face. 'What's going on?'

'Nothing,' he says, draining the rest of his pint, and placing it down with a clip. 'Look, I'm sorry, it's just been a shitty day at the restaurant and it's just not the time to start pushing me on starting my own place.'

'I am not pushing you.'

Robbie makes a face. 'Could have fooled me.'

She reaches her hand across to Robbie's but he pulls it away. *Fuck.* She looks hurt now and quite rightly – she asked him a simple question and now he's being a total dick about it.

I was the one who said I always wanted to own a restaurant. *Scottish with a European twist* – my words, not hers.

'Look,' Jenn says, 'why don't we head home after this drink, we can talk about it on the way back, maybe even pick up some chips on the way?'

She smiles at him hopefully, and I think about all the times we wandered across the road to the fish and chip shop late at night when we realised the fridge had nothing more than some gone-off vegetables in it. It was our treat for having a hard week – always extra brown sauce for me, extra ketchup for her.

But he doesn't rise to it.

I already know he doesn't.

'I might just hang out with these guys a bit longer,' Robbie says after a long pause. 'Liv's only just got here after all.'

There's a distinct emphasis on the *I* and I feel myself recoiling from it all.

'You sure?' Jenn says, as Matt walks back over to the table. She lowers her voice. 'I think it would be good to chat about this, no?'

Robbie's eyes soften finally, and I watch as he takes her hand, squeezes it twice. *I love you*. For a split second, my chest floods with hope, before I remember exactly how the evening ended.

And my heart plummets.

'I'll catch you later on,' he says, 'you need the sleep.'

Jenn's face starts to fall, before she makes a strained attempt to smile again. All I can do is sit and watch as she heads towards the exit alone, giving Liv a small wave and a smile as they pass each other by.

But as she pulls open the door, it suddenly dawns on me: I never did find out what her news was.

JENN

Stepping out into the now-cool night air, she feels like shit. What the hell was going on there with Liv? It all just felt so weird and uncomfortable.

Like she was the literal third wheel.

And she knows they won't talk about the restaurant anytime soon, or anything else really. He'll be too hungover in the morning before she heads to work and then the moment will pass. They'll barely see each other over the next week.

Shit.

As she walks down the quiet street, a familiar churning starts in her stomach.

Did she push him too hard about the restaurant?

If she pushes him, he'll leave her.

Like everyone does.

She turns a corner towards their empty flat, stops outside a shop window full of gardening equipment. Staring at the dull outline of herself in the glass, she imagines another scenario: where they'd left the pub together, laughing away hand in hand, and she'd told him her good news – that she'd re-sat the MRCEM Intermediate in secret and, this time, she'd passed.

SIXTEEN

2007

ROBBIE

My head is thumping, slowing a bit. Vision clears. I'm back in the communal garden and it's hot. Must be summer, or close to it. Marian's over on the far side. She's in a green dress, sun hat and gardening gloves, and she's kneeling on a cushion. Reaching out with a fork thing into the earth, she digs away at something. Lying in the grass directly in front of me in shorts and t-shirts are Jenn and Katy. Their feet are pointed in different directions, with their heads positioned alongside each other. Shadows of clouds scud across their faces. It looks like some idyllic snapshot.

I feel bad about the older version of her walking away down the dark street alone – she looked so sad.

Why didn't I just go home with her?

And why the hell did she never tell me what she'd been meaning to that night?

Because you barely saw her in the weeks after, a voice says.

Looking back, I did start hanging out at the restaurant a lot after that. We were trying to get the place booked out again, and Liv had all these new ideas for how to do it and—

I guess I did get a bit distracted.

'I can't believe that's it,' I hear Katy saying. With a sinking feeling I look over, see her eyes are still shut to the sunlight. 'No more school, ever.'

'For you maybe,' Jenn smiles, eyes also shut. 'I'm back studying again in September.'

'And whose fault is that?'

'Mine,' Jenn sighs. 'But it will be good. I'm looking forward to it.'

This must be just after their last term, which means at this very moment, my other self is gallivanting across the globe with Marty somewhere. Florida maybe?

'But you'll still be living in Edinburgh,' Katy says, 'at home. Why not switch it up for a year?' She opens her eyes now. 'Come with me to Paris.'

'Katy,' Jenn says, and her eyes snap open. 'I'm enrolled for this year. I can't just go to France.'

Katy turns her head to look at her. 'Yeah, you can. Just defer. We'd have a total riot. Picture it,' she says, spreading her hands up in the sky and looking up again. 'You, me, the Eiffel Tower. The French men. My parents just signed a lease on this studio apartment which I get in ten days. We could go together?'

Jenn laughs up at the image, but it's tinged with something else. 'It's a nice idea,' she says, 'but I'm starting that job at the cinema tomorrow, and the supermarket the week after, remember?'

'Ditch them!'

Jenn sighs.

'Even if I could,' she says eventually, a definite trace of longing in her voice, 'there's no way Mum could cope alone. I can't just leave her.'

Oh, come on, Jenn.

Why didn't she go? It sounds like an amazing opportunity. I don't think I thought once about anyone else's plans when I was eighteen, least of all my mum's. The world was my oyster and I was going to shuck it.

'You know,' Katy says, dropping her hands back to her stomach again, 'this is your life too.'

The clouds momentarily float across the sun so that everything is cast into shadow. And although Katy can't see Jenn, I can – and she's frowning.

'Right. Gotta pee,' Katy says jumping up, and disappearing back into their tenement block. After she's gone, Jenn just continues to lie like that on the ground, eyes shut, lids fluttering slightly as though she's still thinking.

Does she ever just stop?

Eventually, she gets up from the grass, tugging her shorts back down awkwardly. She might be eighteen now, but she still seems so young. Walking across the grass, her feet brush through

164

the feathery blades and her mum turns from the beds, smiles up from the cushion. There's a bowl of freshly pulled potatoes beside her.

'That Katy away?' Marian asks, shielding her eyes with her hand. 'She's welcome for dinner, you know?'

She looks healthier than before, a sprinkle of freckles across her nose, arms slightly tanned.

Maybe everything really does just take time.

'No, not yet,' Jenn says, 'I'll ask her though.'

Marian smiles. 'OK.'

'I meant to say,' Jenn says, 'I had a chat with Mrs Barclay at the end of term, you know, my art teacher?'

'Yes, I think I've met her at a parents' evening.'

'Well, she mentioned there's a full-time position going at the school for next term, working with her. Mr Allen's leaving apparently.'

'So . . . ?' Marian's smile has fallen. She looks confused.

'So, you should totally apply for it,' Jenn says brightly. 'You'd be so good at it.'

'But I don't want a full-time teaching job,' Marian says, a firmer note in her voice. 'I need the time to do my *own* art.'

What?

That doesn't seem fair. Why should Jenn have to work two jobs all summer when her mum barely works one? Why is Jenn sacrificing the trip of a lifetime? I just thought her mum *couldn't* get another job. I didn't realise it was a choice. Does she even sell her art for money?

'Would you maybe just have a wee look at it?' Jenn asks instead, smiling.

Marian turns back to the vegetable patch, pokes around with her fork in the dirt again. But I can see her mouth is set in a tight line, and I feel a strange impending fear for Jenn. Something's happened here between them, on this perfect sunny day.

'I'll think about it.'

Five weeks later

JENNY

Jumpers, shirts, dresses. She sifts through her wardrobe quickly, looking closely for that flash of red. Not there. *Shit.*

It's OK, it must be in the ironing pile still. Walking quickly into the kitchen she finds her mum sitting at the table with a piece of paper in front of her. She looks up as Jenn walks in, stands up too. Her eyes are shiny, cheeks flushed.

'Have you seen my waistcoat?' Jenny asks, bending down to rifle through the ironing basket on the floor filled with her mum's floral dresses and her own vest tops – it's been an unusually hot summer. She really needs to find it quickly or she's going to miss the bus.

'I was just wanting to talk to you about something, darling. Just if you have a moment.'

'I don't really have time right now,' Jenny says, trying not to sound irritated. She flips through a few sweaters, down to some pyjamas at the bottom. It's not here. Standing up, she looks around. *It's not in the laundry basket still, is it?* Her mum said she would wash it.

'Jenny, darling, I really think we should talk about this. It's important.'

Opening the door to the utility area, she starts riffling through the basket on the floor. *Ah ha!* Pulling it out she can immediately see it's slightly crumpled; a patch of cola on it still from when a customer at the cinema accidentally lurched into her. It's going to look awful but she can't work without it.

Don't say anything to Mum or you'll upset her.

As she starts to pull the waistcoat on over her blue shirt, she looks back finally.

'Sorry, can we talk after my shift?' She pulls her hair out from the waistcoat. 'It's just . . . I'm going to be really late now. First film starts at five.'

Her mum probably just wants to tell her about an art exhibition she's got a piece into. She's actually been displaying more and more work at small galleries in the city, which has made her mum really happy, she knows, but she never actually sells anything: Jenny's been subbing the gap in their bills for over a year now.

'I'm going to Cornwall,' her mum blurts out suddenly.

Jenny's fingers pause on the buttons. 'Cornwall? Why?'

Her mum is clutching the piece of paper in two hands now. Her green eyes are alight and her red hair seems to shimmer in the hot afternoon light.

'To paint, darling.'

'For a holiday, you mean?' Jenny says slowly. 'I'm not sure we can afford that right now.'

'Well,' her mum says, taking in a breath. 'I was thinking maybe a bit longer than that.'

'I'm sorry,' Jenny says, feeling really confused now. 'What do you mean? Why would you go to Cornwall?'

Her mum swallows, like she's trying to compose herself.

'You see, there are these wonderful studio collectives—'

Jenny recoils. 'Are you meaning to live?' Her heart's beating fast. 'But . . . but where would you stay?' she says. 'How would you earn any money?'

'Well, that's the thing.' Her mum's face lights up again. 'I was just speaking to my friend, Maggie, from art college, and she was saying she has this caravan in their garden I can stay in initially. Just while I get on my feet. Apparently, there's a real market for landscapes and seascapes down there, even from visitors.'

'What's wrong with painting up here?'

Jenny can hear her tone is level but she feels panicked now. Annoyed. All this time, she's been trying to stay here in Edinburgh for her mum, to help her, and it's all for nothing. She could have gone anywhere. She could have gone abroad. Started a new life too.

'Nothing,' her mum says, eyebrows lifting. 'It's just, now seems like the right time to do this, I think. You're eighteen, you're out of school. I wouldn't have considered this before now.'

'OK, so I just stay here and look after the flat while you get to go somewhere new and exciting then?'

Jenny knows she sounds harsh, but she can't contain herself. How can her mum just spring this on her now?

Her mum looks nervous. 'That's the other thing, darling.'

Oh god, there's more.

'There's a small rent on these studio spaces,' her mum continues. 'It's not a lot, but it's something. And the lease on this place is coming to a close at the end of August anyway . . . '

Jenny feels stunned, doesn't know what to say. Frantically, she tries to process what's happening, even as she knows the bus is approaching outside. She hears the roar of the engine, the screech of the brakes.

'But, where will I live?'

'Well, I thought you could go to that Halls of Residence place, that might be fun?'

'Mum, what are you talking about?' Jenny says. 'You have to apply ages in advance? Everything will be gone by now.'

'Oh, oh dear,' her mum says, 'I didn't think of any of that.'

She can feel tears stinging. Why is no one ever there for her?

Because no one cares.

She shuts her eyes tightly for a moment.

'Jenny, darling, are you OK?'

She feels a hand on her arm, opens her eyes again. 'I'm sorry,' her mum says softly, 'I didn't think this through clearly.'

'No, you didn't. I'm leaving now.'

And apparently so is she.

*   *   *

The kernel scent fills the cool foyer of the cinema; a welcome relief after the relentless sun. Standing by the entrance to the main screens, Jenny feels beads of sweat collecting along her clavicle. She'd had to walk up Morningside Road in the end to get here, the waistcoat adding a layer of extra heat she didn't need today. She knew she'd probably still make it just in time – she's a fast walker after all – but out of nowhere she'd found herself jogging, and then the jog turned into a bound and the bound turned into a run and suddenly all that energy and panic was flooding out of her. She didn't care what she looked like because in that second, in that second it was all gone.

But now, that panic is starting to seep back into her again.

What is she going to do?

The first cinema-goers of the night approach the ticket stall, a couple around her age, sun kissed and sipping cool drinks from Coca Cola cups. She gives them as wide a smile as she can manage, before ripping their tickets and ushering them to follow her. As they walk down the red-carpeted corridor, shiny black-and-white images of Hollywood stars look down on them from the walls, and she wonders if they really felt that happy – or were they all hiding something behind that gloss?

She just can't believe this has happened, her mum just leaving her like this. She has this overwhelming feeling like she's done something wrong, like this is her fault.

He left, then she left. The common factor both times is her.

And then the other questions start up. Should she contact the uni and check if any accommodation is still available? Perhaps there's something on a student forum? Shit, she could have had something lined up ages ago.

Katy's voice rings in her ears. *You need to live your own life, Jenny.*

But it's all very well for her now, isn't it? Katy asks for something and her parents just give it to her – no question. She's not even vaguely thinking of a career, or an income, or responsibilities yet, because she doesn't have to.

And the honest truth is, she'd never have gone to Paris with Katy. Because more than anything, she needs to learn how to earn more money now – proper money – so she'll never feel worried about where she's living, or how she's paying for things, ever again.

Katy just doesn't get it.

After depositing the couple to their designated seats in the cinema, she heads back along the corridor, ready to pick up the next group. While she walks, she keeps desperately trying to smooth out the corners of her life again.

Back at the ticket point, she's surprised to find a familiar face is waiting there, even blonder if it's possible, and freckled from the sun. He's wearing beige shorts, a whiter-than-white polo shirt and she can't help but smile.

'Duncan,' she says and pauses, confused. *Is he here to see her?*

As though in answer, he smiles and raises a ticket. 'Too much sun today.'

'Right,' she says and nods, immediately feeling stupid. He'd come to the cinema to see a film. *Don't flatter yourself, Jenny.*

'Well, just follow me,' she says, trying to sound vaguely professional, but she can hear the waver in her own voice, the shock from earlier still lingering in each beat.

As they walk down the corridor together, she feels unexpectedly awkward. She hasn't seen him since school finished a few weeks ago. There wasn't any call to really, and they both knew they'd see each other at the start of the university school semester. But she had missed talking to him, she realises now. He's such a nice guy. From the corner of her eye, she notices his forearms have grown more muscular than before; tanned skin covered in golden hair.

'So, how's your summer going so far?' he asks.

'Oh, fine,' she lies. 'Just working away, you know.'

'Yeah,' he replies. 'Me too. Kind of wish I'd gone travelling or something like that now though.'

The conversation with her mum floods her head again, piercing any enjoyment she might have had in seeing Duncan here today.

'You alright?' he says, as they reach the door of the cinema. His blue eyes are open and concerned looking.

'Sorry? Yeah, yeah, I'm good. Just—'

She shouldn't tell him her problems, shouldn't bother anyone.

'What is it?'

But it's all too much, holding this by herself. She feels so alone. Words start rising in her throat, and it all comes spilling out: about how her mum has only just today decided to move to the southernmost tip of the country away from her; about how the lease on the flat is about to come up and she has

172

nowhere to stay for when uni starts, doesn't know where she's going to live; how this summer is actually looking pretty shitty now as she'll have to save up for accommodation on top of everything else.

When she stops, she realises Duncan's not said a word throughout. *Why did she just tell him everything?*

'Anyway, you don't want to hear any of that,' she says quickly. 'I'll take you in to the film.'

'Jenny,' he stops her. 'Don't be daft. Sounds like you've had a shitty time of it, I'm sorry.'

She tries to smile. 'It's fine, honestly, I'm fine.'

He opens his mouth, pauses before saying, 'Look, I have an idea, but there's no pressure at all if you don't want to.'

She waits for him to speak, curious.

'My parents bought this flat recently, as an investment type of thing for them but I'll live in it while I'm at uni and cover the mortgage. And there's two rooms, which means you'd be welcome to take the other one, if you'd like, I mean. I hadn't gotten around to advertising it yet, so you'd really be doing me a favour by taking it.'

The panic she'd been feeling subsides a little. She can see a light behind the clouds. But would that be weird? Her sharing with Duncan? Plus, she doesn't want him to just do this out of pity, that would be so awkward. But then, Duncan is definitely a friend, they get on well, and if she just sorts this all out now, she can relax. Stop worrying for the rest of the summer. Suddenly, the answer is obvious.

'That would be really good, actually,' she says eventually. 'If that's really OK?'

Duncan's face breaks into a smile, and she knows he actually means it. This isn't any sort of pity offer.

'That's ace, Jenny. You'd be really solving that problem for me.'

'But I'd pay half of everything,' she says, holding a finger up now. 'Down to the penny.'

'Of course,' he says and nods.

'Well,' she says, and opens the door to the cinema. 'I'll walk you into your seat, flat mate.'

'Alright, flat mate.'

They grin at each other, and the two of them disappear into the darkness inside, just as the music starts up.

SEVENTEEN

2018

JENN

'Just here,' she says, and the taxi driver pulls over to the side of Hanover Street. Music is playing quietly from the radio – from some film she saw once. Through the foggy glass she looks for Robbie on the lamp-lit pavement but he's not there yet. *Is he still in the bar?* She starts calling him again, listens to the ringtone for a while before hanging up. Just as she's about to text him, he appears at the window. He opens the door and jumps in.

'Here, I'm here,' he says, sounding harried, and sits back in his seat. He smells like booze and fags, and she can tell he's a little bit drunk already.

Jenn leans forward to the driver. 'On to Fettes Row, please.'

The taxi lurches forward and Robbie rubs his hands together from the November cold.

'How was it?' she asks, even though she's not sure she wants the answer. She thinks of the steaks she bought for them earlier today, still sitting in the fridge. She thought it might be nice to have dinner with him before the engagement party. Maybe the Champagne they'd been saving for a special occasion – it had been idling in the wine rack for over six months after all, ever since Hilary gave it to her for passing the MRCEM Intermediate. (She feels vaguely guilty for not telling Robbie about that yet, but then she still can't quite believe that he's not even asked if she ever did a resit.) They hadn't planned a dinner before or anything, but she knew his shift was finishing at six. Then, at the last minute, he'd texted to say some of the restaurant folk wanted to buy him birthday drinks in advance of tomorrow – he couldn't say no, apparently.

'Good,' he says, 'shame to cut it short.'

She looks across at him, thrown. 'You do realise Hilary and Marty deliberately had their engagement party tonight so it didn't clash with your birthday tomorrow?'

'Eh, yes, Marty is my best friend too,' he says. 'I just meant it's a shame I couldn't do both, that's all.'

'OK,' Jenn says, unconvinced. He always seems to prefer being out with the restaurant folk of late. And they're all single basically, most of them younger, other than Matt. They go out a lot, and it's been getting worse recently. Last Monday he came in at dawn, following some after party. He stunk of weed and booze. *Should she be worried?*

'Hey,' he says, the trace of a slur already in his voice, 'I'm sorry I didn't make dinner earlier, it's just everyone was going. They expected me to be there, last birthday of my twenties and all that. Twenty-nine . . . fuck me. I'll cook for us tomorrow night though, OK? After we get back from lunch at my parents'.'

She can't help but smile at him and nods. He just doesn't like missing out on the fun. Reaching across for his hand she feels calmer. They're OK.

Everything's OK.

Taking another sip of her Prosecco, she half listens as Hilary's bridesmaids – also doctors from the hospital of course – launch into more wedding chatter, a burble of noise around them.

'But what colour scheme do you think she'll go for?' Deepa is saying, her voice thick with excitement.

'Pink, it has to be pink,' Pippa answers. 'That's Hilary's favourite.'

Where's Robbie got to? She looks around the room filled with their friends talking and laughing. Marty and Hilary's flat is so amazing, she still can't get over it. They bought it together a couple of months back – ground floor Georgian flat in the New Town – after just ten months together.

She's not sure her and Robbie have ever discussed owning anything jointly. She doesn't even know where he is right now. He disappeared into the kitchen as soon as they got here.

Suddenly she catches a lyric, a note, one of Robbie's favourites – 'There Is a Light That Never Goes Out' – and she can't help smiling. It reminds her of him every time she hears it. Anything by The Smiths does, or Joy Division.

'Jenn,' she hears a voice saying and Hilary moves through people towards her, a tipsy smile on her face. One pink strap of her dress is falling off her shoulder and Jenn quickly lifts it back up for her.

Hilary hugs her tightly, before taking her manicured hands in her own. 'Dance with me,' she says and starts moving to the music. Her happiness is palpable. Ever since she met Marty, she's had literal stars in her eyes. And he's been the same: Jenn can see that in the way he looks at her. Robbie used to look at her like that too, like he couldn't believe his luck.

As they both start swaying to the music, people look over and smile. The happy bride-to-be dancing with her best friend – her maid of honour.

And suddenly Jenn has a flash of Katy, her sparkly eyes and the lavender scent of her hair. The laughter between them. *Where is she now?*

A loud crashing noise from somewhere near the door. Hilary and Jenn immediately stop dancing, look over to see Robbie standing at the side of the room, hands out in front of him like he's about to play the piano. As people move out the way, Jenn sees broken glass all over the place. She moves quickly across to him.

Not tonight.

Bending down, she starts picking up the largest shards at his feet. People are looking over.

'Sorry,' he slurs, 'it slipped.'

She can't help shaking her head and looks up at him, a palm full of glass held up like a jagged offering. 'What's going on with you?'

He sways a little.

'Well, sorr-Y for having a good time!'

Marty appears with a dustpan and brush. 'Alright, Robbo,' he says, but there's a crease on his brow. 'Must have been my whisky cocktails,' he says to Jenn, as though explaining away Robbie's behaviour; like she hasn't seen this before, like she hasn't seen him wasted. Except she didn't really mind in the first few years when he was in good spirits, a bit too drunk, a bit idiotic, but happy nonetheless.

This is different. This drinking is coming from an entirely different place.

Standing up finally, she lets the spears of glass fall into the dustpan Marty proffers out to her. 'Sorry about this, I think we'll head off now . . . if that's alright.'

'No, don't leave yet,' Hilary cries appearing alongside them, it's not even eleven yet!'

'I know,' Jenn smiles broadly, 'but we've both just been so shattered with work recently. It's been a fantastic night though.'

Hilary and Marty glance at each other briefly, imparting some secret message. Robbie has propped himself up by the radiator and Jenn knows he's not saying anything because he's lost control of his speech.

They have the goodbye hugs, promises to catch up for dinner soon, the *we-just-can't-wait-for-the-big-day* exclamations, before

Jenn quietly guides Robbie by the crook of his arm through the flat, past a few people in the spacious hall who watch them go with raised eyebrows and whispers. She feels embarrassed, angry that the night has ended like this.

But she's worried about him too.

As they open the door and step out into the carpeted landing, she feels a pinch in her palm. A sting. Holding it up to the harsh light above, she sees a small piece of glass wedged there, in the pale creases of skin. It's worked its way in tightly, deep down, where the flesh is raw, where it hurts the most.

The next day

ROBBIE

I'm in my parents' dining room. Everyone's here, the whole crew, sitting around the table. It's the fancy room. No TV. We only use it for stuff like Christmas and birthdays. But it's not Christmas today. No tinsel along the paintings, no red candle centrepiece. And it's daytime clearly. Lunch? A decanter of red wine on the table, the remnants of roast beef, gravy and Yorkshire puddings – my favourite meal. Oh shit, it's my birthday. The day after the engagement party.

The engagement party. Oh god. I had no idea. Why didn't Jenn tell me what I'd been like? All I remember is waking up the next day, with this massive blank.

Are you OK?

That's what she said, not 'you're a dick head,' or 'you behaved like a total tool.' No, she was asking how I was. She made me a coffee. So I didn't think I'd done anything that bad, not really. I thought it was just another Robbie-being-too-drunk night, where Jenn rolls me home and no one really cares because it's all quite funny. It's all banter. I didn't remember any of *that*.

'Sticky toffee, Max?' Mum says, standing above him with a dish.

Max glances briefly up from his work phone. 'Oh, no thanks, Jill. Can't destroy all this,' he smiles, placing his hand on his middle.

Dick.

Across the table, Fi's mouth is set in a tight line.

'Mumma, juice!' says Struan from beside her and she quickly passes him his cup. Still only three, he's becoming so like his dad it's uncanny, in looks at least – thick black hair, coal eyes, squarish jawline. They're both even wearing the same outfit: bottle-green sweaters with checked shirts beneath.

Mum moves along to Jenn hopefully. 'Any for you, honey?'

'Sure, thanks,' she smiles up at her.

Good old Jenn. She doesn't even like dessert.

Dad isn't speaking, weirdly. He just pours more cream onto his plate and eats. Mum dollops some pudding onto her own plate, before going back around to top up everyone's glasses. She's dressed up, like she does for all our birthdays. But there's a stilted air in the room. I can literally hear the scrape of cutlery against plates, someone sniffing. *What the hell is wrong with everyone?*

'I might just go check on him?' Kirsty says and looks to the door. 'He's been gone ages.'

Who?

'I'll go,' Jenn says quickly, standing up.

'Don't you dare,' Fi puts her hand on her arm. 'It's his fault he's like this.'

Who are they talking about?

Not me, surely?

'Must have been a bloody good party,' Max grins, and takes a slug of wine. Fi looks back at him coolly. Oh man, I forgot how hungover I still was at the lunch; everything came back up after the main.

But I thought no one noticed.

'I'm sick of this,' Dad says suddenly, clanking down his spoon in the bowl. 'I thought he'd got past this stage. He needs to just grow up.'

Shit. I didn't realise he was so pissed at me. I remember him being OK; a little overly focused on the test matches on TV, but nothing else.

'Oh honey,' Mum says, as she refill's Max's glass. 'It's his day, let's just leave it this time, please.'

Dad stands before wiping his mouth with his napkin. 'Fine. But I'm going to check the rugby scores.'

After he's gone, Kirsty pushes her chair back from the table. 'I'll just be a sec.' My heart goes out to her. She's so like Mum, always trying to keep the peace. *Go away*, I remember saying when I heard someone outside the bathroom door.

There are three empty chairs around the table now and the atmosphere is even cooler than before. Jenn's still fiddling with her glass of lemonade and there's a small, flesh-coloured plaster on the inside of her palm – the broken glass.

I just didn't realise my drinking would actually have that sort of impact on anyone. It was my birthday after all. Surely I could do what I liked? Wasn't it my prerogative to drink too much?

'Goodness, where's my dessert gone?' Mum says, sitting back down finally. She's looking down at her plate in confusion. Struan beside her has gooey sauce across his face.

Fi laughs quietly from further up the table. 'Sorry, Mum.'

'Sorry, Nana,' Struan says, waving his spoon at her, and everyone starts laughing, a visible crack in the tension. Even Max puts down his phone and shakes his head at his son, amused.

'What's all this about?' a voice says. Robbie has come back into the room holding another beer. He's smiling but he looks horrendous, so pale, and his hair's a state. His eyes are groggy from vomiting up lunch and he's gripping the beer like it's a lifebelt.

Jenn's face drops again, and Mum is looking at her in a worried way.

'Time for tea,' Mum says.

JENN

The lawn is crisp with frost, and Jenn pulls the tartan rug closer around her shoulders. On the wrought-iron table in front of her is a tray of milk and biscuits and the massive red teapot

Jill always uses, despite the chip in the handle. Puffs of steam rise up from it, disappear into the freezing white-grey sky above.

'How's work been?' Jill asks, as she pours the tea into two matching china cups.

'It's good.' Jenn nods, trying to focus on the question. 'I've just got to do my sixth year of specialising and that's me. Well, then it will be consultancy exams next.'

'You never stop, do you?' Jill smiles, taking a sip.

'It's the same for everyone in medicine I guess.'

'But you are special, honey. I hope you know that? I hope Robbie isn't making you feel ... bad about yourself? Because I know he's my son, but if he hurts you, he'll have *me* to deal with.'

Jill is smiling, but there's an edge behind her words – other people have noticed his behaviour too, and for whatever reason, that makes it all worse.

'I just don't know what changed,' Jenn says quietly. 'He was so happy with me when we first met.'

'That's *because* he met you.'

Jenn turns to her. She feels confused.

'You did something to him,' Jill says. 'You brought the best of him out. Because that's the thing, Jenn, I know my boy, and he's got such a big heart. He's got so much potential, and you drew it out of him. I remember him when he was younger,' she says, and smiles like she's lost in a memory. 'He was such a loving child. Always cuddling everyone and making people laugh. That's what he was great at. He lit up any room he was in.'

Jenn can't help smiling at the thought. That's him. Her Robbie. He lights her up too.

Some of the time.

'I will never forget the time he did a stand-up routine at his Aunty Beth's fiftieth,' Mum continues, her eyes dancing. 'He had the whole room roaring, aged ten. Can you believe it?'

She really can. He can make anyone laugh. That's why people just gravitate to him.

'But we spoilt him,' Jill says, and she sits back with her tea. 'I know we did. He was the youngest child and the girls doted on him. Fi used to carry him around in this bucket,' she says and starts to laugh for a moment, before her smile drops. 'He got lost in his teens, everything was too easy for him, everything was done for him. If he needed money, we threw it at him. When he wanted to go travelling, we paid for it, and that's my fault, I know, but I kept hoping he would learn at some point. Like the girls did. I thought perhaps he was starting to do that when he got back from France, but nothing really changed. It was still all about parties and getting drunk. It wasn't until he met you that—'

She looks up at her.

'I really thought—'

Jill stops.

'You thought we'd get married?' Jenn finishes.

Jill's cheeks flush. She looks down briefly, swipes invisible crumbs from her knee. 'Well, yes. I suppose I thought that's where you might be headed. Or something like it.'

Jenn sits in silence for a moment, as she tries to process what's being said. She still has no real interest in getting married, but she does need something more than this, she knows that. She wants Robbie to love her like he did at the start, to make her a priority in his life, like she has made him for the four years they've been together.

But if he isn't doing that that now, will he ever?

Oh god, she just can't face the idea of losing him.

She still loves him so much.

'Will you do me a favour?' Jill says, and Jenn looks up quickly as Jill reaches for her hand on the table.

What is it? Tell me what to do?

'Just . . . give him a little more time to figure it out please,' Jill says finally. 'He'll come around. I know he will. Or he'll lose the best thing in his life.'

Jenn doesn't say anything, just smiles.

Jill's right, she just needs to give him more time, and keep remembering how much she loves him.

Keep remembering what a good guy he really is.

One week later

ROBBIE

People everywhere, outdoor stalls selling soaps and cheese. Still fucking cold. A rich smoky scent drifts towards me – paella. I'm at an outdoor market, that one in Stockbridge.

I can't see Jenn anywhere yet, but I'm just so glad we've left the last place. It was all getting too painful to watch.

I had no idea they'd had that conversation; that my own mother asked my girlfriend to give me time to grow up. She's supposed to be on my side, for god's sake.

My chest tightens.

But is that really how they all saw me? Some spoilt man-child who only cared about himself?

Being hungover on my birthday was one thing, but I'm starting to think maybe I wasn't so great a lot of the time. For them to actually have had that conversation, well – it's not good.

At least it can't get any worse, not in this place at any rate.

I am one hundred percent certain I did nothing wrong at an outdoor market.

Familiar voices behind me. I turn around. Jenn and Hilary are walking towards me, brown coffee cups in hand. They're both wrapped up, noses pink like they've been out walking for a while, which is likely: Jenn and Hilary can spend hours catching up. It used to be mainly about Hilary's break ups, but today she's talking away about the brunch Marty brought her in in bed that morning, coffee from a new place and I can't help smiling to myself: Marty's so good to her.

'There it is,' Hilary cries, cutting into her own thread of chatter.

I look to where she's pointing – a cheese stall.

The two of them walk up and start testing the samples on the counter.

'Any of them?' Jenn says, after the third try.

Hilary peers back at the handwritten names, frowns. 'Don't think so, it was softer than that.'

'Excuse me,' she says to the plump-cheeked man behind the counter and he smiles. 'I'm looking for this cheese my fiancée loves, but I can't for the life of me remember the name. It's soft, but sort of strong too, French name.'

Époisses. That will be the one. We have that on our cheese-board at the restaurant.

Sure enough, two seconds later and the guy whips out a round of it before cutting a segment off for Hilary to try. Her eyes light up as she tastes it. 'Yes,' she grins, 'that's it! I'll take a wedge of it, thanks, large. Oh, and some of that spiced chutney please, yes, that one. Oh, and the oat cakes too, he loves them.'

'Success,' Jenn smiles as the man starts putting it all in a bag. 'What time are his parents coming over later?'

'Oh, probably far too early,' she says, raising an eyebrow. 'They're always far too early, though that's about their only flaw so I can't complain really. Did you see the amount of booze they bought for the engagement party last weekend?'

I think about Marty's parents – Wendy and Bill – and she's absolutely right. They're super kind and generous, always putting everyone else before themselves.

They were like second parents to me.

Hilary pays up and then the two of them start meandering back through the stalls, as the afternoon light begins to fade in the sky.

'You and Robbie doing anything this weekend?' There's a strange note to Hilary's voice.

The engagement party, the glass smashing.

Fuck. Humiliation floods me again. I never even said sorry.

But then I didn't even know I'd done anything to say sorry about.

'Nah, I think just a quiet one,' Jenn says and looks at the paving beneath her feet. 'Think Robbie's working tonight.'

'Well, after everything you've told me, I reckon you need a little evening to yourself. Hot bath, glass of wine, take care of you.'

I forgot how Hilary was the one person Jenn would speak to about things. Only in person though, Hilary once told me. You had to actually see Jenn to break down her barriers. Thinking about it now, I wonder if that had anything to do with her mum and not feeling like she could ever worry her; she got used to holding things back. She was like that about good stuff too actually – she liked to tell you face-to-face, rather than just rush information out over text or a call, and unlike me with my runaway mouth, she only told people she was close to; people who actually cared.

Oh shit – that night she came to meet me at Burn's Bar. The exam result.

Was I being that distant?

Hilary's phone starts ringing – some Ed Sheeran nonsense – and they stop near the exit. 'Hey, you,' Hilary smiles, picking up. 'One hour? Christ, OK. Yes, good plan, thanks.'

Hanging up, Hilary's eyes are wide. 'Sorry, that's Chris saying the in-laws will be here even sooner than we thought.' She shakes her head, but I can sort of tell she's loving it, this in-law stuff. 'He's picking me up on his way back from the gym.'

'No issue,' Jenn says. She looks a little down.

It must have been hard for her, I suppose, seeing how close Hilary and Marty were, while we were struggling.

Because I can admit that now – *we were struggling*.

'God, it's so weird hearing you say in-laws,' Jenn says after a moment. 'It all feels like it's gone so quickly.'

Standing opposite her, Hilary frowns ever so slightly. 'Well, when you know, you just know, right?'

'Sure,' Jenn says, 'it's just . . . making that commitment before you know everything about them. It's big, right?'

I'm not sure what Jenn means exactly, but it's an odd thing to say to an engaged person.

'I don't think that time necessarily has anything to do with it,' Hilary says a little briskly, pulling her handbag up higher on her shoulder. 'I mean, you've been with Robbie for what? Over four years now and you still don't know—'

She stops.

Jenn tilts her head to the side.

Hang on.

'Still don't know what?' Jenn finishes, the smile gone now.

'Bollocks,' Hilary mutters. 'It's nothing, Jenn, I'm sorry. I said I would never say anything.'

Oh fuck.

'No, you have to tell me now,' Jenn says, firmer.

Don't tell her, Hilary.

Images come to me: *a white beach, people dancing. Me and Marty in neon vests. Him grinning at me on a Thai beach.*

Hilary looks up at the sky briefly, back down at Jenn. 'OK, but you can't tell Robbie or Chris I told you. Promise?'

'I promise.' Jenn nods.

As Hilary starts to speak, the rest of the memory comes flooding back; one which I've shoved aside for years – a beer funnel in Marty's mouth, me pouring something strong and unknown down it, egging him on along with a bunch of seedy strangers we'd only met that night.

Hilary tells Jenn the rest of it, that police had found him unconscious and alone later that night. That he was taken to hospital to have his stomach pumped, then put on a ventilator. His parents had flown out the next day, only to be told that if the police hadn't have found him when they did, he would certainly have died.

'And where was Robbie?' Jenn asks eventually, her face impassable.

Hilary just shakes her head, and my stomach flips.

They can probably guess.

I was with some girl I didn't know the name of, in some hostel that wasn't ours. And I had no idea where Marty was.

Hearing it all out loud like this, it just sounds so much worse.

But we were just kids being kids, right?

Right?

'So that's why he went to Chamonix,' Jenn says eventually.

Hilary nods. 'Yes. A couple of days after Chris left with his parents for the UK.'

'And how was Marty, afterwards I mean?'

Hilary shrugs, and with a sickening feeling, I realise that I actually don't know the answer. Marty went home for the summer, then started at Bristol uni in the autumn. I worked the tourist season in Cham and stayed on after. We didn't really speak during that period, which I put down to just being in different places.

Or maybe that's what I told myself.

'He wasn't great, apparently,' Hilary says eventually. 'I don't really know the ins and outs – he didn't go into it – but I do know he spent a lot of time not seeing anyone that summer. Then he just threw himself into course work at uni after that. I reckon that was his way of dealing with it all.'

Jenn bites her lip, and I just wish I knew what she was thinking.

Ed Sheeran's voice cuts through the air again and Hilary answers her phone a little too quickly. 'Hey, you,' she says, mustering a smile. After a second she turns to the road, and Marty's Audi hatchback parks up close by. 'Yes, I see you. Just one minute.'

Turning back to Jenn, her eyes are wide, regretful. 'I'm so sorry I have to run off like this after telling you all that . . . we'd offer you a lift but it's just—'

'No, don't worry, I fancy the walk anyway,' Jenn says, waving vaguely at Hilary. But she still looks thrown, and no fucking wonder. She's just heard that the guy she lives with – has committed to – once left his best friend to die.

'Well, I'll call you later, OK?' Hilary says, hugging her tightly.

'OK,' Jenn says, smiling her smile again.

As Hilary runs out of the gate, sandy hair flying behind her, I stay back with Jenn.

Confusion fills me. I just don't get what I'm supposed to be seeing here. What does my secret have to do with hers?

I have to tell you something.

Jenn's words again, like a siren.

EIGHTEEN

2009

JENNY

She hears the sound of their feet pound along the pavements, as morning light blinks from between sleepy Old Town buildings. The castle slumbers up on its perch to the left of them, and The Cowgate is quiet, the cobbles resting after another night of footfall from the bars. Next to her, Duncan's strides are strong. His breath still even after a 5k that morning. As they reach the sloping street taking them back up onto the Bridges, Jenn feels a final burst of energy flowing through her and she pumps her legs up the hill as fast as she can go, all the way to the top.

Duncan arrives beside her a moment later, and they both take a moment to catch their breath outside Greyfriars Bobby. The sky is a fresh rising blue; their legs pink from the October chill.

'You were really going for it,' Duncan says, and leans his hands onto his knees.

Jenny smiles. She usually runs by herself before classes start, leaving Duncan snoring away in their bed, one hand still resting on the quickly fading imprint of her. But today he seemed weirdly keen to come too. She didn't mind really; they keep the same pace.

He stands up and puts his hands behind his head. 'So, I was just wondering about going out for food this evening? Pizza or something.'

'Not tonight I'm afraid,' she says. 'I'm actually meeting Katy at some club night. Remember she's back in Edinburgh for a few days?' Stretching her legs off, she feels surprised. They don't usually 'go out' for food, given their student budgets and the fact that Jenn still works most evenings at the cinema.

Duncan looks tense.

'Everything OK?' she asks.

'I was going to give this to you back at the flat,' he answers, reaching into his pocket. His blue eyes look earnest suddenly.

'What?'

He hands her a small white envelope, bent out of shape from his pocket.

'What's this?' she smiles. Turning it over, she opens it and tugs out the card. In loopy writing it says, *Happy First Anniversary*, with a bright pink love heart underneath. She has to stop herself from cringing: it's so cheesy, but when she looks up at his open face, his sincere expression, she feels bad and smiles. She had no idea this was today.

She can't really recall the exact moment they got together; it didn't stick in her mind somehow. She just remembers growing closer to him in those first couple of months living together, that easy rhythm which picked up between them. They studied together, went to classes together, came home together. And then one night it just happened: one glass of punch too many at a Hawaiian party in the union and she'd knocked on his door when she got home. Because she knew how he felt. He was just waiting for her to feel it too.

'There's some stuff on the inside too,' he smiles, and she opens the card.

Dear Jenn, thanks for the best year. All my love, Duncan.
She looks up at him.

'I love you, Jenn,' he says quickly, and she feels her heart jolt.
He searches her eyes, as the brisk winds sweep over them.

It's the first time he's said it, as though again, he's been waiting for her. And it feels nice, those words, the feeling she gets when she's with him like everything is OK. But is it supposed to feel like this when you fall in love? Nice, sweet. He's a great guy – the perfect guy really – but she just thought she might feel something else. Something more. She's probably just being overly romantic; silly. She's seen first-hand from her childhood how great romances can end.

Reaching for his hand, she says, 'I love you too.'

Later that night

ROBBIE
Reverberation in my stomach. Electro beats. It's hot, dark. Strobe lights flash, smoke billows, people shout. The sound surges up

in my ears. Bass kicks in. The music goes crazy. The people go crazy. *Fucking hell.* I'm thrown about between bodies. There's a stage ahead of me with a DJ. I'm in a big club – that one on Victoria Street. I've been here before.

But where is she? I need to find her. How am I going to track her down in here? At least Duncan won't be around. An ache in my chest, those words she said to him. *I love you too.* I know she had a life before me, but it's just hard to hear her saying that to another guy.

The light strobes across a face I recognise. Katy. She looks different, older. Her eyes are heavily made up, but in an arty kind of way and there's glitter across her cheeks, on her shoulders. She's dancing away to the music. And then she appears, Jenn, in a black vest top. Her hair is still long but she looks definitively older too: an adult, a not dissimilar version to the one I fell in love with. My heart catches.

The music starts to morph into a different track and Katy slows down, looks across at Jenn. *Drink?* Jenn nods.

Edging their way through the people towards the bar, the noise dims ever so slightly, but I know I'll be lucky if I hear anything much. *Why are we here?* The two of them lean against the bar and Jenn puts her bag on it. She's still got that one actually – a battered brown satchel she won't part ways with.

'Nice,' Katy says, nodding at it. 'Very retro feel.'

Jenn looks at it, smiles softly. 'Yeah, it was my dad's. Mum found it when we moved out and I sort of converted it into a handbag.'

She pulls out her wallet. 'I'll get these drinks.'

'You sure?' Katy drapes an arm around Jenn's shoulders. 'You're a star, mon amie. I'm sorry I've not bought many tonight. Just Paris is proving bloody expensive. Work experience in art galleries does not pay well, let me tell you.'

'Don't be silly,' Jenn reassures her. 'I've barely been going out with all the work on at the moment so my bank balance isn't doing too badly. Anyway, I need to get Duncan a drink before he gets here. Makes sense if I get this round.'

'Duncan?' Katy says, the glitter on her face seeming to dull slightly.

I know the feeling.

'Yeah, I'm sorry, it's just I forgot it was our anniversary today. It's not a problem, is it?'

'No,' Katy says bluntly, 'it's just I thought it was just us guys tonight, you know, having a girls' thing. I barely see you as it is . . . You've still not come out to Paris.'

'I'm sorry about that, it's just I was working all summer and I didn't think it would be a big deal tonight—'

'It's not a big deal, it's just . . . '

'It's just what?'

'Well,' Katy turns to Jenn, takes her hand on the bar. Her eyes are woozy and there's a sway in her step.

'I just didn't think you'd actually *still* be with Duncan,' Katy half slurs. 'I mean, you moved in with him for uni and then you got together like a week later. You missed all the fun stuff.'

'Katy I—'

'We're already in second year and you've never actually experienced anything.'

'What else should I be experiencing?' Jenn asks, her voice harder now. Her eyes are focused and she looks pretty sober. 'I'm here to become a doctor,' she says. 'That's the point.'

Katy doesn't miss a beat.

'Sure, but I'm talking about the living part, Jenny. Random friends, random men, travelling, having fun, you know, all that stuff?'

'I'm out with you tonight, aren't I?' she says. 'Some of us just don't have the luxury of doing whatever we like.'

'But why not?' Katy says, her eyes widening. She grips Jenn's sides like she wants to shake her. 'Why not? There's so much more out there.' She brandishes one hand about. 'Don't you think it's possible that you got with Duncan because he felt safe? I get you maybe needed that after everything that happened with your family, but at some point, you've got to stop letting the past influence everything. Stop being so bloody sensible all the time.'

'Oh, like *you* would understand?'

Katy frowns.

'Some of us actually have responsibilities, Katy,' Jenn continues, 'not everyone's privileged like you are. While you waltz around Paris on your parents' money, I actually have to earn a living.'

What the hell is she saying? She's being so mean. The lights flicker across their faces and I can tell an invisible line has been crossed between them. I've never seen Jenn like this before.

Is this to do with her mum?

198

'You know what?' Katy says, her voice sharp despite the alcohol. 'Why don't you just hang out with Duncan tonight if that's how you feel?'

'OK,' Jenn says, her voice wavering. She swallows. 'I'll leave now, shall I?'

'Please do, and leave me to waltz around Paris.'

For one lingering moment, Jenn looks like she might say something. But then she doesn't, and Katy shrugs, glitter falling off her shoulders and onto the floor below. She turns back into the surge of people again before melting away into the darkness.

Beside me, Jenn heaves in a breath of air. A figure appears at her shoulder and she turns. Duncan.

Ever-predictable goddamn Duncan.

'I know you just got here,' Jenn says, a wobble in her voice, 'but can we go home, please?'

He doesn't try to change her mind or order a drink. He just looks worried and nods. 'Alright,' he says. 'Alright.'

As the two of them disappear together through the mash of people, it occurs to me that Duncan's always been there for her when she needs him most. He's a good guy through and through and the comparison isn't lost on me. *Is her subconscious showing the two of us side by side?*

But what does all this have to do with her secret?

What the fuck am I supposed to be seeing here?

My heart beats faster.

Club lights blind me, flash in my eyes.

* * *

ROBBIE

Back in the car.

Holy shit.

My heart's pounding.

Come on, Robbie. Do something, anything.

But I still can't move my hands. Still can't move my feet.

Those dust particles are still floating in the air and Jenn's just looking straight ahead beside me, the light shining brighter now.

The truck has moved closer.

We're running out of time.

I try to move again, feel myself straining, battling against my own body. But my limbs won't let me. I'm trapped by my own body. *Fuck, I need to do something!* I want to shout, turn to her, speak to her, but nothing is working. It's like there's an upturned hourglass going, and she's showing me I'm running out of time.

I think of Duncan, that calm way he has about him.

I have to stop panicking.

I have to actually think about what Jenn's showing me, what I'm seeing and why: her dad left and there's a mystery around that. Duncan was great and I was a shit.

But how does it all tie together? How does me being a shit connect with her secret?

Oh god.

Another thought, another memory – of my own this time.

My stomach curdles, drops.

As the truck lights shine in my eyes, I have a horrible feeling I'm getting closer to something.

And that something might have to do with me.

NINETEEN

2019

JENN

Her body is aching as she walks up the stone steps of the tenement. It's been a long day at the hospital: one too many Valentine's overdoses. Her neck is stiff, shoulders tense, and the soles of her feet are worn out. She permanently feels too stretched in her job, like a reel of bandage wound tight around a joint. Just as soon as she is trying to deal with one patient, she's called to another one. She sifts through bodily information like a croupier; no time to dwell or think about the actual person. Simply take their history, examine, check records, move on.

It's not what she thought it would be.

Letting herself into the flat, she dreams of a bubble bath and a mug of hot tea. She drops her backpack on the ground with a dull thud, before flipping the light on. In the hall mirror, her reflection looks back sullenly. There are bags under her eyes, and she knows it's not just the job. Ever since Robbie's birthday, she's been trying to spend more time with him and stop worrying so much. Just be present. But it's hard. It all feels so one sided, like she's the only one trying.

Christmas and New Year went in a blur of shifts (her side) and a blur of hangovers (his side). She'd had a nice enough Christmas Day, at least, at his parents', but she was all too aware that she spent most of it hanging out with Fi, who was evidently avoiding Max. Robbie spent most of the day merrily moving between the snug and the kitchen for beers. *Hey,* Jurassic Park *is on again. Epic!*

At least there's one thing to look forward to. Smiling now, she looks along the sideboard for the little packet. But she can't see it. Frowning, she riffles through the pile of mail, in case it got caught up there: they don't do Valentine's really – both of them think it's a ridiculous tradition, which means absolutely nothing – but Robbie always gets her a packet of jellybeans anyway.

But she can't find it. She double checks the side table, beneath it, behind it. Nothing. With a sinking heart, she realises he's forgotten.

Walking down the hall and into the kitchen, she looks around at their lives together: his headphones tangled with hers on the table; silly photos of that trip to Skye from three years back on the fridge; the magnetic beer mat she bought for him with an R on it; the purple statement wall he painted for her while she was at work one day as a surprise. She tries to remember the last time he sent her one of his silly *I like you more than –* messages, but can't.

How did they get here? Where did the warm, thoughtful Robbie she first met go? Does she expect too much from him? Or is she simply one of those stupid girls, who hangs around too long in a relationship, hoping it will get better somehow?

I just can't imagine not loving him.

Flipping on the kettle, she sees a couple of unwashed mugs on the sideboard, some laundry spilling out of a basket. On the pulley up high, Robbie's cycling gear is thrown over the wooden slats to dry, the arms of his top drooping down as though weary. She imagines him up in the hills earlier today, pedalling off somewhere alone. They had sex last night finally, after a fortnight of being passing ships, and although he was physically close to her, she couldn't feel the love like before. He seemed more distant than ever.

Taking Robbie's koala mug off the cup branch, she drops a decaf teabag in and pours hot water over the top. The tannins stain the water and brown tendrils curl out until she can't see the bottom. She pours some milk in at the fridge, before pressing the bag against the side of the mug and dumping it in the bin.

'You're doing it wrong.'

She stops, looks up at the door. Her heart is thumping. *Who was that?*

'Robbie?' she calls out, even though she knows he's not here. He's at the restaurant. All the same, she heads out into the hall, looks at the darkened bedroom and living-room doors. They gape back and her breathing quickens.

Heading into the bathroom, she turns the light on and sighs. She's exhausted, that's all. The mind can play tricks when you're tired, skitter around and make things feel real when they're not.

Just the faraways again.

Moving across worn white floorboards to the bath, she twists the hot tap. With a roar from behind the neck, water plummets onto the hard ceramic curve below and starts rushing down the drain. She reaches quickly for the rubbery plug, stuffs it down as scalding water splashes onto her hand.

Sitting on the side of the bath, she lets her eyes drift back along the hallway towards the table. There was a white letter in that pile of mail, in between the plastic-wrapped magazines and brown circulars, she recalls now; sort of formal looking. But they aren't expecting a wedding invite or anything right now, are they?

Standing up, she finds herself listening out again for that voice. She shakes her head. Robbie's not here. *Stop scaring yourself, Jenn.* Walking back along to the table, she flicks through the post until she finds it. Her name has been typed and the post mark is official looking – *PR Winston Solicitors, England.* She feels confused. Why would a solicitor from England be in touch?

'Open it.'

The letter drops from her hands, heart thumps against her chest.

That was definitely Robbie.

That was definitely his voice.

204

'Robbie,' she says, annoyed now. He must be playing some stupid prank on her. Well, it's not funny anymore. It's freaking her out. Going into the bedroom now, she smacks the light on, fully expecting him to jump out at her. But then it dawns on her: that would be something he would have done before, when everything was alright between them. Not now. He wouldn't do something like this now.

He saves all his fun up for elsewhere.

Closing her eyes tight for a moment, she takes a deep breath in. *It's not real, you're just tired*, she whispers to herself.

She turns and walks back out into the corridor, ducks down to lift the letter from where she just dropped it. She hears the rushing of water like a waterfall in the jungle and steam drifts down the corridor towards her. Her fingers jam into the welded paper, and she tears open the sticky bind.

One hour later

ROBBIE

A clattering of plates. Stainless steel. The scent of chicken. I'm at the restaurant again. *Shit!* What was in that envelope? She was just about to open it, I was just about to read it. And there was something about that moment, something about that letter, which seemed important. I can't think why else I was shown that memory.

But what could it be? Who could it be from? *What if it's the secret?*

I need to find her. I need to find the letter.

But what memory is this? The air is heavy with pan-fried chicken and rosemary, though everything's cleaned up. No one's here. It must be the end of the night.

Moving over to the main restaurant door, I peer through the submarine window. Burgundy walls and tweed material flood my vision. So, this is after the refurb. This could still be the same night.

It's not *that* night is it?

My stomach twists, remembering what I realised in the car.

But Jenn wasn't at the restaurant that night?

Goddamnit, why the hell would she have been there?

A clicking noise. The door opens. Turning around I see her standing there, at the back door. She looks distraught. So very not herself. Something has happened. And then I see it in her pocket – the letter.

It's got to be the secret.

I can feel it.

I just need to get hold of it somehow and then we can wake up. I can stop this.

With visibly shaking hands, she takes a glass from a shelf and pours a water. *What the hell does that letter say?* She has her back to me. Now's my chance. I reach out to her pocket, careful not to disturb her. But she turns suddenly from the sink, looks straight at me, right into my eyes.

My heart stops. *Can she see me?*

Taking a sip of water, she starts pacing up and down the kitchen, getting paler by the second. 'Oh god,' she mutters to herself and covers her face with her hands. 'Oh god.' She can't seem to stand still.

Then I remember.

She texted me that night, while I was at the restaurant, saying she needed to speak to me.

And I ignored it. I was busy, harassed. I assumed it could wait.

But now she's here, trying to talk to him still.

Turning to the restaurant door, Jenn walks across, peers through the glass circle. She looks so panicked.

I just need to get the letter.

If I do, she'll wake.

And if she wakes, we'll live.

I creep up behind her. Shit, she's stuffed it further into her pocket. I'll have to stick my hand right in, to hell with scaring her.

An eerily familiar voice makes me stop. Through the glass circle I can see my other self talking to an elderly couple.

Now he's shaking their hands at the door. He's opening it for them. They head out into the dark night, leaving Robbie alone.

He starts walking towards the door.

Someone else appears from the side.

JENN

It's her.

Liv.

Shit, I just need to speak to Robbie alone.

She's about to push through the door, speak to him, when something makes her stop. A movement. Liv reaches up to Robbie.

She kisses him hard.

Oh god. Jenn stumbles back from the door, breath ragged. She feels faint, holds onto the silver island to steady herself.

I'm going to be sick.

Suddenly everything feels upside down and back to front. Everything feels wrong. That can't have just happened.

But it did.

And there's no time now. They can't see her here – she can't face that humiliation. Not now.

Not after the letter.

She has to get away from here, from him.

As though on autopilot, her legs take her across the kitchen and to the door. Swinging it silently open, she feels something, like a tug on her jacket. Reflexively, she smacks her hand down, looks behind her.

But the kitchen is empty.

Looking back at the kitchen door, she feels sick again thinking about what could be happening behind it. But she doesn't want to know anymore, and after pressing her eyes shut for the briefest of seconds, she disappears out into the alley.

Out into the cold.

Passport, wallet, phone. She ticks off the items mentally at the flat door, heart racing. She's not entirely sure what she's packed in her suitcase; has no idea what she'll need to take, given she has no idea where she'll end up. What she does know is that she can't be here when Robbie gets back, whenever that might be. She can't tell him the truth now, not after what she saw.

She needs to just go.

Leave everything.

But there's one last thing she must do. Lifting the letter from the side table, she takes it through to the living room and crouches down beside the fireplace. There are embers still in the grate and she remembers the first fire they lit together after they started dating – when Robbie got coal all over his face and he kept trying to wipe it on hers, until they tumbled down onto the hearth in a mess of black dust and kisses.

They were perfect once.

Taking a lighter from beside the coal bucket, she holds the letter up and tries to ignite a flame under it.

A shadow.

A movement beside her – something knocks it from her hand. *What was that?* She looks around, uncertain of herself as hot tears start to stream down her face.

Composing herself once more, she tries again and this time it works. She holds the lighter to the letter's edge and watches it blacken first, tinge orange, before charred petals curl over white. The fire moves along the sides, until the words have been eaten, torched. She throws it onto the grating along with the burnt-out embers.

ROBBIE

I'm in a black cab. It's dark outside, lights and houses rushing by, and she's beside me, a backpack resting against her knees – the one she took on our camping trips together. She clutches her satchel to her. She looks pale in a grey zip-up, eyes concentrated ahead of her. But she looks determined too. Where are we going?

The letter. I press my hands to my face. It was right there, within my reach, the secret to save her, and she burnt it. *Fuck*.

The taxi picks up speed and I glance up at a green sign before it vanishes. *Airport*. I have no idea where she's planning to go, and perhaps neither does she, but all I do know is, this time, I'm going with her.

TWENTY

2019

ROBBIE

Mud beneath my trainers. Hot, humid. *Fuck, that's a drop!* I'm
right at the edge of some sort of trail. Beyond it, the ground
falls away to a rocky reddish valley, strange jungle-type trees.
I step back quickly. There are mountains all around, cloudy
skies above. Have I been here before? A clanking noise. Feet
coming. It's Jenn. She's wearing a navy waterproof jacket, shorts
and hiking boots. She's breathing hard, hair soaked, and she's
walking at pace as she passes by. Alone.

My heart is racing, mind spinning still.

Behind us on the mountain, a small trickle of people are
making their way up too. I start walking up behind Jenn so I
don't lose her. Where the fuck are we anyway?

She went to South America first. That's what Hilary told me
after she'd gone.

Yes, there's definitely something familiar about this place,
something knocking at my brain. That hot, rainy smell – almost

tropical. That guy who's just behind Jenn with a badge around his neck. I think he's a guide. We're not in Machu Picchu, are we? I think we are. The Inca Trail. So, I have been here before.

I make sure to keep following just behind her; alert to everything. Her legs work quickly, mud splattered up the backs of them. The rainy season is up until February – of course. The trek's closed then, and the months just after are wet too, the mountain still largely empty. This was the one bit of planning Marty actually left to me when we went away that summer after school.

This could be March perhaps. Just a couple of weeks after Jenn left.

Liv. The restaurant. The kiss. It comes back to me again.

Fuck.

But Jenn got it all wrong; it's not what it looked like.

'What are you doing?' I'd said, stepping back from Liv.

We'd just been talking about how busy the restaurant had been that night, how well it was finally starting to do again. I'd suggested a drink after work to celebrate. I'd absolutely not invited anything else.

'Come on, Robbie,' Liv said, 'don't tell me there's nothing happening between us.'

'Liv,' I said, shaking my head. 'Look, I'm sorry if I gave you the wrong impression, but I'm with Jenn.'

She sighed, looking almost irritated in the dim half-light of the restaurant. 'But you never even see her.'

I frowned. 'I see her all the time.'

'OK, keep telling yourself that.'

She stood there in her black shirt, hair pulled back neatly, lots of makeup on. *For me?* I felt annoyed, flattered. Panicked.

'Just go home, Liv, OK,' I said, rubbing my face. 'I can't deal with this right now. I'll clean up.'

And she just shook her head at me, like she couldn't believe it. 'Fine.'

After she stalked out of the restaurant, I had a think about what to do. Did I need to tell Jenn about this? No, I decided. Jenn didn't need to know. It would only upset her and nothing had happened anyway. Not really.

I didn't go home straight away though. I felt stressed, weird. I could sense Jenn's text still sitting there on my phone unanswered, but the Liv kiss had totally thrown me. So, I did what I was planning to in the first place – went to the bar around the corner and had one pint, three pints, more, until my mind was fuzzy enough to forget about what had happened earlier. I stumbled back home and straight to the spare room, to let Jenn have a decent sleep after her shift.

I remember it being quiet in the flat the next morning, which was odd because I was sure Jenn wasn't working that day. She'd talked about doing some walk together that morning up the Pentlands. The kitchen was empty when I went in, but I kept expecting her to appear with a pile of laundry in her arms or ask me to turn the kettle on for tea or something.

'Jenn,' I called finally into the corridor. Nothing. Wandering into our room, I saw that the bed wasn't made. Odd for her. I went into the living room, feeling slightly more concerned by that point, I think. Or maybe I still hadn't been worried at all – I guess I just like to think I was; had some vague sense of her absence.

It was only then that I found it, the little note on the table with her small, precise handwriting across it. Except it looked different when I picked it up, slightly jagged in places like she'd rushed it.

Dear Robbie – even the way it started made my stomach plummet – *I have to leave Edinburgh for a while. I'm sorry. Jenn.*

No love, no kisses – no fucking explanation. For the tiniest of seconds, the thought of Jenn discovering the kiss with Liv had flashed across my mind, but just as quickly it had gone. We'd been completely alone in the restaurant, and Liv wouldn't be stupid enough to say anything. There was no way Jenn could possibly have found out. In which case, what the hell was going on?

Now, as I watch Jenn walking up this muddy trail in the Andes, I realise she did find out.

In fact, she saw everything.

I feel sick.

But Liv kissed me, not the other way around. It wasn't my fault. I know I hadn't been great before then, I can see that now – that I was stuck in a rut, while Jenn tried to move forward with her life – but surely I deserved more than a note? After all those years together.

I feel so angry. This whole fucking thing could have been avoided if she'd just spoken to me.

Emma Steele

We wouldn't be in this situation.

A scuffing noise behind me, a guide goes past. He looks about the same age, dark hair, beard, red cap. The badge he's wearing has the name Raul on it beside a blurry photo of him. He starts walking alongside Jenn.

'You're number one on the trail for the third day in a row, señorita. Do you ever slow down?'

Jenn looks up, like he's said something surprising.

'I suppose not,' she half smiles.

'Not interested in the chat still?'

Further back on the mountain, a younger-looking trio are making their way up at a slower pace. They're laughing away together, hoods up tight over their heads so they all sort of look the same from afar. Suddenly they stop and cluster together with a phone outstretched, making peace signs and sticking their tongues out.

'Well, you can take a rest soon,' Raul says to Jenn eventually. 'The last campsite's not far now.' He pauses. 'And maybe tonight, stay up with us after dinner?'

'Maybe,' Jenn says, and gives a small smile again. But there's still sadness there, and suddenly I think about everything I've just seen, everything I got so very wrong on the run up to that kiss. I worked a lot of shifts with Liv, come to think of it. She might have switched them sometimes with Craig or Jo, but ultimately, I made the rotas up those days. I dictated who worked with who. I was the one suggesting we go out for drinks after. Of course I'd noticed Liv was attractive when I was with Jenn.

Had I really gone to the spare room that night after Liv kissed me to let Jenn sleep – or had I just felt guilty?

Oh god.

It hits me.

I encouraged the whole bloody thing.

'OK,' Raul says and nods. '*Vamos, señorita.*'

He drops behind her, starts traipsing back down to the rest of the group. I stay close to her, my heart catching painfully in my chest.

Because the secret to save us is gone.

And I think it might be all my fault.

JENN

She feels cold now as they huddle around the campfire on little orange deckchairs. Night three of the trek, and she still can't get over the enormity of where they are, up high in this dark world of cloud and rock. The others are sitting around drinking rum and laughing about their travelling stories: to the salt flats and Lake Titicaca, Potosi silver mines and jungle excursions. All the major hotspots. They're a bit tipsy by now she knows, despite having a brutally early start ahead on their last day. She's holding a cup of hot rum too, but it's more to warm herself than to drink really. She hasn't particularly felt like it since she left Edinburgh. But Raul was right, she should at least stay up with folk one night, instead of going straight to bed. She could use the distraction after all.

Staring into the hot flicker of a flame, she thinks about how, if someone had told her she'd be in the Andes right now, she'd have told them they were mad: she would never just up and leave her job and her life with Robbie. But then she saw him kissing Liv and it was like her entire world had come tumbling down around her. She couldn't breathe.

For a moment, she thinks back to the letter she received shortly before, black beetle words on the crisp white page, *Dear Miss Clark . . .*

Don't think about it. Don't go there.

Her mind pivots quickly to those first moments in the taxi, when she'd decided to do the ridiculous and book the next available flight to anywhere. With shaking hands, she'd checked the internet, looking for anything which would take her away from Edinburgh – and him – immediately.

But, like many other parts of her life, it didn't work like that. It was already late, and the last flight to Heathrow was leaving in twenty minutes. She'd never make it. The next one was to Amsterdam first thing the next day, and so she booked that, hoping that from there, she'd fly somewhere again. She had to go further, much further away than The Netherlands. Checking into the airport hotel that night, she lay on the firm white bed, in that beige and grey room, which so many other people had flitted through before. But she couldn't sleep, her mind ballooning with nightmarish thoughts: Liv's smile, wide and garishly red, Robbie betraying her, a white letter on fire; her insides twisting. And she felt so angry too that he'd let her down like this, when she needed him the most. Every time she started to nod off, her body would jolt awake, and she'd remember it all again. She wondered if the awful panic would ever go; if she'd ever have a moment's peace again in her life.

From Amsterdam, she bought a direct flight to Lima – the furthest-flung destination. Everything went by in a blur still, like she was drunk or drugged or having some sort of out-of-body experience: departure lounge, boarding tunnel, safety demonstration, the deafening roar of the engines and then more half-sleeps. By the time she landed, her nerves were jangling and she was half-sick from exhaustion. She booked herself a private room in a hostel, and at some point, her body had finally given in to sleep. She stayed in bed for what seemed like weeks, but was probably more like three or four days. In the evenings, she would emerge to get a little food and water from a small *supermercado* across the road, only to fall back into bed again like a dead weight.

Eventually, she started to feel slightly more normal again, more lucid. Her heart was beating at a steady rate and the light outside her window had seemed brighter. She had proper hunger again for food. The first thing she did was to message Hilary finally, replying to her one hundred, increasingly panicked texts, phone calls and emails. *I'm OK, honestly. I'll call soon,* she'd said. Then the harder part – her work. She explained the situation as best she could, said she was profusely sorry for her behaviour, whilst mentally accepting that she would most likely never be allowed back again.

And Robbie.

Robbie, who'd been texting and calling just as much as Hilary. *Please let me know you're OK? Call me, please.* What could she say? His worry had quickly turned into annoyance, belligerence even. *How can you do this to me?* Her fingers hovered over the reply button, as she imagined his brown eyes, his arms around her, his scent. The one person who could make her feel better. Then other thoughts bled across her vision: his recent distance, the kiss with Liv. She knew what she had to say.

I'm sorry, I can't be with you anymore.

That same day, she wandered further into Lima finally, enjoying the hot sun on her face. Immediately, she felt the vitamin D working its way into her pores, helping her when she couldn't really help herself. It made her think about how even in her darkest moment, nature still found a way to keep her going. She'd drifted around the old centre, the sun beating down on the pink, orange and yellow stonework. She'd eaten ceviche in a plaza; ordered treacle-like coffee in faltering Spanish and, at some point, she'd spotted a flyer for Machu Picchu.

'How's the rum?'

She blinks away from the fire, refocuses on Raul beside her in the dark.

'It's nice,' she says, looking down briefly at her still-full cup. 'I just haven't felt like drinking recently.'

'It will keep you warm when the temperature drops,' he smiles. 'But it is not as cold as later in the year. Maybe one good thing about coming now, and an almost-empty trail.'

'It must get pretty busy in peak season.'

'Oh god,' he grins, 'so busy, so crazy.' He throws his hands up by his ears to make the point. 'But it's nice to have people to speak to also, no?'

He says it in a way which lets her know he's asking if she's OK. Most people probably join these groups to actually talk to people, she supposes. Not run away from them. Why did she come here anyway if she just wants to be alone? She makes a mental note to avoid the hotspots going forwards – go to some place different.

'Being alone is just easier sometimes,' she replies eventually, and looks up at the night sky, unwilling to divulge further. It looks so impossibly vast in this place, the stars like ice chips on a dark arctic sea. She wishes she could swim in it.

'I'm not sure we can ever be fully alone,' Raul says, and Jenn looks across at him, curious. He's staring up at the sky himself now, but she doesn't reply, just turns her face up again too.

'Did you know,' he says, 'the stars were really important to the Inca. They believed that each one belonged to a different animal. Like that one over there,' he points over to the right, 'that might be a toad or something. They were also one of the only civilisations to see constellations in both the light and the darkness – in the places between the stars. They thought the dark blotches in the Milky Way were actually animals in a river, like the animals down here.'

'I didn't know that,' Jenn says, still looking up.

'Yes, they thought everything was connected,' he continues, 'everything around us. So, maybe we never can be completely alone.'

She smiles to herself, wondering just how many times Raul has told this star story to someone up here. But she appreciates it anyway. It's the first time she's truly felt distracted for a moment.

'Anyway,' she says. 'I might need to head off to bed now.'

His face falls briefly, and she feels bad to cut him short like that but she really is exhausted. They all have an early start, after all.

'OK, señorita,' he nods, before smiling again. 'I'll wake you when it's time to leave.'

After Raul's gone, she gets up from the camp chair, stretches. Setting the cup of rum down on a table, she says goodnight to the others around the fire. They look almost surprised to see she's still there, but smile widely, call out goodnights and *see-you-in-five-hours*!

Lying in her sleeping bag a few minutes later, in the darkness, she wonders if she could try to make a little more effort on the trek back down tomorrow. It might even be fun to have a drink with them back in Cusco or something.

A dull thrumming on the tent soon starts up, growing increasingly louder. There are screeches from around the campfire, footsteps pounding as the others hurry to their own tents. *It's raining again.*

A noise. Jolting up, she looks around. *What was that?* It was like someone was here in the tent with her. Peering around in the patchy darkness, she can feel her heart racing, eyes searching. That prickling sensation again. But there's no one there, of course. After a moment, she lies back down again, tries to sleep.

A piercing trill, a noise in the centre of her mind. The world is black when she wakes. Groping around quickly for her phone, she hits the alarm button – silence. She hears a shuffling, a movement from outside the tent. It comes closer.

'Jenn,' a voice whispers from the other side of the fabric.

Raul.

Sitting up in the tent, she unzips the door. His shadowy face appears under a hat, a tin mug in his hand.

'Tea?'

'Thanks,' she smiles, taking the scalding cup from him.

'Ten minutes until we leave, OK? Time to get the little chicks up.'

With a grin, he disappears off into the darkness again, and she's left with only the dull light of the phone in the gloom still, the tea's steam rising into the tent like early morning mist.

The night is bleeding into dawn as they trudge away from the campsite, the fog around them thick and cloying like a blanket across the mountains. She thought she might be more tired than this after all the walking, but she realises her job has made her used to broken nights, early starts. It's in her system still, like a lot of other things.

Just ahead of her, Raul is leading the way up a steep mountain path, which drops away into green below them. There are a few other trek companies behind them too and she hears the tired silence trailing away back down the mountain like a weary snake. As they walk, the fog starts to lift from around them, and the sky becomes pearly and clear. The scent is like dew and jungle and fresh air combined.

Raul finally raises his hand in signal, before ushering them around a rocky corner. And there, as the sun finally bathes the land in morning glow, she sees it, the place she's seen so many times on cards and brochures; Robbie's pictures. Those strange rocky peaks so high they jut into the lingering clouds.

With the lost city beneath, and the protective wall of the Andes beyond, it's like something out of a childhood dream.

And even though she didn't want to think about him, wanted to completely eradicate Robbie from her mind, she feels him somehow, here in this place beside her, as though the steps he took before her all those years ago are still in the soil. As though he's standing right beside her.

The next day

ROBBIE

It's dark, Reggaeton hammering in my ears, reverberating in my chest. Lights strobe around the place in greens and reds and I can see I'm in a large club, surrounded by people dancing. Every so often the lights stream brightly across the people here, all young, all with bands on their wrists and drinks in their hands. But their features are blurred so I know Jenn's not here yet. It's got that kind of nasty underscent of sweat and toilets, which I don't usually notice when I'm drunk, but is so obvious now that I'm sober. I have a very vague memory of ending up in this place in Cusco, years ago now. Glittering pillars, steel framework. I was probably fucked.

Because I was always fucked, I'm realising.

The blurry bar staff moving around like shape shifters – spirits are being poured and pints are being pulled, and I know in another life, all I'd want to do right now is go get drunk – have fun.

But where did that ever get me?

How did that actually help anyone other than me?

Memories from before keep crashing into my mind: the pub with Liv, Marty and Hilary's engagement party, my birthday, the kiss with Liv.

Turns out repeatedly being shitty doesn't make me feel very good.

Scanning the darkness now, I wait for Jenn to appear. It only takes a few moments. Raul and the cagoule trio too. She's wearing a strappy blue dress now, which shows off her long legs, and her short hair is wavy. Her eyes are slightly nervous, but she's smiling about something Raul has said, head inclined in his direction. A pang in my chest.

How could I have let this happen? How could I have let the person I loved the most get this far away from me?

She thought I didn't care.

The group traipse across to the dance floor now, and I follow behind them. The music's pumping as they find a space in the middle. Jenn starts to move, dance like she's allowing her body to loosen up for the first time in ages. Strobe lights throw rainbows of colour across her skin, and I can't help thinking how beautiful she is

She told me something about light once – about how a phosphorescent object would absorb energy when exposed to it, and that's what would make it glow.

I think that's how I was, looking back.

Her light made me glow.

After a moment, Raul leans over to her, shouts something in her ear and points to the bar. She looks at him and smiles, then points at the floor, mouthing, *I'll stay here.*

'And I'll stay with you,' I find myself saying. But she doesn't hear me above the bass. Raul walks away, and we're left under the flashing lights together, the cagoule trio doing stupid dancing nearby.

I start dancing too, because I used to love going out with Jenn to clubs, spinning her around the sticky dance floors of Edinburgh until the lights came up. We would go congratulate the DJ for an excellent set after, pick up some chips on the way home. We used to be perfect.

Then I messed it all up, like I always do.

But if I'm going to die – if *we* are going to die – because I lost her secret, then I'd like to think that my last moments on this earth might be spent doing things right, finally. Because I know I missed everything the first time. I know I never really listened properly or tried hard enough to understand her, or anyone else I loved for that matter. I know I wasn't interested in dealing with anything hard or serious or uncomfortable; I couldn't be counted on in a crisis.

And that's why she couldn't tell me the secret in the first place.

Maybe that's part of what she's trying to tell me? Maybe this whole thing is actually bigger than one secret.

So with all the time we have left in these memories, I'm going to do things differently this time. I'm going to stop being consumed by some secret I might never actually find, but, more than that, I'm going to see everything she wants me to see, understand everything she wants me to understand, go where she wants me to go. And I'm going to be fully present the whole time, taking every single second in.

Like I always should have been.

Why the hell were you ever with me in the first place? I want to say to her, but don't.

I feel the music in my arms, my legs, my whole body, taking me over like there is no tomorrow and no car and no truck coming towards us. I raise my arms high and for a moment it's like we are dancing together, just the two of us, in the strobe-lit dark.

TWENTY-ONE

2010

JENNY

The red light from the iron blinks at her as she sits at the kitchen table, steam coming up in little puffs above the ironing board.

'Did she say why she couldn't come?'

She looks up to see Duncan standing topless behind the board, watching her. A creased shirt is laid across the top, waiting for the hot iron to smooth it down.

'No,' she says eventually and takes another quick spoonful of porridge from the bowl in front of her. She knew the conversation wouldn't stop there.

Duncan grimaces slightly, before taking the iron across the length of the shirt, pressing it down firmly into the corner. It sighs loudly when he sets it upright again.

'Well, maybe you should speak to your mum about it?' he tries. 'It's clearly stressing you out. She can't keep cancelling trips up here.'

Looking down into the bowl, she sees how little she's actually eaten, the apple Duncan chopped earlier still balanced precariously on the top. Her mum makes her feel like that sometimes. Precarious, like she can't quite get her balance. She wants to ask her why she doesn't bother to come and see her in Edinburgh, but equally she doesn't want to know the answer. It's not normal, she knows. Most parents seem to make huge efforts to see their children. Duncan's are always popping over to say hi, and even when they go off on one of their cruises, they're always phoning him to check in. She hasn't seen her mum since their visit down to Cornwall last summer, and even then, it had all seemed a bit of a hassle.

Still living in the caravan, there'd been no room for her and Duncan to actually stay, and her mum had been so caught up with some exhibition coming up anyway, so they'd skipped around some cheap B&Bs in the area: Carbis Bay, Porthcurno. It turned into more of a summer holiday for them, and she found she loved waking up to a glimpse of the sea over rooftops, that dull roar of the waves.

But there was a moment one night, when Duncan was sound asleep in bed and she just couldn't sleep. The mattress was too small, the room too stuffy, and so she slipped out and onto the cold wooden floor, tip-toed across to the window and quietly opened it. She felt the cool air drifting in, before ducking down and pushing her head out into the darkness. A winding street lay below her, the sea across the horizon, and she just had this feeling that perhaps somewhere out there in the world was something larger, something bigger than she knew. Her heart was thudding in her chest and she had this sudden rush of inexplicable joy, like maybe something wonderful was still to come.

But she had immediately felt guilty, because that something wonderful didn't feel like it included Duncan. It was disloyal to the man she loved and had a future all mapped out with. Only one year to go of university and then they were done, free to go wherever they wanted. And he was OK about her wanting to leave the UK. The plan was to do their two-year training here in Edinburgh and then go to Australia and specialise there. That was the dream: the money was better, the lifestyle was better and finally, *finally*, she could be away from it all. Leave all these ghosts from the past behind.

'Jenny,' Duncan says, and she looks up to see him hanging his shirt on the back of a chair. 'Are you sure you're OK?'

She doesn't know why exactly, but he's irritating her now. Sometimes it almost annoys her how attentive he is, like he's always watching to see how she's feeling, how she's coping. And it makes her feel vulnerable. It would be easier if he just distracted her, or made her laugh.

Keen to change the subject, she says, 'you all ready for the big day?' and gets up from the kitchen table. It does its obligatory wobble as she does so, and in a second Duncan's there with a coaster, kneeling down and sticking it under the table leg. Water still glistens on his back from the shower.

'Your big day too,' he says from the floor. Standing up again, he walks over to the ironing board and folds it up, before tucking it back away neatly in the pantry.

Thinking about the day ahead gives her a thrill of excitement at least – the first emergency medicine attachment she's had at university. Despite the traumatic injuries she knows she'll see, there's something about it which draws her in: she can learn to help people at their crisis point, and no day will ever be the same.

'Shame we'll see less of each other now,' he says, turning around again.

She nods, but secretly she's sort of glad of it; she's glad Duncan wants to do cardiology and not A&E, because medicine is about her, not them as a couple. *A couple.* That constricted feeling starts in her belly again, the one she had in Cornwall. What's wrong with her?

'Right, I'm going to head off now.' She picks up her phone and her wallet, dumps them in her handbag hanging on the side of a chair.

'Let me know how it goes today anyway,' Duncan says. Reaching up, she gives him a quick peck on the mouth. He's thoughtful. She's ungrateful, and she doesn't deserve him.

'Will do,' she smiles and heads out the door.

ROBBIE

A woman on a bed. A hospital bed. She's completely battered, all bruises and drips and casts. She's hooked up to a machine which bleeps, her jet-black hair fanning out around her.

Where's Jenn?

There, at the foot of the bed, with a few other stiff-looking students in blue scrubs. I smile with some relief – we're still together at least. Is this the 'big day' her and Duncan were talking about? A guy who looks to be in his forties, with short ginger hair and wearing scrubs, runs over the accident like he's going through a shopping list: multiple contusions, multiple abrasions, multiple fractures – what the hell happened to this woman?

I really hate hospitals, but I'm glad we left the last place at least. It made me feel a bit ill seeing Jenn and Duncan living together. In my head she'd only ever lived with me.

And he's so incredibly nice to her, all the time.

I don't think I ever actually thought about the nature of her relationship with him before; how it was day to day. But it sure as hell looked more peaceful – more caring – with him, than with me.

He was always looking out for her; thinking of her first.

'Any questions at this point?' the doctor says finally and I look up. His name tag says Doctor Burden. I remember Jenn speaking about him. He seems worn out but his eyes spark when he looks at the students. I can imagine that's what Jenn will be like when she's older. Always wanting to help no matter how tired she is.

Or what she would have been like.

I swallow back tears as she raises her hand, and he nods at her. 'Which injury is the worst?' she asks.

He ushers her closer and I edge over beside her. The woman's a total mess, with her leg in a cast thing and her foot a nasty shade of purple. There's some sort of brace on her neck too, blocks on either side.

I wonder what it will be like when the truck hits. Over in a flash, I suppose.

Lights out.

I never really thought about it before, how brief life is. How it can be there one moment, and gone the next. Just like that.

'This is the real danger area,' Doctor Burden is saying now as he points to the torso. I look down absently.

'She's got significant pulmonary contusions and is already requiring high ventilatory pressures.'

Bizarre to think there could be something catastrophic going on under the skin that no one can see.

'It's incredible the damage car accidents can do,' Doctor Burden continues.

My heart stops.

My head starts pulsing.

The last thing I see, as the room starts to blur and distort, is Jenn's eyes trained; locked on that woman.

TWENTY-TWO

2019

JENN

'Arepa, empanada, a la orden.'

She passes a woman with jet-black hair behind one of the many beach stalls on the sand. They're all selling the cornmeal cakes she's seen everywhere in Colombia, along with mango, pineapple, coconuts, bananas – all sorts of beautiful, technicoloured fruit and juice cups. For a moment she's tempted: she only had one coffee at the hostel and now she can feel her stomach rumbling, urging her to eat.

But her watch tells her she doesn't have time, and she walks a little faster past the vivid green palm trees to her right; the indigo, boat-speckled sea to her left.

Further along the beach now, and she sees the hut the man at the hostel told her to find. There's a flurry of people around it, chatting, exchanging money for tickets and, for a moment, Jenn feels nervous. But then she remembers her Spanish is coming along pretty well now. She thinks back to the start, how stilted she was in Cusco – it's almost laughable. She had barely been able to ask for a coffee. But little by little it's improved. The more she forces herself to use it, the easier it's become. Like a welcome new challenge: it's hard to dwell on troubles when you're mulling over the present perfect, preterit and imperfect tenses.

She goes up to the stall, manages to squeeze through close to the front. A man with shaggy dark hair glances at her.

'*Una ida*,' she says.

Two seconds later and she's exchanged money for the one-way ticket, the man pointing her in the direction of a rickety speed boat behind them. It's pulled up close to the sand, but she sees she'll still need to wade through shallow water to get to it. Heading over, she slips into the almost bath-like sea. She'd kill for a swim right now. She's so sweaty in her white sundress and it's not even ten.

A guy standing on the side takes her ticket, glances at it briefly, before gesturing to her backpack. She passes it to him and he swings it up and into the boat.

'*Vamos, señorita*,' he says, turning back to her with an outstretched hand.

Jenn takes it and steps up.

'*Gracias*,'

'*A la orden*,' he smiles.

Finding a seat on a wooden bench, the boat fills up quickly around her: men, women, children, perhaps one other tourist, all packing in so that she's right up against the side. She feels slightly nervous – apparently people have actually died on these, flipped off at speed. But she quickly pushes the unease down. Other boats come and go, dropping people off and picking them up; men call out to each other and motors buzz. A warm breeze tickles her face and she looks back to the dusty town she arrived in last night.

Two months in and she's still not really following any particular plan – but there's something about it which feels right. For the first time in her life, she trusts the chaos of not knowing what's ahead of her. It feels good to do exactly what she wants, when she wants. And after Machu Pichu, she decided what she really wanted was more heat, less British tourists. So, she'd headed north to Colombia. To Medellín.

She hung around for longer than she thought she would – in the city of eternal spring, as she heard it called – enjoying the sprawling city along the valley floor, the way the office towers and apartment blocks were scattered all the way up the jagged green peaks. It was like no place she'd ever seen. She went dancing with a couple of German girls she met at the hostel, rode the Metrocable across the communes, looked over the city from high up a mountain as the sun set and the lights twinkled; she saw Botero's art work and thought for a moment of her mum.

She'd received a few messages from her by that point, asking her to call. She'd let her mum know she was abroad, that she was OK, but she was still unable to bring herself to speak to her over the phone.

She needed more time – time to decide what to do after that letter, time to stop reeling from Robbie's betrayal. Maybe at that point she'd be able to make some sense of what had happened to the life she thought she knew, form some sort of new plan. But, until then, it was best to stay far away from everything, and everyone.

And that appeared to include Hilary too.

She felt awful for not calling her, of course, but she'd emailed and texted at least, told her what she was doing and where she was going. She told herself she just didn't want to get into it all with anyone, but the honest truth was that it was hard to talk to someone about how your life is falling apart when that person's dreams are all coming true.

After Medellín, she headed briefly to Bogotá, more because it seemed like the underdog city than anything else. No one really recommended it. But she'd found brilliant street art and chilled cafés. Then finally, she'd heard about some remote hostel in a beautiful cove on the Caribbean Sea.

The sound of the motor starting on the boat rings in her ears, and she realises that everyone is finally on. There's a collective lurch and the boat moves out from the cove.

Their progression is calm initially, punctuated by the chatter of Spanish around her, then there's a rush of wind in her ears as the boat speeds up into the blue. It starts to skip over the waves, the whole thing flying up in the air for a moment and crashing back down. Water sprays up and over the sides, into Jenn's face and the elderly woman's beside her and they both start laughing – the kind of hysterical laughter of two people who don't even know each other. Then it happens again. Hop, slam, sea spray across everyone and Jenn is grinning to herself now, feeling nothing but the wind on her face and the sun on her skin. She looks out across the water and has the distinct feeling that she's supposed to be in this exact place, at this exact point in her life.

Half an hour or so later and the numbers on the boat have whittled down. They've gone by six coves or so already and, each time, she's strained to hear the name of it, keen to not miss her stop. The woman beside her went at the one before. With a curly grin, she'd pressed an orange into Jenn's hands before she went, holding on for a moment longer, as if to say *enjoy it*.

She takes her time peeling the fruit now, realising how fresh it must be, likely from some sun-saturated grove not too far away. She breathes in the scent: *Robbie, Christmas*.

Her heart catches.

Even here on the other side of the world, he's always with her somehow, like he could be sitting there beside her on the boat. She wonders what he's doing at this very moment.

She hears a shout from the front.

Her stop.

'*Sí, señor*,' she shouts over the sound of the engine, as the boat starts to slow into a cove. Looking ahead properly, she's amazed by the seclusion of it all, the way the green hills roll up around the cove, sheltering the white sandy beaches and small wooden huts. There's no jetty as usual, but a man wades out into the warm sea, salt water slopping up and onto his blue shorts. He's thick set, a bit older – in his forties perhaps – with greying hair, leathery skin and a big smile. Before they've quite reached the beach, the driver turns the engine off, and she knows she'll be disembarking the way she got on.

The driver chucks her backpack to the man coming towards them, who props it on his head like it weighs nothing. Tipping one leg over the side, she plops down into the water beside him.

'*Gracias*,' she says.

He grins. '*Bienvenidas.*'

Welcome.

ROBBIE

I'm on the beach now. The guy's gone, Jenn too. I'm wet, sandy, too hot. I take off my hoody; dump it on the sand. It seems insane that I can feel so much in a memory. My clothes are completely wrong for this climate. But I'm glad I'm on dry land at least. I thought I was going to fall out the boat and into the sea just there – I don't know if I actually could drown in a shared-death experience, but I really don't want to find out.

It's not like I can go to a hospital.

Those injuries in Jenn's hospital – I didn't quite realise the extent of damage a car crash could cause, that you might not even immediately die, you might just be completely broken and in excruciating pain.

Which means she would be in pain too.

But I've tried – fuck – I've tried to figure out her secret. And now I need to stop messing about trying to find something I might never find.

I need to focus on her; make the most of the time we have left.

A movement nearby. Jenn comes out of the water in a purple bikini and I stop. She looks incredible: toned, lean, relaxed. Did she have that bikini before? I can't honestly remember the last time we had a holiday before she left, just the two of us lazing around together somewhere hot with no hospital, no restaurant and no dramas.

Come to think of it, how did she pay for eight whole months away? She was always the most money conscious person I know, down to the penny. I suppose that means she probably had a lot of savings, but still – to blow it all like that. It's just not like her.

It's probably past the point of questioning that now though.

The beach around us is pretty stunning. I never went anywhere like this on my travels – everything was tourist heavy, easy to get to and boozy. But then, that was always my main priority back on my gap year, of course. Getting pissed and meeting girls.

Jenn stops at this open wooden structure, with a thatched roof like something out of Robinson Crusoe. There are two hammocks strung up beneath, one green and one orange. Is she sleeping here? Shit, this is cool.

A pair of black swim shorts hangs across a line strung up between us; large flip flops are lying in the sand. Hang on. Who's sleeping there?

After throwing on a sundress she heads along the sand, and I follow. Colourful bean bags come into sight, the odd person lounging back in them. Wooden swings are strung up between two tall trees towards the sea, and a long rustic table is already filled with a few people, chatting and eating plates of fresh fish, rice and salad.

'Please, just pick up some food at the kitchen,' the man from earlier calls to her from a table, and Jenn nods before walking towards the hatch nearby. I watch her as she goes, and I can't help thinking how much I would have loved doing this whole thing with her; the fun we would have had. We always enjoyed going to new places together, trying new food.

'*Bonjour*,' a girl in sunglasses says as Jenn sits on the edge of a bench. She has long dark hair, lean, tanned arms. She looks around the same age as us.

'*Bonjour*.' Jenn nods back.

'English?'

'Yes,' Jenn smiles apologetically. 'Sorry.'

'Do not apologise,' she says politely. 'I am Mathilde and this is my boyfriend Fabien,' she indicates, waving her hand lightly beside her. 'And Isadora and Matteo here are from Roma.'

'*Ciao*,' says the younger couple beside Jenn in unison, smiling widely. Everyone looks so bloody healthy here.

'Are you travelling alone?' Mathilde asks.

Jenn nods. 'Yes.'

'Super, I travelled alone when I was twenty. Best time of my life.'

'*Pardon moi*,' Fabien says, throwing up his arms in what I assume is faux annoyance.

'What?' she says bluntly. 'It was! You cannot understand yourself until you, how do you say?' She holds her palm up to her face, 'see yourself in the mirror. And the best way to do that is to be completely alone. No friends, no family, just you and you.'

'You might be right,' Jenn smiles and takes another mouthful of food.

'Hey,' Isadora says, leaning forwards, 'has Juan come back from his hike yet?'

'He will be away for hours yet,' Mathilde says. 'He said he was trying to find that hidden beach you can apparently see from the top of the hill.' Mathilde points vaguely to her left, looks back at Jenn. 'Juan's Colombian actually. He's staying in one of the hammocks. That's where you are, yes?'

Jenn nods and Mathilde smiles.

The sun is dipping in the sky, and the heat has lessened slightly. Beside me, Jenn is lying on her hammock reading a book. She seems so peaceful, so content. The air is still warm, her skin is glowing and, for a moment, I imagine if I'd been on this trip with her too – if I'd been in that hammock across from her and not some Juan guy. Her phone is lying against her leg and, very carefully, I reach over to press it. She only vaguely flinches as the screen lights up, too engrossed in her book. April.

What was I doing then? Those first couple of months are all a bit blurry, just drinking and pizza deliveries and missed shifts. Matt had been pretty cool about it, initially. He'd roped in a mate from another restaurant to cover me for a bit – I just couldn't face going into work, couldn't be bothered doing anything really. Marty would come over now and then with some cans. We'd watch stupid cop films and play on the Xbox.

Thinking about it now, he was really there for me when it all got shitty.

A scuffing noise on the sand behind me. I turn swiftly to see a youngish guy walking up to Jenn's hammock. He has hiking boots on, shorts and a sweaty grey t-shirt. His skin is mahogany, black hair pushed back, very lean. Good looking. I swallow.

He passes so close to me I can smell that sweaty man scent on him.

'Hello,' he smiles down at Jenn and she finally looks up from her book, a surprised look on her face. He takes a slug from his water bottle.

'Hi,' she says.

Did she just blush?

No, Jenn would never go for this type of guy, all suave and exotic.

Never in a million years.

'You must be Juan,' she smiles.

'Mathilde said I had a new sleeping friend,' he replies.

Jenn laughs. 'Yes, that's me.'

He lifts one arm and holds onto the wooden hut above so that his triceps flex. How old is this guy anyway? He's got to be a good few years younger than us. *Fat chance*, I want to say to him.

'You just here for the night?' he asks.

'I don't know actually. I'm just seeing what happens.'

'Great, great.' He ducks across to where the black shorts are hanging. 'I'm going to for a swim before dinner if you fancy it?'

He peels off his t-shirt without warning, exposing cast-iron abs.

'I'm alright.' She smiles. 'I went in earlier.'

After taking off his boots, he walks back out onto the sand in his shorts, rakes a hand through his hair. He wanders down to the water, smiles back briefly at Jenn. 'Maybe later then.'

In the hammock beside me, Jenn covers her face with her hands, and for a moment I think she's about to cry. Has he upset her? *Dick.* But looking closer, I see that she's not crying, she's smiling. Then she's laughing to herself silently, like it's the funniest thing in the world.

Suddenly, I get it.

I get what's going to happen here.

And my heart sinks as low as it can go.

JENN

Light from the little kitchen bar nearby illuminates the table in front of her, filled with empty plates and full glasses. The stars above look spectacular and the air is still warm. The sea hums in the cove, a soothing backdrop to the post-dinner chatter.

The evening has been so relaxed. There's only about eight of them here in total, a mixture of French, Italian, Colombian, British and Dutch, all lured by the seclusion of the place.

She hears something about Medellín from down the table.

'Didn't you say you'd been?' Juan says, turning back to her again. She's spoken a lot with him in particular, his intense green-brown eyes focusing on hers for most of the meal like everything she said was fascinating.

'Yeah, I did,' she says, 'loved it.'

'Well, just make sure to go to Cartagena while you're here too. It's a fun place.'

'I will do,' she smiles.

'Hey, do you want another drink?' he says, indicating at her near-empty glass.

'Sure.'

As he gets up, she feels the brush of his hand against her thigh and an unmistakable current goes through her.

But what the hell is she playing at? She doesn't do flings. Never has done. And besides, she's just not in the zone for that type of thing right now. Is she?

Quickly, she drinks the last of her wine, noticing a trace of dirt on her wrist as she places the glass down. She didn't bother washing earlier, just let the sea salt stay on her skin, her hair. When she checked herself in a hand-held mirror earlier, she suddenly noticed how long it had gotten. It's just touching her shoulders now. *Katy would approve.*

Katy. She gets the sudden image of her in that club night in Edinburgh, glitter around Katy's eyes and that excited look behind them. *There's so much more out there*, she'd said.

She wishes she could tell her she'd done it finally, and she has a sudden urge to text her. Not that she actually could from this cove – the signal is patchy at best – but in the next place maybe. She still has her number, and it's probably the same knowing Katy; she wouldn't have bothered changing it after all. She was always so wonderfully laissez faire – still is, from what she's found online. Photo after photo of Katy in France, sipping coffees under green awnings, or drinking wine on some fabulous sun-soaked veranda. Always with stylish, just-threw-it-together clothing, always with a slick of scarlet lipstick. She was always fabulous.

Her stomach curdles.

What if she doesn't want to speak to me again?

A noise.

She looks up sharply to see Mathilde watching her carefully, chin resting in the palm of her hand.

'Sorry,' Jenn says, 'did you say something?'

Mathilde smiles her wide smile. 'I said, what's the plan tomorrow, Jenn?'

She seems so very comfortable in her skin, so luminescent with life. Jenn wishes she could be more like her.

'Some trekking nearby maybe,' she says eventually.

'Ah, yes, it's beautiful, but just watch out for the leaves.' Mathilde raises her eyebrows.

She frowns. 'Leaves?'

'Yes,' Mathilde nods, 'so many leaves.' She smiles at Fabien and he shakes his head.

'Mathilde was convinced a snake would jump out of them and bite her.' He makes the snapping motion with his hand and laughs.

'I just like to know what's beneath my feet is all,' Mathilde continues. Then pauses. 'I think Juan's leaving tomorrow actually.'

Jenn doesn't know how to respond. *Why is she telling her that?*

'May I ask,' Mathilde says, lowering her hand. 'What happened, before you came here?'

She feels confused.

How can she possibly know?

'I am sorry,' Mathilde says, pulling her hair up into a bun and sticking a pin through it. 'It is not my place. But I can always tell when a girl is running from something. I have a . . . how do you say – instinct. My mother always said so. From a man, yes?'

Jenn nods slowly. It's the first time she's actually spoken to anyone about any of it. Even in her emails to Hilary, she doesn't mention anything about Robbie. She can't bring herself to. Remembering that moment she saw him with Liv – it just hurts too much.

Mathilde takes another sip of wine. 'And you cared for him very much?'

'Yes,' she pauses. 'But I'm not sure he cared about me. Well, not as much as I thought he did.'

'Do you want to know the good news?'

'I guess.'

'That pain you feel, right here,' she says, tapping her chest. 'It will go.'

Jenn smiles sadly. 'When?'

Mathilde takes another drink of wine. 'In time. Time is good.'

She feels deflated. 'So, no magical cure then?'

246

No way to heal that open wound.

'Well,' Mathilde says, eyebrow arched. 'There's always distraction. Another moment, another person. That can be pretty magical.'

Jenn realises now why she was talking about Juan, and feels a flush creeping up her neck. But she can't. Even though Robbie was disloyal to her, even though they've broken up, she still feels completely tied to him by some invisible string.

'I'm not ready for that,' Jenn says and shakes her head.

'Well, just don't wait too long,' Mathilde says, the gold specks in her eyes flashing in the kitchen light. 'Because he won't think twice about moving on. Don't miss out on a moment of joy when you have it, because you never know what might happen tomorrow.'

Something resonates in Jenn, like Mathilde has said something that makes sense at another level. But she doesn't know why.

Juan appears beside her at the table with their drinks, and she can't help but feel a burst in her stomach, like Mathilde has given her a pass to let go of it all for a moment, even if it's just for the night. Her head feels filled with a happy cloud of wine and sea and warmth.

'Fancy taking our drinks down onto the beach?' he says, with a smile.

Without another thought, she nods.

'Sounds good.'

They meander a little away from the table, until the chatter fades out and the sand becomes wet beneath their feet.

She pauses in front of the water and he stops besides her. When she looks across at him he smiles, his almost-perfect features slightly blurry in the dark. And suddenly it seems like a great idea – diving in head first with him. It makes no sense, really, because she'll never see him again after tonight and this can only be a cliché travelling fling; a brief moment of joy.

But that's why she trusts it.

'Time for that sea swim?' she says and he grins.

She takes off her sundress, so she's just in her bikini again, and he swiftly removes his top. And then they are splashing into the water, running towards the depth. When they're in fully, he swims to her and she feels his hands go around her waist, his face so close to hers now that she sees the water on his dark lashes. Putting her hands onto his strong shoulders, she can feel them both kicking in the water below. He kisses her, and the world swirls around them into starry darkness.

TWENTY-THREE

2012

ROBBIE

Throbbing in my head. Voices all around me. Cool air again. I open my eyes to see blurry faced people in black robes everywhere. Blue skies sit above an imposing grey building ahead. We're in a courtyard that I've definitely been to before, for some festival show I think – we must be back in Edinburgh somewhere.

Is this her graduation?

Thank god the last memory cut out when it did. Fucking hell. I feel sick. What happened next? Did they sleep together? I know I was a shit by kissing Liv, I get that, but I didn't sleep with her within two months.

Did I?

An uncomfortable knot starts to build in my stomach. Something Mathilde said to Jenn. *Just don't wait too long . . . because he won't.*

I blow air out. Shit, when did it actually happen with Liv in the end? It can't have been as early as this surely – or was it?

I just remember being bored and pissed off about everything. Then suddenly I had been back there, like I was pre-Jenn, scanning through my contacts on a Friday night to see who might still be out. My thumb hovered over Liv's name. I couldn't really see why I shouldn't speak to her at that point: I wasn't with Jenn anymore, she'd made that crystal clear, and I'd been friends with Liv for years. It was about time we made up. And she'd definitely be out.

Liv was always out.

Almost immediately after texting her, she replied: *George Street. Come join?*

I met her in a basement club in town. It was dark and dingy. We had too many shots. But even though I was half-cut, I knew I was standing on one side of a line and if I crossed it, that would be it. Me and Jenn. Done. For good.

I can't really remember how it happened exactly, just that suddenly we were all over each other in front of the bar, kissing like we were starved.

My stomach sinks.

It's strange when I think about it all now. How everything had seemed so certain at the time: Liv had been at fault, not me; Jenn had left for no good reason and therefore I was entitled to do as I liked. I'm starting to think maybe I'd looked at it all through my own self-made prism. Only thinking about my side of the story, remembering it the way *I* wanted to.

But after seeing it all through Jenn's eyes, it's clear to me now how much I got wrong.

A few faces around me suddenly become clear, and Jenn and Duncan appear through the crowd, black robes and pink sash things around their shoulders.

I feel awful.

At least it's Duncan here and not Don Juan, who's only after one thing. Duncan actually cares about her.

Unlike me evidently.

An older couple appears behind them. The woman has the same pale blonde hair and blue eyes like Duncan. She smiles sweetly, ushers them to stand together for a photo. Must be his parents.

'Well,' she says, stepping back. 'Are you two excited to graduate? Jenny, you look so pretty today.'

She's right. Jenn does. But I can't face looking at her right now, knowing how I let her down in the future.

His parents start talking between themselves about lunch plans after the ceremony.

'You alright?' I hear Duncan say.

'Yes,' Jenn replies, 'it's just I really thought she'd come.'

Finally, I look up.

Shit, her mum's not here. *Did she not even make her graduation?*

'I know,' Duncan says softly, 'but today will still be good, you'll see. We'll have a nice meal out after with my parents. They're so proud of you too, you know.'

She nods, but she looks so lost somehow, amongst all these graduates smiling and calling to each other.

'And focus on the good stuff ahead,' Duncan adds, taking her hand. 'Sunny beaches in Australia. Waking up to those views of the sea you want.'

Jenn finally smiles and it's clear how important her happiness is to Duncan. I'm not sure if I ever said anything even half so committed to Jenn. I was always just joshing around, being an idiot. I didn't think about the future. Or what she wanted.

A noise beside me. Jenn suddenly launches forwards into the crowds. *Where is she going?*

'Jenn,' Duncan calls after her, but she doesn't look back.

Feeling slightly dazed, I follow her.

'Excuse me,' she keeps saying, moving past people, 'excuse me.' She seems alarmed, frantic almost. 'Excuse me!'

I see what she's looking at. A man hovering behind the gate. I don't know why, but something about him is odd. He's wearing a red cap, a scruffy-looking jacket. He looks familiar. There are people everywhere but he's just standing there, watching. I look at Jenn and her eyes are trained on him too.

Then, quite suddenly, he walks away.

She moves quickly forwards, pushing past people, and I follow behind, until she runs out onto the street. But it's busy, people coming and going everywhere on this sunny day. Breathing hard, she looks frantically around.

But the man is gone.

Like he was never there in the first place

JENNY

The arced ceiling is vast and beautiful above her, soaring to a height that feels impossible. Murals line it and an enormous cascading chandelier falls from the centre. It twinkles above the rows of smiling relatives and friends. Morning light streams through windows high up, and she feels an overwhelming sense of possibility.

'For the Bachelor of Medicine and Surgery.'

Looking down at the robed presenter behind the lectern, on the grand stage ahead of her, she realises it's time. The line of graduates she's standing in falls silent. This is the moment she's been working so hard for, for so long.

'Archie Abdul.'

First alphabetically on the list, she watches her classmate go up. Bending his neck slightly, he's met with the light tap of a cap from their professor; a sign that he's made it.

As the list continues, she looks out into the paper chains of well-wishers, the rows upon rows of mothers and fathers, siblings and grandparents. That familiar disappointed feeling rises up in her; that hollow sensation at the pit of her stomach when, yet again, no one is there for her.

But who was that man? She still feels unsettled. It looked so much like him – her dad. But that's impossible. Isn't it? She's scoured the internet for him routinely for years now and nothing. She forces the image of him away, just as she arrives at the front of the line. This is everything to her. This is the moment she's worked so hard for.

'Jennifer Clark.'

Applause floods in her ears, a whoop from somewhere. Silently, her feet carry her up the red carpet and she dips her head in front of the professor. It feels more intimate than it looks from afar, more human. She can smell rich perfume, the trace of coffee as she gently knocks the cap against her head.

Stepping past the professor quickly, she continues on the path back to their seats. Sitting down between other robed students, she hears Duncan's name being called, looks up to see him walking up the ramp, the golden rails there to guide him. His black gown swells behind him. She claps as hard as she can, smiles until her cheeks ache. And she's proud of him, she really is.

It's just she's not in love with him.

The thought arrives with such ferocity, such weight, that she's caught off-guard. Her hands slow to a pause against each other.

The list continues on, as though nothing has happened, as though her carefully crafted life hasn't just exploded around her. But, deep inside, she knows this has been coming. It's been creeping up on her like ivy on a wall for months now.

For so long, this has been her plan: graduating, becoming a doctor, training in Edinburgh with him, creating a life with him in Australia. But it was all a bit of a foggy image before. Now she's pressed right up against the window of her future and there's something missing.

She feels so awful, like the worst kind of person.

But maybe it will go away? Maybe this is just because they're about to start a new stage of their lives? Maybe this doesn't have to mean anything, and she can just ignore it.

As Duncan walks back to his own row, he smiles at her, an expression as if to say, *this is it.*

But a voice at the back of her mind is saying,

No, you see, this isn't.

And she knows that she'll have to address this soon. Because whatever's going on, she still loves Duncan, as a friend. None of this can ever change that. But that's exactly why she also needs to let him go now; let him move on. She needs to cut ties fully, live completely independently of him, or he'll still try to take care of her. She knows he will. She has to do this for her, and for him.

ROBBIE

Fresh coffee. Wobbly table. Their kitchen. Light is pouring in. Must be morning. Jenn's at the table in a T-shirt clutching a mug. She looks far away, somewhere else. Jaded from graduation drinks perhaps?

Duncan's at the hob in his boxers and a t-shirt, pouring porridge into two bowls. He throws apple on the top, turns to her, and her face just crumples.

What's going on?

He says something, which looks like, 'Are you OK?' But it's so weird. It's like everything's on mute. I can see everything, but I can't hear it.

Almost like she wants me to see something, but doesn't actually want to recall what was said.

She starts crying, and he's over by her side immediately, throwing the bowls down on the table and putting his arms around her.

She pulls apart from him, says something else from her seat, something which makes his hands fall down by his side. He goes so still.

Hang on, is she breaking up with him?

But nothing bad happened with them. There's been no argument, no problems. They just graduated together. They had a perfect plan.

I don't get it.

I always thought there had to have been some reason they didn't work out, like he had some secret flaw, or became a dick, or cheated on her.

Perhaps I even wanted him to do that – to know I'm not the only arsehole.

She gets up quickly, moves towards him, but he steps back. Shuts his eyes for a moment. She's crying so hard now, wrapping her arms around herself like she's trying to hold herself together. He looks at her sadly for a moment – it's hard to watch. He nods once, walks past me and out the kitchen.

My head starts to pulse again. She's sitting there all alone, crying. I want to reach out to her, help her in some way. But what the hell can I do? After everything shitty I've done.

The past is the past.

So how the hell can I possibly help her now?

* * *

ROBBIE

Honking. Darkness. Bright lights. I'm back in the car.

I try moving my feet again, still nothing. Try lifting my hands.
Fuck.

The truck's definitely closer now – the driver must be pressing
the horn. And Jenn's just sitting there. I can't even see her face. I
wish I could just see her, then maybe I could get through to her
somehow – tell her time is almost up and I tried to work out
her secret but I blew it. Tell her I know it was all my fault but
I tried.

I'm still trying – to find the secret, to be present for her; be
that man she needs me to be.

That noise!

What else am I supposed to do?

The past is the past.

That thought I had in the kitchen.

Something clicks over in my mind.

What if there is actually something else I can do before time
runs out? Some other reason I'm in this shared-death experience
with her, that I just couldn't see before because I was too
self-involved and too selfish?

The past might be the past, but I'm still here with her now.

For as long as I can be.

Just as I feel myself being pulled away somewhere else, a new
type of urgency floods me.

Because all I need is a little more time.

For her.

TWENTY-FOUR

2019

ROBBIE

Rows of seats. Ears popping. A plane. Jenn's asleep beside me and the sky through the cabin window beside her is a deep blue. The truck and the car all melt into the horizon.

The pounding in my head lessens, heart slows.

And then I feel it.

Something else.

Something like relief.

Because that wasn't the end for us. The truck hasn't killed us yet. Which means we still have time.

I have time.

Jenn makes a noise beside me. Is she shivering? It is kind of cold in here actually. I hate that on planes, how sleeping is always so bloody uncomfortable. I'm either too hot or too cold, and typically wake up with my head lolling forwards and my mouth hanging open. Not that she's doing that, but she does look a bit awkward; her head's at a funny angle.

As gently as I can, I pull her blanket up from the floor in front of her, lay it on top. I nudge towards her, and it's funny because it's as though she realises I'm here, and her head falls gently onto my shoulder. I can hear her breathing quietly, smell the fruity scent of her hair. I feel myself smiling. I take her hand; squeeze it twice. *I love you.* She murmurs something and I immediately freeze. I don't want to wake her. She seems so peaceful.

A pinging noise. Tinny voices come over the flight speakers. 'Ten minutes to landing.'

The little red signs above go off and a member of the crew goes by, checking over each row methodically, before disappearing out the back. Where are we going anyway?

The cabin plunges into darkness. Early morning descent. The plane drops down again, changes direction in the sky. And despite that sinking feeling in my stomach, I feel lighter suddenly.

Perhaps I can change, even now.

Perhaps it's not too late.

Because even if this is all about to end for us, and even if there's nothing I can do about the actual past, maybe I can still do something good in her memories.

And that's what she'll remember.

Forever.

JENN

The light outside is dimming now and she shifts position in the driver's seat. It's the first time she's actually driven since she left the UK, but she knew there was no real better way to get around Australia than a car. This one's a bit run down, and slightly musty, but she's glad she bought it cheap rather than hiring.

No need to worry about what happens to it.

She still has no idea what she's doing from one day to the next, and even more so now, she wants to push it; see just how far she can go alone. For so long there was Duncan, and then just two years later, there was Robbie.

But there's a possibility that something hard lies ahead in her future – and then she'll need to deal with it alone.

Out of the window, the sky is a soft navy blue, a silhouetted landscape of trees and bushes below. Checking the sat nav, she sees she's a few hours south of Darwin now. As soon as she landed something inside her made her want to bolt from the city, head into the remoteness of the Outback. The frenetic travelling through South and then Central America invited all sorts of new connections; and she's not sorry for that, but just for a while, some alone time would be good.

Some alone time is necessary.

ROBBIE

It's light now. We're blasting down a road which seems to go on forever. The sky above is a hot blue and there's just endless red dirt and rocks on either side. How long has she been driving? From the change of landscape, I'd guess she's already stopped in a few places along the way. I know enough about Oz to know that we're somewhere in the middle now – some place I never bothered to go and see. It sounded a bit dull. Just endless nothing, with a big fucking rock in the centre.

But sitting beside her now, in the middle of all this great nothing, I feel a deep sense of calm. I'm still here with her; still close to her.

I can't help thinking how chilled she seems. She's wearing a white vest, skin slightly bronzed and hair ducking past her shoulders now.

This trip was good for her; I can see that now.

I can see Fi was right.

It was the first dinner Liv and I had had at home since things had started up, and I remember it all feeling a bit weird. Liv had been coming over to the house since we were young, but suddenly the atmosphere was stilted, odd even, with Fi and Struan there too – they were there quite a lot from what Mum said. Max had more business in New York.

Dad had started his usual *where are you working now?* shit with Liv over Mum's lasagne and when she'd said she worked part time at the restaurant, he'd made this face that said everything. I'd flown off the handle, accused him of being a snob and said the only reason he'd liked Jenn was because she was a doctor; said he'd always hated the fact I only cooked for a living. He'd told me he wouldn't care what I did as long as I did it with some dignity and stopped getting pissed all the time.

It must have been so awkward for Liv. For everyone.

And I'd gotten no sympathy from Fi later on. I couldn't believe she was taking Dad's side. We'd always joked about how snobby

Dad secretly or not-so-secretly was. Then she'd said it was shitty of me to start dating Liv when I clearly wasn't over Jenn. I'd got angry and tried to tell her I was just getting on with my life: Jenn had left me, not the other way around.

'Everything's always about *you*, isn't it?' Fi had said. 'How you're feeling, what happened to poor Robbie. Did you ever stop to ask yourself what *Jenn* was feeling to make her leave?'

A cloud of mist appears on the horizon ahead of us.

'Shit,' Jenn says, 'shit, shit, shit.' She slows so rapidly we both lurch forwards as the car veers off the road. It bumps along to the side, just as an enormous vehicle suddenly appears out of the cloud.

What the fuck is that?

'Road train,' she mutters beside me, almost like she heard.

The rumble of the engine gets louder and louder until suddenly it's flying past us, a massive truck with a never-ending string of trailers behind. I can literally feel the car shaking, even from the distance we're at. *Fuck.*

Eventually it passes, and she takes a breath, drives the car back onto the road.

I can't believe she's just out here alone like this, driving in the bloody outback with no help for miles. It's so isolated. No other cars. No other people. Just her and the dirt and the sky. I wonder what she did between South America and here. Where did she go? What did she see? It's hard skipping over parts.

It's hard that we barely got one night together after she arrived back in Edinburgh. I didn't manage to ask her anything.

But then I suppose it's like that with everything in life. Unless you ask the people you love questions when you have the chance, the information goes – just like that.

A familiar note – The Beach Boys, 'Wouldn't It Be Nice.' It's only then that I realise there's been low-level singing from the radio this whole time. Making sure Jenn's not looking, I fiddle with the volume control and turn it up. She immediately smiles, which makes me smile, and suddenly it's like we're really on a road trip together. Jenn and Robbie. Robbie and Jenn – dream team.

The most intense excitement floods through me.

This is actually working. And it didn't scare her, or jolt her out of the memory.

Something I did simply made her smile.

After a while, the car begins to slow again and she drives off the road towards what looks like a sparse designated stop. Someone's there, by the water tank. A man. I look at Jenn beside me and feel worried suddenly. Nothing bad happened on this trip did it?

She parks up the car and gets out. When she's a few metres away, I quietly do the same. It's incredibly hot and I'm sweating already. Christ. You wouldn't stand a chance out here exposed. Didn't she think about that?

I hang around near the car as she heads off to use the toilet, keeping my eyes on this guy the whole time. He's a bit older, gangly, with long-ish salt-and-pepper hair and one of those floppy sun hats on. He's wearing shorts but it's not that obvious really because he's covered in dust. I look around for his car but can't see one. A bike lies in the dirt nearby, a backpack. He can't seriously be cycling? Jenn walks over to him smiling, but I can tell she's wary too from the slight frown line on her forehead.

She's not completely lost her mind then.

'G'day,' the man says and smiles at her. It seems like a normal enough greeting – no crazy *Wolf Creek* grin at least.

'Hey,' she says. Her eyes dart to his bike in the dirt and widen. 'Are you cycling along here?'

He takes another sip of his water, nods. 'Yup. Length of Australia, Darwin to Adelaide.'

'Oh my god,' she replies, her eyes widening. 'That's amazing.'

It really is. Jenn driving it alone is one thing, but this guy cycling it – well that's something else.

I guess there's always someone out there to raise the bar that little bit higher.

She looks concerned suddenly.

'Do you have enough water there? I mean, do you need any more? I've got plenty,' she says, indicating at the car.

'That's alright, I'm sorted. People've been very kind. Just stopping off here before the next bit, not many places to pull over after this one.'

'Yeah I've seen that on the map,' she says, nodding.

He looks at her curiously and my danger antennae raises up again.

'What brings a young woman like you out here all by herself?'

She pauses, like she's about to run off a rehearsed answer, then her face sort of falls.

'Do you know, I'm not sure anymore,' she says. The man doesn't reply, just takes a swig of his water, like he's waiting for her to speak.

She won't though. Not to a stranger.

But then suddenly she sighs, looks around herself, back at him.

'I was having a hard time with some stuff,' she says eventually. 'So, I left. I didn't really think it through too much. Probably should have.'

The man nods at that, like she's said something which hits home and he takes another glug of water.

I'm shocked. It's just so wildly open for her to say this kind of stuff to a stranger. But perhaps not knowing this guy also means it doesn't actually matter what she tells him.

'You know,' he starts, 'when I told my wife that I was going to do this – cycle down the middle of Australia – she said I'd lost it. But the thing was, doc told me I was probably going to die last year. Bit of bowel cancer. I'd been working round the clock before they picked up on it. Another couple of months in me and I'd have been a gonner, they said. They removed the sucker in the end but, after that, I think I did need to lose it all. Give myself a break finally.' He takes another drink of water, before looking back at her and smiling. 'I reckon you're just doing exactly what you need to – giving yourself a break.'

For a random Aussie in the outback, he's really pulled out some deep shit. But he might have actually tapped into something in Jenn, because her shoulders seem to drop, like she's relaxing finally.

And he's right. Jenn never just stopped when we were together, she was always going, going, going.

Like she never felt she was good enough.

Was it because of her dad leaving? Her mum ditching her for Cornwall? I'm no psychologist, no Doctor Fiona Stewart, but from everything I've seen now, I guess that's got to have some sort of lasting effect on a person. Did she think it was her fault?

And then I let her down. I abandoned her too.

Fuck's sake.

Why couldn't I just have made life a little easier for her when I had the chance? Been there for her when she needed me?

Well, I'm here now. And there's got to be other things I can do for her.

'I think you might be right,' she says finally.

He grins. 'Even a stopped clocked is right twice a day,' he grins.

I want to laugh. This guy.

My head starts to pound again.

'Anyway,' he says, like nothing has passed between them. 'I'd better hit the road again. Long way to go.'

He walks over to his backpack, hoists it onto his shoulders, before picking the bike up from the ground. Flinching slightly, he sits on the saddle and lurches back onto the road. Briefly, he looks back over.

'Remember, you're exactly where you need to be right now.'

'Where's that exactly?'

He pushes his hat up. 'Middle of bloody nowhere.'

She laughs as he cycles away, the form of him getting smaller and smaller into the shuddering horizon.

TWENTY-FIVE

2014

JENNY

After securing her bike at the rack, she walks across to the hospital and into the heat of the building. She goes straight to the staff room where she says hi to a few people and makes herself a quick coffee. She always has two coffees before a shift starts. It's probably not great for her, that double hit of caffeine, but there's something about that little rush to the system that really gets her going.

As she sips the hot black liquid, she thinks about how weird it will be next year to leave this place behind – leave Edinburgh behind. She'd been keenly aware of it on her cycle up this morning. As the autumn air had whipped over her face, the Meadows had disappeared in a blur of green and gold to the left, then Bruntsfield, with its old Victorian buildings, cake shops, interior designers, people wrapped up in scarves carrying morning coffees or walking dogs: they'd all whizzed by in a blur of sandy brick and quaint shop signs.

She loves this city, she really does. And perhaps in other circumstances, she might have stayed. But there's nothing to keep her here anymore.

Hopefully it won't be too long before she hears about the Sydney jobs.

Will Duncan still go to Australia too?

She has a flash of the break up, the awful move out the flat eighteen months before. It had been about the worst thing she'd ever experienced. But she'd moved in with a girl who would be starting with her at the hospital, and she'd got her head down. It was easy enough to keep her distance from Duncan in such a big hospital, and she deliberately avoided a lot of the nights out so she wouldn't bump into him too much. If they saw each other it was OK at least. Duncan always smiled, asked how she was. And after a year or so she heard he was seeing a pretty blonde girl in obstetrics called Lizzie. It stung initially, that natural pain of feeling forgotten, but she reprimanded herself quickly; it had been her choice, and it was about time he met someone else. Soon she'd be gone anyway, and all of this would be a distant memory.

The locker room is busy when she goes in and she immediately starts unzipping her thick jacket. It's been ridiculously cold this October but she kind of likes it, the way the air is so fresh suddenly, how the world turns orange and gold.

Casting around for an empty locker she catches a set of familiar wide-set eyes looking at her, a big smile. Hilary. She's only met Hilary a handful of times on the wards since they started their A&E rotation, but she seems friendly, kind, and Jenn has this strange feeling, like she could imagine them being great friends. Shame she's leaving for Australia so soon.

Hilary points at a locker beside her. 'One here, Jenn.'

The name Jenn makes her smile. Hilary just seems to have decided that's her name for some reason and not Jenny. But she doesn't mind, she kind of likes the change, like she's starting a new chapter of her life already.

Maybe she'll go by Jenn in Sydney too.

She walks up to the locker and starts slipping off her jacket, her hat.

'Oh, your hair looks amazing!'

Looking around at Hilary, she touches the feathery ends. She'd forgotten she'd had it cut.

'I got it done yesterday,' she smiles, feeling self-conscious. 'You don't think it's a bit short?'

'No,' Hilary gushes, 'I absolutely love it. Seems very you.'

She doesn't entirely know what *you* means, given they don't know each other that well. But then maybe the 'her' she thinks she is, isn't the one that other people see. She wonders what it would be like to truly see herself from the outside.

What would she think?

'What prompted the change?' Hilary asks, pulling her sandy hair up into a ponytail.

Jenn shrugs, as she starts to get changed into scrubs. 'I dunno, I suppose I started thinking about Oz, how hot it would be,' she says and laughs. 'That's stupid isn't it?'

'Oh, yeah, I forgot you're applying for jobs there,' Hilary says, arms dropping to her sides.

Jenn feels bad for a moment; perhaps it's not just in her head that they have some sort of connection. Of course, she'd made a few friends at the hospital during her two years' training. She went out with them occasionally, grabbed a coffee on days off – but no one she particularly got on with.

'Hey,' Hilary says, as Jenn shuts the locker, secures it. 'Don't suppose you're free tonight at all? It's my birthday and a few of us are heading out. I mean there's nothing exactly exciting about turning twenty-five, I realise. God how old does that sound. Twenty-five!'

She smiles but somehow that age suddenly feels so young, like she's hearing Hilary's words through a funnel, and she's already completely aware just how fast time passes, disappears.

'It was actually my twenty-fifth last week,' Jenn says, after a moment.

'What?' Hilary's eyes widen. 'You never said?'

'I'm not huge on birthdays to be honest. My flatmate made me a cake though.'

'Right, that's it,' Hilary says, clearly horrified, 'you're definitely coming out.'

Jenn smiles, but she's just not sure she's in the mood to go out. Work has just been so stressful recently; so insanely busy. All she wants to do tonight is look up amazing apartments in Sydney with a big mug of tea. She's not in the headspace for boozy Edinburgh bars.

'You know, I've just had so many shifts recently,' she starts, 'and I'm not—'

'Oh, come on,' Hilary smiles, almost hopefully. 'It'll be fun! You're not working tomorrow, are you?'

She feels bad for a moment. Although they're not close, it feels a bit shit of her to say no. Plus, what's she doing tomorrow? Nothing.

She doesn't have to stay out late anyway.

'Alright then,' she nods.

Just as she's turning to leave, she sees something, up on the pinboard. A handwritten note.

And although her heart's racing with confusion, she can't help smiling at it.

'I love you more than anything, Jenn. Have a great day.'

ROBBIE

A bar. Loud, dark. Guinness signs everywhere. Irish. Lots of people and loud cheesy music. The Cowgate. I've been here before, definitely. I'm standing near a table littered with drinks. Jenn and Hilary are beside me with a bunch of girls I recognise from parties and stuff; Deepa and Pippa are here.

It must be late here because it's dark outside and inside's already rowdy. The girls are all shouting over the music at the top of their lungs – The Killers, 'Mr. Brightside.'

Jenn and Hilary start dancing around together and I actually feel happy. No Robbie getting drunk and ruining their night, no cutting her hand on broken glass or shitty awkward hungover lunches at my parents' the next day. She even smiled at my note in the hospital.

At the words I should have told her every fucking day.

But it's still not good enough; not big enough.

I need to do something more.

Hilary dances past me suddenly. She's wearing a giant HAPPY BIRTHDAY! badge.

Hang on.

Hilary's birthday. The Cowgate.

It's not *that* night is it?

But this isn't the bar. It wasn't here.

'I might go outside for a smoke,' Hilary says suddenly. She's a bit unsteady on her feet.

'I'll come with you,' Jenn says quickly.

I follow the two of them outside, lost details leaking back into my head: Hilary stopped smoking not long after I met Jenn. We met on Hilary's birthday.

Out on the cold cobbled street, Hilary pulls a packet from her handbag and lights up.

'I'm glad you came tonight,' she says, after she's taken a drag. 'We never really get a chance to talk in the hospital. You don't go out much, do you?'

Jenn smiles. 'Not a lot, no.'

'You used to date Duncan Anderson, I think?'

Jenn pauses, and Hilary reddens. 'I'm sorry, I shouldn't have mentioned it.'

'Don't worry at all,' Jenn says. 'We broke up ages ago now.'

'Oh, that's a shame.'

'It's fine,' Jenn says, batting it away. 'My choice.'

'God, I wish breaking up was ever my choice,' Hilary says woefully. 'That's sort of why I came here tonight actually. There's this guy I've been seeing recently, said he'd be here. But he's quite clearly not. I never have any luck in that department.'

'Well, he might still show,' Jenn says hopefully, but Hilary doesn't look convinced.

After a moment, Jenn says, 'I heard you got onto the A&E programme for next year. You must be chuffed?'

Hilary glances at her, takes another drag. 'My dad thinks I should be going into something I can make more money at privately. Like orthopaedics.'

They share a look between each other, both start laughing.

Bloody doctor humour.

'You've got to do what you enjoy,' Jenn says. 'Who cares what other people think?'

'I know,' Hilary smiles woozily. 'It's just a bit tricky when your step-siblings are perfect though.'

'Parents divorced?' Jenn asks carefully.

'Yeah,' Hilary says. 'My dad left us when I was little. I've probably got all sorts of man issues because of that, right?'

Jenn smiles a little sadly. 'My dad actually left when I was thirteen,' she says eventually.

Wow. It took me ages to get that stuff out of her.

Or maybe I never tried hard enough.

Hilary looks almost relieved. 'It's shitty isn't it? Everyone else always seems to have these cookie-cutter families, and I feel like some sort of outsider.' She chucks her cigarette on the ground, heels it.

'I get what you mean,' Jenn says.

'You know, it's a real shame you won't be staying here,' Hilary says, through woozy eyes. 'We could have specialised together.'

A couple of guys walk past the bar, and suddenly Hilary clutches at Jenn's arm. 'That's him,' she whispers, then walking forwards she says, loudly, 'Harry!'

One of the guys stops and looks over at her. He smiles and they start chatting together for a bit, but his body language is all off. He's just not interested. Oh Hils, Hils, Hils – back here again.

Eventually the guys walk off again, and Hilary comes back over to Jenn, eyes alight.

'So, they're headed to an Irish bar near here apparently. We should go too?'

Jenn looks uncertain, glances at her phone. 'I guess I could come for a bit,' she says. 'Shall we go tell the others?'

Hilary shakes her head. 'It's fine,' she says urgently, 'I'll drop them a text. Let's just get going now.'

Watching the two girls hurry off along the cobbles, I suddenly can't believe how random life can be. How a guy passing by a bar at an exact point in the night can change the futures of two people forever.

The chances of me and Jenn meeting tonight were so incredibly slim.

But we did meet.

It did happen.

And for some reason I can't understand, given everything I put her through, she's circled right back to it.

To us.

JENNY

Inside the Irish bar she's hit by the warmth after the cold. It's a rammed vaulted space, like they've walked into a stone barrel. Flags from different countries are strung up from wall-to-wall and there're framed sports strips behind the bar. Live music playing from somewhere: fiddles and drums. Everyone's drunk. Everyone's smiling. It's an end-of-the-night sort of place.

Immediately Hilary spots the guy from earlier at the bar and squeezes her hand. 'He's here! Come on.'

She pauses, doesn't know if she has the energy to pretend to flirt with this Harry guy's friend.

'I'm just going to the toilet quickly, OK?' she says.

'Alright,' Hilary smiles, eyes shiny with expectation. 'I'll get you a drink.'

Jenn walks through the crowds, hopeful that by the time she gets back, the others will be here and she can head home.

Before she goes into the toilets, she glances back once just to make sure Hilary has started chatting to Harry. They seem to be speaking at any rate.

Inside the bathroom, she takes a moment in front of the mirror. She's still getting used to the new haircut. It tapers out at her neck, so incredibly short for her, and she keeps feeling for the rest of it still, like a phantom limb.

But it's good. It's different. And if she needs anything in her life right now, it's different.

Because she doesn't want to keep plodding along on the same safe life track, knowing exactly what will happen at every step of the journey.

It felt necessary when she was younger – having a plan and sticking to it – but then she'd missed out on so much too. She wants something more now, to shake her to her core.

To make her feel alive.

TWENTY-SIX

2019

ROBBIE

We're back on the road. Looks different. It's dark, but a dingo sign confirms it's still Australia. Low bushes rush by outside, a stretch of nothing beyond them. The sea. My head's still thumping, but it's lessening now, dimming, along with the image of Jenn in the Irish bar.

Just moments before we met.

I can still remember the taste of her when we kissed in her flat later on, that exhilarated feeling in my chest. I'm not sure anything will really top the feelings I had with her at the start.

She was the best thing that ever happened to me.

Beside me, Jenn makes a gear change and starts fiddling around with an app on her phone. She looks over to the coastal side before slowing the car right down. Everything is murky and it all feels wildly unsafe when she pulls over. There are no other cars. It's so late.

Is she trying to attract danger?

The car stops and Jenn opens the door and gets out. It's so hard to see anything, the only light coming from the moon up above. She darts away, past more low bushes, presumably to pee, and I get out too. The land ahead of me tails away to a huge beach, the ocean beyond it. I can hear the waves crashing, imagine how incredible this place will look in the morning.

She's picked some spot.

When she gets back minutes later, she goes around to the back of the car – gets inside; shuts the door.

Pulling up a blanket, she lies back and closes her eyes. Behind me I hear the roar of the ocean, imagine her walking down onto the beach in the morning.

I have an idea.

My heart leaps, because I've realised what else I can do for her. And even though I can't find her secret, and we may have very little time left on this earth, I still feel happy for a moment.

I just hope this works.

I hope we don't leave this place quite yet.

JENN

Light. A rushing sound. For a moment she feels confused, disorientated and she wonders if she's in still in South America, up a mountain again. She opens her eyes, sees the metallic roof of a car. Western Australia. A beach. She remembers now. And suddenly she's excited, like she was as a little girl and they'd go away to this cottage up on the north-east coast. She'd wake

278

up in the morning to the sound of seagulls, the smell of freshly brewed coffee and knowing the beach was all hers for the day. There was this spiral conch shell in that place, which her mum used to put to her ear when they got there. *Can you hear the sea, Jenny?*

She sits upright.

She gasps.

The car is there somehow, on the beach, like someone has actually reversed it down. The door is open and she can see she's on the firm part of the sand, the waves ahead gently lapping at the shore. *How the hell did I get here?* For a moment she feels panic. Did she sleep drive her car? Did it roll?

She looks up at the sky, how it's a warm gold on the horizon, seeping into pale blue above. The water ahead of her reflects the same, shimmering where the new sun hits it directly, and suddenly this strange peaceful feeling comes over her. She doesn't care how she got to this exact spot on the beach, or the fact that it's probably a little dangerous. Because somehow, she feels safe. And just this once, it's incredible.

Standing up now, she feels the day's heat already settling along the beach, and without even a glance about the expanse around her, she strips off her t-shirt, her shorts, until she's completely bare. She walks across the sand and runs into the surf, the cool water rushing up her legs, her thighs, her belly. Her heart is racing and she shrieks to no one. Sinking down into the salty water, she sees the sky above her, vast and wonderful and she listens to the sound of the sea in her ears.

ROBBIE

A street. A busy street, in a city. A bus is pulling away and Jenn is standing beside me on the curb, checking a map on her phone, totally unaware of me still.

But I feel amazing.

It worked. She woke up to a view of the sea, just like she always wanted: just like Duncan said they'd have one day, and I'm sure he would have got for her, given half a chance.

Watching her splashing around in that water was amazing – getting to see how happy it made her. If this is what she remembers at the end, I think she'll have some joy at least.

This is what it's about.

This is all it's about.

Jenn starts to walk off and I follow. Where are we?

I feel like I've been here before.

A luggage tag hangs off her now dusty-looking backpack: Sydney. September. She's been here for four months now.

And that also means we're edging closer to November – when we get in the car.

Only two months to go.

Shit.

But it's OK. We keep going back into her past too. Which means there's still time. We have time.

Hot sun breaks from the clouds and I squint up into it. It's weird because I always assumed winter was a bit shit in Sydney. We pass a line of twisted, odd-looking trees. Fuck, I'd forgotten about the city trees. I remember when I first arrived in Sydney with Marty how bizarre I'd found them. Like I'd gone into upside-down land.

People with blurry faces are walking about with their morning coffees, suits on, off to work. Jenn glances at a girl cycling by in leggings and trainers, backpack on; how Jenn would look going into the hospital. She watches the girl go a moment too long.

Was she starting to miss her job?

Crossing a busy street alongside her, we head into a bog-standard café. She orders a black coffee at the bar and a pastry before sitting down at one of the long benches at the front.

I bet if I were here, I would have insisted on finding some artisan place, where they weigh out the granules one by one.

Jenn was always far too forgiving of my bratty shit.

Unlike my dad.

I think back to his seventieth birthday in September. My parents had been planning it for ages – caterers, marquees, bands, the whole package. It practically felt like a fucking wedding by the time it came along. All the family had been invited, loads of my parents' friends too.

It had been one of those Indian summer evenings and I'd been out in the garden drinking champagne with Liv. She'd started talking about holidays, asking if I wanted to go on a long weekend to Rome. And all of a sudden, I just felt really claustrophobic. We'd been loosely seeing each other for about six months by then but I was happy with it being just that: loose.

Rome had felt romantic.

I tried to make an excuse about the restaurant or something and she got mad – accused me of leading her on.

She disappeared into the house not long after so I got drunk by myself. I was pissed off with everything. Work was going nowhere, Liv was annoyed at me, and I was starting to realise I was still in love with a girl who had vanished off the face of the earth.

By the time I got into the marquee, the party was already in full swing.

And I was leathered.

I vaguely recall Kirsty and Fi trying to get me outside again. But that had pissed me off even more. I could feel Mum and Dad's pretentious friends looking at me, judging me. All any of them cared about was appearances; all my dad cared about was appearances.

Or at least that's what I thought before. Perhaps he just didn't want an arse for a son.

I started dancing, but I couldn't see straight. I think I might have tried to do an arm spin with someone, but the next thing I knew I was flying off to the side and straight into the band. I remember yelling, cymbals crashing, hard wooden floor beneath my face.

Silence.

For a moment I just lay there until someone hauled me up. And Dad was just standing there, his face puce.

I knew I'd done it this time.

Last chance saloon.

'Get out,' he'd said quietly.

And this time when I'd left, no one had come after me.

No one had come to check.

The clink of a spoon. Jenn takes a sip of her coffee beside me. Just as well I never got to go travelling with her really.

All I ever seem to do is fuck everything up, ruin everyone's day because I'm too bloody selfish to think about how my actions might affect other people

She pulls her phone out of her satchel, starts typing a message. She pauses, deletes most of it, starts typing it again. *Who is she messaging?* I lean over to read it. I can't quite see what it says, but I can see who it's going to.

Duncan.

JENN

Walking up the driveway, she sees traces of sand in between the neatly placed grey stonework, tropical plants to the side of manicured grass. And there in front of her, is his house. Big, but not in a showy way. White stone and windows seemingly everywhere. She looks out for the sight of him at one of them, feels her heart beating in her chest and wonders again if this was the right decision – coming to see him after all this time.

But it had felt weird being in Sydney and not at least texting to say hi; the last thing she wants is to make him feel like she never cared at all. They went through so much together: school, university, and everything in between.

She should have known he'd suggest catching up – being anything other than polite would be weird for him, unless he'd had a personality transplant in Australia. And she hadn't felt too bad imposing; after all, she'd heard on the grapevine that he'd split up with Lizzie about a year before. They'd ended up going to Australia together, instead of him and Jenn.

And for just a moment, she'd imagined if she'd come here five years ago. If she'd never met Robbie, and never fallen in love, and never had all those wonderful moments together.

Never felt the pain of losing them all.

Just as she reaches the wood-panelled door, it opens. And there he is: the same pale blue eyes, white blond hair and wide smile she'd known at twenty-three. She can't believe that was seven years ago now, and for the strangest moment, it feels like mere seconds. But his physique alone tells her this is a very different time. He's sun-kissed, broader, like he's filled out his soft lines; grown into who he was becoming.

'Jenny,' he says and grins so widely she can't help doing the same.

He reaches out to hug her and she remembers the clean scent of him, like washing powder and toothpaste. His sturdy arms fold around her, strong and supportive.

'How are you?' he says. 'What's it been?'

'A while,' she smiles, and they pause like that for a brief moment.

'Well, come in,' he says suddenly, and stands aside to let her by. Walking into the cool, airy space, she sucks in her breath. It's stunning. The room is huge and open plan, all white floors and white walls. There's a pristine looking kitchen to one side and an enormous L-shaped sofa in the living area at the back. It should be clinical but, somehow, it's not. It feels light and peaceful – like him.

Tropical foliage outside the floor-to-ceiling windows at the far end of the room makes it very private. Has she just stepped into some sort of dream house?

'Duncan,' she says finally, looking up from a shelf of medical books. 'This place is incredible.'

'I'm not going to lie, I kind of like it too,' he says. He looks so at ease here, hands in his navy shorts pockets, and she can totally picture him at night, reading his books, the sound of the sea somewhere nearby. *With someone?*

She feels bad for a moment. She should never have just assumed he hadn't started dating someone else. Her waltzing in here could be an imposition. But looking around the place, at the severe lack of extra bits and pieces, she feels instinctively it's not. Plus, he would have mentioned that when she texted. She knows he would have: there's not a deceptive bone in his body.

'Tea?' he asks. 'Or wine? It's the afternoon now,' he smiles.

'Yes, actually,' she says after a moment. 'A wine would be lovely.'

'Great, take a seat,' he says, indicating at an expensive-looking glass table, and moving into the kitchen. 'Still a white drinker?'

He remembers. 'Yes, white would be great, thanks.'

As she sits down, he goes to open the fridge and she gets a glimpse of greens and neatly stacked Tupperware boxes: healthy, clean living. She thinks of hers and Robbie's fridge back in Edinburgh, the messy, colourful shelves. The rows of beers.

Duncan pulls the only bottle she can see out, and goes over to another closed panel white cabinet. Inside is a large array of expensive-looking glassware. He takes down two long-stemmed white wine glasses and sets them on the side. Unscrewing the cap, he pours in the pale-yellow liquid and takes them across to her at the table.

'Bit of a change from the wobbly one,' he says, taking a seat across from her.

Her brain triggers, a memory sparking and expanding suddenly: the coaster under the table leg. 'Oh, I'd totally forgotten about that,' she says and laughs. 'Please tell me you got rid of that table.'

He passes her a glass.

'Well, I will admit, a few things may have been chucked during the move out of there.'

'Surely not the cat pictures?'

He nods solemnly. 'They'd had their time.'

She laughs again and a strange silence falls between them. They're talking about the home they shared for five years.

'Well,' he says after a moment, and clears his throat. 'Cheers.' He raises his glass to hers. 'Lovely to see you again, Jenny.'

'Cheers,' she says back, and clinks her glass lightly to his. She takes a sip. It's crisp and floral – *bloody perfect*, Robbie would say.

Stop it.

She doesn't know why her mind keeps coming back to Robbie, here in this place with Duncan.

'You OK?' Duncan asks, and she looks over to see him watching her carefully.

She doesn't immediately answer.

'I heard what you did,' he says, after a pause. 'Leaving work and everything. I wanted to message to check you were OK, but I wasn't sure . . .'

She grips the stem a little tighter, knowing how easily she could just pour everything out to him. And he would listen, he would understand. He would make her feel better.

But looking at his sun-kissed face, in his gorgeous home, in this perfect new life he's built for himself, she knows that this is no longer his concern. She's nobody's concern but her own.

'I just needed a little time out,' she says eventually and tries to smile convincingly.

He pauses, as though waiting for her to say something else, and when she doesn't, he nods.

'Yeah, I get that sometimes. It would be nice to disappear for a while.'

'And take a break from all this?' she says, glancing about.

'Well, you've still not seen the best bit.'

'There's more?'

'Come on,' he says, and inclines his head at the floating staircase to the side. 'And bring your wine,' he smiles.

Curious, she follows him up the white steps. Light from a huge window floods in on her as she goes, and she sees another big white house next door, tall trees. Turning left on the landing, he heads into an enormous bedroom, with more panelled white and a gigantic bed at the back. Glass doors stretch from one side of the room to the other.

Sliding them open, he walks out onto the balcony and she heads out after him. The clouds still hang heavy in the sky, rolling and tumbling on a breeze, but it doesn't detract from the sight in front of her: the sea, vast and grey, only one line of houses away.

'It's not quite a beach house,' he says quietly after a moment, leaning his elbows onto the stainless-steel railing.

'But it's a sea view,' she almost whispers.

Her dream.

Their dream.

He turns to her and, for a moment, she thinks he might be about to say something serious; something she just can't handle right now. Then, like the clouds above them, his face changes – he smiles. 'So, have you been to any of the sights yet?'

She feels herself breathing out.

'Not really, I mean, I went on a guided bus tour today, which lasted about ten hours, but I'm not sure if that counts.'

He laughs, a deep rumbling noise.

'Well, as it happens, I've got the next few days off,' he says. 'I'd be happy to be an unofficial tour guide if you'd like . . . ' He pauses. 'And you're more than welcome to stay here? In the spare room I mean.'

She feels surprised. She wasn't angling for an invitation by any stretch. But then, the hotel in town is pretty soulless; it would be so nice to stay in an actual home again for a bit. Somewhere solid after all her travels.

And it's been so long since they broke up. They're just two friends, surely, catching up for old time's sake.

'Are you sure?' she says eventually.

He smiles. 'Definitely, no point you paying money for some overpriced hotel. We can drive to get your stuff soon. I've only had a sip,' he says, indicating at his glass.

'Well, thanks,' she says. 'Thanks so much.'

'No problem . . . flat mate.'

Her stomach flips. *The cinema, that summer.*

Why is it always him who's there for her when she needs it?

She turns back to Duncan, to the solid form of him against the darkening clouds, and smiles.

The next few days are brilliant with him as a tour guide. Predictably organised, he has them up and out to see the city early in the mornings after a plate of eggs and avocado, or porridge. She laughs when he produced the packet of oats from a cupboard the first morning – *you can take the boy out of Scotland*, she says and he smiles at her, chops up some apple to put on the top.

The weather's a bit shit really, rain and a bit chilly, but she doesn't mind. It almost feels like home again in a way. Duncan deftly navigates their way through the city's sights, the Opera House, the Bridge – they don't actually bother going up it – a trip to Manly, a trip to The Rocks; she loves the funny little houses, the young history of it all. The city's so fresh and new still. Even the ghost tour they do one evening is hilarious, the alleged dates of the deaths ridiculously recent. But she's OK with that. She likes leaving the really terrifying ghosts back home.

In the late evenings, they hang out at Duncan's, watching movies on his enormous flat screen or just reading books quietly together. He makes her a tea and then, at the end of the night she goes to the spare room upstairs, aware that he's just there on the other side of the wall.

The lights of the city shimmer across the dark water now as they walk along the harbour. People sit in bars, sipping drinks and finishing dinners as they pass, while across the water, office and apartment blocks twinkle against the night sky. Just ahead of them, a brightly lit Ferris wheel turns round and round. She still can't get over the sheer scale of everything in this city, how the buildings seem taller, the lights seem brighter and everything is what she dreamed about when she was younger – and more.

As they walk along quietly together, it almost feels like they'd never split up. Like all those years in between never actually happened, and now they're just a normal couple, walking along Darling Harbour on their way back from a dinner out. It feels odd; surreal even.

'So, what do you think you'll do?' Duncan asks suddenly, stopping in front of the railing. Jenn stops too, looks up at him.

'What do you mean?'

He smiles, hands in pockets.

'You're thinking about moving here still, right?'

Dear Duncan. He knows her so well still, can see every part of her. And he's right. She is thinking about it again. Perhaps that's what she was doing when she left Edinburgh, following her nose until she literally landed in the place she'd always wanted to be.

She nods slowly.

'Thought as much,' he says.

She pauses, the enormity of it all settling into her; this dream of hers from years ago finally coming true.

'But I haven't actually considered it all properly,' she says, and moves across to the railing, leans out over the glittering water. 'I have no idea what I'd do about work,' she says quietly. 'I sort of fucked it up a bit when I left.'

Duncan comes and stands next to her, leans his elbows on the railing. 'You'll figure out a way to sort it. You always do.'

'I'd need to do my final year back in the UK.'

'Australia can wait a year.' She hears him pause, breath in. 'I can wait a year.'

Looking around at him sharply, she realises she's not actually surprised by what he's said. She'd tried to pretend the looks he gave her were just friendly, that the care he offered her was purely platonic. But now she knows for sure; her instincts were on point. And hasn't she had a great time too? Wasn't everything basically perfect? No fights, no arguments. Just plain sailing.

Robbie. His face flashes across her mind – his eyes, the freckles on his shoulders, the touch of his hands on her, hysterical laughter under covers. A feeling like nothing else. Her heart jolts painfully.

She has the strongest sense of him suddenly, like she can actually feel his physical presence near them.

'Look,' Duncan says, when she doesn't immediately speak. He takes her hand. 'I'm not saying it will work out. But all I do know is I'd like to give it another shot. I think we're good together, you and me. I've thought that ever since I drew that hideous portrait of you at school,' he smiles.

She laughs then. 'You remember that?'

'Sure,' he says quietly, 'I remember everything.'

She wants to say something, but she just isn't sure what. She feels so very loved suddenly. It feels good.

Before she can reply, there's a rumble in her handbag.

'Sorry,' she says, smiling at him, 'I'd better check that.'

He nods. 'That's alright, take your time.'

As she pulls her phone out of her bag, she knows he's not just talking about her messages. Pressing the screen on, she sees there's a message. It's from her mum, with just one line.

We need to talk.

ROBBIE

Standing beside them on the Harbour, I see the lights on the Ferris wheel starting to flash.

I've been so fucking blind.

This whole time I've believed the secret was the bloody letter, when she never said anything about a letter. I saw what I wanted to see as usual, put two and two together and got twenty.

But I know what her secret is now: she's going to Australia to be with Duncan. That's what she was trying to tell me in the car. That's what she was so panicked about.

That night we had together before this whole thing started was perfect. But that was it – a perfect goodbye.

She's shown me all my failings, all my flaws, shown me everything Duncan can give her instead.

I get it now.

My throat catches, chest crushes inwards.

I know what else I need to do for her.

I need to save her, but not for me. I need to save her so she can have the life she always dreamed of; the life she deserves, with him.

Turning back to her, I see the way she's smiling up at Duncan, her eyes focused on him so intently.

'I've figured it out,' I say and she flinches, turns. She glances around wildly, but I don't care right now.

'If you live, you can go to him,' I say breathlessly. 'I won't stop you. I just want you to be happy, even if that's not with me.'

'Robbie,' she whispers, her face contorted with fear, and something else.

'Jenn,' Duncan says, reaching out for her shoulder, 'are you OK?'

The people passing along the harbour become hazy. The orange lights of the Ferris wheel go faster, like some sort of acid trip and I shut my eyes, ready myself for motion.

Ready myself to drive.

TWENTY-SEVEN

2014

JENN

The orange leaves above her head flutter as she walks, sunlight glinting at her through the row of trees lining the path. The Meadows is already filled with people jogging, walking or playing football – their skin red raw from the chill. Over to the right, Arthur's Seat rears up into the white sky. She pulls her blue coat tighter and wonders if he's there yet.

Images of the other night at the Irish bar flash into her mind again, his brown eyes sparkling as he'd talked, his hand in hers – she could feel the callouses from working in kitchens for years. And then that kiss on her sofa later on. It was like nothing she'd experienced before, that feeling of free falling with someone she'd only just met; an electric current which went through her whole body. She'd never felt so alive, and she wondered if perhaps he might be it; that person who changes everything.

They didn't sleep together in the end, even though she wanted to. *Oh god, she'd wanted to.* It just seemed too fast, too rash, when she didn't even know him yet; didn't know if she'd even see him again. But she had a feeling she would, she could sense it deep in her gut, like something she knew innately. Perhaps he knew that too, because he didn't push it, didn't press it. And she liked that. They just lay in her bed kissing, talking, then kissing again, until dawn light crept through her curtains. Then finally they fell asleep in each other's arms.

The next morning, as he put on his coat, he'd said, *when can I see you again?*

So impulsive and enthusiastic. She'd laughed, said she was on nights the following week, but maybe Sunday brunch the next day would work.

Her heart thuds now as she walks up the tarmac of Meadows walk, until she reaches the glass-fronted shop. The tables bustle with adults and children. She can't immediately see him, but perhaps he's at the back. She checks her watch – right on time. Going inside, she looks around properly, waiting to spy that mop of dark hair, that cheeky smile looking up at her. But he's not here yet.

Is he running late? She checks her phone for a message – nothing. Odd. He'd been texting for most of yesterday, their messages pinging back and forth like he just couldn't stop. But then they did, in the evening at some point, when he went out again with some friends. She didn't know how he had the energy to go out for the second night in a row; not after they'd been up all night. But she liked that attitude he had, that slightly reckless air about him, like everything he did was for the moment. She feels excited just thinking about him.

She orders a black coffee and takes it over to a table near a window. As she sips it, she checks her phone. Still nothing. On the other side of the glass people are ambling by, cycling, dog walking. She feels around for a book in her satchel, but she doesn't have one, didn't think to bring one today.

Where is he?

She drinks her coffee slowly. Of course he'll come.

What if he's standing her up?

She places her cup down. Maybe he does this with girls. Maybe she made that incredible feeling all up in her mind. What was she doing getting all worked up like that about a guy she just met? She doesn't even know him.

She watches people walk in, the same people walk out.

Thirty minutes.

He's not coming.

There's just a trace of coffee lying cold now in her cup, and she slugs it down, puts on her jacket before heading back out into the cold. Lots of life admin to do today before her night shifts start. Better get on with it.

This is so shit. I really liked him.

Just as she starts walking back down Meadows Walk, she sees a flash of green; she stops breathing for a moment as a familiar figure pelts up from the Meadows – messy hair, puffer jacket.

Eventually he comes to a halt in front of her.

'I'm so sorry,' he says, breathing hard.

He looks rough, like he's had a big night again. She feels annoyed and delighted in equal measures.

'You could have messaged,' she says, keeping her voice steady.

'Well, I lost my phone and my wallet in a club last night and I just . . . ' he says, then stops, takes a breath.

'The thing is,' he says, 'I'm not very good at this.'

'This?'

'Dating stuff. I've never actually had a relationship before.'

She pauses. Maybe she didn't imagine that feeling between them.

'Well, no one's forcing you,' she says.

'Yeah, I know,' he nods. 'But I do really like you, and I'm sorry for being late today. I promise I won't do it again, if you'll give me another chance some other time. This week maybe?'

'I can't,' she says, and he looks immediately crestfallen.

'I'm on night shifts for most of it,' she explains after a moment.

His eyes light up again, and her heart sings quietly.

'Well, next weekend then? We could make a day of it.' He clicks his fingers like he's thought of something brilliant. 'We could go to Camera Obscura, that illusion place on the Royal Mile. Ever been there?'

'No,' she smiles, fighting down a bubble of laughter.

'So, will you come?'

She really wants to. 'I'll think about it.'

He grins. 'It will be a great day, I promise.'

'Well,' she says, after a moment, 'I've really got to get going.' She hooks her satchel back up on her shoulder.

'Can I walk you back?' he says, a hopeful look on his face.

She's wants him to, but she doesn't want him to know that, yet.

But it's just a walk. It doesn't mean she'll definitely meet him next weekend.

'Alright,' she says eventually.

She sets off towards the Meadows, and after a moment she feels him step into pace behind her. He slips his hand into hers. Just like that, like it's the most natural thing in the world. And it does feel natural.

It feels like breathing.

ROBBIE

What's happening? Why am I back here again in her past? Where's the car?

I figured it out. The secret was Duncan.

I watch my younger self walk away with her, swinging her hand like he hasn't got a care in the world, and I want to shout at him to hold onto her, to never let go of her.

My head starts to thump again, stronger than before. I'm going somewhere. The trees around me are fading out. It's getting dark.

Please let it be the car. Please let us get away.

The outlines of Robbie and Jenn walking together go fuzzy, then disappear.

TWENTY-EIGHT

2019

ROBBIE

Darkness.

Motion.

A feeling of moving through time and space.

My head feels heavy with the pain. It hurts. Where am I? I blink around. Dashboard, windscreen, radio. I'm in a car. It's moving.

I can move. My hands, my feet.

Fuck, yes! It worked; we're driving away from the truck. We're alive. She's alive. It's all going to be OK. I hear the comforting rumble of the engine, other cars passing by. My heart is still beating so fast. *Jesus Christ.*

Got to drive, Robbie. Got to concentrate. Can't crash now. I feel for the steering wheel, pedals. Not there. *What the—*

My eyes focus. A kaleidoscope twisting. I'm in the passenger seat, but Jenn was in the passenger seat before? Jenn's driving – that doesn't make any sense. It's night time though, that's right.

Countryside. Hang on, this isn't Edinburgh.

A sign we pass says Carbis Bay.

Cornwall.

Fuck!

I thump my hand against the window beside me hard. Jenn looks across briefly, hearing the noise. She turns back to the road, eyebrows furrowed.

I hold my head in my hands. I can't believe this. I figured her secret out.

Didn't I?

A dull niggle starts in my gut, works its way up. The night she left Edinburgh so suddenly – that was before she went travelling. Before she saw Duncan in Australia. Before he suggested anything to her about moving to be with him.

I tip my head back against the car seat and shut my eyes. My stomach sinks. I feel like I'm back to square one. It's like when I played Snakes and Ladders with Fi and Kirsty when I was younger. I'd think I was winning and then *bam*. Kicked down to the bottom again.

Whatever made Jenn come to the restaurant that night had nothing to do with Duncan. Or Liv. This is still all about that fucking letter she read. The letter she burnt.

That's where her secret died.

I feel desperate; close my eyes briefly, because I have nothing and no one to help me figure out how to fix this.

It's just me, and me alone.

Lights flicker and I open my eyes again. Houses outside. We're in the town. Jenn turns up a road. It's hilly. We drive along for a while, turning here and there until finally we slow to a stop. She peers out her window to the lights of a little cottage set back from the road.

I look out the other side, tip my head against the cool glass. What the hell am I going to do?

What the hell are you going to do now, Robbie?

JENN

There it is. The cottage her mum rented. It's so *her*, with its old traditional stonework and haphazard windows. A clapboard galley bit protrudes out from the ground floor, next to which is a weather-beaten garden table and chairs.

No more caravan.

She gets out the car and breathes in the fresh night air once again. It was a relief coming out of Newquay airport earlier, into the almost immediate wildness of the Cornish roads. Heathrow had been jarring and soulless after the long-haul flight back.

As she walks up the cobbled garden path, she sees hanging baskets at the door, plant boxes on a window and, for a moment, she feels like it could almost be their old home back in Edinburgh. She stops, breathes it all in for a moment.

A noise ahead of her. Her mum appears suddenly at the top of the path in a floral dress and too-big cardigan. She looks uncertain, then smiles widely.

'Jenny,' she says, enveloping her in a hug.

She can feel her mum's thin arms around her even under the scratchy wool; that scent from childhood: sweet perfume, paint and hairspray. She breathes it in briefly, before pulling back.

'You're here,' her mum says, gripping on to her hands still.

'I am,' Jenn says, but something is different about her mum. Something she can't put her finger on.

'Well, come in.'

Inside she's met with exposed brick and low beams. An old table sits at the centre, covered in papers and paint pots, a green Aga is nestled at the back, and a dresser packed full of random plates and cups stands at the side.

'Tea?' her mum asks, tucking her greying red hair behind one ear.

'Yes, thanks,' Jenn says, still glancing about. 'The place is great, by the way.'

'I'm glad you like it,' her mum says, going to put the kettle on. 'Just take a seat.'

Jenn sits down at the kitchen table, feeling a twinge of recognition. She looks at it closely, the swirls in the wood. *This was ours in Larchfield.*

'When did you move in?' she asks.

'Oh, a couple of years ago now,' her mum says without looking up. She moves around with quick, bird-like movements, her thin hands wrenching open a tea jar, before she puts two teabags into mismatched mugs. 'It was good because I could finally pull our things out of storage. I wanted to surprise you with it the next time you came.'

Has it been that long?

She's about to say sorry for not having come to stay earlier, when she stops herself. It's time to give herself a break. She can't keep being the adult in their relationship. She's the one who's visited after all. Again.

As though sensing her thoughts, her mum turns to look at her. 'I'm so glad you've come . . . and I'm sorry I haven't been up to Edinburgh recently.'

Jenn traces a dent in the table with her eyes. *Mum made that dent when I was little.* 'Well, I've been away travelling in fairness,' she says, looking up.

Her mum pours hot water into the mugs, before looking across, an almost determined look on her face. 'Yes, I want to hear all about it. I really hope you can stay for a bit, Jenny. There are things to say.'

They talk for the next hour or so, her mum lighting candles around the room and putting out bread and olives to keep them going before dinner. As Jenn plucks one of the glistening olives from an earthen bowl, she thinks how odd it is that her mum has actually thought to buy this stuff. It's so . . . prepared.

Jenn relays all her travel stories to her – like a normal person would with a parent when they get back from abroad. She tells her mum about the Botero artwork in Medellín, the National Gallery in Melbourne, and her mum eventually shows her a couple of pictures from her recent exhibition: she's been doing quite well apparently, selling lots of paintings of Cornish scenery.

That's how she met Frank, about a year ago now. He came into the gallery one day, and the two of them got chatting. He's from the area, the owner of a small hotel, a widower. They'd started going out for dinners once or twice a week, slowly at first, until a few months ago he finally asked if she wanted to meet his kids – now all grown up and both living in London. Jenn can't help feeling a tinge of regret, hearing about them all having dinners here in the heat of summer and visiting beaches together. It's everything she wanted when she was younger, but her mum's doing it years later. With another family.

Her mum goes on to tell her Frank is looking after her admin now so she can paint more, and Jenn smiles ruefully to herself at that. Her mum has clearly come a long way, making decent money and renting a proper house, but perhaps some things are too much to change in a person.

'So, what was the other thing you wanted to talk about?' Jenn says eventually. She thinks about the text she got at Darling Harbour, that plea for Jenn to go back to the UK.

Her mum's face falters.

'Why don't we talk about that another day,' she says, and before Jenn can respond, she continues, 'let's just enjoy this evening.'

ROBBIE

I'm sitting on the sofa in the kitchen, head in my hands. I've been wracking my brain since we got here, trying to think what that letter could possibly have said. If there's some sort of copy out there.

Don't be stupid, Robbie.

She must have burnt it for good reason.

Sizzling in the background. Someone's cooking. But it doesn't matter who. It doesn't matter what. The chatter between them goes in and out my ears because I need to figure out what to do now. I need to figure out how to save her. I close my eyes, try to steer through the fog of my mind.

TWENTY-NINE

2019

JENN

She wakes to the smell of coffee and bacon and blinks around
the little bedroom. Jam jars of seashells sit on the window
sill and her mum's paintings of Cornwall float all around the
violet walls, above the wooden dresser and behind the rocking
chair. There's even a little one of Edinburgh Castle. A proper
spare room.

For me?

Throwing on an old dressing gown from the back of the door,
she heads down the stairs into the kitchen. Her mum is already
at the Aga, scraping overdone scrambled eggs, bacon, sausages
and French toast onto two plates.

'Morning,' her mum says, glancing up from the steam. She
looks frantic. 'I just thought I'd cook up a few things in case
you're hungry.'

'Thanks,' Jenn smiles and takes a seat at the table, before
pouring herself a cup of strong looking coffee. Her mum brings

the mountainous plates over and sets one in front of her. It feels weird. They never did anything like this in Edinburgh. Her mum pokes at her own plateful for a moment as though she's not quite sure what she cooked herself.

'So,' she says eventually, placing her fork down. 'What would you like to do today?'

'I don't know yet.' Jenn forks a mound of eggs and ponders the question. 'I hear the coastal route to St Ives is nice. But you just do what you need to. Don't mind me.'

Her mum looks sad for a moment, the lines by her eyes deeper grooves now. 'I'd like to go with you today, if that's OK?'

She feels surprised. 'You don't need to do your art?'

'No.' Her mum shakes her head and smiles. 'No, I don't need to do my art.'

'OK,' she nods after a moment. 'OK.'

The weather has turned even cooler than the day before, she realises as they stride along the path. It's flanked by shrubbery, growing high and wild, and overhung by trees, which spill out from one side. She can smell the salt in the air, damp earth and greenery. She wishes she could bottle it all.

'I can't believe you still have that,' her mum says, and Jenn turns to her see her pointing down at her satchel.

Looking down briefly, she touches the cool leather, which once belonged to her dad. 'It's stood the test of time, hasn't it?'

Her mum says nothing for a moment, and she hears the scuff of their feet on the pathway, the cry of a gull in the sky.

'Some things last longer than others, I suppose,' her mum says finally.

Images of the letter appears in Jenn's mind suddenly, and her throat catches. Guilt bubbles up from inside. She opens her mouth to speak, then stops herself.

Not yet. Not now.

'Look,' her mum says and points over to the side. With some relief, Jenn follows her finger across.

And there between the treescape, where the foliage scrabbles steeply down to the white sands, is St Ives. The water is dotted with the odd surfer still, the headland wrapped around the grey water, white buildings speckled along it, and she lets her mind stretch out to them, leaving the dark thoughts behind, once again.

Walking around the harbour, they eventually find a café to sit at with tables outside. Across the water, little boats and buoys bob around in the breeze, while people wander up and down the beach. As her mum goes to order inside, she feels her phone buzzing in her bag and pulls it out. Hilary.

Hen party starting at two on Saturday. You going to make it?

It feels so bizarre suddenly, the idea of actually being back in Edinburgh again, and in just a few days' time. Being at Hilary's big day, like she never left. But she did leave, and although they managed to speak over the phone a couple of times when she was in Oz, things weren't quite the same; she could feel herself holding back, and she could tell Hilary was confused by it.

She thumbs in a quick response now though – that she'll definitely be there, wouldn't miss it. She feels bad enough as it is that she wasn't around to help plan it all. She's the maid of honour after all.

'Here we are, darling,' her mum says, carrying two shaky-looking cups and saucers. Her multi-coloured scarf drifts in the breeze behind her and her cheeks are pink from the walk – *Cornwall suits her.*

Setting them down on the table, they sit in silence for a few amicable minutes, drinking their tea and taking in the harbour. She wonders again what her mum wanted to speak to her about, thinks about raising it, but she got the impression last night that she was in no rush. And if she knows anything, it's that forcing the truth out of someone isn't helpful.

It needs to come in their own time, when they're ready.

'So,' her mum says, after a moment. 'What are we going to do on Wednesday?'

She shrugs, smiles. 'We don't need to do anything special. It's just another birthday.'

'No, it's not,' her mum smiles. 'It's your thirtieth.'

THIRTY

2019

ROBBIE

Green Aga. Messy table. Grey light coming in the windows. The scent of coffee and baking. I'm standing in the middle of her mum's kitchen again. Jenn's reading on the sofa. In the corner of the kitchen, her mum's working away at something.

I feel a little better now after the enforced walk to St Ives, a bit less frantic, which is good. Mum was right – fresh air is good for the soul. We used to go on these big rambles in the countryside when I was a kid. We'd pick blackberries and raspberries, and then make some sort of pie with them at home – with the ones I hadn't eaten already.

It feels weird thinking about normal stuff like that right now, stuff I might never get to do again. I don't really think I ever really appreciated it all before, those little ordinary moments with the people I love.

A clatter in the kitchen, and Marian walks proudly across with some sort of tiered cake monstrosity. It's leaning precariously to the side, purple icing dripping onto the board.

Jenn's thirtieth.

October 17*th*.

How the hell didn't I notice it was October? I think back through the recent places: the darker nights, the thicker jackets. Shit, how out of it was I?

My heart beats quicker. This means she probably had a whole month in between Darling Harbour and here that I didn't see.

I don't know why, but there's something about this particular time jump which throws me.

What was she doing all that time?

She was with Duncan, you idiot.

I force down the lump in my throat. It's a good thing she was. She'd have been happy at least.

Jenn turns a page of her book and I look across at her, at the way her eyes are focused on the words as she's chewing her nail absently. She squints slightly as light from the window shines in her eyes. *Is it annoying her?* I go over to the curtains and twitch them forwards just a little. She smiles.

Sitting down next to her, I think about where my other self would be right now. I remember waking up today in Edinburgh feeling weirdly agitated. I kept wondering if I should send her a birthday message; wondered if she even wanted me to.

In the end, I think pride got the best of me. I decided if she wanted contact, then that was up to her. Looking back now, it seems pathetic and childish. Why didn't I just rise above it all? How hard would it have been to send a simple *Happy Birthday*?

Her phone starts going on the table and Jenn looks up sharply, shoots up to check it. She smiles and picks it up.

'Hey, Duncan,' she says.

Of course.

A pain in my chest.

'Oh, thank you,' she's saying, 'it must be so late for you . . . yes, I'm all good. Just hanging out for a few days with Mum still.'

She wanders off down the hall, still talking away to him, but it's like it all goes mute again. Her mouth is moving but I can't hear it.

Like everything with her and Duncan, this conversation is just between them.

A knock on the door.

'That will be Frank,' Marian calls, interrupting the silence. Jenn looks up, before making audible goodbyes to Duncan. Marian walks hurriedly across to the front door and flurries her fingers at the locks. After a few tuts and sighs, she finally opens the door to reveal a man on the step. He's quite short, but trim. Smart looking, with red hair like Marian. I stifle a laugh.

'Hello, hello,' he says and embraces Marian warmly before giving her a kiss.

'And you must be Jenn,' he smiles widely, turning to her. 'Happy birthday.' He gives her a kiss on each cheek before holding out a silver bag to her. 'I hope it's OK,' he says, as Jenn takes it. 'I asked my daughter what to get and she said I couldn't go wrong with candles.'

'Oh, thanks so much,' Jenn says, genuine surprise on her face. 'That's so kind.'

Marian looks up at him adoringly, and I'm sure I see a look of sadness pass across Jenn's face. It must have been hard for her, I suppose, watching her mum move on with someone new, feeling like she'd forgotten about all those happy early years as a family.

The thing is, though, I remember the photo of Jenn's mum and dad, and nothing here would even come close to the look they gave each other. Marian won't have forgotten it. But she has clearly found something else in her life now, something solid and real. And while that might not be the great love she once had with Jenn's dad, it's a different kind of love. One that's made her pretty happy from the looks of it, and I can't help thinking how much it's like the love which Duncan and Jenn shared; how it would be far better – far less traumatic – for her to have that type of love in her life once again.

'Well,' her mum says after a moment. 'Cake?'

A few minutes later and they're around the table, with the Leaning Tower of Pisa creation at its centre, a fire hazard of candles across the top of it. It's nice to see Marian trying for once but she really is shit at baking. I guess Jenn seems happy with it, so that's all that matters right now. I'd probably have gotten too drunk if we were still together – ruined it.

This is better.

Marian and Frank do a tuneless rendition of 'Happy Birthday' together, and I sing softly under my breath so I don't freak Jenn out. At the end, Marian looks across at her.

'Make it a good one,' she says quietly, and Jenn leans forwards, before blowing them all out.

JENN

Salty wind billows into her face and cold sunlight gleams in her eyes before she closes them for a moment. Somewhere nearby her mum is combing the beach for shells, and she hears the occasional plunk of one into her bucket.

She knows she'll have to tell her what's going on eventually, but just for today – her birthday – she wants to enjoy the moment, feel every bit of joy she can. From her mum's hilarious attempt at baking, to the pretty seascape she painted for her, to being on this beautiful beach in this deserted cove in Cornwall, this day has been perfect.

Almost.

She checks her phone again; her stomach sinks. Still nothing from Robbie. She really thought he might get in touch on this day, her thirtieth. After all the years they spent together. After all the memories they shared.

It's probably for the best.

But does he ever think of her? He's not with Liv anymore, she knows – Hilary mentioned that had all come crashing down in the summer.

She shakes her head. Why is she even thinking about this? He betrayed her trust, let her down when she needed him most. And that's not what she needs in her life right now. It's pointless dwelling on him.

'Jenny,' she hears her mum calling, and she turns around, smiles at the small figure off in the distance. Her mum is beckoning to her across the empty beach, and she heads towards her.

Something in the sand makes her stop.

Writing.

Her spine tingles.

Happy Birthday Jenn x.

ROBBIE

A garden. Her mum's garden. The sun is overcast now, and Marian is digging in a flower bed, an oversized jacket on. Frank's? Jenn's at the little garden table reading another battered-looking book. I'm starting to realise that the memories from her past have stopped – at the point we got together. At the point the two timelines merged.

Time is only moving forwards now.

And we're only weeks away from getting in the car.

Do something.

But what else can I do? I have no idea what the secret is, or how to find it.

In front of me, Jenn turns a page, and something falls out onto the table. It's square, pink. She picks it up, eyebrows furrowed, then gasps and puts her hand up to her mouth.

Her mum looks up from the flower bed, shields her eyes with her gloved hand. 'Jenny, are you OK?'

But Jenn doesn't speak. A tear falls down her face.

What's happened?

'Jenny,' her mum says again, more worried sounding this time. She lifts herself quickly up from the ground and walks over.

'Jenny, I—'

Her mum stops, looks down.

Then I see it too. Looks like one of those old-fashioned library cards. I peer closer. A name.

David Clark.

All the stuff from storage – Marian must have kept his books.

'Jenny, I'm sorry,' she says, wide eyed. 'I didn't know that was there.' She tries to take it quickly from the table, but Jenn grabs it.

'No,' she says. 'No, I want to keep it.'

'Why?' Marian asks, looking confused. 'It's just an upsetting reminder.'

Jenn closes her eyes for a moment. 'Because,' she starts, 'because—'

Because what?

'Jenny, there's something I have to talk to you about,' her mum cuts in, and Jenn's eyes snap open. Like a train of thought has been severed.

What was she going to say?

Jenn looks at her curiously, face blotchy.

Marian stands still as a statue, like she's scared to move. 'It's about your dad, about when he left.'

'What about it?'

Slowly, Marian moves over to the seat opposite Jenn and sits down on it. She looks up at the cottage for a moment, before looking back down at Jenn and sighing.

'You see,' she says eventually, 'I didn't tell you everything, I'm afraid.'

Jenn's face is rigid, unreadable. 'What do you mean?'

Marian falters, and I realise this is it, the thing Marian texted Jenn about at Darling Harbour.

'Well,' she starts slowly, 'your father didn't actually leave us with nothing.'

A look of surprise passes across Jenn's face. 'I don't under-stand,' she says.

Marian shifts position, her face suddenly pale and drawn.

'It was maybe a week after he left,' she says, 'I had a look at our bank account, to check what we had left, and there was suddenly this big lump of money there.'

'Money?' Jenn says, 'but we didn't have any?'

Marian takes a breath in. 'We did actually, at the start.'

'From Dad,' Jenn says, more like a statement than a question. There's something odd in her expression.

'I think so, yes. It can't have been anyone else.'

'What happened to it?' Jenn says steadily.

Her mum hesitates. 'I was just so sad back then, Jenny,' she says, 'I wasn't in my right mind.'

Jenn takes a deep breath. 'Mum, what did you do with the money?'

Marian's face crumples. 'I went to this independent financial advisor to understand what to do with it. He told me that if I invested it all in this fund thing that we could double it. I was just so sad; I didn't think it through. I thought I was helping us. But the thing was, after I sent over the money to him, he just disappeared. I tried to track him down, but he completely vanished. I wanted to tell you, but you were young at the time so—'

'So you just let me believe that Dad didn't care about us. About me,' Jenn says.

'Jenny, I'm sorry,' Marian says, moving her hand towards Jenn's. 'This is all just so hard to bring up again. After what he did . . . '

Jenn pulls her hand away. 'I have to go out for a bit,' she says and stands up quickly.

Marian's crying now. 'Jenny, I—'

'I need some time,' Jenn says, almost to the air.

She turns and walks down to the gate. I follow after her.

I just can't believe what her mum's just told her. I'd have gone nuts if that had been me; being lied to all these years, and by her own mother. All this time, Jenn thought her dad walked out without even a look back. But that wasn't the case. He cared enough to make sure they were OK.

It doesn't make any sense.

Jenn walks around the area for a while, along streets which look out over the bay, the crashing waves, down steep hilly bits where she almost has to trot like a mountain goat. A sea shower comes and goes, soaking us both. But I keep with her all the way.

Eventually, we end up back where we started. Her mum is still sitting in the garden, and she looks up sharply when Jenn walks up the path; stands.

'Jenny,' she says as her daughter comes towards her. 'I'm so sorry, really. I should have told you before now, it's just time went on and it became so hard to say anything.'

Jenn comes to a standstill.

'No,' she says firmly. 'Hard was my dad walking out without any explanation at thirteen. Hard was looking after my mother alongside everything else too. Hard was working two jobs while I was at school so that you could keep doing your art. And then you just left. You left me.'

Her mum looks taken aback. I'm not surprised – Jenn never speaks like this.

'We still saw each other, Jenny.'

'Only because I made it happen,' Jenn says. 'Do you know how unloved that made me feel? That you couldn't be bothered to come and see me.'

'It wasn't like that,' Marian says, shaking her head.

'Well tell me what it was like then?'

Her mum opens her mouth to speak, but says nothing.

Jenn nods, like something's been confirmed to her. 'I'd better get my stuff together now. Remember, I'm leaving for the airport in an hour.'

She walks towards the kitchen door.

'Don't go,' I say.

Immediately her eyes snap back, look right through me and I freeze. She looks so panicked. *Idiot*. I know not to do that. I know not to speak to her. But I couldn't help it. I wanted her to keep talking.

Because I've had an idea.

319

JENN

Her backpack appears on the carousel and she moves in between people so she can grab it. In one swift movement, she hauls it up and onto her back. Turning to the grey sky out the huge windows of the airport, she takes in a deep breath. This is it. Edinburgh again.

Heading towards Arrivals, she smiles at the familiar sound of Scottish accents. But as she walks through the doors and sees the people standing on the other side, mothers, fathers, siblings, friends, she feels her stomach sink a little: no person here for her. No Robbie standing there, grinning widely at her.

She's being silly really – Hilary would have come if she wasn't working today. And anyway, she doesn't need anyone to take care of her. She's quite capable.

Plus, there's something important she needs to do before she leaves the airport.

Walking quickly, she heads towards the coffee shop they'd confirmed by email a few days before. It's colder up here already, even in the airport, and she crosses her arms over her jacket. She bought it in Cornwall, at a shop in St Ives with her mum, but she suspects very much that it's built more for English winters.

Mum. She feels bad about how they left things, but for once in her life, she doesn't feel the same sort of desperate urge to fix it. She can forgive her mum for making an error with the money, but not for keeping that sort of information from her. For so much of her life, she believed her dad didn't even care.

Walking into the chain shop, she finds an empty table. Wiping a little spilt sugar to the side of the wood, she takes a nervous breath in. Should she go and get the coffees now or wait? After all, the order might have changed by now. In the end, she decides to just get them – two black Americanos – because despite their many differences, some things about them were always just the same.

Just as she sits down at the table, she catches sight of a figure rushing towards her. Chunky boots, short skirt, sparkly tights and bomber jacket.

The two of them clock each other at the same time, and grin.

Katy.

'Jenny,' she cries and immediately reaches in to double kiss her in the French way. She smells of rich perfume. 'Oh my god, it's so good to see you.'

'It's so good to see you too,' Jenn says, her heart immediately swelling.

Katy sits down, looks at the coffee in front of her and grins. 'This for me, I take it?'

'It is indeed.'

'*Merci beaucoup.*'

As Katy takes a smiling sip, she knows instinctively that this was the right decision, reaching out to her old friend at the end of her trip. Turns out they were both coming in on a flight the same morning, Katy from Paris, Jenn from Cornwall, and it just seemed almost fateful to meet at the airport. No point leaving it until another time, when it might not happen.

After all, contacting Duncan had been a great decision too, and perhaps it's never too late to make that first move.

Try while you still can.

'How have you been?' Katy says, glancing curiously at her backpack. 'Or should I say, *where* have you been?'

'Oh, just various places.'

Katy raises one eyebrow and Jenn can't help smiling. *If she only knew.*

'Do you need to get away soon, or have you got some time?'

Katy's eyes immediately light up and she smiles. 'Yeah,' she nods. 'Yeah. I've got time.'

An hour later and Jenn's grinning so hard her face hurts.

'That's my kind of sea swim,' Katy says, and laughs. 'Oh, Jenny.'

'And the worst part was, everyone knew the next morning. It was so horribly obvious. I went trekking as soon as I could.' She half covers her face with her hand.

'I think I'd have happily taken some breakfast embarrassment for a little Juan time,' Katy winks, her eyelashes fluttering with glitter.

'You *would* think that,' she says, lowering her hand and the two of them grin at each other.

She takes the last sip of her coffee and thinks how easy it's been seeing Katy again, like they'd never been apart. It's funny how it's like that with some people. They've covered pretty much everything over the last ten years: from Katy's failed career in art, replaced by a step into the wine industry (she can just picture Katy, waltzing around vineyards at the weekend and at Parisian dinners through the week) to Jenn's recent break from medicine and her travels abroad.

And she could see it in Katy's eyes, this look that said, *you did it*.

There's a short silence, then both of them speak at the same time.

'I'm sorry about—' Jenn starts.

'About that time—' Katy finishes.

They both laugh.

'I'm sorry for saying what I said,' Jenn finishes finally, 'I think I was just taking my problems out on you, and that wasn't fair.'

Katy shrugs. 'That's what people do sometimes with the people closest to them though, isn't it? I knew that really ... but you were right about me too. I was totally privileged and irresponsible back then.'

Jenn shakes her head. 'God no, I should never have said that.'

'No,' Katy says firmly. 'I really was. I was spoilt, and clueless about money and work and actually being an adult. Probably still am, if you ask my parents. But ... I'm learning,' she smiles. Then adds, with one eyebrow raised, 'Maybe when I'm ninety I'll get the hang of it?'

Jenn smiles and sighs, imagining the two of them when they're old and wrinkly. Maybe still in touch, maybe not, but at least she knows now that it will be on good terms.

At the taxi rank a few minutes later, Katy turns to her.

'Please let me know if you're ever in Paris,' she says, a sincere look in her eyes. 'I'll show you the sights.'

'Of course,' she replies, whilst already knowing somewhere inside herself, it will probably never happen.

At that moment, two taxis pull up.

'You going to Edinburgh?' Jenn asks, 'we could always share?'

'No, actually, I meant to say, my parents moved across the bridge to Fife.' Katy points a finger in a random direction. 'More space for their dogs apparently.'

Jenn nods, smiles.

And so it is.

'God, it's been great seeing you,' Katy smiles, and Jenn can see on her face that she really means that.

'Say hi to your mum for me,' Jenn calls, as Katy hops inside her taxi with her fancy wheelie case.

'I will, *mon amie*.' Katy grins, pausing for a brief moment, before she shuts the door and the taxi drives off.

As the black cab disappears, Jenn smiles to herself, thinking of all the memories they shared together as kids, hanging out for hours in Katy's room listening to music, chatting about boys and eating ice creams on Cramond beach. She loved her like a sister, still does in a way. Katy was there for her at a difficult point in her life, and she'll never forget it; never forget that close bond she had with her. But perhaps not all types of love are supposed to last forever.

Sometimes, you just end up going in different directions.

'You ready?' the man in the other taxi shouts.

'One minute,' she says and looks down for her bag.

It's not there. She frowns, looks up at the driver.

'It's in here already, hen.'

What?

Confused, she heads over to the car and gets inside. Just as the driver said, the bag is sitting there propped up against the seat. The engine gears up, and they start to move out and away.

Back to Edinburgh.

Back to him.

THIRTY-ONE

Two weeks before

ROBBIE

Flowers. Warmth. Chatter. A room with high ceilings and bay windows – a private room. Somewhere in town from the looks of it. Women are standing around a long table filled with flowers and greenery and ribbons. They're all making wreath things and drinking champagne.

Jenn's here, sticking berries into her own creation. She's wearing a fitted green dress – so formal for her after all the travelling around, but she looks so pretty. My stomach flips.

Hilary's beside her in a tight sparkly number as usual, a silvery sash across her saying 'Bride to Be.'

It's her hen party.

Two weeks before the wedding.

Two weeks before the car.

Shit.

But we might be in just the right place. It all seems so obvious now, how I'll find out her secret and stop this shared-death experience. I may have been wrong about it being Duncan, but I was right about one thing: I was blinded by the letter. Because the secret didn't burn with it.

It's still in Jenn's head.

And even if she didn't tell her mum what it is, she's surely going to tell Hilary, her best friend; the person she shares everything hard with. Jenn might not have told her anything while she was away, but that's what it was always like. Hilary didn't stand a chance from the other side of the world.

I walk around to where Jenn and Hilary are standing, try to listen in over the din. If they get drunk at this thing, then something's bound to come out.

'How's everyone getting on?' a voice calls from the top of the table. A smartly dressed woman is looking around. The organiser I presume. The girls all nod away and smile, keep drinking. A young waitress is going around topping up all the glasses and handing out fancy canapés. Everyone's faces are crystal clear here I've realised too – I guess because this all happened so recently.

Jenn looks across at Hilary. 'This was a great idea, who thought of it?'

'Oh, Deepa and Pippa,' Hilary says, without looking up. She fiddles with some berries in her creation.

'Well, they've done a great job of everything,' Jenn says.

'Yes, they've been brilliant bridesmaids.'

Ouch. That undertone. What's up with her?

Jenn pauses. 'Well, I'll speak to them tonight and see what I can help with over the next two weeks. I'm totally free before I start up work again.'

'You're starting work again?' Hilary says, turning to her finally. Her eyes look a little softer.

'Yes, and I wanted to speak to you about that actually.'

Hilary looks at her expectantly.

'You see,' Jenn says slowly, 'my first day back is the day after your wedding. But don't worry, I'll be at the whole thing,' she says quickly, seeing Hilary's alarmed expression.

Hilary turns back to her wreath, prods at it. 'It's fine. I get it honestly.'

'You sure?'

'Yeah,' Hilary says quickly. 'I'm a doctor too, you know. I know how it works.'

The two girls go silent again, as the happy chatter carries on all around them.

Shit, this is not good. I need them to be talking normally – getting drunk and spilling information. But even though they're standing right next to each other, it feels like they're still worlds apart.

JENN

The dinner goes well, at yet another fancy private room in town. It's all dark oak interiors and white table clothes. Everyone only paid a moderate amount towards the hen costs so she suspects Marty's injected money somewhere. Waiters fawn over them all evening and, at the end, the Maître d' surprises them with custom-made cocktails, ordered in by the groom, of course.

Deepa and Pippa have organised everything perfectly, as she suspected they would in her stead. But as she sips the sweetly alcoholic liquid (aptly named Hilary's hen-tail) she can't help feeling a bit unnecessary, like perhaps no one needed her to come back at all. She imagined her and Hilary having this drunken, fun reunion tonight, but she's been giving her the cold shoulder all day.

Is it because I wasn't here to help with anything?

It dawns on her that perhaps she's been so consumed with escaping her own life, she's forgotten about other peoples'.

The party games start up next, slickly done like everything else. They kick off with a game of Mr and Mrs: Deepa asks Hilary questions with Marty giving his pre-recorded responses over a flat screen at the side of the room. His answers are all insanely sweet, and funny too, but she's surprised to see Hilary looking stiff throughout, a forced smile on her face. It's odd because Jenn always imagined this would be such a happy time for Hilary. She'd spent the whole of her twenties dating idiots and now she's about to marry the perfect guy for her and she's just subdued.

Has something happened with Marty?

After the meal, the group head off to a slightly rowdier bar, finally. It's dark and sticky and the music is pumping – *this is more like it*, she thinks. More like the places she and Hilary used to drink in when they were younger. It sort of reminds Jenn of the first time they went out together five years ago.

The night she met Robbie.

Someone passes her another drink and she takes a sip, tries not to think of him. But it doesn't go down well. *I'm so tired.* It's late and all the travelling has taken its toll on her. Is her body clock still on Sydney time somehow?

Her stomach plummets.

Duncan. Australia. The truth.

She really needs to speak to Hilary about it all. But not tonight. It's her hen after all, and anyway, she's not entirely convinced Hilary's OK.

She looks around the group to check where she is; they're all drinking away at the bar, a couple of them are dancing nearby already, but she can't see Hilary.

Where has she gone?

Suddenly she sees a shimmer of pink heading out the door. Putting down her drink, she walks quickly after her.

Outside, she spots Hilary standing at the side, cigarette in hand.

'There you are,' Jenn says, wrapping her arms about herself. It's freezing.

Hilary smiles, like she's been caught out. 'I know, I know,' she says, indicating at the cigarette. 'I quit.'

'No judgement,' Jenn says. 'It's your hen night.'

Hilary takes another drag, her hand shaking slightly.

'Is anything wrong?' Jenn says finally, hesitantly. Hilary doesn't reply immediately. 'I'm really sorry I haven't been here to help with the wedding planning,' she adds.

Hilary blows smoke into the night air. 'It's not that,' she says quietly.

'Then what is it?'

Hilary takes a breath in, turns to her. 'You just took off, Jenn.' she says. 'It wasn't just Robbie you left with no explanation. I appreciated the travel updates and everything, but you shut me out. You're supposed to be my best friend, my maid of honour, and I felt like you'd just abandoned me.'

She doesn't say anything for a moment. 'I'm sorry,' she says, 'I'm sorry for leaving you without saying anything.'

'It's OK,' Hilary says finally. 'I'm just glad you're back now. I've really missed you.'

'I've missed you too,' Jenn says, relief flooding over her.

'So, why did you go?' Hilary asks levelly.

She wants so badly to tell her what's happening. *If I just said it.*

But no.

She can't overshadow Hilary's hen night.

'Things with Robbie had just gotten difficult,' she says finally, 'and you know work was insane. It just all got too much. I needed some time.'

As soon as the lie comes out, she knows she wants to tell Hilary the truth, but she's already taking another drag of the cigarette, a distracted look on her face.

Just as she opens her mouth to tell her what's really going on, a guy comes out of the bar and stops in front of Hilary.

'Mind if I bum a smoke?'

Jenn assumes she'll say no, stub her cigarette out and continue speaking to her.

But instead she says, 'Sure.' Hilary flicks her packet open and takes out two.

What's she doing?

Jenn hovers, uncertain what to do.

'Don't worry, I'll see you back inside,' Hilary says easily.

It's then that she notices the 'Bride to Be' sash has gone. 'You sure?'

'Totally sure,' Hilary says, 'I'll catch you in a bit.'

After a final torn moment, she finally heads back in. Looking back through the door at her friend blatantly flirting with a stranger off the street, she knows her instincts were correct – something's definitely going on with her and Marty.

And right before the wedding.

ROBBIE

Standing beside Hilary and that guy, I hold my head in my hands. *Fuck.* Jenn didn't tell her. And she was so close, I know it. I could see it on her face. Something was about to come out.

Why couldn't Hilary see she was trying to tell her something?

Then again, she hasn't even really pushed Jenn on what happened with us at the end; how I blew it. And I think it's pretty obvious Jenn is holding something back, like she tends to do.

I never told anyone what happened that night in the restaurant either, come to think of it, not even Marty. At the time, I think

I told myself there was nothing to tell, but now I can see what was really happening.

Deep down, I was ashamed.

The pink of Hilary's dress starts to blur into the orange tip of her cigarette. I'm fading, but not before I glance one final time at Hilary.

What the hell is she doing?

She's about to marry the best guy in the world, and she's blowing it.

Just like me.

THIRTY-TWO

One week before

JENN

'How many hearts have you got now, Wendy?' she asks across the checked table cloth. At the other side, Marty's mum silently counts the row in front of her, peering through her glasses as she does so.

'That's another ten, dear.' Marty's mum smiles, looking up. 'We're almost done. Bravo.'

Jenn looks down at her own work: little stuffed hearts made of world-map material.

Things weren't quite so organised with the wedding as she'd been led to believe at the hen. But she was glad to find herself useful again, running between the cake maker and the wedding-dress shop. Then when she clocked the table favours had still not been made, Marty's mum had immediately come to the rescue with her crafting skills, inviting Jenn over to their enormous house for the last few days to work on them. Hilary's mum, on the other hand, has proved pretty useless with the wedding preparation, spending most of her time moaning to

Hilary, or whoever's around, about how stressful it will be seeing Hilary's dad there. Jenn's tried to shield Hilary from the worst of it, but there hasn't been much she can actually do.

She hopes it doesn't throw Hilary.

'They're a sweet idea,' Wendy says, examining one of the hearts, 'but I still don't totally understand them.'

'I think Hilary's implying they mean the world to each other.'

'That's nice,' Wendy says, a bemused expression on her face. 'We just did sugared almonds in my day.'

Jenn smiles, glances up at the clock. She'll need to leave shortly if she's going to meet Hilary on time.

Something's still not right with her. Thinking back to the hen night, she goes over it again in her mind: nothing happened in the end with that guy, thank god. Hilary just drank too much and then passed out in Jenn's bed. She tried talking about it with her the next day, but she just pretended like everything was normal, a bright smile plastered across her face. So, what's going on?

Does she actually want to get married?

'Would you like another tea, dear?'

She looks up at Marty's mum sharply. 'Oh, no thanks. I'd better go meet Hilary in town soon. But I'll come by tomorrow to take these to the venue.'

'Oh, lovely. Are you two out for dinner?'

'Yes, it's kind of a belated thirtieth birthday meal for the both of us.'

As she gets up to put her coat on, she glances at the photos of the family on the sideboard: a spectrum of Marty and who she assumes is his younger brother, Jamie: in swimming pools and on beaches as kids; fishing with their dad as teenagers; at a rugby match more recently. They're a good-looking pair of boys.

One photo in the corner catches her eye, and she can't help picking it up.

Dark messy hair, sparkly brown eyes.

Her Robbie. But a kid version of him, with one arm around Marty. She feels herself smiling.

'He was a cheeky wee thing, Robbie,' Marty's mum says, appearing alongside Jenn.

'Oh, sorry,' Jenn says, placing the photo down again. Her cheeks feel hot.

'Don't be silly,' Marty's mum says, picking it back up, 'photos are supposed to be looked at.'

Jenn smiles.

Marty's mum nods at the photo. 'I remember when Chris was fourteen, he broke his leg badly playing rugby. Robbie visited him every day in the hospital for months.'

'I didn't know that,' Jenn says softly, feeling her heart swell a little. That sounds like her Robbie; the real Robbie from the start. Loving, loyal.

'Yes. But he just needs to stop falling into drum kits now,' Wendy says, a bit more briskly.

Drum kits?

'Sorry?' she asks.

'Don't you worry about that, dear,' Wendy says, 'as long as he gets a haircut for the wedding photos, I'll be happy.'

She feels curious, but suspects Marty's mum isn't really the gossiping type. Still, she wonders if Robbie's OK. *Has he been struggling without me?* She quickly dismisses the thought. She hasn't heard from him for a long time now; he probably doesn't even think of her anymore. And even if he did, so much time has passed. So much has happened.

Things are different now.

She hasn't heard from her mum since Cornwall either – but then, she didn't really expect to after what happened. Although she can't deny she had an unexpectedly lovely trip for the most part, she's starting to accept that some things may never change. Her mum may never step up the way she needs her to, not like she suspects Wendy would, but she can't change that. All she can change is herself, and for once in her life, she's not going to do the heavy lifting between them.

With a last glance at the photo, she says her goodbyes to Wendy and heads off into the night.

Glancing around the bar-cum-restaurant, she sees Hilary waving from a back table. As she weaves between the other diners, she thinks how long it's been since she was in this place. It was one of her and Robbie's go-tos back in the day: great music, awesome food and a buzzy feel to it. Just being in here gives her a little pop of happiness. She can practically see a faint image of them over on the sofas, him telling her some stupid story and her doubled over laughing.

She thought they'd be like that forever.

'I can't believe you're late,' Hilary says with disbelief, as she sits down and starts unravelling scarves from her neck. 'Is this new *Travel Jenn*?'

'No,' she says and laughs. 'Just sorting some wedding stuff with Wendy.'

'Oh god,' Hilary says, her face falling, 'I'm sorry for all the hassle.'

'Don't be silly. It's your wedding. Anyway, I kind of think Wendy likes getting involved.'

Hilary takes a big gulp of her wine. 'Well, thanks for that. I do really appreciate it.'

'No problem.'

She's about to ask how everything's going when the waiter comes over to take their order.

After he's gone, Hilary turns to her, a meaningful look on her face. 'So, have you bumped into him yet?'

'Who?' Jenn says, knowing full well who Hilary means.

'Oh, don't give me that,' she says. 'I wish you'd just tell me what actually happened between you two at the end.'

'I told you,' she says, feeling a knot form in her stomach. 'It wasn't working between us anymore.'

Hilary rolls her eyes. 'Not buying it. You guys were mad about each other. Anyway, at least he's not with that awful *Liv* anymore,' Hilary says, saying the name like it's an offensive term.

Jenn feels her stomach turn over at the idea of the two of them together, but then she sighs. 'She's not awful, honestly. She's just young and fun.'

'You're young and fun too,' Hilary says.

'Sort of,' she agrees slowly. 'But I think I was too caught up with working hard all the time. I never really stopped to enjoy the moment.'

Hilary looks sad for a split second and then opens her mouth to speak. But then her eyes alight on something at the bar. 'Bollocks,' she says.

'What is it?' Jenn turns to where she's looking.

She stops breathing.

It's him.

Robbie, with Marty, at the bar.

They've got their backs to her and Hilary. She takes in the familiar broadness of his shoulders and mop of hair.

'I'm going to kill Marty,' Hilary says suddenly and Jenn turns to look her, heart still pumping.

'What are you talking about?' Jenn asks, momentarily distracted from her own shock.

'I told him we might be coming here tonight. I can't believe he's brought Robbie.'

'Maybe he just forgot,' Jenn says, blood rushing to her head.

But Hilary doesn't seem to hear, and two seconds later she's up and over to the bar. The boys look around with surprise and Hilary starts speaking really quickly to Marty with a lot of gesturing.

Robbie looks over and their eyes connect. His mouth parts slightly like he's seen a ghost.

She turns quickly back to the table, unsure what to do. This is the first time she's seen him in almost nine months.

Since she saw him with Liv.

Her heart is thumping in her chest, and she prepares herself mentally to speak to him. A few seconds later and she looks up to see him standing beside the table with his pint.

'Mind if I sit down?' he asks, pointing to Hilary's seat.

'Go for it.' She nods.

Sitting across from her, she can see he's nervous too and, for a moment, she feels bad for him. She left the country without even saying goodbye to him.

But he kissed Liv. This isn't my fault. I deserve more than what he gave me.

'How have you been?' he asks.

'Good. You?'

'Yes, good,' he says, and nods.

They look at each other.

'This is so bloody awkward,' he says finally, and pulls a hand over his face.

She can't help smiling. It really is awkward. Her heart is still thumping wildly.

'Why did you do it?' he says after a moment. 'Why did you leave?'

'Robbie, I . . . ' she starts, feeling herself being pulled in by his brown eyes.

Liv, the restaurant, that kiss.

Torturous images flash into her mind and, for a moment, she wants to shout at him, tell him exactly why she left that night.

But what's the point? She can't ever let herself get back with him anyway.

Not now.

His eyes are focused on hers and he looks so pained.

'I've missed you so much, Jenn.'

He reaches for her hand, squeezes it twice. It sends tingles up her arm, across her body.

Those words – it's so good to hear.

She's missed him too.

But at the end of the day, they're just words. Not actions, and they were struggling long before Liv. How can he not see that?

'I can't do this,' she says, pulling her hand away. Opening her wallet, she takes out some cash and puts it on the table for the food. Tears well up behind her eyes.

'You're leaving?' he says, a look of surprise on his face.

She stands up and takes her coat from the back of the chair.

'Yes, Robbie,' she says as steadily as she can. 'I'm leaving.'

'Oh great,' she hears him call as she moves away from the table, tears starting to fall. 'Just walk out on me. Again.'

ROBBIE

Jenn disappears out the door. *That idiot.*

Incredible. After everything he put her through, then kissing Liv in the restaurant, how can he say that to her?

How can he not see what a shit he's been?

Uncommitted, self-absorbed, selfish.

He should have gone after her, told her he was sorry for everything and he'd been a dick. But he doesn't – he just sits there looking lost.

I run to the door, out the bar and onto the pavement. It's dark outside, busy. I look left, right. I see her – away down the street. She turns a corner onto the Royal Mile and I sprint as fast I can. She's all alone and upset. Even if she can't see me, even if I can't speak to her, I need to be with her right now.

I pass newsagents and bars, feel the cold whip of wind in my face. Rounding onto the Mile, I scan the cobbled area for her, bar entrances, cathedral, monument. Where's she gone?

She was just here.

Fuck.

Lost her.

Wandering down the street, I wonder where she went, what was going through her mind. Why am I still even in this memory if she's gone?

I come to a stop finally at a monument and sit down on the stone edge at the base of it. I let the wind chill me, sink right into my bones. Looking across at the warmly lit bars, I see hazy figures behind the glass; a blurry couple leaning in for a kiss.

We always loved the Royal Mile. It was one of our places. We had a few of them dotted around the city: places we laughed, places we fought, places we kissed – had sex. Places which haunted me after she left Edinburgh. I avoided coming this way for weeks. Somehow memories seemed to have a way of lingering in the cobbles, or a café we went to once to get out of the rain, the bar we were just in around the corner.

Maybe people never truly leave that way.

I think about what happened in the bar after she'd gone. I'd walked back over to Marty, just as Hilary stormed off in the direction of the toilets. He'd looked pale, stressed. He asked me what had just happened with Jenn and I just remember being so frustrated with the whole fucking thing. I took another drink and told him that Jenn clearly had no interest in speaking to me. He went quiet for a long moment after that, before he said the strangest thing.

'I used to be jealous of you guys.'

I felt totally thrown. Marty was the one with the fancy job, and the fancy flat. He was the one with the perfect relationship. When I asked him what he was on about, he explained that it was obvious we were crazy about each other from the first time he saw us together at my Christmas party years ago – he said not everyone gets that type of relationship. 'What about Hils?' I said, and he just smiled at me sadly. Said he loved her with all his heart, but something about me and Jenn was just 'magic', and that I'd regret it if I didn't at least try.

I had felt something like hope grow in me then, but it had quickly faded. I just couldn't see what I could do. I'd been too humiliated, too proud to go after her.

'Fucking tool,' I mutter to myself now on the monument.

I hear an intake of breath.

'Robbie?'

Oh my god.

It's her.

Where is she?

'Jenn?' I say, in disbelief.

'I don't want to see you right now, OK?'

Her voice is coming from the other side of the monument. It's thick and muffled like she's been crying.

But I don't understand.

She's speaking to me.

She's not freaked out.

Because she wouldn't be able to see Robbie anyway – the monument's between us.

Shit.

How did I never even think of this? She's been able to hear my voice all along. It's just she can't see me. Right now, she thinks I'm him – my other self in the memories. She thinks he's followed her here.

My heart is racing.

'Jenn,' I say again.

She doesn't reply. *Maybe I've got it wrong?*

'I just wanted to check if you're OK,' I say quickly.

A pause. Then I hear a sniff from the other side, a shuffling sound.

'I'm OK,' she says finally. 'Thanks for asking.'

Holy shit, I'm speaking to her. Oh god, I wish I could hold her, comfort her properly. But I know what I have to do – and quickly.

'Jenn,' I say and inhale. Exhale. 'Why did you leave Edinburgh?'

'Robbie, I said I can't do this.'

'But I need you to, Jenn. I can't explain right now but it's so important,' I say, 'and I know it's not just because of Liv.'

I hear her intake another breath.

'How did you . . . '

'It doesn't matter, I'm so sorry about her. I'm so, so sorry for putting you through that. But I never loved her, I love you. Please, Jenn, just tell me what really happened that night.'

My heart is thumping. *Please tell me, or we'll die.*

There's a long pause, and for a moment I wonder if she's disappeared somehow. Gone again.

'Let's chat,' she says eventually.

Yes, yes, yes!

'I'm coming around.'

No!

'Just chat to me from where you are,' I say quickly. 'Right there is good.'

'No,' she says, and I hear the tread of shoes on the cobbles.

Appearing out of the shadows, her face is still blotchy with tears, but her eyes are alight with something else – something like hope.

I can't stand this.

Can't handle that I've made her feel like shit, yet again.

But all I can do is watch her as she looks about herself, searching the area for the man she was just speaking to. Her lips part, eyelashes flutter in confusion. 'Robbie?'

I'm here Jenn, I want to cry out, moving quickly towards her, *I'm right here.*

I'm so close I could touch her, so close I could just wipe that last tear from her cheek.

But I can't.

I need to focus on finding a way to speak to her again – finish that conversation.

Because she was about to tell me the truth.

And it's our only hope.

THIRTY-THREE

The day before

ROBBIE

Chandelier. Marble floors. Mahogany check-in desk. People buzzing by.

Where am I?

I look around. A giant Christmas tree almost touches the ceiling – *ridiculous putting decorations up in November*, Marty had said.

A sign nearby says *The McFly-Davidson* wedding.

We've jumped.

This is Marty and Hilary's wedding day.

The day before we get in the car.

I can't breathe suddenly. We're almost out of memories and this so-called shared-death experience will surely finish soon. I have to find a way to speak to her again. It has to be somewhere my other self already is, so that it's plausible, but in a place he wouldn't be visible.

Where is she?

347

A figure in purple appears from the back of the foyer – Jenn. She walks towards me. She looks amazing, like some sort of Roman goddess, with the silky material pulled over one shoulder and white and gold flowers in her hair.

She stops in front of the desk and the older man behind it immediately looks up and smiles politely.

'Hi,' she smiles back, 'I just wanted to check if the celebrant had arrived yet? She said she was running late. Ice on the roads apparently.'

The man checks something with the girl beside him, and I look around the foyer again.

Where the fuck is Robbie anyway?

'Yes, don't worry,' the man says eventually. I turn back to him. 'She arrived about five minutes ago. She's just setting up now.'

'OK, great,' Jenn says, clearly relieved. She starts to walk away and I follow. My mind whirls with possibilities. Could I speak to her over a phone somehow? Whose would I use? But the computer didn't work, so why would a phone? Another monument then. But why the hell would that happen again? And will she even speak to me again after what just happened on the Royal Mile?

Shit, shit, think, Robbie.

'Jenn,' a voice says loudly, and we both turn to see a woman all in mint with short sandy hair and wide-set eyes behind her. Hilary's mum. She's wringing her hands, expression pinched.

'Hi Sue,' Jenn says, 'everything OK?'

'Not really.'

'What's wrong?'

'It's Hilary,' Sue says. 'She's refusing to get ready.'

Jenn's face furrows. 'But I just saw her. She was just getting her makeup done with the other bridesmaids.'

Sue shakes her head. 'She asked them all to leave.'

What the hell?

'It's OK,' Jenn says, laying a hand on Sue's. 'I'll go and speak to her.'

'Would you?' Sue says hopefully, visible relief across her face. 'I just don't understand what's going on with her. Her father will go mad if he hears about this.'

'It will all be fine,' Jenn smiles encouragingly.

A few minutes later and we're in the lift together going up. It feels so odd to be so close to her; if I spoke, she would hear me. If I touched her she would feel it. It would be so easy to do. But no. I can't risk anything now, I have to do this the right way. This is about saving her now.

Fuck what I want.

The lift finally comes to a stop and the doors slide open, before I tail out behind her. Walking along the plush corridor, I hear a familiar noise – the other Robbie laughing – and Jenn pauses for the briefest of moments outside the closed door. His door. Marty and the other Robbie are in there right now, having a whisky, getting ready for the ceremony.

Shit, how do I make this work? Could she think he was speaking to her from the other side of the door?

Get a fucking grip. Why would he do that?

Jenn sighs, moves on anyway, down to the next section of the floor.

I just need to think of something else.

We round a corner. *What's this?* A trickle of concerned-looking women line the wall down from the bridal suite: the other two bridesmaids in matching silky dressing gowns and a couple of women with hair brushes and makeup in hand.

Hilary's mum was right. Marty certainly didn't say anything about this though. *Did he even know?*

Suddenly his pale face in the bar the other night makes sense. He and Hilary were having issues.

And I didn't even notice; too wrapped up in my own shit as usual.

The bridesmaids pounce on Jenn as she arrives.

'We don't know what to do,' Deepa says.

'She won't come out,' Pippa adds.

'Just leave it with me,' Jenn says calmly and knocks on the door. 'Hilary,' she calls. 'It's me.'

A long pause. Eventually I hear padding across carpet, metal scraping. The door opens and Jenn slips inside before I squeeze in behind her.

Hilary looks nuts. She's in a white towelling robe and her hair's all sticking up at odd angles. Only one eye has makeup on it and there are black smudges beneath like she's been crying.

'What's going on?' Jenn says softly and takes her hands.

Hilary grabs a Champagne from a table and takes a long swig, shakes her head like she doesn't want to speak.

I think about the night before. Hilary had been totally fine then, or had she? It certainly wouldn't be the first time I missed something. I play it back: the wedding party got together for a fancy Italian in town, fine. But then Marty's brother had gotten a bit too drunk and mouthy, and Hilary's dad had never showed. OK, so maybe not the best the night before a wedding.

I was just so concentrated on Jenn all night – the way she'd tilt her head slightly when she spoke, that dimple appearing on her cheek when she laughed; how our eyes had seemed to catch each other's across the table constantly. But after she'd run out of the bar a few days before, I didn't know if I was imagining it. I didn't know what to do. Then, before I'd known it, dinner was over and Jenn and Hilary had left to get an early night.

'I don't know,' Hilary says finally, and I look up. She's shaking her head.

'What don't you know?' Jenn says.

'If I can do all this.'

'All this what?' Jenn's eyes widen. 'The wedding?'

'The wedding, the marriage,' Hilary says. 'It's such a massive headache for everyone. Why am I even doing it at all?'

Her eyes tell me she's actually looking for an answer here from Jenn.

'Because you love Marty,' Jenn says steadily.

Hilary starts pacing around the room, taking short sips of Champagne. 'But really, does that mean you have to actually get married? Plenty of people never get married and they're perfectly happy. I mean, look at you?' she says spinning round to her.

'Me?'

'Yeah, you went off travelling alone and do you know what, it looked really fun. Maybe I'd like to go travelling.' Hilary's voice is so frantic it's almost breaking. 'I could go to Colombia too. I could just fly away right now,' she says, flapping one white robed arm up in the air like a seagull.

'But what about Marty?'

'What about Marty?' she says, a hard look in her eye. 'This is a woman's world after all. I don't have to be some wife of a fund manager, do I? Giving up all my dreams for him.'

'No, you don't,' Jenn says slowly. 'But he does know you're a doctor. He's always been so supportive of your career.'

'Yes, right now he is,' Hilary says, stabbing her finger at the ground. 'But what about if we have kids?'

'Look if you don't want to marry him you don't have to,' Jenn says.

'Try telling my parents that.'

'They'd get over it.' Jenn pauses.

Hilary looks unconvinced.

'Come sit,' Jenn says eventually, perching on the edge of the enormous bed. Hilary slowly walks over and sinks down beside her.

'What's all this really about?' Jenn asks. 'You adore Marty and, when I left, everything was fine?'

Hilary keeps looking at the floor. 'I know,' she pauses. 'But that's the thing.'

'What's the thing?' Jenn says.

Hilary takes a deep breath.

She looks up finally. 'It was you leaving, you see. It made me think . . . '

'About what?'

Her shoulders sag. 'About everything that could go wrong.'

'Wrong?' Jenn says, 'but you and Marty are great together?'

Hilary smiles sadly. 'Right now we are, maybe, but what's not to say it all falls apart in a few years? What's not to say he doesn't just leave me, like every other guy has? If you and Robbie can't make it, with all your fireworks, then why the hell should we make it?'

Jenn looks sad for a moment.

'Crap, I'm sorry,' Hilary says, shaking her head. 'I shouldn't have mentioned him, it's just—'

'It's fine,' Jenn says quickly.

'I think that's maybe why I've being picking fights with him, testing him.' Hilary sighs.

Jenn stretches her hands out, as though to look at her nails. But I know she's not. And I also know she's about to say something very wise – because that's the thing about Jenn, she truly sees what people need.

'The thing is,' she says eventually. 'Robbie and I were great for a time . . . but there's a lot more to love than what we had in the end. It's the other stuff in a relationship, the stuff you also have with Marty, which actually matters in the long run.' She looks up at Hilary. 'It's obvious how much he loves you. Like how he always picks up that butterscotch ice cream you love on Fridays, or how he did your hair for a month after you broke your wrist?'

'Oh god, yes,' Hilary laughs, her eyes lighting up.

'Well,' Jenn says. 'I think that's the kind of love which goes the distance.'

Hearing Jenn's words, everything becomes so clear suddenly: we had the big fireworks, we had the stuff from the movies, even. But there was more to it than that, and I just couldn't see it. Perhaps I did OK at the start, but then it's easy for everyone at the start – when it's fun and new and you have no responsibility to each other. But as time goes on, and things get harder, you need to work at it.

Like that unfinished Gaudí cathedral Jenn wanted me to see, the work love requires never really stops.

'But what about my parents?' Hilary says eventually, and I blink.

'What about your parents?'

'They hate each other. They can't stand being in the same room as one another.' Hilary turns to Jenn, eyes wide with concern. 'What if that happens to us in the end too?'

Jenn pauses.

'I think that's the risk everyone has to take to be happy. Everything in life's a gamble . . . and sometimes things just don't work out, people go in different directions. But you and Marty are brilliant together. Wouldn't you rather try?'

The hint of a smile finally appears on Hilary's lips.

'Look,' Jenn says, placing her hand on Hilary's. 'If you want me to go out there and tell them all that you're not up for it today, I'll do that. You don't need to get married to anyone, ever, so it's your choice.'

Hilary takes in a deep breath and looks out the window into the wintery white sky, and I wonder if she can remember what I saw: her chasing after guys who made her feel like shit, that giddy smile on her face when she first met Marty, the way he still takes care of her every single day. They adore each other, and while nothing in life is certain, I'm pretty sure the kind of love they share will see them through.

Hilary looks back at Jenn, finally. 'I don't want to let Chris down today,' she says softly.

'You can, if that's what you want,' Jenn smiles. 'Think of *Mamma Mia?*'

Hilary laughs then, her one black eye crinkling up.

'No,' she says eventually and shakes her head.

'So, is that a yes to the wedding?'

A pause.

'Yes,' Hilary says finally, nods, and she turns to pull Jenn into a big flannel hug. The two of them stay like that for a moment.

'I'm so glad you came back for this,' Hilary whispers.

Jenn closes her eyes. 'Wouldn't have missed it for the world.'

JENN

Harp music starts up from behind the doors, and she hears a call to stand. Turning back to Hilary, she smiles widely. She's looking so happy now, so calm. Her dress is perfect – a simple backless number – and her sandy hair cascades down in waves, with a few gold flowers pinning it to the side. It's everything Hilary wanted and more.

Deepa and Pippa are just behind Hilary in their sparkly gold dresses and Hilary's dad is standing a little to the side, fiddling with his work phone still. Jenn feels a stab of regret for him already.

He'll never get this moment with his daughter back.

From everything Hilary's told her, he's been all-but invisible on the run up, other than firing the odd antagonistic email to her mother about costs. Jenn can't help wondering what *her* dad would have been like before her wedding – in the event that that ever happened. In spite of everything, she suspects he'd have been as he always was in her childhood – quietly smiling, always helping, and ultimately wanting only the very best for her.

But that will never happen now.

Her eyes start to fill up with tears, and so she's relieved when the wedding planner appears with her headpiece, in her crisp suit. She gives them a weirdly large grin, as if to signal *smile girls*, and Jenn feels Hilary smirking beside her; is relieved to find herself almost laughing now. The wedding planner nods at something in her earpiece suddenly and turns to them.

'Time to go,' she whispers, and opens the doors with a flourish.

The ornate room is packed with people all smiling back at them. White pillars loom high, and another grand chandelier floats down. The chairs are tied with pale purple sashes, set on either side of a white runner which guides their path to the front.

Butterflies bloom inside her at the sight of Robbie again, despite the weirdness of the last two times she's seen him since she got back. He just looks so smart in his kilt and formal black jacket. And when he looks back briefly from beside Marty, she sees that he's actually cut his hair and shaved for the occasion. With a sickening feeling she realises she's just as attracted to him as she ever was.

Leading the way up, she passes colleagues from the hospital, mutual friends of Marty and Robbie. Campbell and Jill are standing near the front and she takes a breath in.

But as she goes by, she catches Jill smiling at her – a look which is still just as fond as before, and she feels herself exhale.

Coming to the front, she stands on the opposite side to the boys, and without thinking she glances at Robbie. Their eyes connect.

Oh, my heart.

Hilary and her dad reach the top and he dutifully kisses her on her cheek before walking quickly back to his seat.

'Good afternoon, everyone,' the celebrant says warmly. She's quite young looking, with a blonde bob and smart grey trouser suit on. She talks them through the 'boring house rules,' for the venue, before telling them a bit about Marty as a child, always cheeky, always getting into trouble with his best friend, Robbie. Then Hilary, who excelled at the violin, and adored animals – but eventually found she liked talking to patients more.

There's more chat on the relationship, a couple of readings: one by Jenn and one by Hilary's cousin, followed by a piano piece by a family friend, which is hilariously aggressive for a wedding and sounds more suited to a horror film – she knows how Robbie will be thinking the exact same thing as her and when she looks over, she sees he's trying to suppress a smile. He glances at her, a knowing look passing between them.

The celebrant goes on to talk about the true meaning of love: how it's making that cup of tea for someone, getting a blanket when they're cold, the little things that make someone's day. And the bigger things too – supporting each other's dreams, and allowing each other to change too. It's being there for them even when things get hard. It's thinking about that person's happiness over your own.

At the end of it, Jenn feels a wetness in her eyes again and realises she's crying. She feels embarrassed for a moment; exposed. But all the attention is on Marty and Hilary today. No one is looking at her.

Other than him.

She feels Robbie's gaze on her as the more formal vows start, and Marty agrees to spend every day of his life caring for Hilary.

'And do you Hilary, take Christopher Peter McFly to be your husband?'

'I do,' says Hilary, her voice cracking. But it's not with fear anymore, Jenn knows. Because the love her and Marty have for each other is the real kind of magic, and it burns brighter every day.

THIRTY-FOUR

The night before

ROBBIE

Same room, but it's different now. I'm standing in the middle. Everyone's sitting at circular tables with white linen cloths, other than the wedding party who are at a long table at the front. It's covered in candles and flowers. They're all still eating, the other Robbie chatting away to Hilary.

It's odd watching myself from only yesterday. I look exactly the same, but I feel so different to this guy sitting in front of me. It's amazing how much can change in the blink of an eye.

But I need to focus now. I need to work out how to speak to Jenn again. It was impossible while she was talking to Hilary, impossible during the ceremony – her and Robbie were always in each other's lines of sight – but she's got to leave this room soon.

I just have to wait.

Walking closer to the head table, I see the largely uneaten trio of desserts on their plates – all of them too big and too dry-looking. If I'd catered this wedding, I'd have done something much simpler, but packed with taste. Something for Marty and Hilary to remember.

I had so many fucking chances to start my own business up, do something with my life. Why did I never just do it?

The photographer comes around, still snapping away, but no one's really aware now. The main photos had been on the Royal Mile earlier in the day. It had been freezing cold I remember, the bridesmaids all slipping on the icy cobbles in their heels and laughing. Marty had carried Hilary up part of the way to stop her falling in her dress, and they'd just looked so happy together – her in his arms.

I suppose I must have seemed pretty tense, because during the groom and best man photos Marty had asked me what was wrong. Even on his wedding day he was thinking about me and my shit.

'Is it Jenn?' he'd said.

I hadn't replied.

'Just talk to her.'

'Already tried that the other night, didn't work,' I muttered.

'Well, fucking try again.'

'No,' I said. 'I'm not putting myself through that humiliation again.'

'Oh, too proud for that?' Marty said, eyebrows raised.

'No? Maybe. What's the point if she's just going to say no?'

'The point is you love her.'

At that moment the photographer told us to start heading up the Mile together. As we turned, the camera snapping behind us, I said, 'I just don't know what to do.'

'Well try and do something nice.'

'What do you mean?'

'Use your head, you dafty. What does she like? What makes her smile?'

It was at that point I'd spotted something in a tourist shop.

'You're a genius,' I'd said, gripping his arm.

'Go on,' he'd smiled, 'at least someone can miss a few of these bloody photos.'

A tinging noise sounds from the wedding table and Jamie stands up. He starts tapping his knife lightly against his water glass.

Shit, not the speeches.

People around the room stop talking and start to turn.

'Good evening ladies and gentlemen,' he says. 'I'd like to thank everyone today for being at my big brother's wedding.'

He makes a couple of cracks about Marty when they were younger, how Marty always ended up taking the rap for things he'd done.

'Sorry, Mum,' he says, grinning across at Wendy. She makes a face, then smiles.

'Anyway, I won't harp on,' Jamie says, 'I'll leave the comedy for Robbo at the end.'

There's some cheering from back tables, drunken laughter. Robbie smiles, but then fiddles with a card in front of him, a strange expression on his face.

It's weird. I really can't think what I said now.

I came up with it on the day pretty much, after speaking to Marty on the Mile.

It's all sort of hazy.

Jamie goes on and introduces the father of the groom (Hilary's dad was reluctant to speak) who does a fairly textbook speech about being proud of Marty and all his accomplishments, but that Hilary might just be his best one. Then Marty speaks for a while after that. He talks about how thoughtful Hilary is, but also how hardworking; how dazzled he always is by everything she does; how lucky he is to have her and how he wants to spend every day of his life with her.

And I wish in this moment that I had the kind of strength of mind that he does – to know what makes me happy and just go for it.

By the time he's finished, a lot of wine on the tables has been drunk and there's a buzz around me.

'And now,' Jamie says dramatically, and takes the microphone from Marty. 'Over to the best man.'

He makes a big deal of passing the microphone to Robbie. Clapping and cheering rings out from around the room.

'This is going to be hilarious,' I hear someone mutter, and turn to see some guys from school all grinning away. A few of them push money across the table. A bet sealed.

I feel nervous.

'It's a real honour when your best friend asks you to be best man,' Robbie starts and takes a deep breath.

A pause.

'Marty and I have known each other since we were kids, always had each other's backs. And I think that's really important in life . . . ' he says, clears his throat. 'Being there for people when they need you is really important.'

Muttering beside me. The guys look confused.

What's he doing?

'When Marty and Hils first got together,' he continues, 'it was obvious how much he loved her. How much they both loved each other, and they've been inseparable ever since.'

Along the table, Marty and Hilary look at each other, smile.

He goes on to talk about their relationship, the places they've been together, the memories they've shared. And there's none of the stupid stuff. None of the anecdotes to embarrass Marty.

The whole time Jenn just stares up at Robbie, with this look on her face I can't quite read.

It almost looks like love.

But it can't be, not after what I've put her through.

'I won't hog the microphone for too much longer,' Robbie says and there's a small ripple of laughter around the room.

This has got to be the shortest best man speech on record.

'But I'll leave you with this,' he says, and swallows. 'A wise man once told me that not everyone finds a certain type of relationship. The magic type.'

Marty gives a small nod, smiles.

'And when you find it,' Robbie says, 'you need to do everything you can to hold onto it.'

He glances at Jenn, and I'm sure she's breathing a little faster.

'So, would everyone be upstanding for the bride and groom,' he says, looking away. He charges his glass.

There's a collective rumble, as chairs are pushed back and people get off their seats.

'To Marty and Hilary,' he says into the room, 'and their magical kind of love.'

'To Marty and Hilary,' people say in unison, and drink their Champagne.

Marty leans over to kiss Hilary and, for the first time, I almost feel a moment of pride.

This was good.

This was right.

I look at Jenn and she's smiling up at Robbie, an expression that says she's proud too.

But the thing is, I can see the whole picture in a way I couldn't before. This is typical Robbie, thinking he could make one speech, make one quick fix and magically become the right guy for Jenn. But the truth is, he still has no idea about love. About what it takes to actually make something work, or make another person happy. It's all just words; hot air.

And somewhere out there is Duncan – the perfect guy – just waiting for Jenn to get back to their dream life.

For me, it's all just too little, too late.

The room has changed again. Tables gone so there's space to dance. I'm standing on the edge of it, people sipping after-dinner cocktails and chatting either side of me. There's a fizz in the air. The lights are low and the band strikes up a song.

'And now for the first dance,' a voice booms from somewhere, and Marty and Hilary appear on the starry floor. They look giddy with happiness, in a way I didn't notice the first time.

Because Hilary had come back to him.

For a few minutes the two of them sway around together. They don't take their eyes off each other. Then finally, Marty looks across at the side of the dance floor, beckons to the wedding party with a grin.

Marty's parents appear first, followed by Hilary's mum. Hilary's dad reluctantly goes to her, the two of them still avoiding eye contact. The groomsmen and the bridesmaids are next, then I see Jenn and Robbie tentatively looking at each other, hesitating, before Robbie takes her hand.

I don't need to go over to hear them. Because I remember every word.

As they start to dance together, I think how bizarre it is that she has two Robbies looking at her – the one who cares about his happiness, and the one who cares about hers.

'You have a good time today?' he's saying to her nervously.

She smiles up at him. 'It's been perfect.'

'Hils didn't have some massive makeup disaster or anything? No drinking in the bathtub?'

She lets out a laugh. Pauses only briefly. 'No. All smooth sailing.'

As I watch them spin away, I wonder if perhaps some lies are OK, in the right circumstances.

Another song comes on now. I know it. My spine shivers. Robbie and Jenn look at each other. It's 'Fisherman's Blues':

the first song we danced to on that first night we met five years ago.

And suddenly we're properly dancing together, twirling around and around, grinning at each other like no one else is there in the room.

I smile at them, because it feels good seeing us again together like this for a moment. Happy, like we once were.

But I feel sad too – my other self has no idea about Duncan and her plans to go to Australia. It's funny how you can never truly understand what's going on in someone else's head.

They can always surprise you.

At the end of the song they clap for the band and Robbie whistles loudly.

Jenn's grinning away to herself, clearly caught up in it all, then suddenly her face changes, falls. Her shoulders stiffen. And without warning, she starts to walk away from him. A second later he looks around, sees her going and heads quickly after her through the mass of people. I follow too, because I can't lose her now. I have to try and speak to her.

Off the dance floor, he calls out. 'Jenn.'

She turns and looks at him with sad eyes.

He spreads his hands to the sides. 'Where are you going?'

'What do you want, Robbie?'

He looks confused for a moment. 'I want to spend time with you, Jenn. I want to see you.'

Her eyes flicker across his. 'Is that it?'

'What do you mean . . . is that it?' he says, frustrated looking. 'I've missed you, Jenn. I still don't understand why you left?'

It's so insanely clear now.

He just doesn't get it; was never going to get it. Everything is just about him and what he needs.

He never thinks about what she wants or needs.

In some twisted way, I needed this all to happen.

I can see that now.

'And I've missed you too, Robbie,' Jenn says quietly. 'But I just don't know if this is a good idea again, you and me.'

'Why not?' he says, reaching for her hands. 'Why can't we just have fun tonight? See what happens?'

She pauses, looks over Robbie's shoulder at something. He doesn't notice, but it's quite clear from where I'm standing now what it is: Marty and Hilary, still twirling around in each other's arms under the soft lighting. Marty kisses her and it's so obvious she's the most important thing to him.

Jenn looks back at Robbie. 'I'm sorry,' she whispers. 'I can't.'

She turns and walks away, leaving him standing there looking confused. And despite finding this all painful to relive, I know I have to focus. This is my chance to speak to her.

This is it.

I follow the back of her purple dress as it swishes away. She's almost out the room when I hear a voice I know very well.

'Jenn.'

I turn to see Mum walking towards her, with a big smile on her face.

Shit.

'Jill,' Jenn says and stops. She looks nervous. 'How are you?'

'More to the point how are *you*, sweetheart?' Mum says, holding onto Jenn's arms. 'Look at your hair! It's so long. It's gorgeous.'

Jenn looks a little thrown but smiles back at her. 'Thanks, I'm good.' A glimmer of something in her eyes. 'I'm sorry I didn't get in touch.'

Mum sighs. 'And I'm sorry about Robbie's behaviour. You put up with it for long enough.'

I stop dead. My stomach sinks. She's actually given up on me.

But then, I've given up on the old me too. This is exactly why she should be with Duncan.

I'll fix it, I want to say to Mum. *I promise I'll fix it. That's what I'm trying to do right now.*

Dad appears, lit up at the sight of Jenn. 'Hello there. Lovely to see you.'

'You too,' Jenn says.

I look at his careworn face, the additional worry lines from everything I've put him through. I can't believe that I never even apologised for ruining his birthday. I pretty much avoided going home between then and now.

'How are Kirsty and Fi?' Jenn asks.

Mum and Dad glance at each other.

What's going on?

'Kirsty's well,' Mum starts, 'but I'm afraid it looks like Fi and Max are . . . separating.'

What the fuck?

'Oh, I'm so sorry to hear that,' Jenn says.

'I don't think things have been right for a while, in fairness,' Mum says, looking sad. 'But it's still hard. Tough for Struan too.'

Struan. I think of the first time I held him in my arms at the hospital, how protective I felt. I told myself I'd always be there for him. When was the last time I saw them? How the fuck could I have missed this?

It all just keeps getting worse.

'And how was your travelling?' Dad asks Jenn, like he can't bear to talk about it. 'Did I hear you were in Australia?'

She nods, and my chest tightens: that missing month.

Her with Duncan.

But she'll be happy with him.

'I hear there's excellent jobs out there for doctors,' Dad says. 'Is that something you'd be interested in?'

Jenn pauses. 'I'm thinking about it actually.'

Mum looks sad for a moment, then she beams. 'Good for you.' She grips Jenn's hands. 'You need to do whatever makes you happy.'

God, they're actually telling her to go. My own parents think so little of me that they're actually pushing the love of my life away from me.

But I can still do something about all of this though.

I can still make things right.

This isn't over yet.

THIRTY-FIVE

The day of . . .

JENN

Her arms are crossed in front of her, hands held by Hilary on one side and Marty's brother on the other. They shake them up and down. *For Auld Lang Syne*, everyone sings in a massive circle, *for Auld Lang Syne*. She missed all the little Scottish traditions while she was away.

Even if she does end up in Australia, she'll always hold a piece of this place in her heart.

It's her home.

The music kicks up a gear and suddenly everyone runs into the middle, and she lets herself be dragged in, laughing and grinning. In the centre she ends up directly in front of Robbie. They look right at each other.

Her stomach flips.

Everyone runs back again and the music finally cuts out, signalling the end of the wedding. At least for some – she's sure lots of people will be kicking on either in the hotel or in town, but she's got a big day ahead of her and it's already after midnight. First day back at the hospital and she has to be on form.

Will Robbie go out?

Don't think about him.

She says her goodbyes to the bride and groom's parents, hugs the other bridesmaids, the groomsmen. Then onto the newly married couple. Hilary gives her a teary look. 'I love you so much,' she says to Jenn, her lip wobbling with emotion, with happiness. 'I don't know what I'd do without you.'

Jenn glances at Marty standing at her side, holding Hilary's hand even as he says his goodbyes. 'I think you'd be just fine.' She smiles.

They hug each other tightly, Hilary promising to message from Mauritius.

From the corner of her eye, she notices Robbie saying his goodbyes, growing steadily closer. But she can't talk to him again. Because she knows what will happen if she spends one more second with him – she can feel it.

She's about to leave, when she hears his voice. 'This yours?'

Her heart leaps as she turns to see him holding something small and sparkling up to her.

'My earring,' she says, taking it from him and hooking it back in. 'Thanks.'

Her skin tingles where their fingers brushed.

'That's OK,' he says, eyes focused on hers, searching.

She pauses. 'I'd better go.'

Turning swiftly, she can feel the form of him watching her go, but she can't look back. Can't see those eyes again. She walks out of the room, down the corridor towards the lifts, breathes a sigh of relief to see no one's there. In front of the double doors, she pushes the button for her floor.

Suddenly, she senses him along the corridor. They glance at each other, before he starts walking towards her.

Shit.

She stabs the button again.

'Jenn,' she hears him call, as the door opens finally and she hurries inside. She hits her floor number twice, heart beating fast.

The doors start to shut.

The last thing she sees is his confused face in the diminishing space between them.

ROBBIE

Lost him. Good. *That was the right call,* I want to say to her here in the lift. But she seems upset. She's breathing hard, eyes tearing up. I wish I could hug her, but I know I can't. I can't risk freaking her out, not when I'm so close to speaking to her again.

If she could just go into her room, perhaps I could speak to her from the other side of the door?

There's got to be a way.

Two more floors to go. *Come on, come on.* The elevator lights ping on one by one like it's counting down time. So little left. It's got to be around one in the morning, meaning we're into the day itself now.

Less than twenty-four hours until we get in the car.

The lift finally stops and she gets out, walks down the corridor to her door. She stops, just stares at it.

What's she doing?

Just go in.

And then I remember. I know where she went next.

She looks over at something, frowns; a table at the far end of the corridor. There's a plant on it with red spade-like flowers. I recognise it. *They're leaves, not flowers,* she'd told me that first Christmas together. She'd smiled at my mistake, then kissed me.

It's a Poinsettia. Her Christmas star.

Before I can stop her, she gets up off the floor in a blur of purple, and heads back towards the lift.

JENN

Standing outside his door, she wonders what exactly she's doing here. This wasn't supposed to happen; she'd promised herself this wouldn't happen.

Duncan. Australia. The truth.

But other words muscle in, fight for space in her mind.

You never know what will happen tomorrow.

It still hurts her to think of Liv, she can't deny it. Those images of them together still haunt her mind. But everyone's human after all. Everyone's flawed. And everyone's also capable of change, surely? If they're open to it.

She doesn't know what the right thing to do is, only that when she sees Robbie, her heart still sings.

Maybe it always will for him.

Knocking on the door, she hears a noise, feet coming towards it. Metal scrapes and then he's there. His tired face a picture of disbelief. He's changed into a navy t-shirt, his boxers, and he looks so vulnerable suddenly. Like he hasn't a clue what's going on.

She kisses him, and the familiar feeling of it all comes flooding back to her; his scent, his taste, the feeling of his body against hers. She feels him pick her up, hears the click of the door shutting, and without any words he carries her back into the dimly lit room. And then they're stumbling towards the bed, clutching at each other, his strong hands feeling for her skin under the silk of her dress. They stop for a moment, and without saying anything she removes his t-shirt slowly, revealing his firm chest, the winter paleness of his shoulders. She pulls her own dress down over her body so it slips onto the floor. For one brief moment, they just look at each other, his brown eyes trained on hers in the soft lighting, and then they are pressed together once more, tipping down onto the soft white of the hotel bed.

She feels the weight of him on top of her, that instinctive way their hips press together, meld into each other. She kisses his neck and he lets out an almost pained noise.

The last of their clothes hurriedly come off, leaving them both exposed, as close as they can get, looking into each other's eyes. He kisses her softly this time, for what seems like the longest of moments, and then like a thousand other times before, he shifts above her, and her whole body hums with life.

ROBBIE

I'm lost in them. Drowning. I can feel her fingers on my skin, her lips on mine, her body arching up; a tormented ecstasy I'm not a part of.

I can't look away.

After it's finished, I realise I'm just sitting on a desk chair at the side of the room. They're wrapped up together on the bed. He's got one arm protectively around her, while she strokes his shoulder, and it's like we were at the start. The place that was so easy for him.

He starts to roll away to get something.

'Where do you think you're going?' she smiles, and he looks back briefly.

'Just wait and see.' Reaching down off the bed, he roots around in his sporran, pulls something out.

Turning back, he hands her a packet of jellybeans.

He spotted them in that shop on the Royal Mile, during the photos.

Her face breaks into delighted understanding.

'Oh, the beans,' she says, and grins so widely. And I see it; how just one little gesture makes her so incredibly happy.

It was always that simple.

He pulls her into his chest and they kiss again, softer this time, lingering over this moment together. Moonlight creeps across their bodies and I know, this right here is my favourite place. Just the two of us wrapped up in each other in the dark. This is the place in my life I'd come back to every single time.

And I'd do anything to keep that smile on her face.

To make a moment like this last forever.

THIRTY-SIX

ROBBIE

Noise. Blinding lights. The car. The truck.

Shit, it's coming for us. It's so close.

I try to move, press the pedal, shout, scream, anything. But I'm still frozen.

Dust particles hover.

Jenn keeps watching.

We're almost out of time.

THIRTY-SEVEN

The morning of . . .

ROBBIE

Her bedroom. The rented place. He's lying on her bed looking at his phone. Red hoody, like mine. New Balance trainers, like mine.

Shit, shit, shit. It's the morning after.

It's all going too fast.

Time is moving too quickly now.

And the car – the car is almost on us.

But I can still save us if she wakes up in time. If I just swing right, away from the truck.

What if it clips her side?

I've got no option. This is the only plan I've got.

I need to find her. I need to speak to her. Where is she?

We came back here the next day. She needed to get changed before work. First shift back started at eleven.

Robbie gets off the bed suddenly, goes into the corridor and I follow. 'Jenn,' he calls, loudly. 'Just off to get coffees.'

Water running. 'Alright,' I hear a muffled voice say from somewhere.

She's in the shower.

As soon as he closes the flat door, I sprint out of her room towards the bathroom, the water louder now. I go in. It's steamy already. I can barely see the outline of her behind the misted curtain.

'Jenn,' I say.

She laughs. 'I thought you just said you were going for coffee. You know I don't have time for shower sex.'

My heart bleeds.

Pull it together.

Pull it together for her.

But I can't. I can't.

'Jenn,' I say, 'Whatever you do, do not open the shower curtain.'

'Oh really?' I can hear the smile. 'Are you naked again? You've got to let me wash.'

She thinks I'm messing about. For once in my life I need her to take me seriously.

'Jenn, you have to listen to me, OK?'

I hear the shampoo being opened, the scoosh of it into her hand. 'I'm all ears,' she says. 'Fire away.'

I take a breath.

'The other night, at the monument, you were about to tell me something,' I say, and try to exhale. 'I need you tell me what that something was. I can't explain it all now, but trust me when I say it's important.'

My heart races. The shower keeps going. I imagine her telling me the secret, the world around us shaking then fading away, the car appearing – for real this time – and us speeding off into the distance together.

Just say it.

'What monument are you talking about?' she says.

I freeze.

What?

'The monument,' I say quickly. 'The one on the Royal Mile. After the bar.'

A pause.

'I went there,' she says, after a moment, 'but you didn't. I was alone, Robbie.'

Another pause. 'Hang on, how did you know where I went?'

It comes me to me, slowly at first, then all at once.

She doesn't remember.

She doesn't remember any of it.

Each memory remains as it actually was.

Nausea rising. My head's bleary. I hold onto the sink to keep me steady. Images rush through my mind: smacking the firework out of her hand, stopping the waltzer car, holding her arm in the Sagrada Familia, the blanket on the aeroplane, waking up on the beach, the words in the sand in Cornwall – none of it.

She remembers nothing I've done for her.

The shower goes off.

But how? I saw it all change. I saw it all happen. It affected her. And she could hear me, feel me, see things I altered just like I could.

I pull my hand down over my face, a lump rising up in my throat. I'd just started to get things right with her and now everything's gone forever. I can't stand this – back down the fucking snake I go.

I thump my fist into the mirror in front of me, and she pulls the shower curtain back. I stare into the nothing in front of me.

Lying on her bed a few moments later, I feel like I'm sinking into it. My body feels heavy, like I've been running for days, months. I'm so tired, in that way I used to get after some massive bender weekend. Before Jenn.

She's the most wonderful thing to ever have happened to me. The most amazing person I know, will ever know. And all I did was let her down. Gave her some half-hearted attempt at love. I always thought there would be another day, another moment. But it turns out there's not. Life isn't a game. There's no second roll of the dice, no surprise ladder to climb up. Everything that happened in the past is still the same. I am not god. I don't have some time travel car to go back into the past with and change all my mistakes. Every time I let her down is still a real memory to her. Every time I fucked up, I still fucked up.

And if I don't save us, that's all she'll remember about me.

But I'm out of ideas.

I'm out of time.

'I'm sorry, Jenn,' I say, as I hear her walking down the hall. 'I'm so, so sorry.'

JENN

In the bedroom she towels her hair and thinks of his touch again on her skin, how amazing she feels in this moment. So very alive, like she could just soar out that window and up into the sky, a bird tumbling on the breeze.

And she knows he's the only person who's ever made her feel like this.

She doesn't want this feeling to end. Maybe things could work with him this time?

Maybe she could give him another chance?

Duncan. Australia. The truth.

Her stomach plummets.

She has to tell him.

But not now. Not before her first shift. She doesn't want to ruin what they just had.

Tonight though. She'll tell him tonight when he picks her up.

Going over to her door, she lifts her satchel from it and takes out the envelope inside it – the one she's kept by her closely this whole time.

She needs it with her today.

More than any other.

ROBBIE

A letter.

She's holding the letter, slightly bent now and discoloured. With the name *PR Winston Solicitors, England*, on it.

My heart is pounding.

Her secret.

Holy shit.

But she burnt it. I saw her do it. I saw her set it on fire before she went travelling.

Or did I?

Little pieces of thought, images I've seen, all circle my mind.

I've missed a fuck load of stuff so far. *Did I miss something else?*

Think, Robbie, think. What did I see that night she left Edinburgh? She came to the restaurant, the letter was in her pocket, she saw me with Liv. Then she burnt the letter in the living room. That's it, that's all I saw.

What about before?

She'd just got back from the hospital, came into the flat, made a tea, ran a bath. The mail. She went to look at the mail. That's when she opened the envelope.

The envelope.

It was big, slightly bulky.

Oh my god.

There was something else in there.

Shit, that's it! There wasn't just one bit of paper, there was more. There was another letter inside. Like fucking Russian dolls.

And it was in her satchel.

She's had it on her the whole time.

I just never thought to look.

But what was it? Why a letter inside a letter?

I don't get it.

Watching her hold it now, I feel a surge of energy. I have to read it before the memories stop.

Even milliseconds will help; get her a fraction away from impact.

I have to save her.

She goes to put it in her backpack and I reach out to grab it. She looks up, startled.

Stars appear like I'm passing out.

THIRTY-EIGHT

Two hours before

JENN

'What are your thoughts on this lady?'

Beside her, Doctor Burden casts his eyes over her now-sleeping patient.

'Looks like she's got a moderate exacerbation of her asthma,' she replies easily. 'We're giving her some steroids, but I'd be quite hopeful that we'd be able to turn her around.'

He smiles and nods. 'It's like you've never been away.'

But I have, she thinks. In so many ways. She feels so different, like she's found a part of herself she never realised she'd lost.

Doctor Burden's right in one sense; the knowledge she's taken in over the years hasn't disappeared at all. It was always there, secreted away until she needed to use it again. Because caring for other people – making broken people better – feels like breathing to her. It's what makes her tick.

'We've missed you around here,' he smiles, before his look changes to one of concern. He glances briefly at the patient – still sleeping.

'If you need to speak about it all at any point then just let me know,' he says quietly. 'Have you considered what we discussed?'

She nods. A small lie.

'Yes,' she says.

'Well, just take your time. It's a big decision.'

She pauses. 'I know.'

A vibration in her pocket. She pulls her phone half out.

Mum calling. She hesitates.

'I'm sorry, do you mind if . . . ' she says, looking up.

Doctor Burden smiles. 'Of course. Go take it.'

'Thanks.'

Walking out of the ward, she heads quickly along the corridor. *Why is Mum calling?* Part of her thinks about ignoring it – she's not sure if she can deal with the stress of it today, and she knows she doesn't have to deal with that stress anymore; she can give herself a break, say no. But the other part of her knows that this is still her mother: the woman who carried her for nine months and planted a new flower on each of her birthdays; who twirled her around the hall to sixties music and painted her face like a butterfly any day of the week; who despite being irresponsible and unpractical, still made everything a little bit magical in Jenn's childhood.

When he left, her mum's life changed forever too.

And despite everything her mum's put her through, despite all her failings, Jenn still loves her.

She finds a quiet corner finally, hovers in it.

She answers the call. 'Hi, Mum.'

A silence.

'Jenny?'

'Yes, I'm here. I'm at work.'

'Oh, I'm sorry,' her mum says. 'I forgot it was today, I can call you back later if that's easier?'

'No, it's OK,' she says. 'I have a few minutes.'

'OK.'

Jenn doesn't say anything else, simply waits for whatever it is. It's been two weeks since Cornwall and not a word. *Will she pretend the conversation about Dad never happened?*

'I'm just calling,' her mum starts, and Jenn hears her take a breath. 'I'm just calling to say it was really hard for me too.'

Jenn's stomach sinks. *Here we go again.* Still all about her.

'I'm not doing this again,' Jenn says wearily. 'It was shit for me after he left, it was shit for you clearly. Let's just leave it there.'

'No,' her mum says, 'I meant living with your dad became hard.'

That's not what she was expecting to hear. 'What are you talking about?'

'I tried to talk to you about it in the garden that time but . . . surely you remember some of it?'

Jenn shakes her head. 'Remember what?'

'His temper, Jenny, the mood swings. He lost his job because of it. You must remember this.'

Jenn frowns into the phone. 'No, no he was always so gentle and kind.'

'When you were younger, yes. But he changed, Jenny. He was different by the time he left us.'

Fragments begin to float around in her mind. Lost pieces of a puzzle she's been trying to click together for a long time.

Suddenly she sees a flash of something; him shouting, stressed, Mum crying. Her running to her room.

A lost memory.

'But,' her mum continues, even as she's still thinking about it, 'I just wanted you to know, I am sorry, about leaving. It wasn't about you. I was running away from everything, you see. Edinburgh haunted me after your dad left – the place just seemed filled with all these memories. They were everywhere. I needed to get away . . . somewhere I could start again,' she says. 'But I never meant to get away from you.'

Jenn feels a tear slip down her face.

'Thank you,' she whispers and shuts her eyes for a moment.

'Anyway,' her mum says falteringly, 'This is your first day back, so I'll let you go. But I'll try to come up and visit soon.'

Jenn nods, knowing it will probably never happen. But the idea of it is nice; the idea of it is something.

'That would be great,' she says.

A pause.

'I love you,' her mum says.

'I love you too.'

THIRTY-NINE

Fifteen minutes before

ROBBIE

I'm outside her hospital. It's icy cold, dark, but I can see Jenn ahead of me, walking quickly towards the car park – Robbie promised he would pick her up, take her home.

This is it.

If I let them drive away in that car together it's all over.

I chase after her. And this time I know exactly what to do. That letter is in her backpack, right there in front of my eyes, like it was the entire time she was away travelling.

I catch up with her, unzip the pocket, stick in my hand, pull it out.

My heart is pounding, but Jenn doesn't even flinch.

She doesn't feel it.

Oh god, oh god, just keep walking.

I open it up, keep walking behind her. And for a moment, the world around me stops.

Dear Jenny,

I hope this finds you well wherever you are now. I'm currently sitting in my little room, at my desk overlooking the gardens. I can see hydrangea and honeysuckle, and there's a little herb garden too, like the one your mother used to keep.

I'm afraid if you're getting this letter, then I'm no longer here. I don't know how many years I have left. Perhaps a few, perhaps more. But I'm writing this now (or rather, I'm writing to you again) because I don't know how many able-bodied years I have left. It's to be included in my will.

I'm fully aware this might all be pointless, given I already wrote to you last year. And I understand why I heard nothing back, after what I did.

But I can't help wondering if you did actually get the letter. Did it get lost in the post? Did you and your mother move? Perhaps it's selfish thinking on my part — a naïve hope that if you'd heard from me, you would have responded in some way. And if there's even a vague possibility that that is the case, then I'm glad I'm doing this all over again.

Jenny, you'll know I was never one for a heart to heart. I was more comfortable with stone and mortar than people. Building things came naturally to me. Talking about them didn't. But I need to tell you something important; something which you need to hear. Maybe I should start at the beginning.

For as long as I can remember, my father was an alcoholic. For the large part he was harmless; drinking large quantities yet still managing to hold down his job. But, over time, his behaviour became more and more aggressive. He started to lose jobs.

Then one day, when I was twelve, he beat my mother. I remember screaming at him, shouting at him to stop, and when he finally did, it was almost like he was coming out of some sort of trance. My mother threatened to leave him, but he convinced her to stay with apologies and promises of never doing it again.

And he didn't do it again, for a while at any rate.

My mother shielded me from the worst of it in my teens, but I saw the bruises on her neck, her arms. I believe she lived in a state of perpetual fear for years. We both did. I never did quite understand why she stayed with him for so long – I guess love makes us do funny things. At any rate, I spent most of my teens trying to avoid my father when he was in one of his moods. I learnt to be quiet, for fear of aggravating him.

Then, when I was seventeen, I made a wrong turn. I went out with friends and came back late. And he beat me, badly. My mother finally moved us out of the family home that night, and we never returned.

I suppose you're wondering now, why I'm telling you this tale, one I never wanted to burden you with. But I do have a point, Jenny, so please keep reading.

I finished school, but not before my teachers had encouraged me to apply for architecture. I was always sketching buildings – the idea of creating something so solid, so real, appealed to me. I gained a bursary for Edinburgh University and never looked back. We never saw my father again either.

I met your mum one autumn day in the Meadows. Perhaps she told you already? I was twenty-five and she was twenty-three. I was reading, and she wandered by, looking lost. I'd never seen anyone more beautiful in my life, with that red hair and big smile. When she asked me how to get to the train station, I couldn't believe she was even speaking to me. I offered to walk her, and she said yes. By the time we got to the station, I knew I'd met the person I wanted to marry.

I loved the way she was always dreaming, always away in the clouds. So very different from me. All I wanted to do was take care of her and make her feel safe. I proposed six months later and we were married six weeks after that.

My mother sadly died a short time after the wedding, of a heart attack, but I was glad she got to see it. I was glad she had a number of peaceful years in the end.

When we found out we were having you, I can't tell you the happiness I felt. We immediately bought Larchfield where you grew up and I spent the next seven months renovating it, replacing each wobbly floorboard and removing each rogue nail. I can still remember seeing your mum out in the garden, her belly full of life and the sky full of sunshine, and I couldn't believe just how wonderful life could be.

We had a perfect life for a time, your mum and I. Watching you grow up, so happy and healthy, meant the world to me. All I wanted for the two of you was to feel loved and safe, without any of the burdens that I'd suffered, any of the fear. I never told your mum about my past, and she never pushed it. We lived in a bubble, and I tried my best to protect it.

It started so slowly I didn't really acknowledge it: confusion over a simple crossword, anger over a forgotten shopping item. It would catch me off guard, and I would suddenly realise I'd been shouting at one, or both of you. I'd take myself away off to my study when it happened, try to compose myself. I know I withdrew.

But it just kept happening.

I was so scared, Jenny. Scared I was becoming like my father somehow, that there was something in me which could be bad – which could hurt you.

Then one night, the worst happened. I hit your mother.

I didn't quite realise it had happened after I'd done it, almost as though I'd blacked out for a moment. And that's when I knew I had to leave. I had to make sure I could never hurt you, or your mother, ever again.

I stayed in a small flat in Glasgow for a time, close by, but not so close that you'd find me. Because I couldn't let you near me until I knew it wouldn't happen again. What if I did something worse?

I tortured myself for weeks. I'm afraid I even considered taking my own life. After that, I went to the doctors and explained what had been happening. The doctor was kind to me, and asked about my family's medical history. But I had very little information. You see, my mother's surviving sister was adamant that there was nothing peculiar on their side of the family and I had no connection to my father's side at all.

Eventually, they ran numerous tests, and there is no easy way to say this, but they discovered I have a genetic condition.

Called Huntington's disease, Jenny.

I'm not sure if you're aware what that is, but I will attempt to explain as plainly as I can: Huntington's is a rare, inherited condition, which causes the progressive breakdown of nerve cells in the brain. For whatever reason, Scotland has some of the highest rates in the world.

Early symptoms — mood changes, memory lapses, and involuntary shaking, to name but a few. Depression is common, as is aggressive behaviour, which would account for the mood swings I experienced, as well as the violent behaviour towards your mum. Medication has given me some reprieve in recent years.

Later features of the condition are, I'm afraid, much worse. It takes away your ability to walk, talk, eat and function, with a life expectancy of around fifteen years from onset. People have described it as having motor neurone disease, dementia, Parkinson's and depression all rolled into one. The normal age for symptoms to start are in your thirties, but it could be earlier, or later.

There is no cure yet, but science is making progress — great progress. There are clinical trials coming down the line. There is hope.

I'm so sorry to tell you also, that because it's hereditary — passed down from generation to generation — any child of mine would have a fifty percent chance of developing the condition too.

Which means you are at risk, Jenny.

When I found out the truth, I had a choice. Should I go back home? And explain why I'd been the way I'd been, before putting you through years of pain and trauma? I loved your mum dearly, and still do, but I also knew my condition was not one she could deal with. If I'd stayed, then the caregiving would have ended up falling to you. I think you know that too. And I just couldn't bring myself to let that happen.

The other option, the only other option, was to stay away.

You'd been hurt and upset initially, but you'd be ultimately happy and safe with your mother. I just couldn't bear the idea of ruining your childhood the way mine had been ruined.

It's the most painful decision I've ever made in my life, but all I could think about was your smile when I told you something interesting, that look of wonder on your face at the world around you. I wanted you to keep that wonder, until the point when you truly needed to know.

In the end, my symptoms didn't progress quite as fast as they could have, and I spent a few years still managing to work in Spain, still saving money for your future. (You'll know from the solicitor's letter that I've enclosed some of that amount now for whatever you wish.) I checked in on you as much as I was able to, from afar I realise, but I read all about the science fair you won when you were fifteen, and that charity event you did with your friends the year after; I discovered you got into medical school too. As your eighteenth birthday approached however, and my health started to deteriorate, I knew it was time.

I wrote to you. I couldn't in good conscience let you meet someone, perhaps even start a family of your own, without knowing what that might entail.

So, I really do hope you did get that letter. I hope you did find out the truth, and took decisions about whether or not to get tested.

I hope it made you do all the things you wanted to now, because the thing I've realised, Jenny, is it's not about the length of time we get on this planet — it's about what we do while we're here. I hope you climb mountains and swim in the ocean. I hope you see cities and jungles, and places that take your breath away. I hope you find something to do with your days which makes you tick — something which gives you quiet internal joy. I hope you take every moment and treat it like your last one. I hope you find someone you love, who makes your heart sing when you see them and makes everything that little bit brighter. But most importantly, I hope you know just how loved you already are. And that even when my memories fade away, even when I leave this earth, I will still find a way to love you.

I will always be with you, wherever you are, my Jenny.

Your loving dad.

FORTY

ROBBIE

I grip the letter. Heart still pounding – all the memories of her dad, the way he vanished from their lives.

He had Huntington's disease.

That's why he left money for them.

That's why he hit her mum.

But how did Jenn never notice his temper getting out of control before? Why did I never see any of those memories? Everything seemed so happy in her childhood, so idyllic – her dad seemed perfectly normal.

It dawns on me.

She rose tinted them.

She remembered all the best bits about her dad and their relationship. Just like I did after Jenn left. I couldn't see the problems I caused. I just remembered the happy moments we shared; the good times together.

I remembered I loved her.

And that person I love might get sick. That's why she ran away from everything.

From me.

She needed me to be strong for her, and I fucking wasn't. She needed me to hold her and I was holding someone else.

Suddenly the paper in my hand blurs, the writing seems to bleed and images flash into my mind: dark skies and twinkling lights across water: Darling Harbour. Duncan. Australia. That night. The missing month.

It's like I'm still standing here in the car park, but I'm also not. She's showing me something else.

She's not finished yet. Even if she doesn't know it.

FORTY-ONE

Two months before

JENN

Putting her phone back in her satchel, she looks back up at Duncan's expectant face and feels a pang of guilt. In the background the bright lights of the Ferris wheel turn slowly around and around.

And she knows in her gut that this will never work out between them.

She'll admit there was a moment there, when she really thought about it, when she wondered if she could find a way to love Duncan the way she would need to.

But she just can't.

She's still in love with Robbie, after all this time.

'I'm sorry,' she says. Reaching for Duncan's hand, she looks up at him. 'I'm sorry.'

Duncan takes a breath in, smiles sadly.

'But we're so good together,' he says quietly, still holding her hand.

'I know, we're so alike. But the thing is, I'm not sure that's what I actually need.'

As soon as she says the words, she realises how true they are: she needs someone different to her, someone who'll take the piss when she's being too serious, someone who'll help her slow down and have fun, someone who'll bring out the silly side of her, and make her feel alive.

But she also needs someone who's seriously in love with her. And if that's not Robbie anymore, then she's prepared to go it alone. Wait until the right person comes along.

Because she's realised something lately: for a long time now, she's had this feeling deep inside her gut, that she's not quite good enough to be loved. She's never given herself a break before, never allowed herself to just think about her, never experienced a moment of joy without feeling slightly guilty; never offered herself any compassion. She's always tried and tried and tried to please everyone else.

And she needs to stop.

She needs to love herself.

It won't happen overnight of course; she can still feel it niggling there, pulling at her, but at least she can see it now.

She's held it up to the light.

And she knows she has to change.

'I'll pack up when we get back,' she says to Duncan eventually. The last thing she ever wanted to do is hurt him again.

'Don't,' he says quickly, and takes her hand. She looks down at it.

'Please stay longer,' Duncan says, his blue eyes focused on her.

She feels confused.

'Just because we're not a couple,' he says, 'doesn't mean we can't still be friends.'

She pauses. 'But I don't want to hurt you . . . '

He smiles finally, lets go of her hand. After a moment, he turns back to the railing again, leans over it.

Slowly, she does the same.

'After you broke up with me when we were younger,' he says, turning to look at her, 'do you know what hurt the most?'

'What?'

'Never speaking to you again,' he says. 'I know you were trying to do the right thing, but we'd been through so much together and then suddenly we were like strangers,' he says, shaking his head. 'I was worried about you, but you wouldn't let me in. I was so happy when you looked me up in Sydney. I missed our friendship. And . . . I don't want to lose you again.'

'But what about—'

He waves a hand. 'I'll deal with it.'

Relief fills her.

Perhaps she doesn't have to say goodbye forever? Perhaps she doesn't have to lose yet another person.

As she finally allows herself to hug him, breathes in the familiar scent of him, she realises there truly are all types of love in the world.

A week or so later and the afternoon sun is beating down on her as she lies on a lounger in Duncan's garden. The tropical trees wave at her against the wide expanse of blue above. She looks down at her long legs and wonders how they can still be so pasty after all this time away. *Her dad's skin.*

Her stomach churns, a knot forming.

Like mirror images.

'Hey,' she hears Duncan call from the sliding doors. 'You do realise this is basically still our winter?'

When she doesn't say anything back, he walks out into the garden.

'You OK?'

That question he always used to ask.

'Yes,' she says quickly, 'I just need to email Doctor Burden, remember him? We're setting up a time for a call.'

The hospital emailed her back quite quickly after she'd told them why she'd left the country. They've been very understanding of her situation, and after months of regular check-ins, she's finally felt ready to start engaging in proper conversations around a return to work.

Duncan sits down on the lounger opposite her, looks at her. 'Do you want to discuss it before you speak to them?' he says quietly.

She stays silent for a moment, because she knows what he's really asking her.

What happened?

And suddenly she doesn't want to hold it in anymore. She can't bear this load by herself; this horrendous knot in her stomach which pulls at her over and over again every single day. She's tried to stem it, pushed it down this whole time with travelling and fun – paid for with the money her dad gave her of course, because wasn't that what he wanted after all? For her to see the cities and the jungles, and to go to all the places she's never been before; make the most of this short life. And it worked for a time she guesses, that distraction. But suddenly on this bright, sunny day, in this beautiful new place, she can't hold it anymore. The knot starts to unravel inside of her, slowly at first, then faster, faster, faster: her dad had Huntington's, he left because he didn't want to put them through it, he died all alone in some hospice somewhere, without any friends or family around him. And he was wrong, so wrong to do that to them, to her, to himself. She would have been able to take it. She could have looked after him. Because that's her thing, taking care of people.

Helping people in a crisis.

She missed so many good years with him, so many memories they could have still had together. She felt like he didn't love her, but he did. He loved her so much. More than she could have imagined. And she misses him.

She still misses him so much.

But she knows that's not the end of it all either. She might have the condition too, and if there's one thing her dad absolutely should have done – which she also needs to learn to do – then that's talk to someone.

Let them help.

She puts her head in her hands, and in a second, Duncan's got his arm around her shoulders.

'What is it?' he says. 'You can tell me. I'm here.'

And just like that, she cracks open like one of her mum's shells, washed up on the beach.

After all has been said, Duncan holds her while she cries in his garden; lets her speak when she needs to, and be silent in between.

Then later that evening, they start talking about her options together. Should she continue to live her life, without knowing if she's got the condition?

Or get tested and find out the truth?

She knows herself well enough to realise that she can't just leave it – as a doctor, every ailment she has in the future will be a symptom in her mind, every spark of temper the beginnings of something dark. She will forever be haunted by the thoughts.

Which only leaves testing.

There's the longer, more advisable route they discover online – multiple counselling sessions followed months later by the blood test itself. It would be a lengthy process, filled with frank conversations and the turning out of herself.

She would probably not know the truth for some time.

This is what Doctor Burden suggested she do; this is what she knows most people do.

But then there's the shorter route – private and expensive, and potentially done right here in Sydney, if she wanted.

Looking across the kitchen table at Duncan, she knows that whatever she chooses, she'll be supported. Whatever happens, he'll be there for her. And in a way, with his letter always close to her, her dad will be too.

Two weeks later and they're standing on the pavement outside the Neurology building in the city. She pauses for a moment to look out at the busy road, the people walking up and down the street, chatting on their phones or listening to music – going about their normal day, their normal lives. The morning sun is high in the sky and, despite the churning in her stomach, she feels a little lighter.

Because that heavy weight she's been carrying around the world with her – the not knowing, the denial – has eased slightly.

'So, just a few weeks to wait until the test results then,' Duncan says, looking at her. 'You'll let me know as soon as you hear, right?'

She thinks about where she'll be at that point – possibly back in the hospital working, possibly alone in her rented flat in Edinburgh. After Hilary's wedding at any rate.

She turns to him and nods. 'I will.'

'So, what do you want to do now?' he asks. 'On your last day here.'

She takes a deep breath – imagining white beaches and salty waves, cold beers and BBQs with her good friend – and smiles.

Because when she thinks about it, this day right here, this moment, is really all anyone has.

FORTY-TWO

ROBBIE
'Robbie?'

Her voice. Somewhere near me.

The sunny street, Duncan, Australia all starts to fade out slowly, like a dream at dawn.

Everything's so dark suddenly.

Are we in the car?

We must be, of course we are, because I know her secret now: about her dad, about Huntington's, about telling Duncan first, about the test. I know the results are ready – that's why she was so panicked in the car. She must have received a message to contact the neurologist in Sydney.

But where's the car? Why is it still so dark?

My eyes start to refocus.

She's there.

We're in the car park still, and she's smiling up at me.

I don't understand.

'You didn't need to get out, it's freezing,' she says, and reaches up to give me a kiss so sweet I feel it in my entire body.

She can see me.

What does this mean? Are we awake? Has it all stopped?

I look over at the car park – my car's there. A shadow, movement inside. The other Robbie.

My stomach drops.

We're still in her memories.

Why isn't she waking? I know everything. I know her secret. I did it. Didn't I?

'You have to wake up, Jenn,' I say, reaching out to her. 'We have to get away.'

She frowns. 'What do you mean? Get away from what?'

'I don't have time to explain,' I say urgently. 'Please just trust me. Please just wake up.'

'You're scaring me,' she says, her voice shaking.

'I'm sorry, I'm so sorry. But none of this is real, can't you see that?'

'See what, Robbie?' she asks, her hair blowing in the breeze. 'You're not making any sense.'

I need to make her see.

'Where did you just come from?' I say, gripping her cold hands. 'Where were you just before you walked over here?'

Her smile wavers. 'I was in the hospital. You know that.'

'But where, Jenn?' I say. 'Where exactly? What were you just doing?'

She opens her mouth to speak again, then she stops, blinks.

She touches her head. 'I'm feeling a bit odd actually,' she says softly. 'We'd better get back home.'

I can't stand seeing her like this, confused and disorientated. But I have to get through to her somehow. I have to do this.

'We can't go home,' I say. 'Not unless you wake up. I can't drive us away from the truck unless you let me. And we have to, Jenn. Because I just want you to be happy. Even if that's not with me, even if you did want to go back to Duncan—'

'Duncan?' Her brow furrows slightly then she smiles. 'Robbie,' she says slowly. 'I love you. It's always been you.'

My heart sings for joy.

Suddenly all the memories – the way they kept moving between her childhood and our story – make sense.

In the moments before death, her mind always pulls back to us. To me.

Because she loves me.

Despite all my flaws.

Despite everything.

'I love you too,' I say, voice cracking. 'So much.'

Oh god, we can be together again, we can have it all. I'll love her every day, I'll support her through her results – I don't care what they say – I just want to be with her.

I'd do anything to make her happy.

Something crosses her face, a shadow, and she looks away, over my shoulder.

'A truck,' she says, so quietly I almost don't hear her. She seems glazed for a moment, lost. Then she looks back at me sharply, and it's like she's coming out of a fog. 'You were driving us somewhere . . . we were speaking. I was about to tell you . . . '

She cuts off.

She starts visibly shaking. 'Oh god.'

Her face crumples, and she looks up at me. There are tears in her eyes.

There are tears in mine too.

Because I see what's happening now. Finding out her secret was never going to stop the crash. Nothing I did was ever going to change anything, because she still thinks this is it for her.

And it's time to say goodbye.

Just as Fi's book said.

That's why she can see me now.

'What's happening to me?' she says.

Then I'm holding her, so tightly I can smell the woolly scent of her hat, the floral scent of her hair. She's shaking against me.

But we have to move quickly, because this can't be goodbye.

I pull back, take a deep breath. 'Do you think you can wake up? If you can just wake up, I can think we can get away. Even if I move the car just by a small fraction—'

'Robbie,' she says, and I stop. There's a look there that I don't understand.

'Front impact hit,' she mutters, almost to herself.

'What is it?'

Wind sweeps across us from the car park. I hear the hum of traffic in the distance, people walking across the car park to the hospital. And somewhere in the corner of my vision, I see my other self still sitting in the car; waiting for her to get to him.

'Robbie, we're not going to survive this,' she says.

I flinch. 'Of course we are. I can do this, I can swing the car right into the other lane.'

'No,' she says softly, and a tear rolls down her cheek. 'I've seen this so many times. Not with the speed and size of that truck, we won't get away from it in time.'

'But,' I start, still at a loss, 'there has to be something we can do? Some way to fix this. There *has* to be a way?'

I'm crying too now but I can't seem to stop talking. 'You're so smart, Jenn, you must know how to stop this happening.'

She shakes her head at me, tears streaming down her face.

'I don't,' she gasps, 'I can't fix this.'

I hold her to me for what seems like the longest time. I don't want to let go. I never want to let her go, because somewhere inside of me, I know this is the last memory.

And, in a moment, this will all be over – for both of us.

Eventually, I feel her pulling back from me again. Her face is blotchy but she's the most beautiful I've ever seen her.

'How long do we have?' she says softly.

My heart is bleeding, and I'm terrified of what's to come. But it's not really for me – it's for her.

I'm not sure I can speak yet, but I force myself to.

'Maybe minutes, maybe seconds.'

She nods, reaches up a hand to my chin, traces the line under the stubble where she knows my scar is.

It's like you're always smiling somewhere. I remember those words, how loved she made me feel every single day I spent with her. She always believed in me.

She loved me no matter what.

A flutter in my hand. She clocks the letter.

'How have you got that—' she starts.

I shake my head, reach out for her. And I can see it on her face – she was scared to tell me. Because Robbie of before – that Robbie in the car right now – would have run a mile from it.

'You don't have to explain anything,' I say. 'I'm so sorry about your dad. I'm so sorry I fucked everything up.'

'I wanted to tell you, it's just . . .'

'I was an idiot,' I finish. 'You gave me a chance, so many chances, and I blew them all. But I'm here for you now, I'm here. And I'm not going anywhere.'

She starts crying again, presses her head against my chest. And I hold her to me, try to cling to this moment forever.

'What can I do?' I say eventually, putting my hands gently on either side of her face.

She starts crying again, but she's smiling too through her tears, gripping my wrists, kissing my palm. She lowers my hands into her own, stares up into my face.

'Just hold my—'

FORTY-THREE

ROBBIE
Bright lights.
Car.
I swing the wheel.
I stamp down.
Now.

FORTY-FOUR

After

JENN

Ringing in her ears, darkness, glimmers of light. Pain. She moves her head slowly, but it jars. *Shit, that hurts.* Her mind is muddled, groggy.

Where am I?

Airbags. Burnt rubber smell. Fractured glass, light spilling in from somewhere. It's shining in her eyes, making everything hazy.

When she was young, her mum accidentally broke a mirror in the hallway – it shattered into a thousand pieces. Her mum got upset over it but Jenn couldn't get over how something so flawed could still be so incredible.

She blinks.

The car.

The truck.

Robbie.

She turns quickly in the seat, pain searing into her neck, head, chest, but she doesn't care. He's there, right next to her.

Like he's been pushed across the car. He's covered in glass; everything is. He looks like he's sleeping, eyes shut, head tilted onto his shoulder. His side of the car is crushed, mangled, up against his body.

Those frantic final seconds before the crash come rushing back to her. She was sure that was it. Her life had literally flashed before her eyes, and then—

The car had slowed at the last second.

Her eyes dart now to Robbie's broken legs, to the steering wheel.

She lets out an animal noise.

He braked. He swerved the car around so it would hit him.

So it would save me.

'Robbie,' she says, her voice coming out in a croak.

Nothing.

'Robbie,' she cries again, feeling like she could almost shake him. He has to just wake up. But he's not moving.

Suddenly all the years of training take over.

Airway, breathing, circulation. Have to check him.

Reaching out for him, she cries out, pain radiating down her shoulder. The seat belt's digging into it. She fumbles at the clip blindly until it's done, airbag up in her face. Her hands are covered in blood; she doesn't know what from, she doesn't know who from. Turning to Robbie again, she sees blood on him too, in his hair, on his skin. He's so close it's like they could be cuddled together on the sofa.

414

But he's not moving. His eyes are shut.

Oh god, he can't be dead already.

She goes to check in his mouth.

There – a rasp of breath.

Still alive, but his chest has obviously been crushed. Badly.

'Robbie,' she says, her voice strangely steady now. 'Stay with me.'

Noises from outside, people shouting. Sirens. *Hurry up, hurry up.*

She feels for the pulse in his wrist, but it's gone.

Blood pressure falling too fast.

He's clammy looking. Pale. She's right.

Shit.

She feels for his neck next, in the vulnerable spot under his chin she's felt a thousand times before.

Please.

A flutter of life.

A beat.

Could he?

Can he?

Her hand falls, slowly.

No.

She's seen this type of crash – many times before.

They should both be dead.

But he saved her.

And now he's bleeding internally. *Catastrophic injuries.*

'Oh god, Robbie,' she sobs. 'What have you done?'

She shuts her eyes for a moment, presses her mouth to the top of his head, as what's about to happen sinks in. Breathing in deeply, she can still smell the scent of him through everything – that earthy warm one she loves so much; the shampoo he must have used at her place this morning, after they had made love again. As the winter sun had leaked in the window, they'd lain in each other's arms, and she'd wanted to tell him everything, about where she'd been, what she'd seen, but she also didn't want to break the spell they'd been under. She'd thought she would have a thousand more moments just like that. So, she tells him now, while she still can. She tells him all about the remote beaches and the endless oceans, the jungles so dense she could barely see the light. She tells him about rooftop mountains where she could see the entire sky and had felt at peace for a moment. She tells him about the people who she'd spoken and laughed with, who opened her up inside in a way she didn't think was possible, healed a wound she didn't know she carried, and made her feel strong enough for what might lie ahead. But, out of all the people she'd met and the places she'd seen, she'd realised nothing compared to the feeling of just sitting right here next to him. And no matter how far she'd distanced herself, she'd always come back to him in her mind; as though he was with her the entire time, cheering her on and making her seize each tiny moment of joy. Because some types of love are like that. They imprint on your soul and change you forever. Even if you can no longer see the person, even if you can no longer feel them, they still make the world a wonderful place to be in.

Shouting from outside the car, muffled words, sharp and urgent. Paramedics. They want her to turn around and talk to them. But she can't. She won't turn from him. Because she knows instinctively that they've run out of time. He won't make it to the hospital. This is it; this is where they say goodbye forever. She just hopes he doesn't know what's happening. She hopes he's thinking of something great, and she'll be there for him the whole time, holding his hand tightly.

'I love you,' she says, tears falling steadily onto him. Her Robbie – her stupid, hilarious, warm-hearted, wonderful Robbie. Her most favourite person in the whole world.

She kisses his head again, willing him to come back to her, to just feel how much she needs him to defy everything. Because she loves him too much, and this can't be it, just like that. 'I can't let you go,' she sobs raggedly, clasping his stubbled face in one hand, feeling his hair against her face. 'I can't do it.'

And then—

The faintest of feelings in her other hand, the lightest of squeezes. She's sure of it.

Another one.

His hand in hers.

I love you.

She sits back slowly, gazes at Robbie's stilling form, as memories from across her life come to her like fragments of a forgotten dream.

He was there. She was there.

Was it real?

As she hears him take a final breath, the hard edges of the car seem to blur through her tears, and the light shines on his face so brightly.

FORTY-FIVE

2014

ROBBIE

It's a beautiful sunny day. The air is crisp and a strip of blue sky runs the length of the Royal Mile. The cobbles are busy with tourists and locals, all smiling in the October light, wrapped up tightly from the cold. Standing outside Camera Obscura, a little down from the Castle, I scan the crowds. My head's hurting, oddly, but the light is helping. The pain is fading.

And then I see her, Jenn, weaving up the Mile towards me. She's got that blue coat on, a yellow woolly hat and she's craning her neck into the crowds ahead of her, searching. Then her eyes find mine, and an amazing smile spreads across her face. As my chest fills with excitement, I walk slowly down to her. And she's walking up to me, never taking her eyes from mine, as everyone else seems to disappear. Then we're standing in front of each other, and sunlight shines on our faces so I feel warm suddenly; the cold has gone.

'Didn't think you were going to come,' I say and gently reach out to touch her arm.

'Neither did I,' she says.

'So why did you?'

She shrugs, smiles. 'I just thought it sounded like a fun way to spend the day. I've never been to Camera Obscura before.'

'Oh really?' I say, 'well, you've got a treat ahead of you then. It's going to blow your mind.'

She laughs, but there's a trace of something across her face – a sadness almost. 'We'll see about that,' she says softly.

Taking her hand, I feel the warmth of her touch, this strange feeling inside like I love her already, and I'd do anything for her.

'Shall we go?' I say.

As we walk, hand in hand, I think about how happy I am that she came today; that a girl like her took a chance on an idiot like me.

As we walk towards the door of Camera Obscura, I look up into the bright sky and I'm glad we picked this place, a place filled with colour and light and cobbles steeped in memories of everyone who has come before us, everyone who has loved and lived. And I know, deep inside of myself, that today is going to be a good day.

Today is going to be great.

ACKNOWLEDGEMENTS

I've always said that writing a book is more of a team sport than a solo activity, and that can absolutely be said of this book. To my wonderful agent, Tanera Simons, thank you for taking a chance on the bud of an idea, and seeing what it could grow into. I'm so grateful to you and everyone at Darley Anderson, in particular Mary Darby, (who sent me an email, which made me cry with joy) as well as Georgia Fuller, Kristina Egan, Salma Zarugh, Francesca Edwards and Laura Heathfield.

To Rosa Schierenberg, I will never forget your first email about the book, and how you felt it captured that 'gut-punching moment of falling in love'. To Catriona Camacho and Caroline Kirkpatrick, thank you also for your astute eyes on the novel, and for making it shine. And to Jennifer Edgecombe, Caroline Hogg and everyone else at Welbeck, thank you so much for all your hard work and enthusiasm in taking this story out into the world.

A very special thanks has to go next to my lifelong friend, Jennifer Gibby. I'm genuinely not sure that this book would be in existence without you. Thank you for your painstaking reading, troubleshooting late into the night, and endless excitement for my ideas. This story will always be part you too.

To my other first readers and plot spinners – Angie Spoto and Toni Marshall – thank you for your incredible feedback and encouragement along the way, and for answering all my weird and wonderful questions.

Which leads me onto my writing groups (I told you it wasn't a solo sport!). Firstly, Skriva Writing School, led by the incredible Sophie Cooke. Thank you for teaching me how to actually write, and for all those cosy workshops up in the eves of The Sir Arthur Conan Doyle Centre. To my first writer friends, Sam Canning, Jo Cole-Hamilton, Lyndsey Croal, Erica Manwaring and Anthea Middleton, thank you for helping me create this book.

To CBC writing school, thank you so much for lifting my writing to another level. I am forever in Suzannah Dunn's debt, and to Nikita Lalwani, thanks for opening my eyes up to the real detail of stories – it truly brought my book to life. To my fellow CBC writers, it was that friendly and nurturing environment which gave me the courage to actually begin this book in the first place.

On the aspects of the book, I had to research, particular thanks goes to Helen Harvey for plugging several travelling gaps – your memory truly is incredible. On medicine, thank you to

Dr Angela Ruthven and Dr Diane O'Carroll, and special thanks to my patient big brother, Dr Mark Mitchelson, for answering all my questions in such detail. To Dr Rebecca Pryde, those walks and talks about psychology were so helpful.

Massive thanks to my parents-in-law, and in particular my brilliant mother- in-law, Paula, who spent many hours entertaining the girls while I snuck off to write. Your endless cheer and kindness was so appreciated.

To my parents, Anne and Alan, I'm not sure I can put into words how thankful I am to you for all your love and support. Thank you, Mum, for teaching me the love of reading, and for all your article clippings on writing – I've kept them all. To my sister, Sarah, only you know how many times I've called you to chat about plots or writing worries. You always make everything feel lighter, and I will never forget it.

And to Ben, thank you for all the dinners cooked and bedtimes covered so I could write, and for your unwavering belief in my dreams - that really is a magical kind of love. And finally, to Flora and Daisy. You are the reason I write, so you always know to follow your heart.

I love you forever.